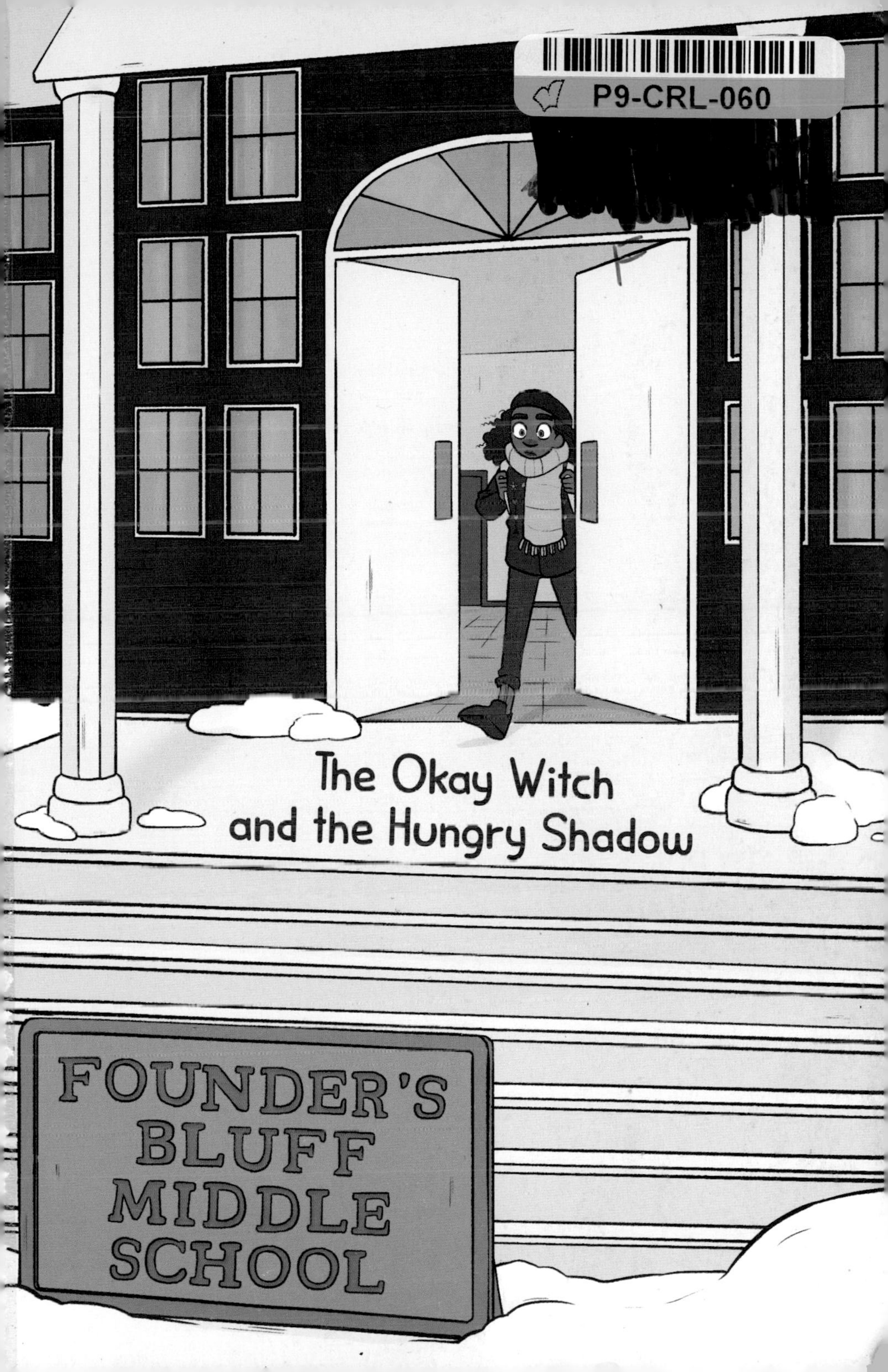
The Okay Witch
and the Hungry Shadow
FOUNDER'S
BLUFF
MIDDLE
SCHOOL

To Team Steinkellner.

I love this family of ours.

Also by Emma Steinkellner

The Okay Witch

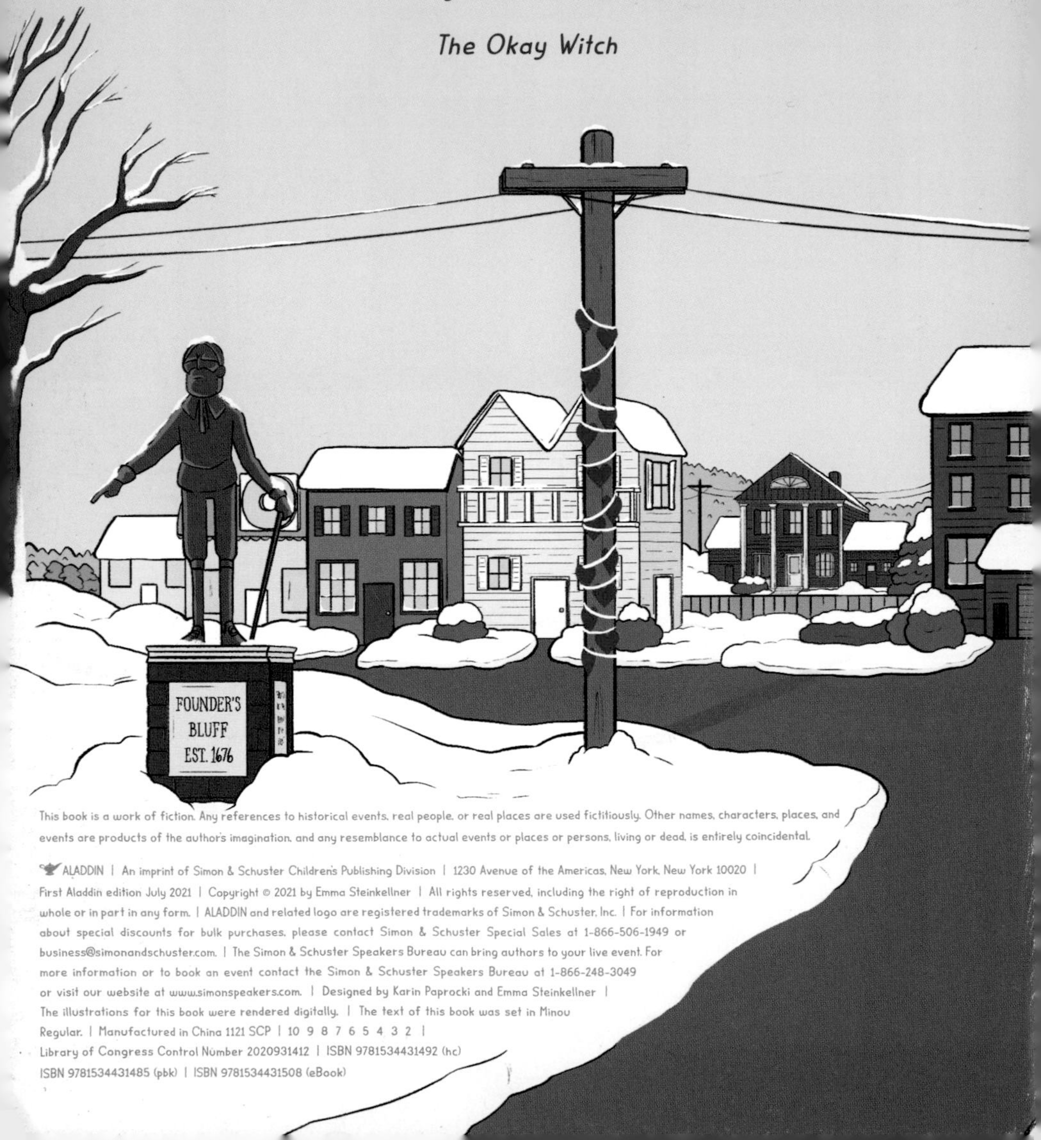
FOUNDER'S
BLUFF
EST. 1676

This book is a work of fiction. Any references to historical events, real people, or real places are used fictitiously. Other names, characters, places, and events are products of the author's imagination, and any resemblance to actual events or places or persons, living or dead, is entirely coincidental.

ALADDIN | An imprint of Simon & Schuster Children's Publishing Division | 1230 Avenue of the Americas, New York, New York 10020 | First Aladdin edition July 2021 | For information about special discounts for bulk purchases, please contact Simon & Schuster Special Sales at 1-866-506-1949 or business@simonandschuster.com. | The Simon & Schuster Speakers Bureau can bring authors to your live event. For more information or to book an event contact the Simon & Schuster Speakers Bureau at 1-866-248-3049 or visit our website at www.simonspeakers.com. | Designed by Karin Paprocki and Emma Steinkellner | The illustrations for this book were rendered digitally. | The text of this book was set in Minou Regular. | Manufactured in China 1121 SCP | 10 9 8 7 6 5 4 3 2 | Library of Congress Control Number 2020931412 | ISBN 9781534431492 (hc) ISBN 9781534431485 (pbk) | ISBN 9781534431508 (eBook)

THE OKAY WITCH AND THE HUNGRY SHADOW

By Emma Steinkellner

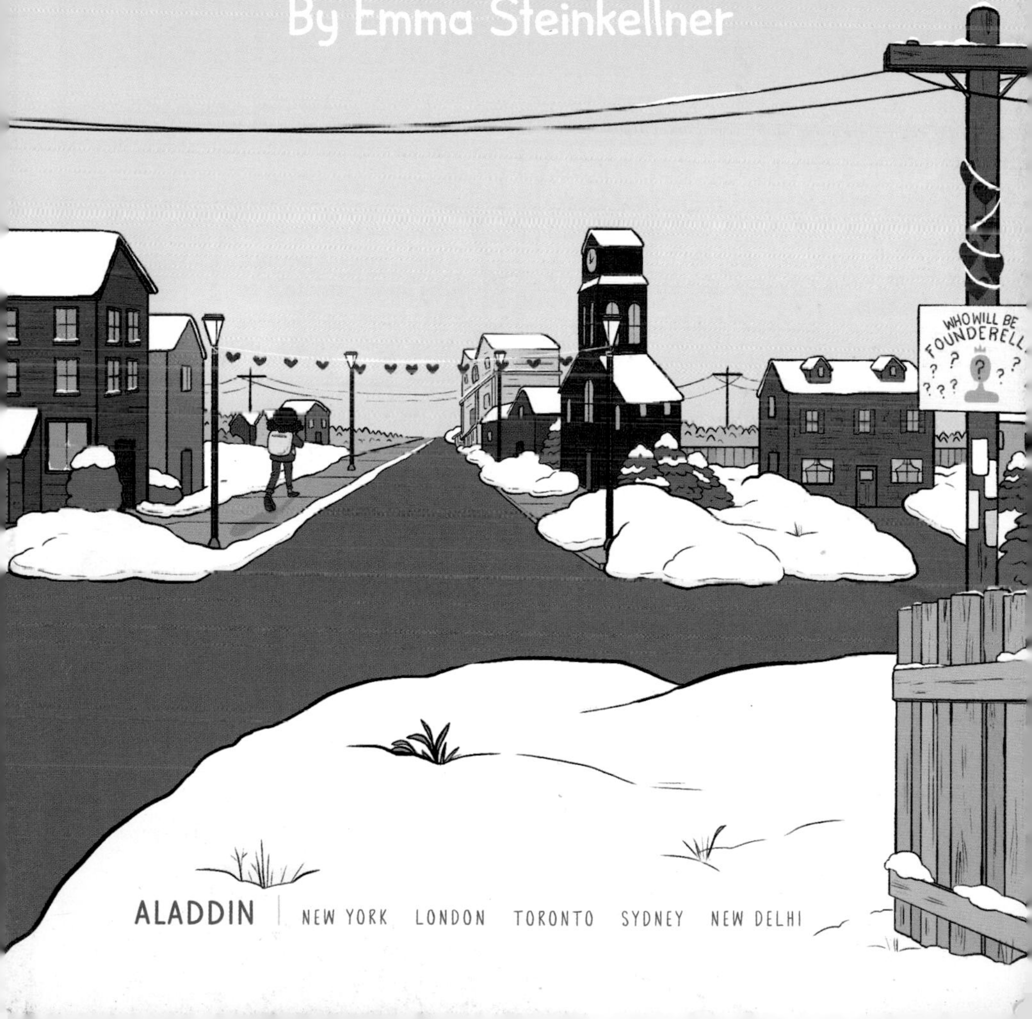
WHO WILL BE
FOUNDERELL

ALADDIN | NEW YORK LONDON TORONTO SYDNEY NEW DELHI

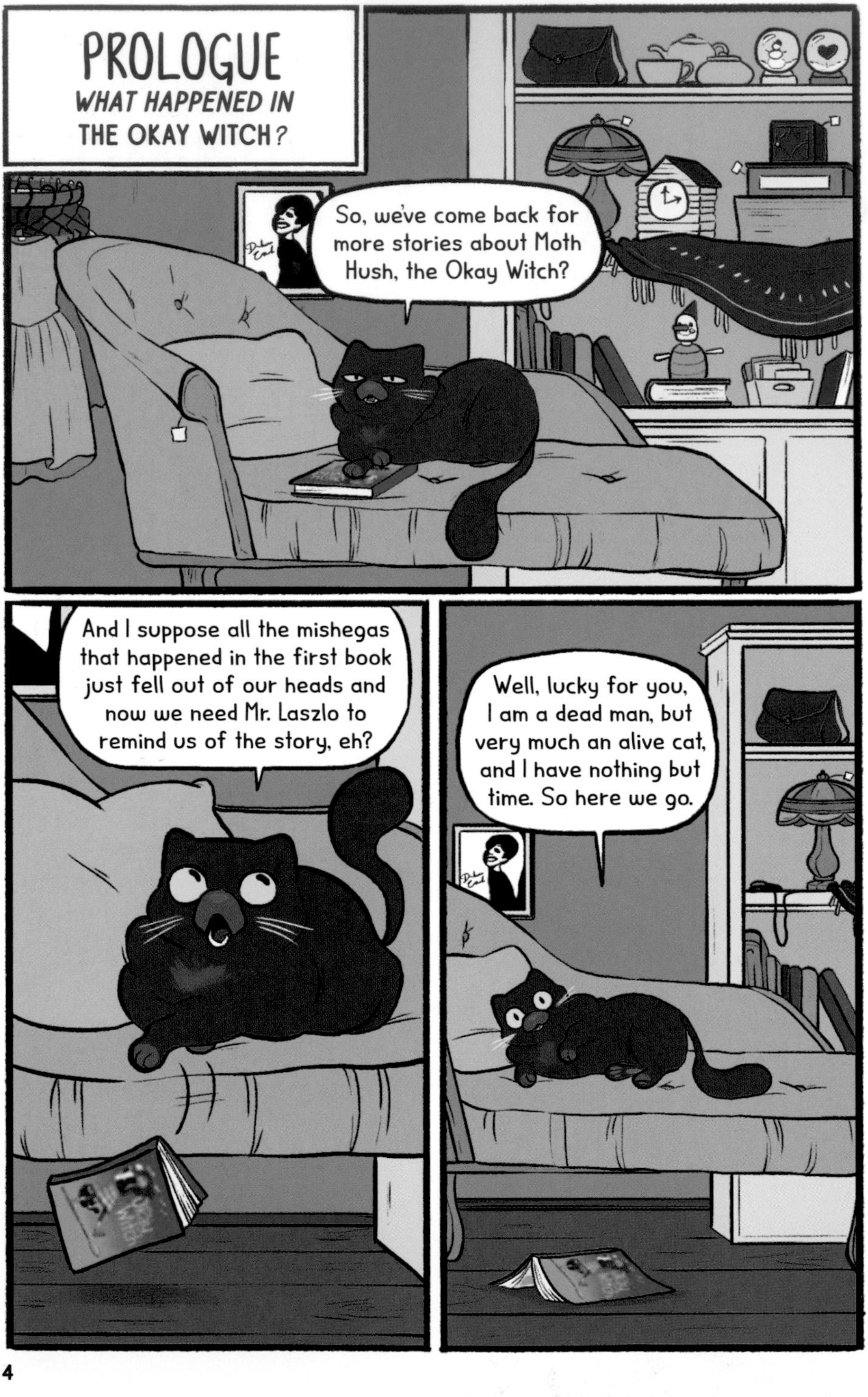
PROLOGUE
WHAT HAPPENED IN THE OKAY WITCH?
So, we've come back for more stories about Moth Hush, the Okay Witch?
And I suppose all the mishegas that happened in the first book just fell out of our heads and now we need Mr. Laszlo to remind us of the story, eh?
Well, lucky for you, I am a dead man, but very much an alive cat, and I have nothing but time. So here we go.

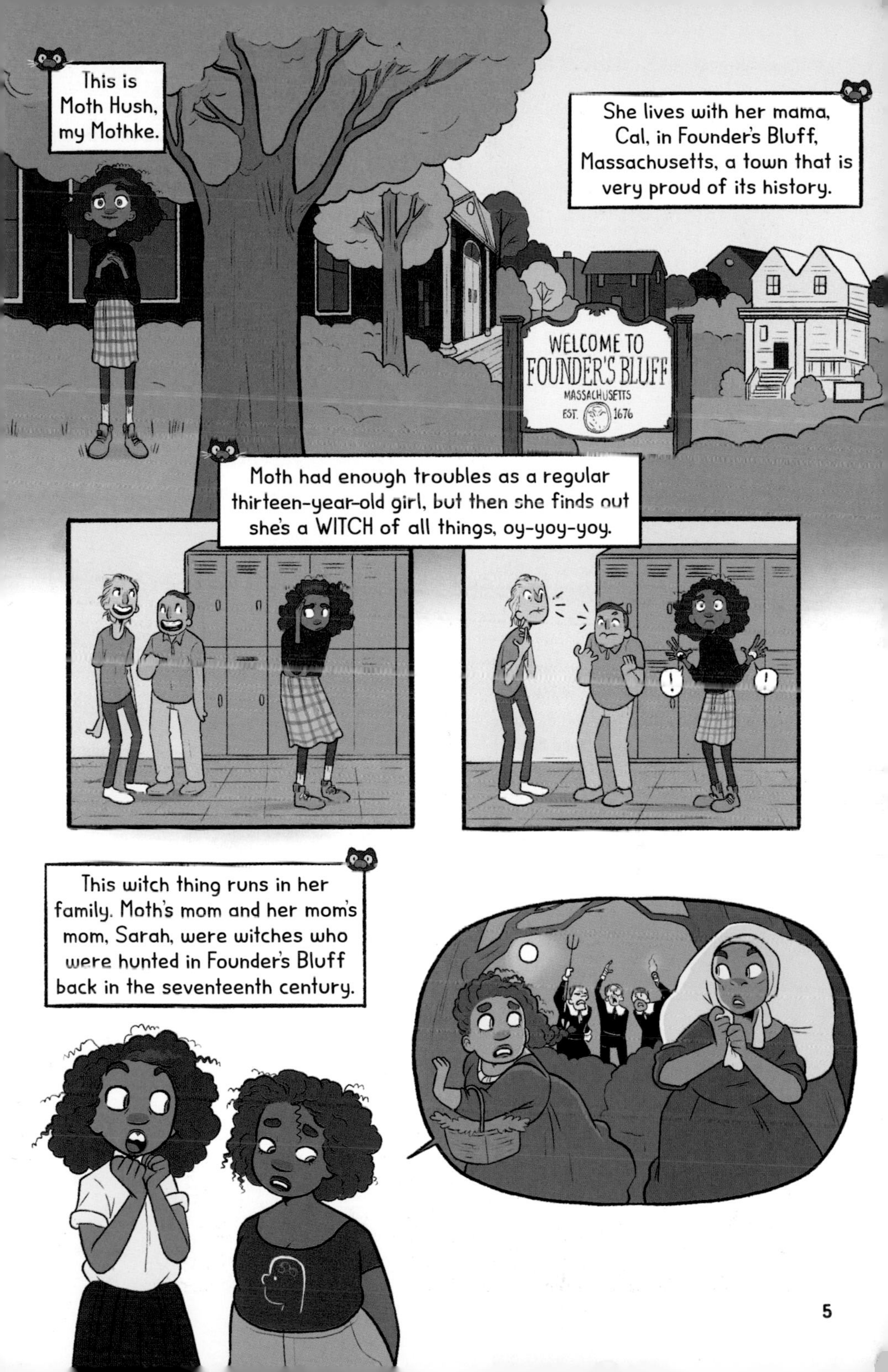

This is Moth Hush, my Mothke.
She lives with her mama, Cal, in Founder's Bluff, Massachusetts, a town that is very proud of its history.
WELCOME TO FOUNDER'S BLUFF MASSACHUSETTS EST. 1676
Moth had enough troubles as a regular thirteen-year-old girl, but then she finds out she's a WITCH of all things, oy-yoy-yoy.
This witch thing runs in her family. Moth's mom and her mom's mom, Sarah, were witches who were hunted in Founder's Bluff back in the seventeenth century.

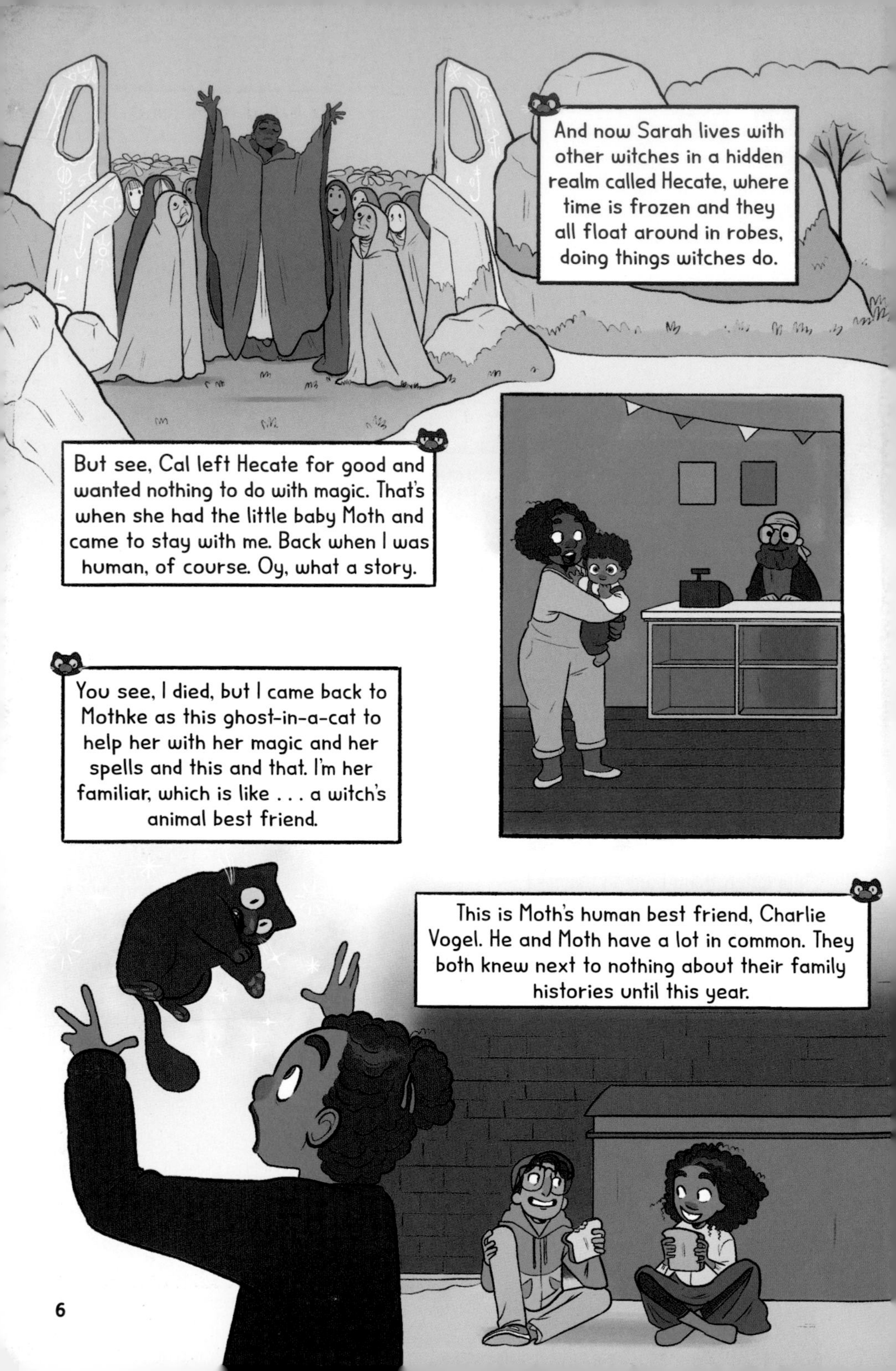
And now Sarah lives with other witches in a hidden realm called Hecate, where time is frozen and they all float around in robes, doing things witches do.
But see, Cal left Hecate for good and wanted nothing to do with magic. That's when she had the little baby Moth and came to stay with me. Back when I was human, of course. Oy, what a story.
You see, I died, but I came back to Mothke as this ghost-in-a-cat to help her with her magic and her spells and this and that. I'm her familiar, which is like . . . a witch's animal best friend.
This is Moth's human best friend, Charlie Vogel. He and Moth have a lot in common. They both knew next to nothing about their family histories until this year.

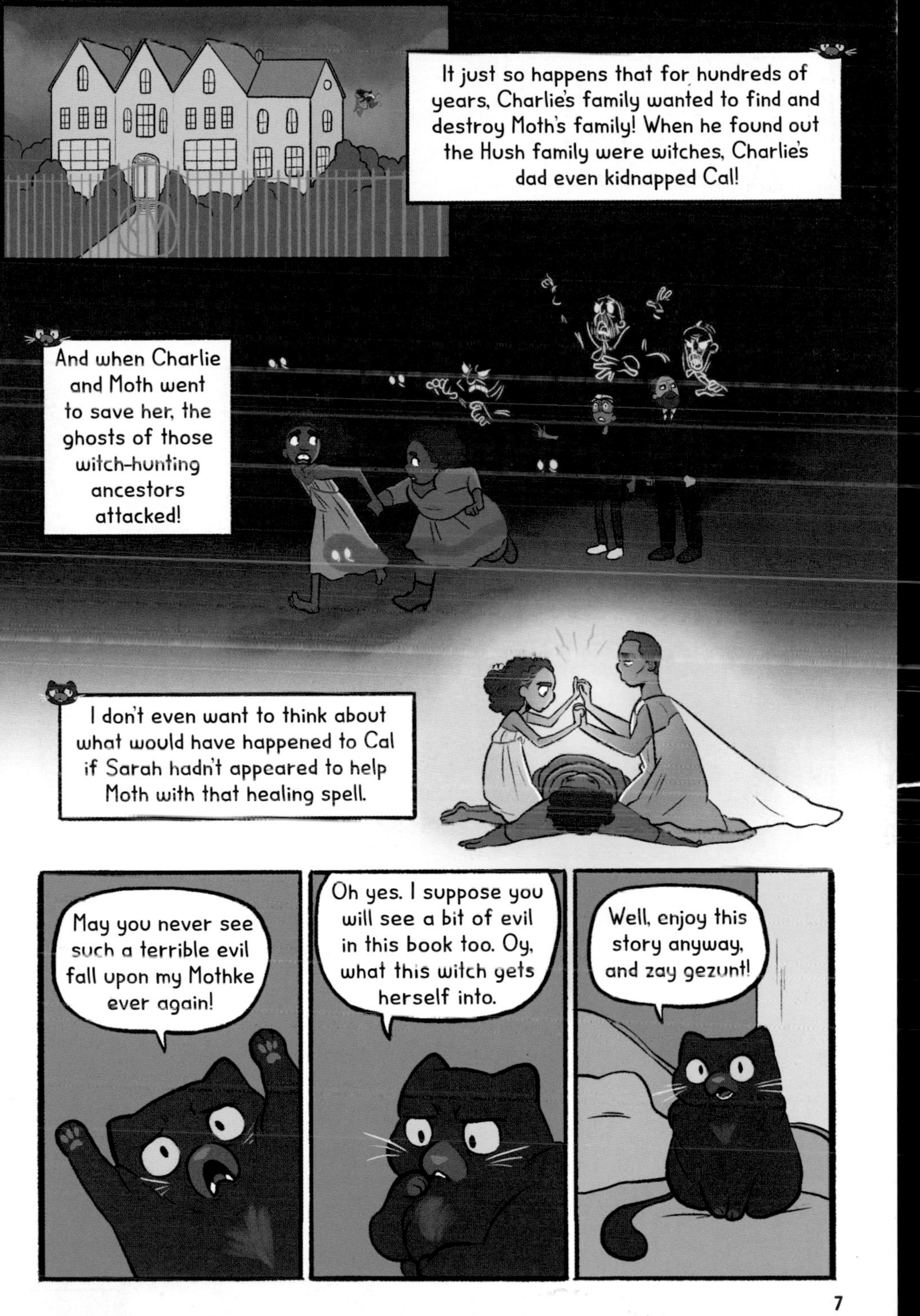
It just so happens that for hundreds of years, Charlie's family wanted to find and destroy Moth's family! When he found out the Hush family were witches, Charlie's dad even kidnapped Cal!
And when Charlie and Moth went to save her, the ghosts of those witch-hunting ancestors attacked!
I don't even want to think about what would have happened to Cal if Sarah hadn't appeared to help Moth with that healing spell.
May you never see such a terrible evil fall upon my Mothke ever again!
Oh yes. I suppose you will see a bit of evil in this book too. Oy, what this witch gets herself into.
Well, enjoy this story anyway, and zay gezunt!

CHAPTER 1
Her Greatest Enemy

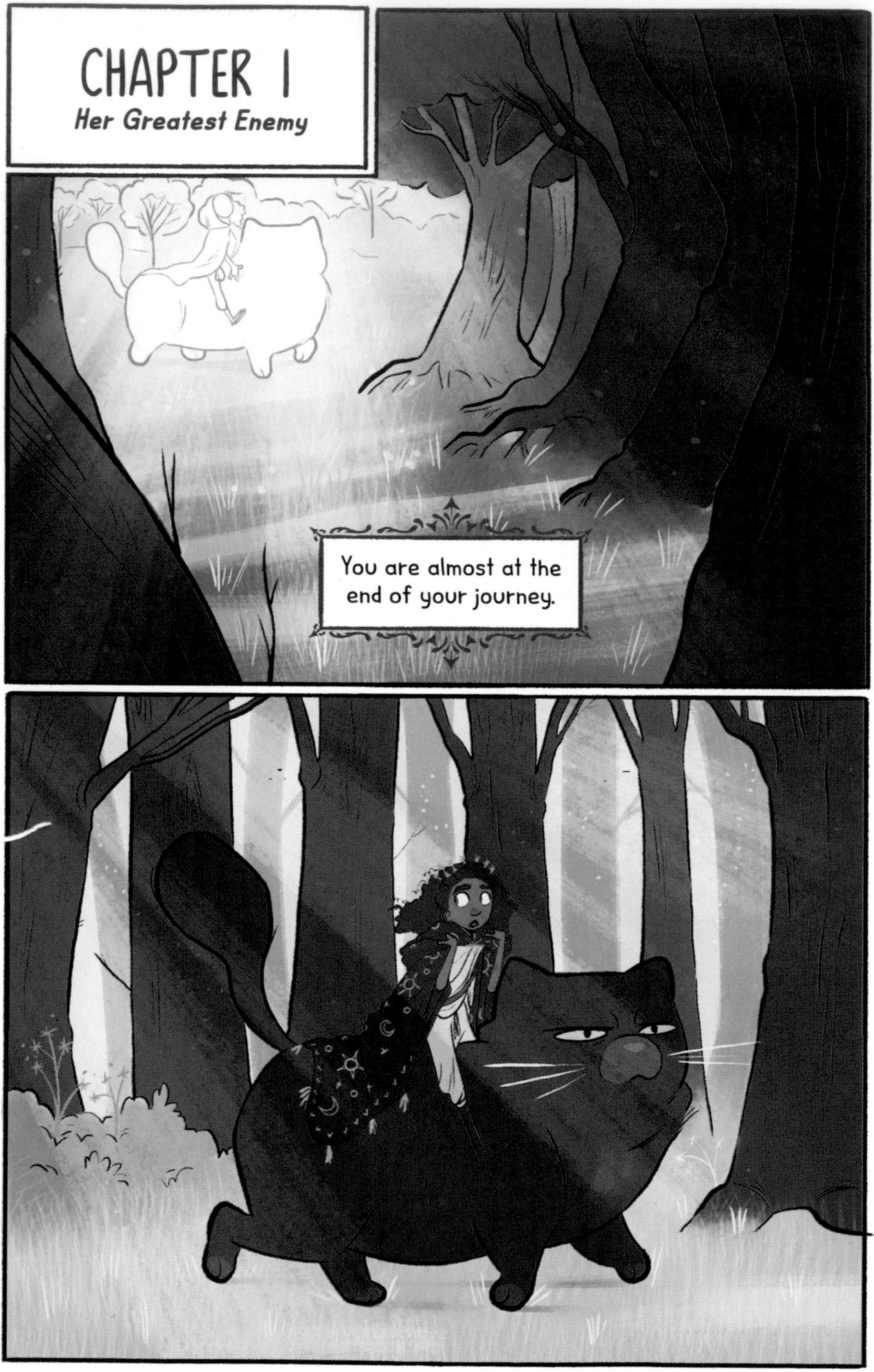
You are almost at the end of your journey.

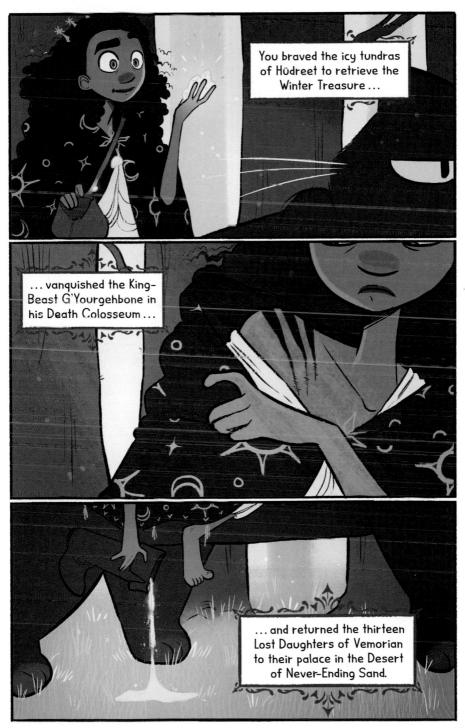

You braved the icy tundras of Hüdreet to retrieve the Winter Treasure...

...vanquished the King-Beast G'Yourgehbone in his Death Colosseum...

...and returned the thirteen Lost Daughters of Vemorian to their palace in the Desert of Never-Ending Sand.

9

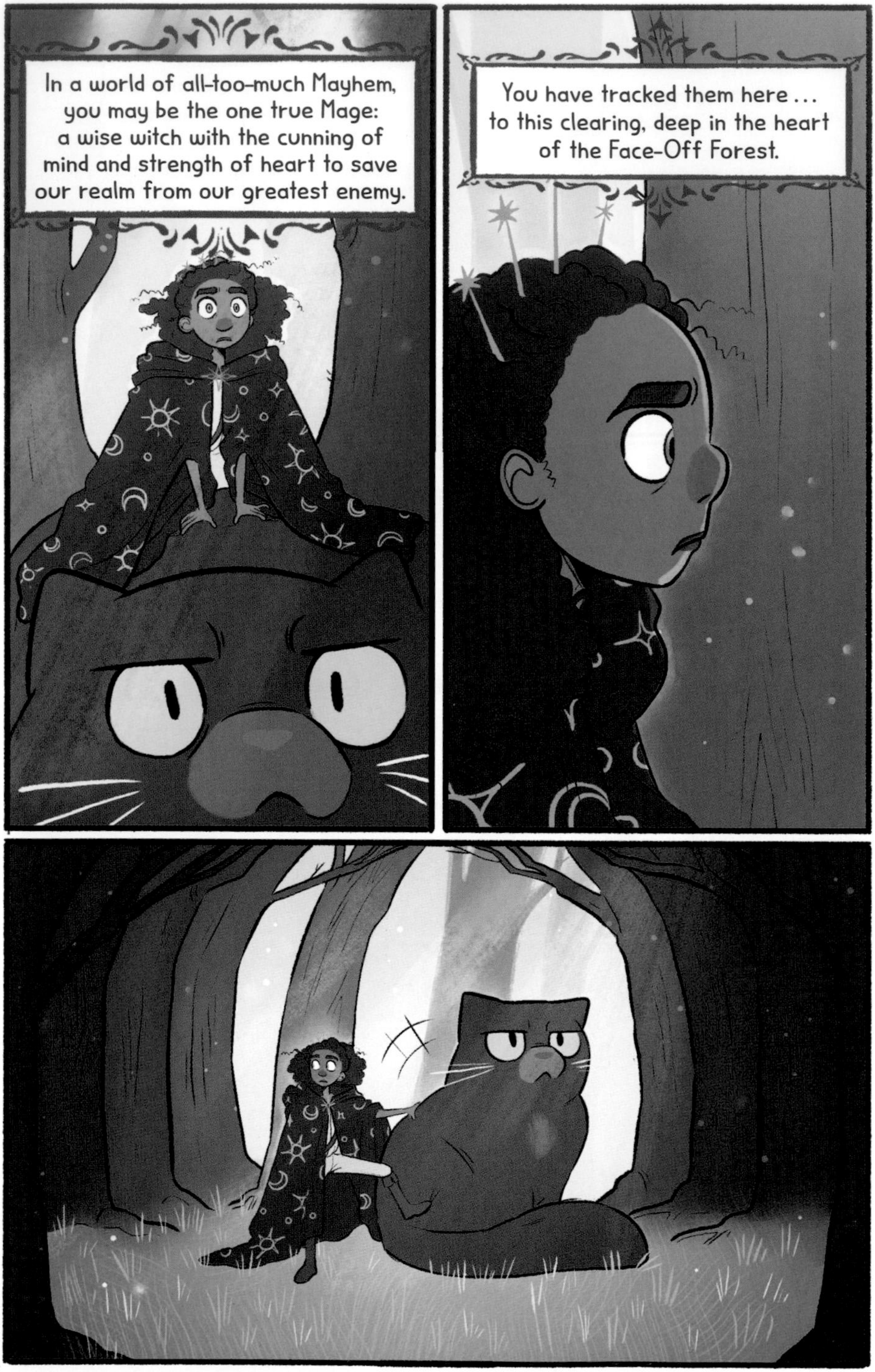
In a world of all-too-much Mayhem, you may be the one true Mage: a wise witch with the cunning of mind and strength of heart to save our realm from our greatest enemy.
You have tracked them here . . . to this clearing, deep in the heart of the Face-Off Forest.

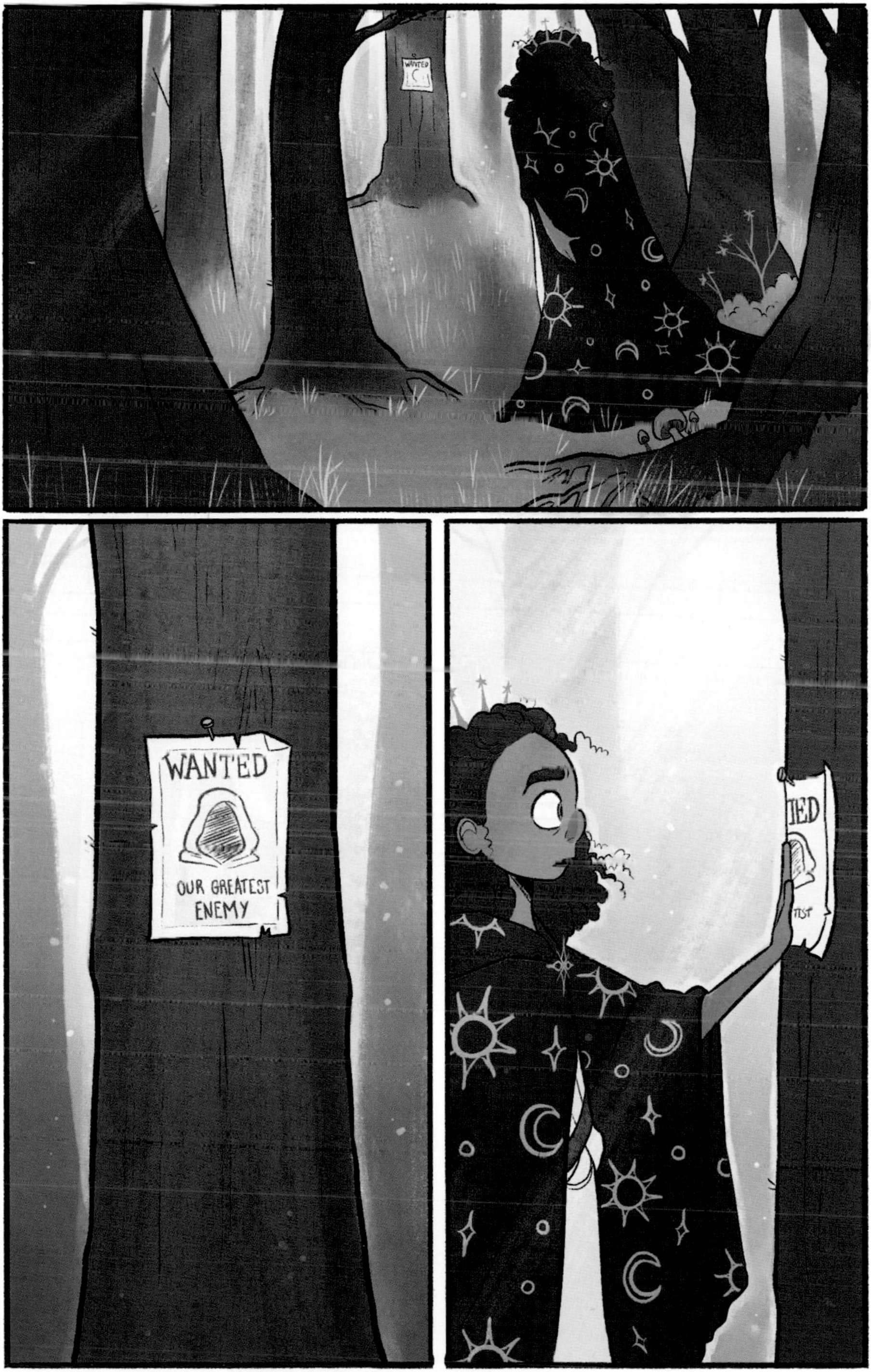
WANTED
WANTED
OUR GREATEST ENEMY

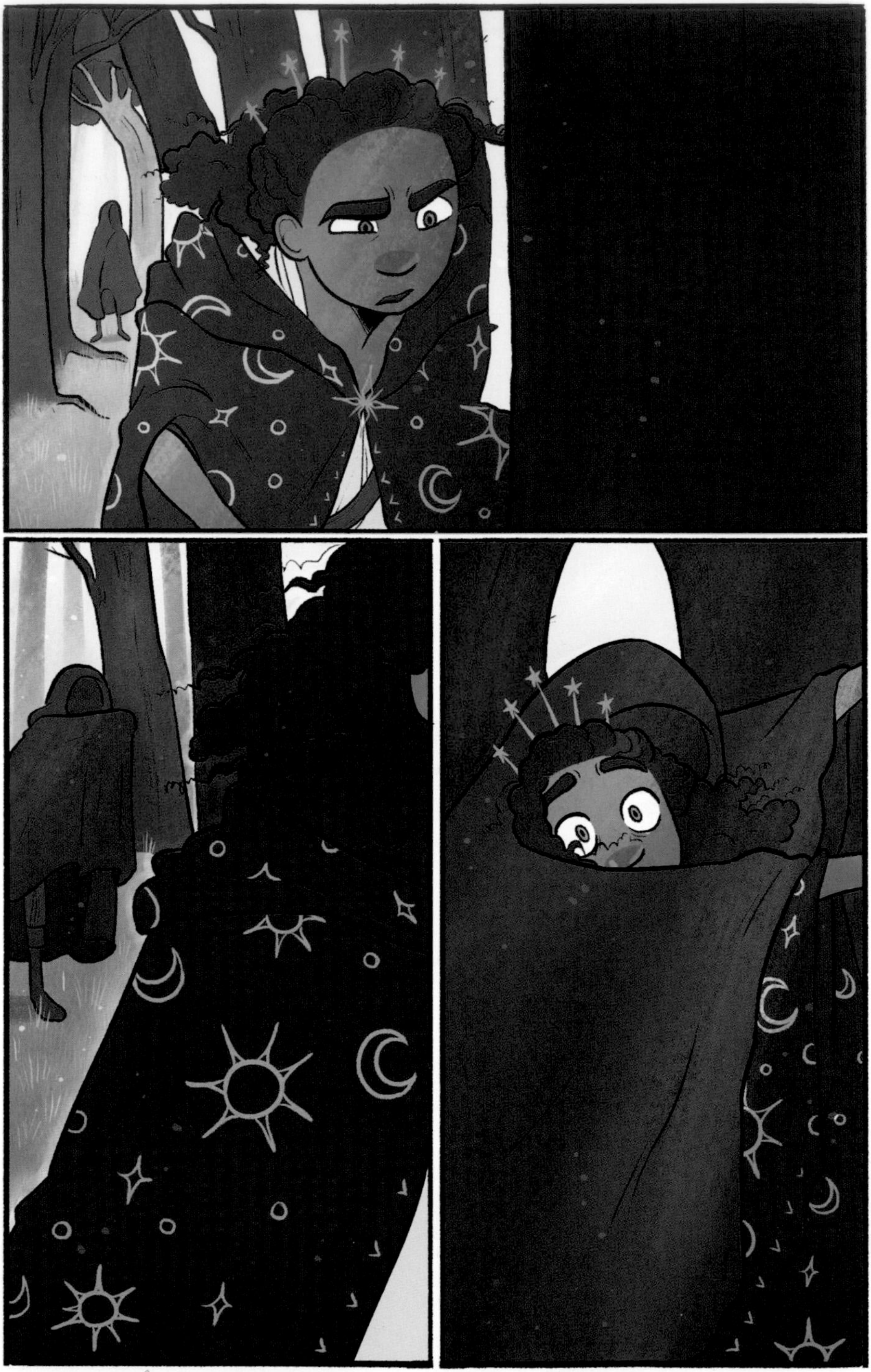

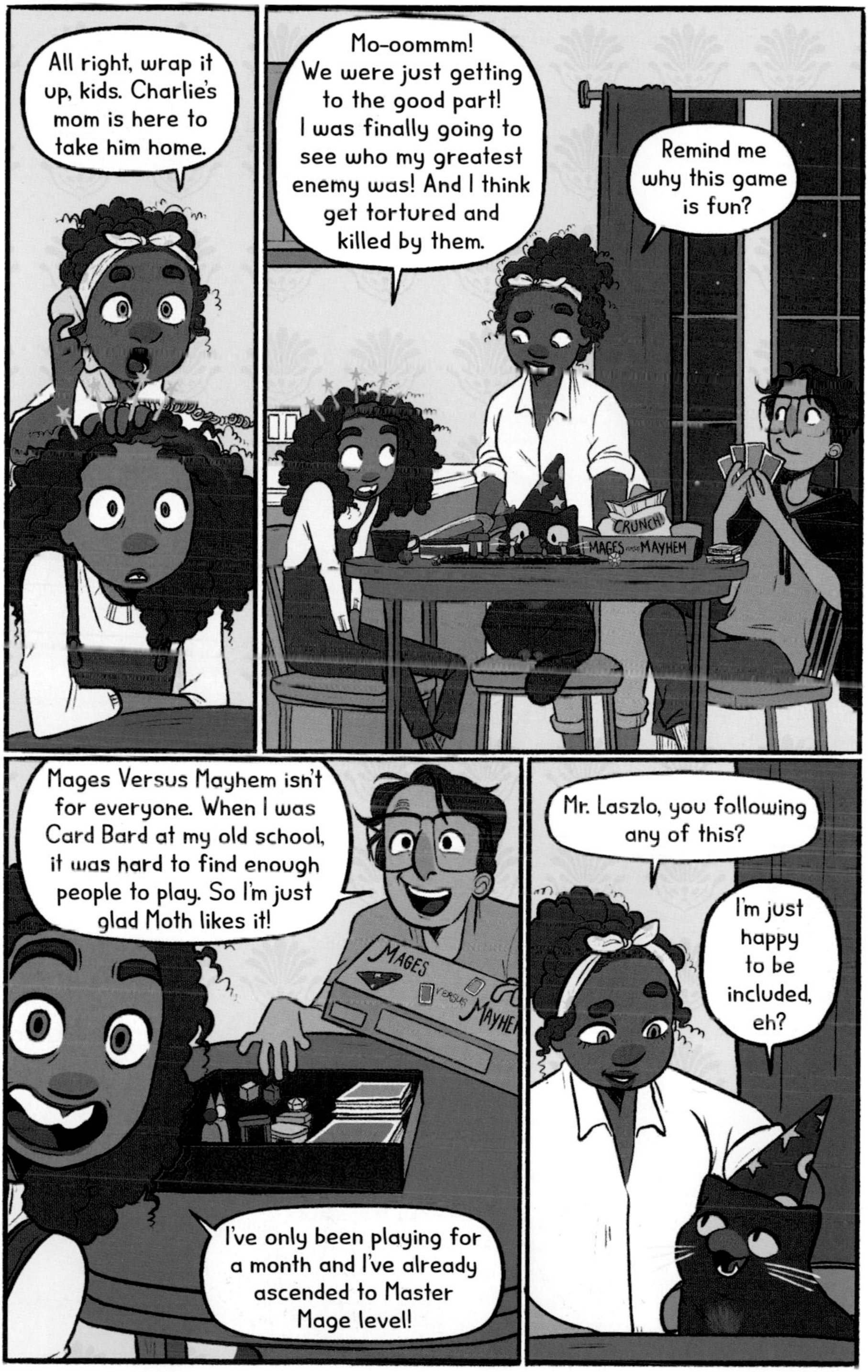
All right, wrap it up, kids. Charlie's mom is here to take him home.
Mo-oommm! We were just getting to the good part! I was finally going to see who my greatest enemy was! And I think get tortured and killed by them.
Remind me why this game is fun?
CRUNCH!
MAGES VERSUS MAYHEM
Mages Versus Mayhem isn't for everyone. When I was Card Bard at my old school, it was hard to find enough people to play. So I'm just glad Moth likes it!
MAGES VERSUS MAYHEM
I've only been playing for a month and I've already ascended to Master Mage level!
Mr. Laszlo, you following any of this?
I'm just happy to be included, eh?

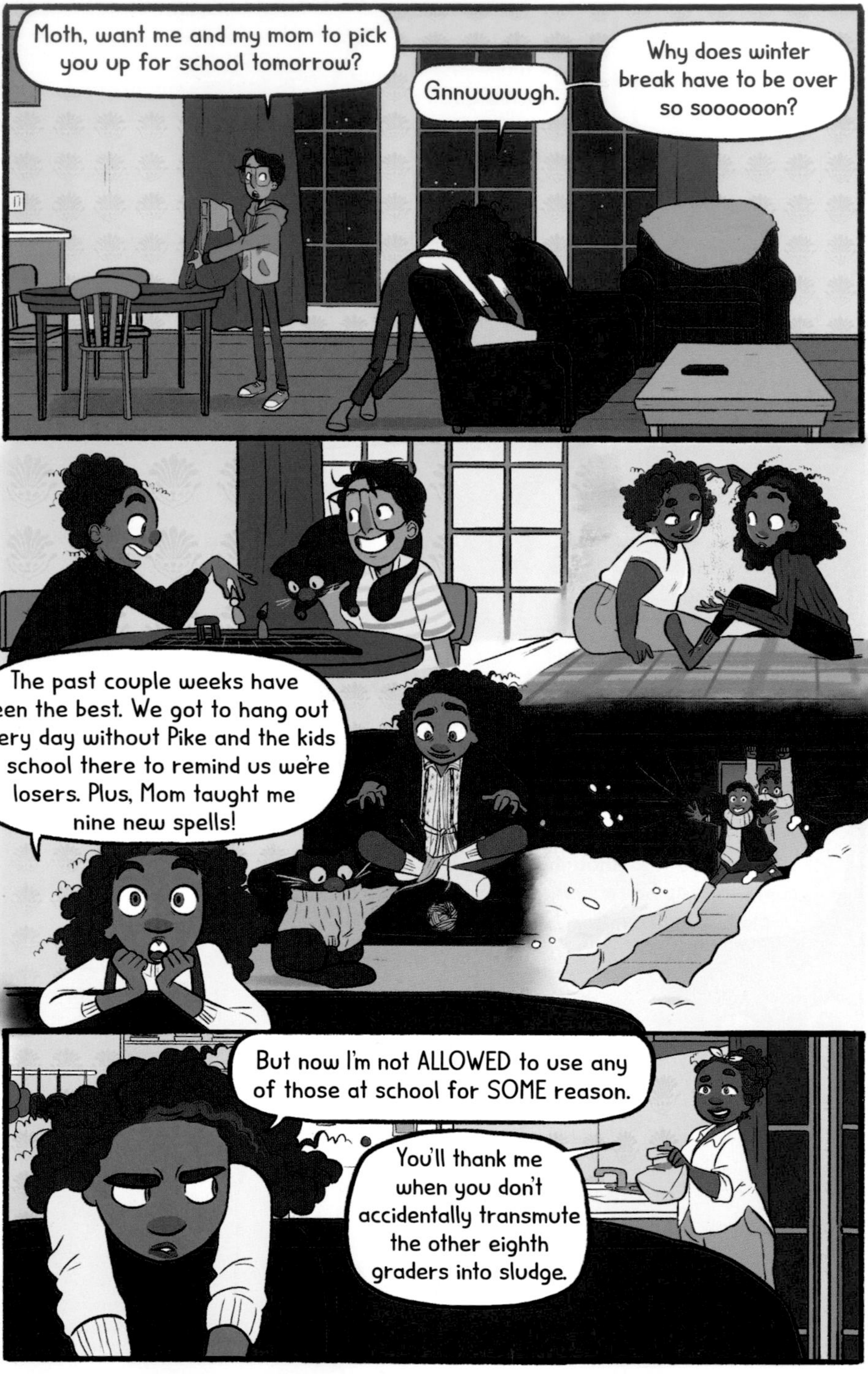

Moth, want me and my mom to pick you up for school tomorrow?
Gnnuuuuugh.
Why does winter break have to be over so soooooon?
The past couple weeks have been the best. We got to hang out every day without Pike and the kids at school there to remind us we're losers. Plus, Mom taught me nine new spells!
But now I'm not ALLOWED to use any of those at school for SOME reason.
You'll thank me when you don't accidentally transmute the other eighth graders into sludge.

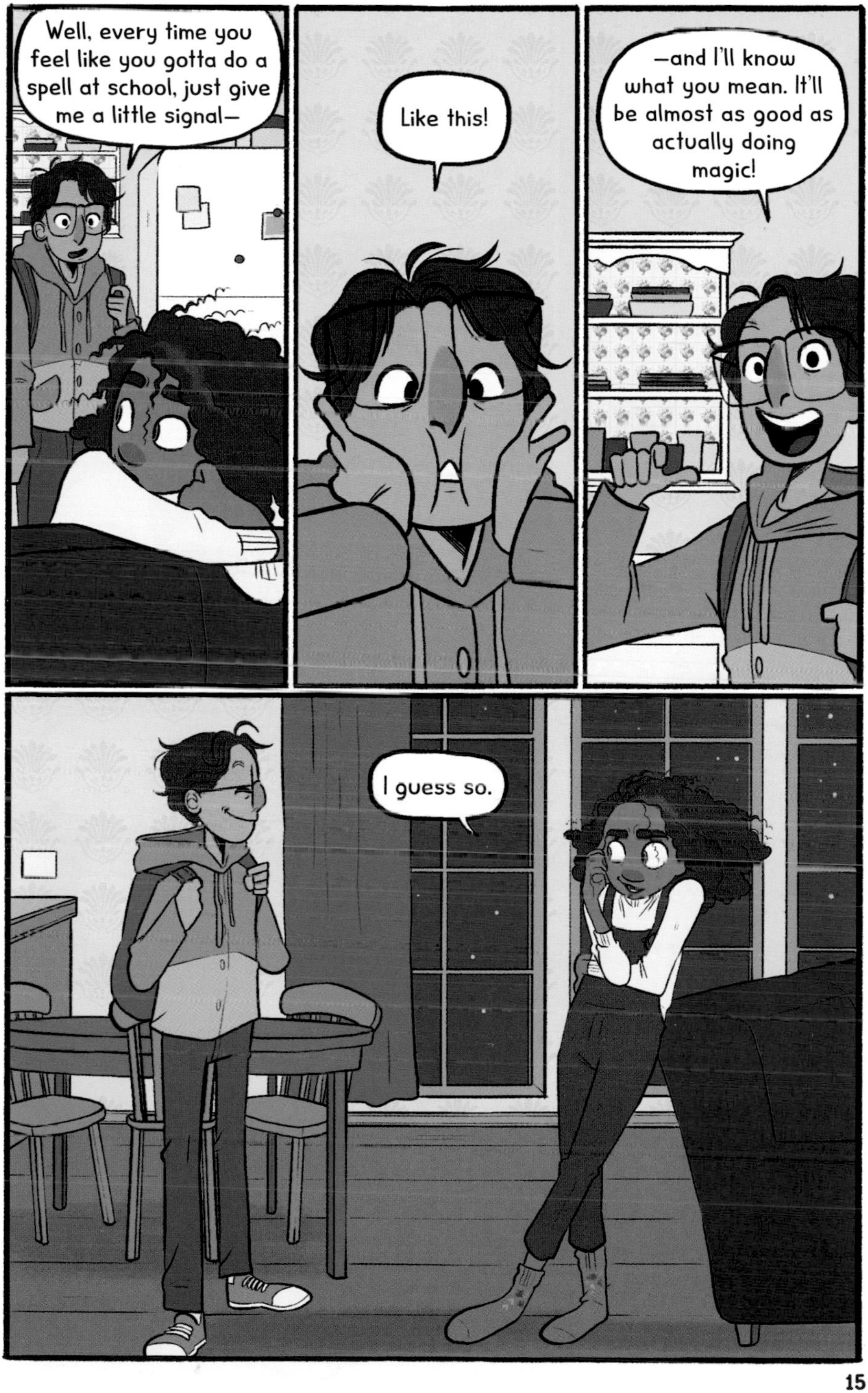
Well, every time you feel like you gotta do a spell at school, just give me a little signal—
Like this!
—and I'll know what you mean. It'll be almost as good as actually doing magic!
I guess so.

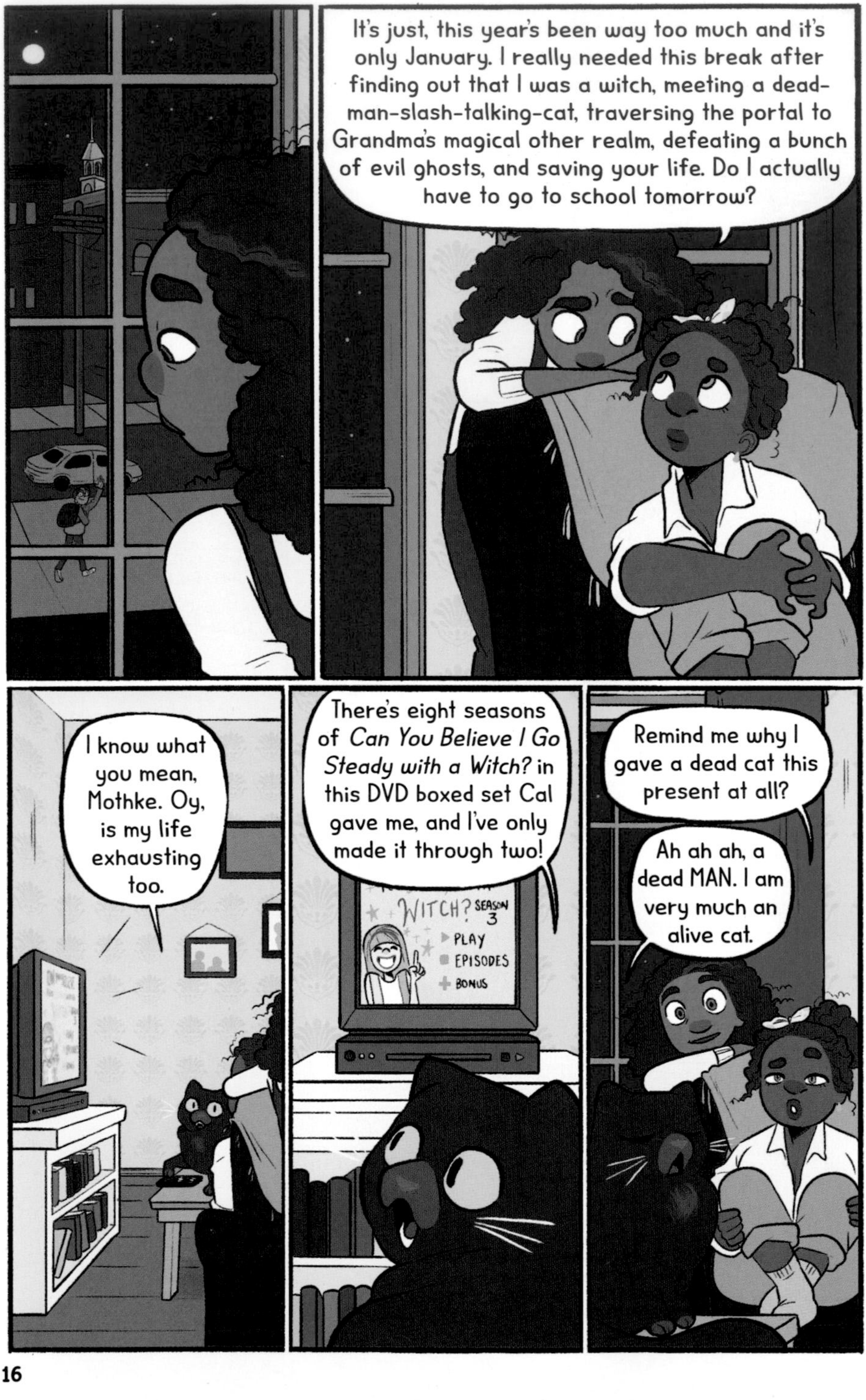
It's just, this year's been way too much and it's only January. I really needed this break after finding out that I was a witch, meeting a dead-man-slash-talking-cat, traversing the portal to Grandma's magical other realm, defeating a bunch of evil ghosts, and saving your life. Do I actually have to go to school tomorrow?
I know what you mean, Mothke. Oy, is my life exhausting too.
There's eight seasons of *Can You Believe I Go Steady with a Witch?* in this DVD boxed set Cal gave me, and I've only made it through two!
WITCH? SEASON 3
PLAY
EPISODES
BONUS
Remind me why I gave a dead cat this present at all?
Ah ah ah, a dead MAN. I am very much an alive cat.

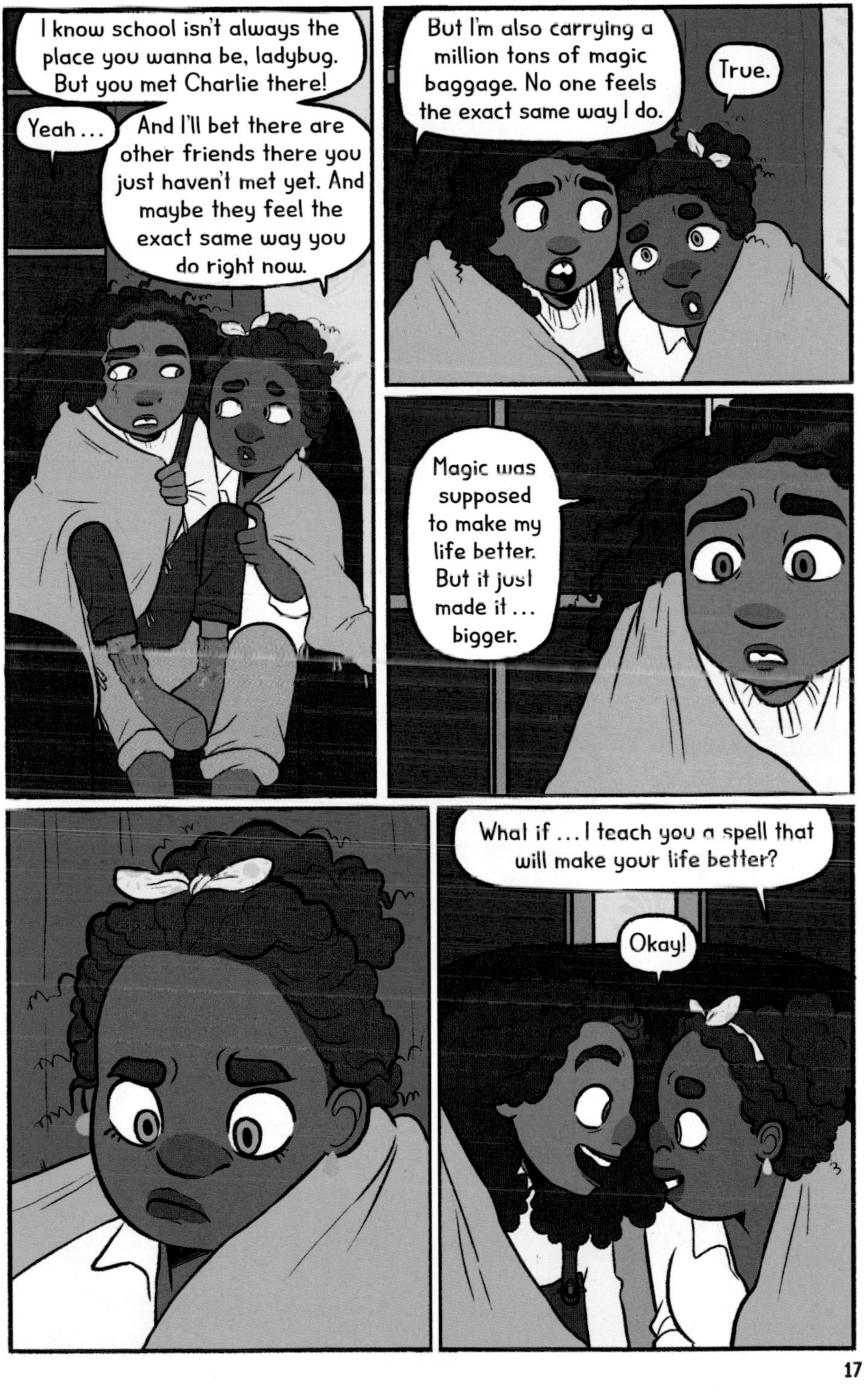
I know school isn't always the place you wanna be, ladybug. But you met Charlie there!
Yeah . . .
And I'll bet there are other friends there you just haven't met yet. And maybe they feel the exact same way you do right now.
But I'm also carrying a million tons of magic baggage. No one feels the exact same way I do.
True.
Magic was supposed to make my life better. But it just made it . . . bigger.
What if . . . I teach you a spell that will make your life better?
Okay!

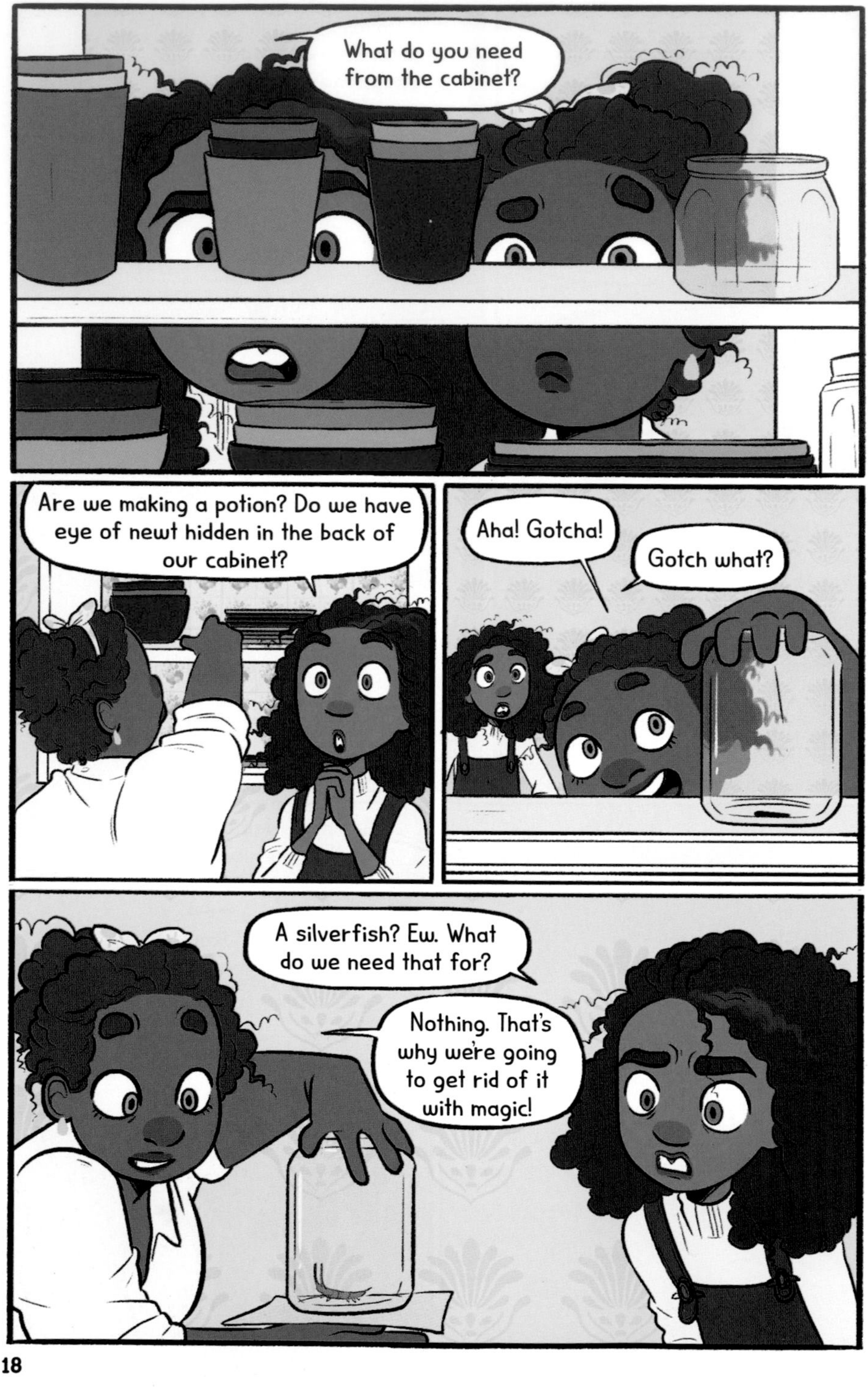
What do you need from the cabinet?
Are we making a potion? Do we have eye of newt hidden in the back of our cabinet?
Aha! Gotcha!
Gotch what?
A silverfish? Ew. What do we need that for?
Nothing. That's why we're going to get rid of it with magic!

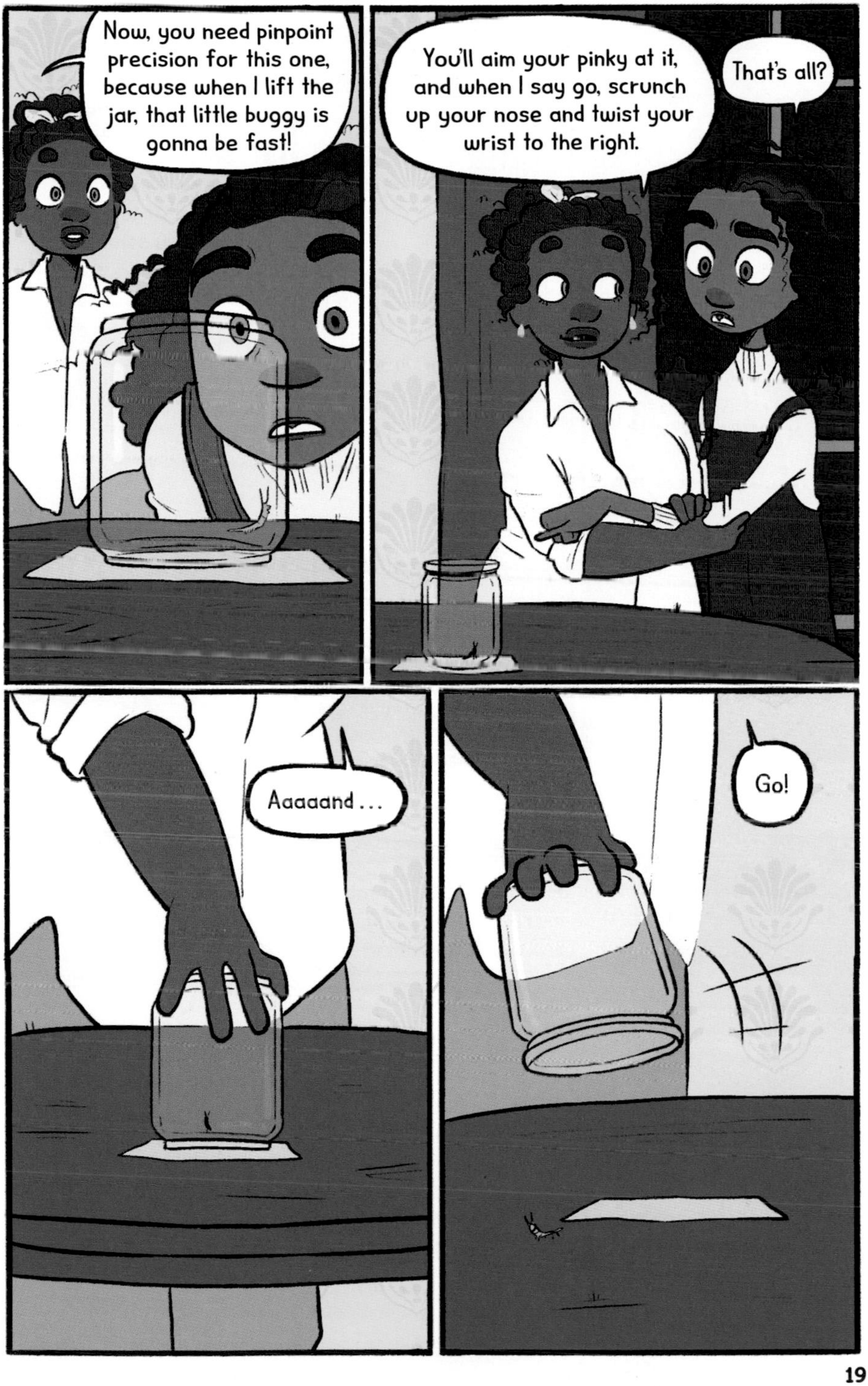
Now, you need pinpoint precision for this one, because when I lift the jar, that little buggy is gonna be fast!
You'll aim your pinky at it, and when I say go, scrunch up your nose and twist your wrist to the right.
That's all?
Aaaaand . . .
Go!

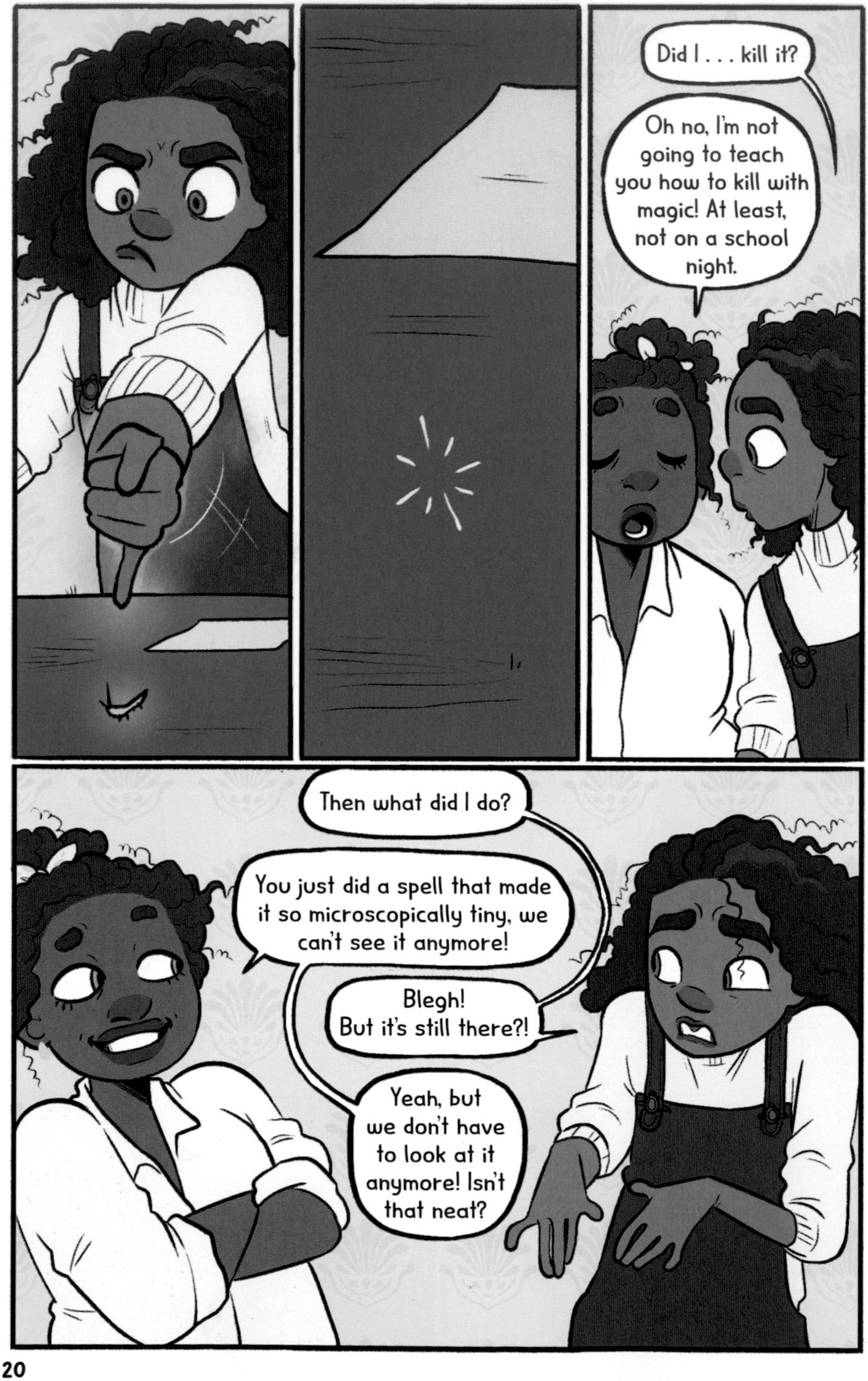
Did I . . . kill it?
Oh no, I'm not going to teach you how to kill with magic! At least, not on a school night.
Then what did I do?
You just did a spell that made it so microscopically tiny, we can't see it anymore!
Blegh! But it's still there?!
Yeah, but we don't have to look at it anymore! Isn't that neat?

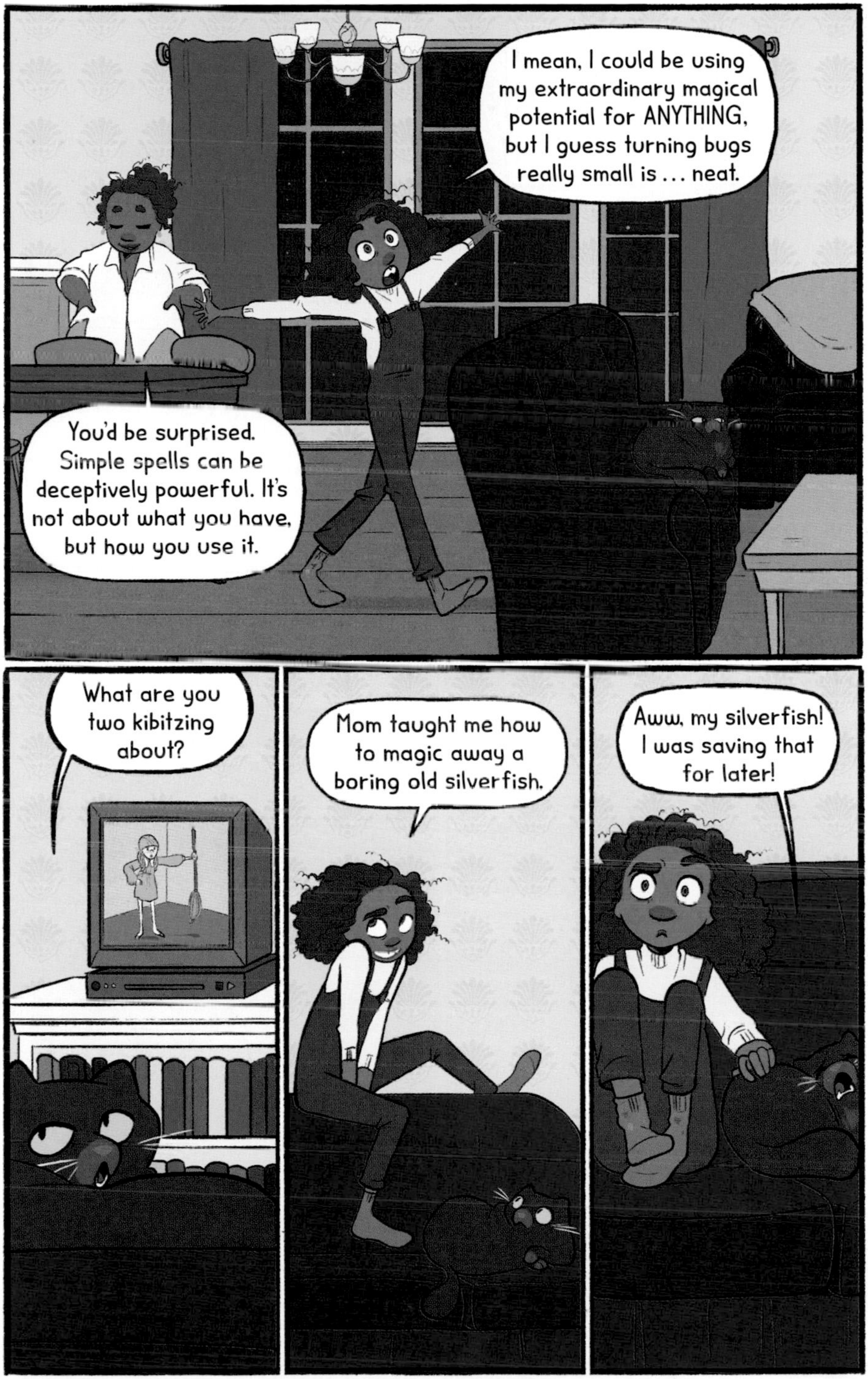
I mean, I could be using my extraordinary magical potential for ANYTHING, but I guess turning bugs really small is . . . neat.
You'd be surprised. Simple spells can be deceptively powerful. It's not about what you have, but how you use it.
What are you two kibitzing about?
Mom taught me how to magic away a boring old silverfish.
Aww, my silverfish! I was saving that for later!

CHAPTER 2

Moth, the Meme

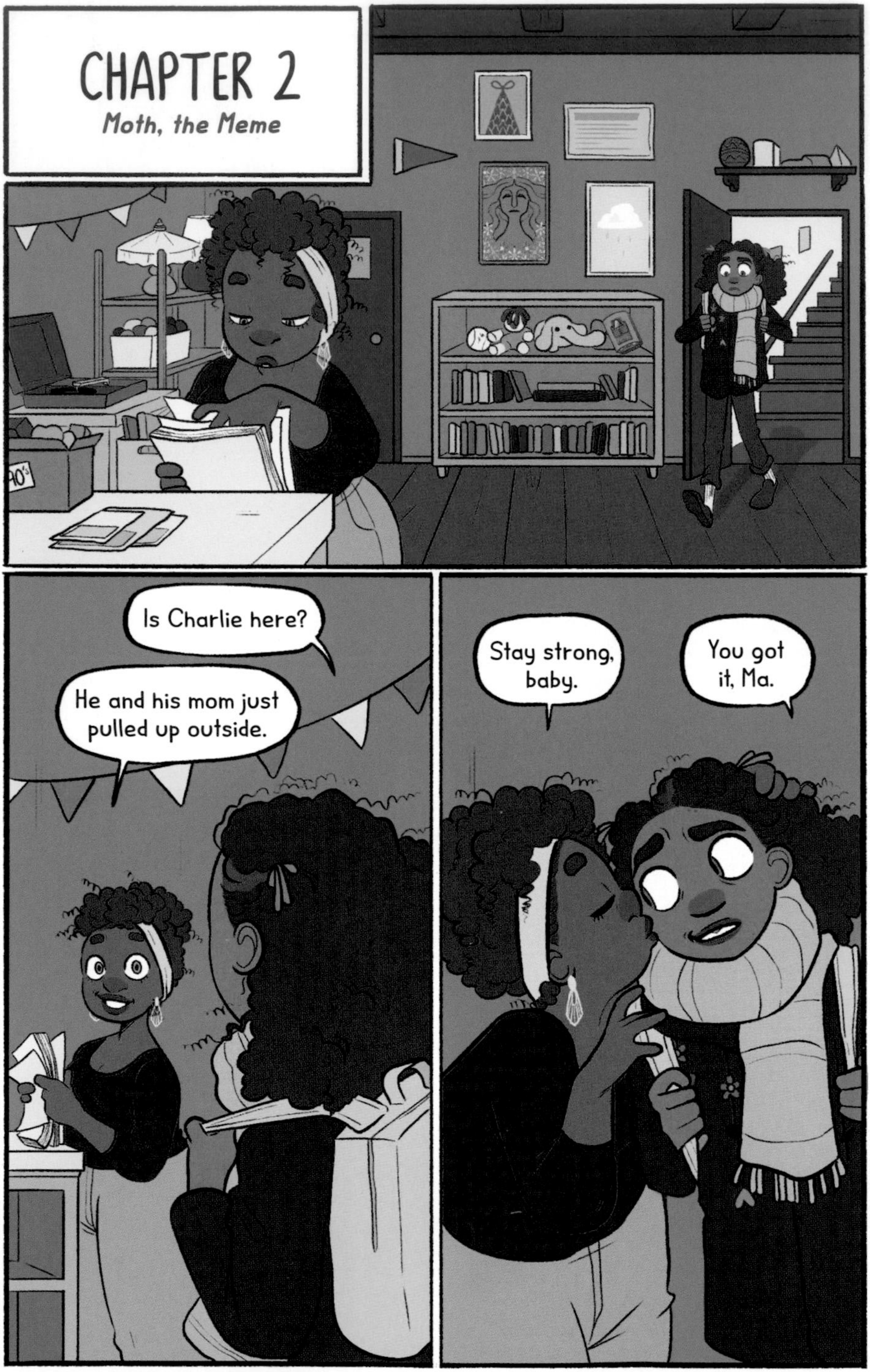
Is Charlie here?
He and his mom just pulled up outside.
Stay strong, baby.
You got it, Ma.

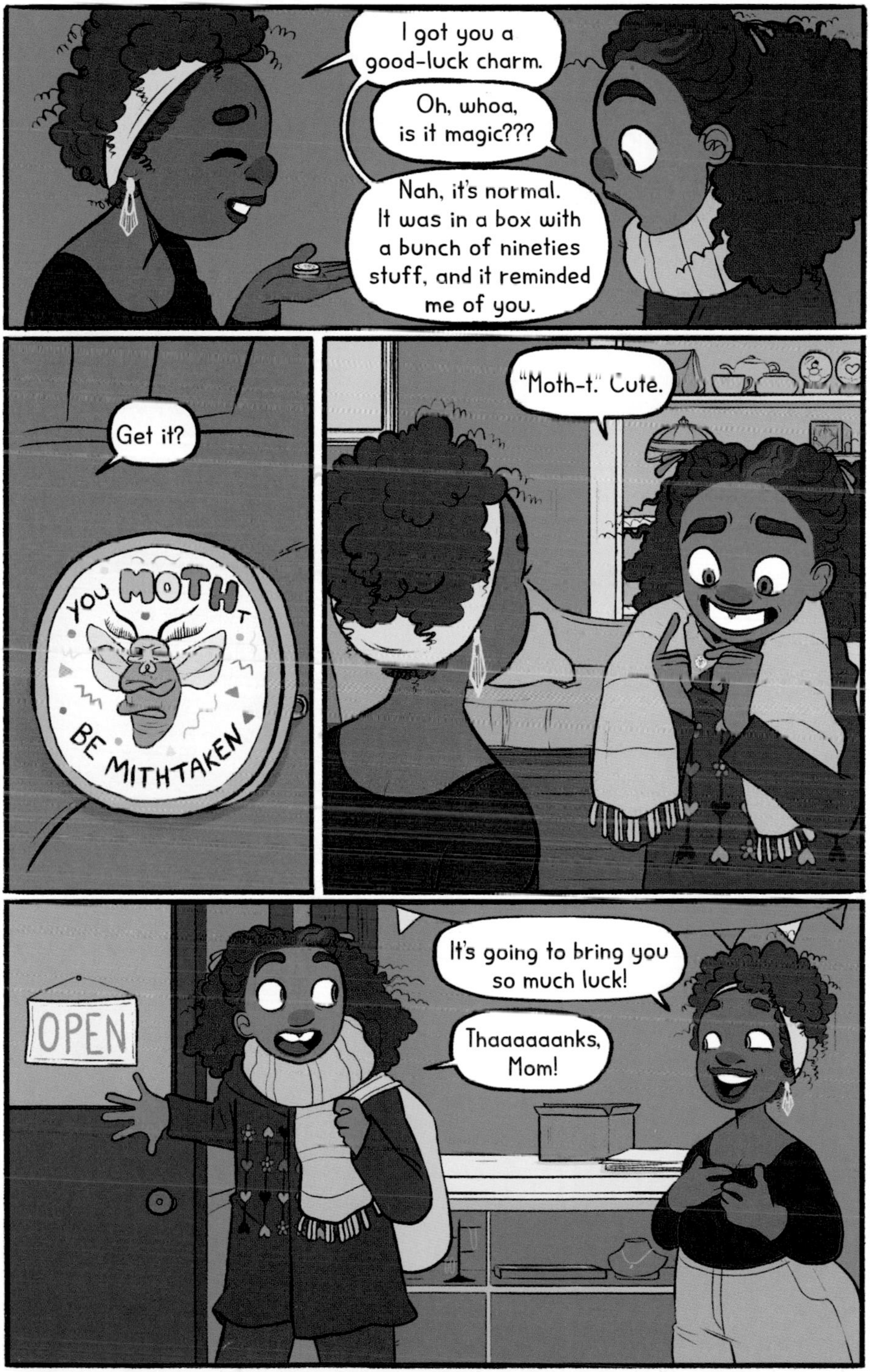
I got you a good-luck charm.
Oh, whoa, is it magic???
Nah, it's normal. It was in a box with a bunch of nineties stuff, and it reminded me of you.
Get it?
YOU MOTH T BE MITHTAKEN
"Moth-t." Cute.
OPEN
It's going to bring you so much luck!
Thaaaaaanks, Mom!

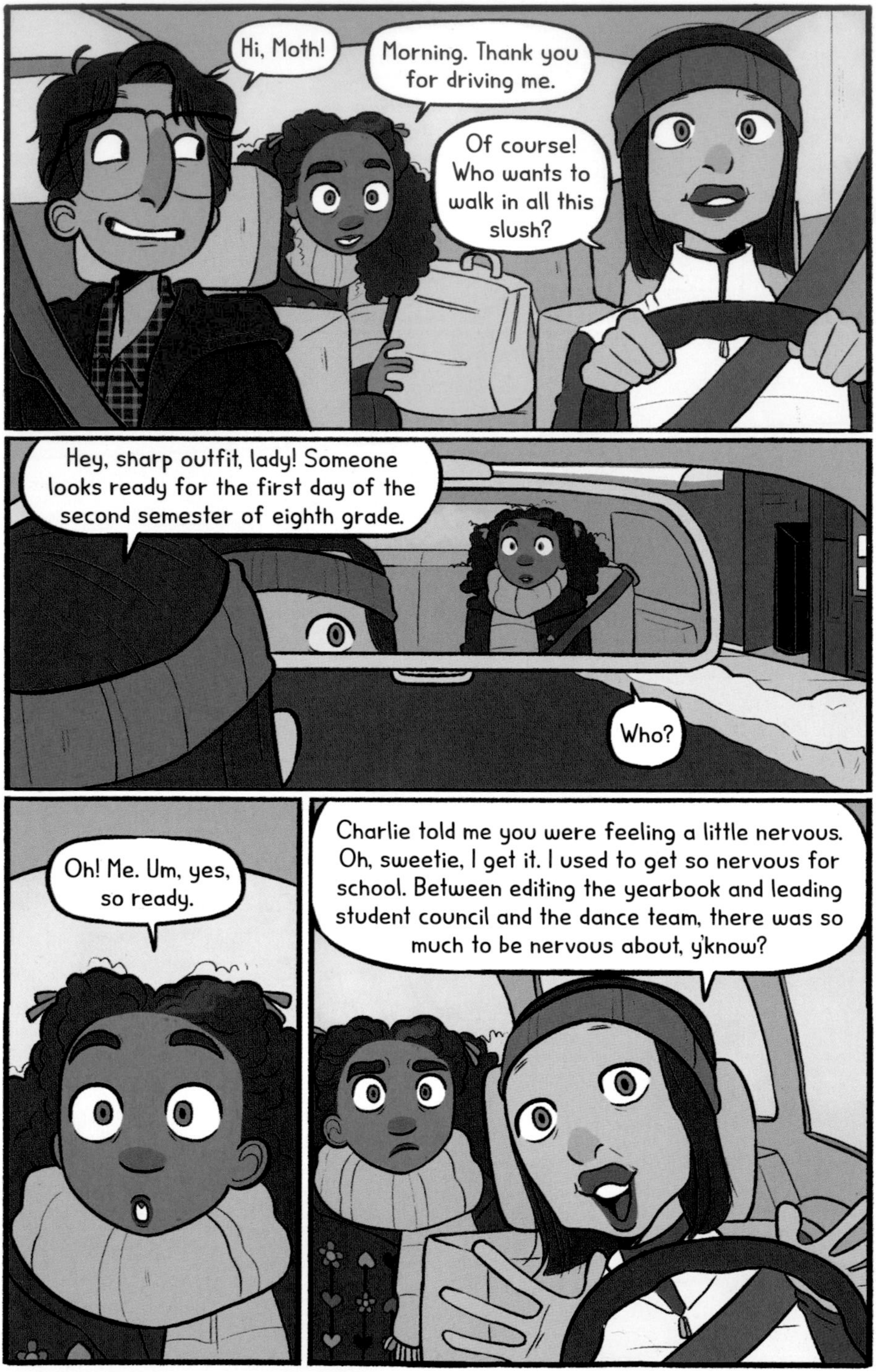
Hi, Moth!
Morning. Thank you for driving me.
Of course! Who wants to walk in all this slush?
Hey, sharp outfit, lady! Someone looks ready for the first day of the second semester of eighth grade.
Who?
Oh! Me. Um, yes, so ready.
Charlie told me you were feeling a little nervous. Oh, sweetie, I get it. I used to get so nervous for school. Between editing the yearbook and leading student council and the dance team, there was so much to be nervous about, y'know?

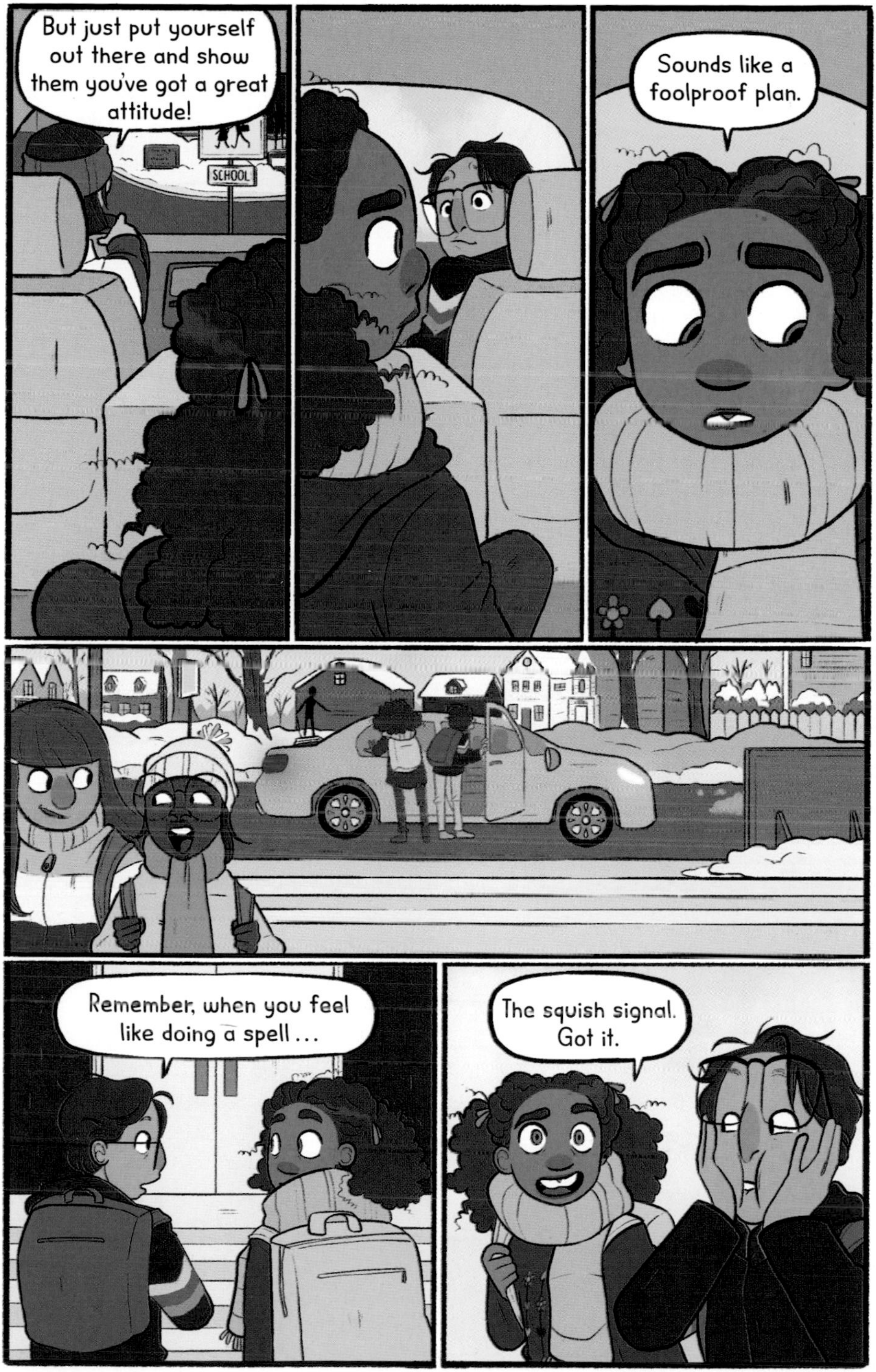

But just put yourself out there and show them you've got a great attitude!
SCHOOL
Sounds like a foolproof plan.
Remember, when you feel like doing a spell . . .
The squish signal. Got it.

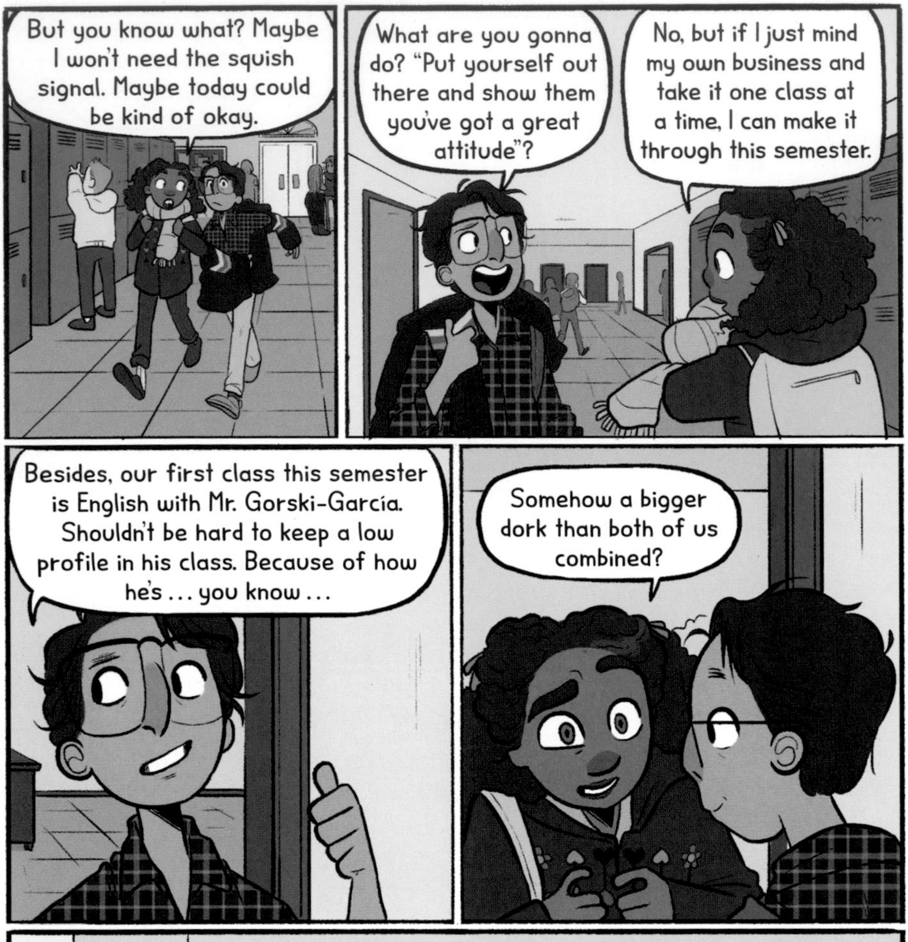

But you know what? Maybe I won't need the squish signal. Maybe today could be kind of okay.
What are you gonna do? "Put yourself out there and show them you've got a great attitude"?
No, but if I just mind my own business and take it one class at a time, I can make it through this semester.
Besides, our first class this semester is English with Mr. Gorski-García. Shouldn't be hard to keep a low profile in his class. Because of how he's . . . you know . . .
Somehow a bigger dork than both of us combined?
Exactly. He'll probably draw most of the attention.
LOSER

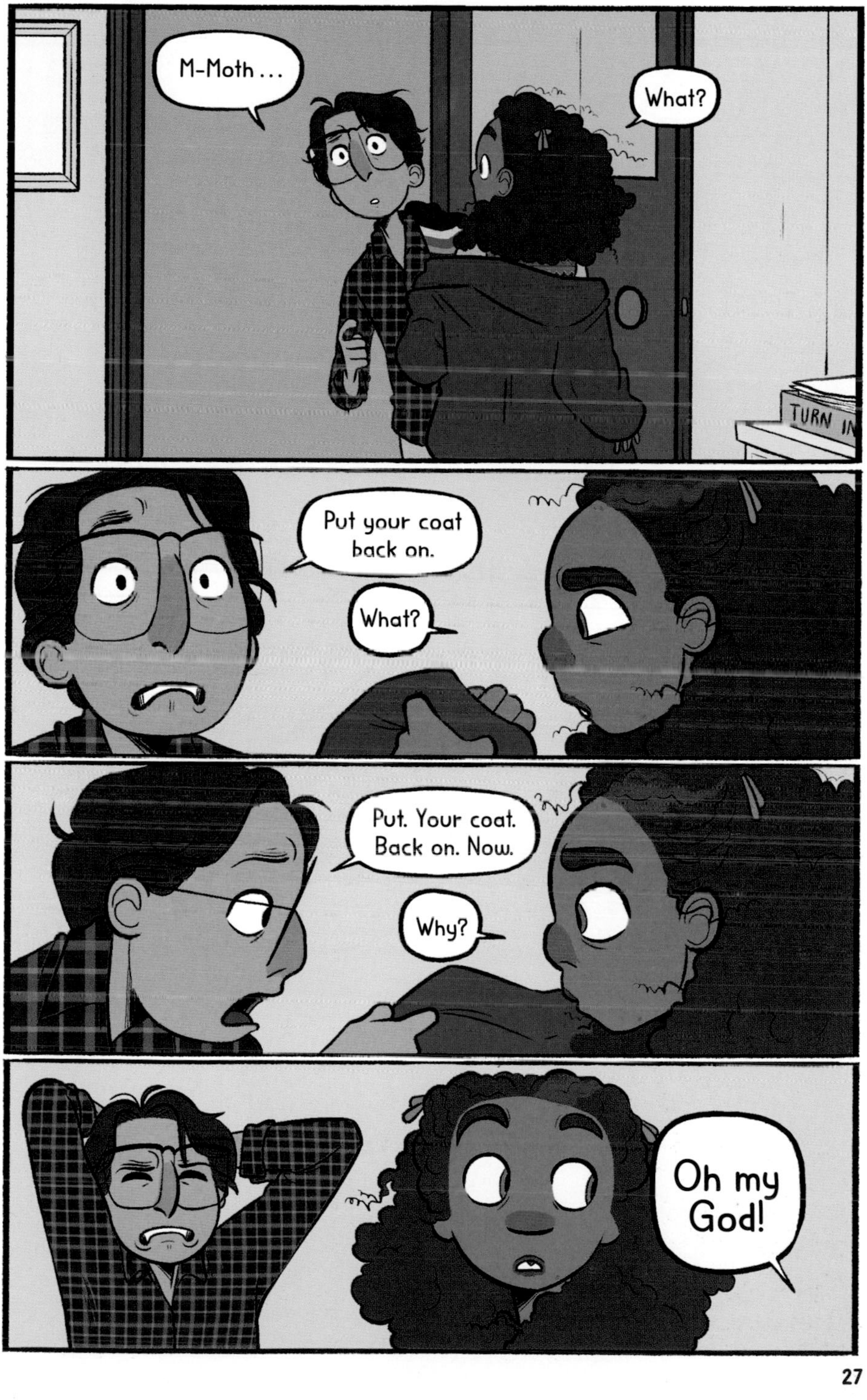
M-Moth . . .
What?
TURN IN
Put your coat back on.
What?
Put. Your coat. Back on. Now.
Why?
Oh my God!

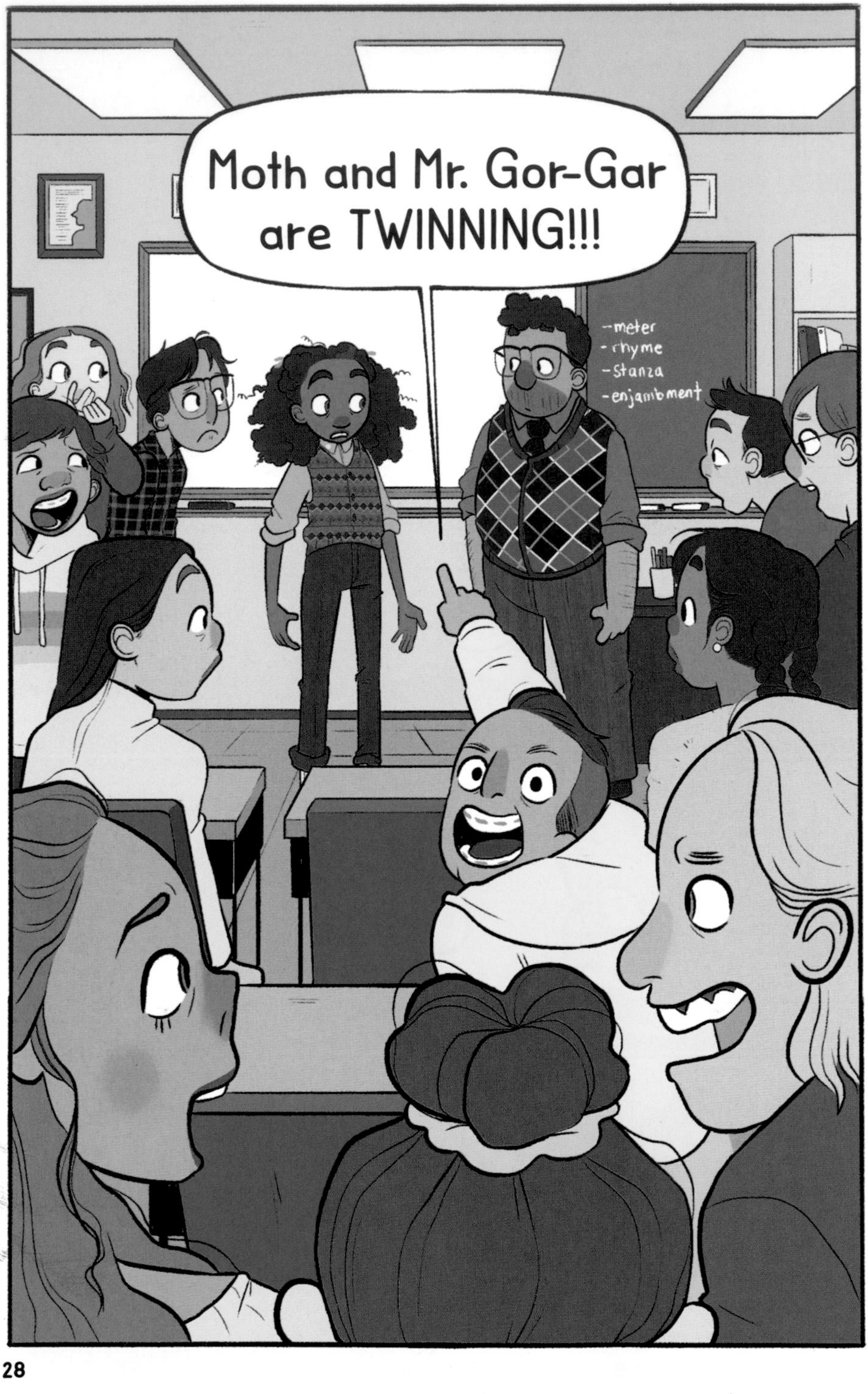
Moth and Mr. Gor-Gar are TWINNING!!!
-meter
-rhyme
-stanza
-enjambment

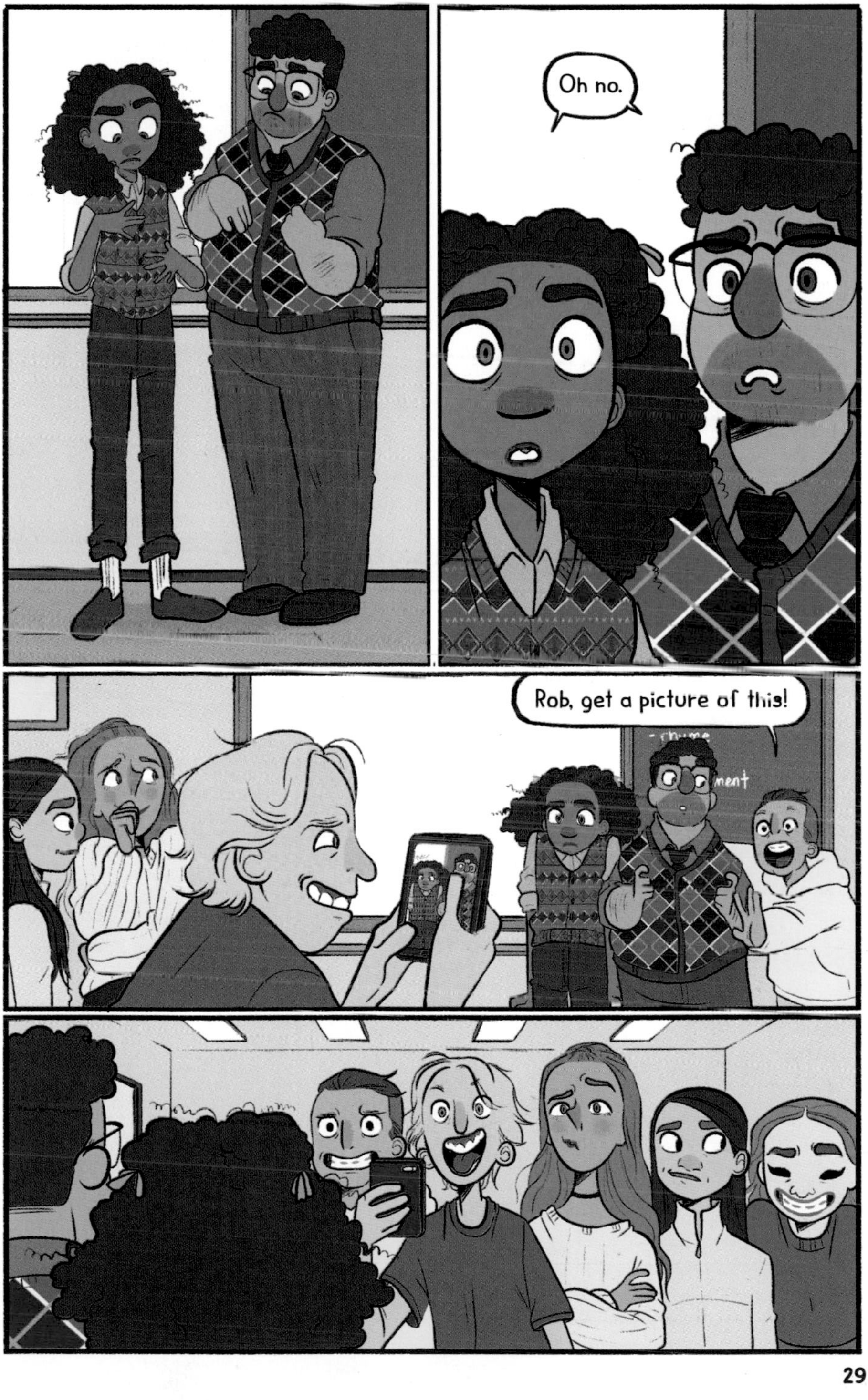
Oh no.
Rob, get a picture of this!

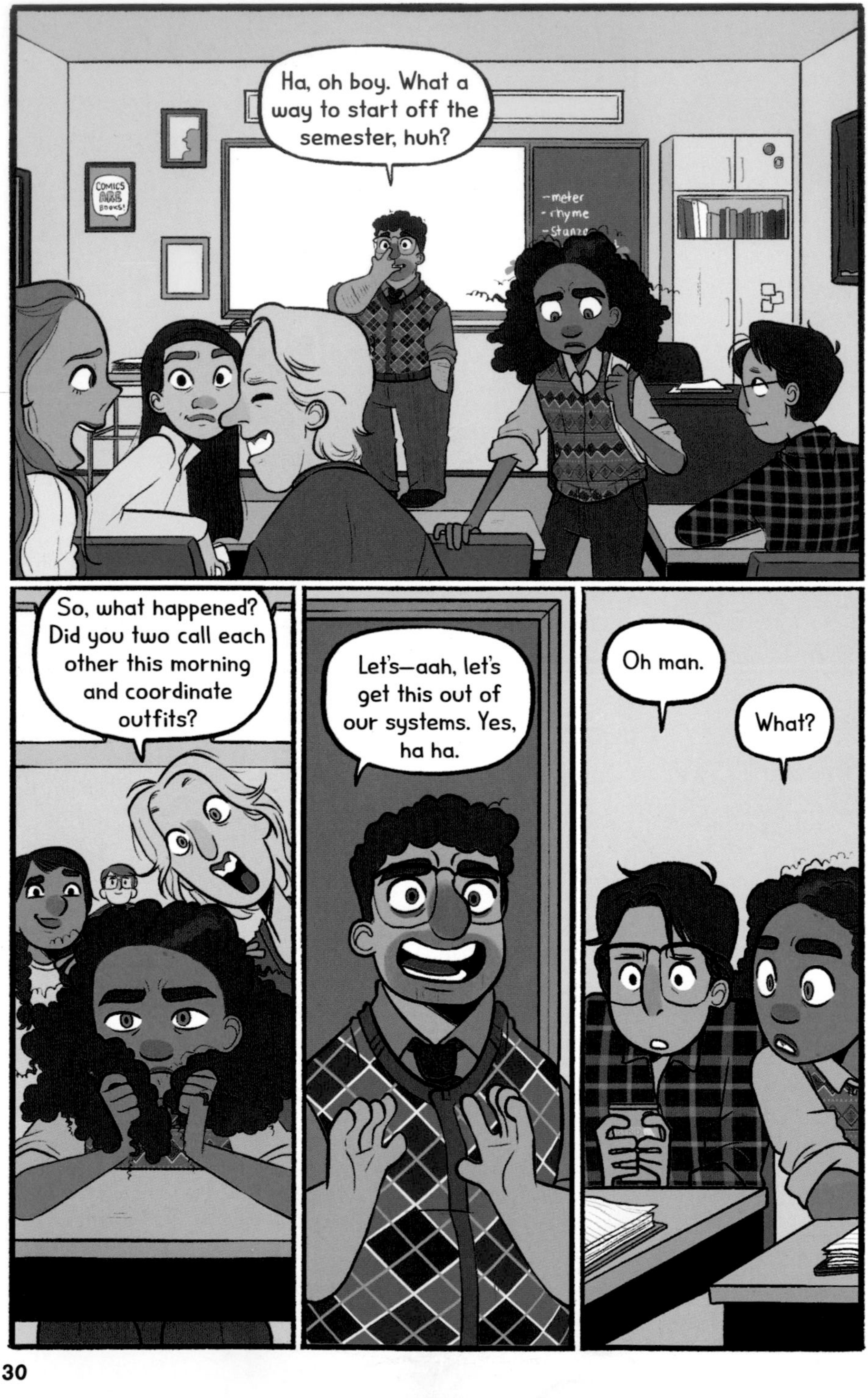
COMICS ARE BOOKS!
-meter
-rhyme
Ha, oh boy. What a way to start off the semester, huh?
So, what happened? Did you two call each other this morning and coordinate outfits?
Let's—aah, let's get this out of our systems. Yes, ha ha.
Oh man.
What?

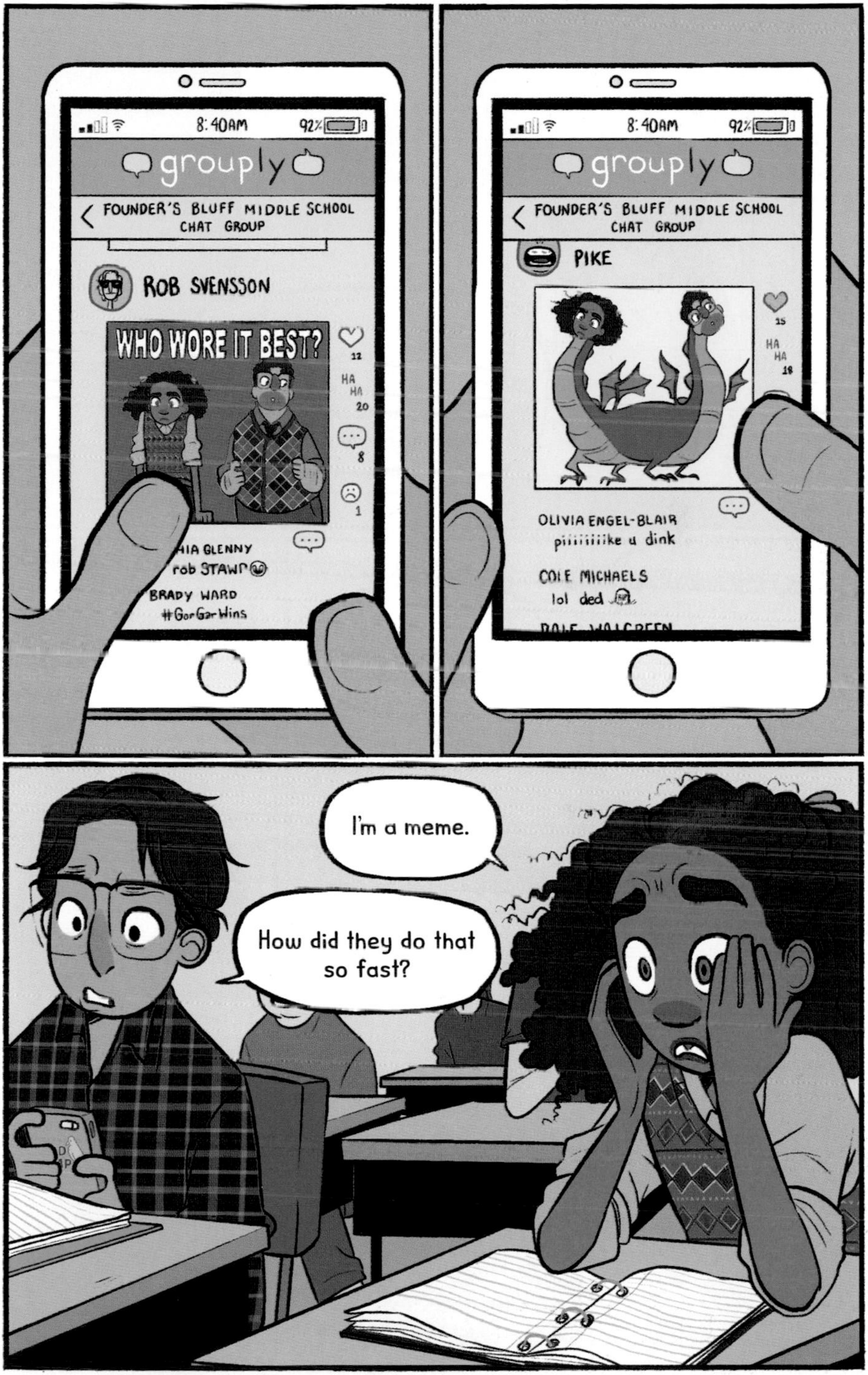
8:40AM
92%
grouply
FOUNDER'S BLUFF MIDDLE SCHOOL CHAT GROUP
ROB SVENSSON
WHO WORE IT BEST?
12
HA HA
20
8
1
rob STAWP
BRADY WARD
#GorGarWins
8:40AM
92%
grouply
FOUNDER'S BLUFF MIDDLE SCHOOL CHAT GROUP
PIKE
15
HA HA
18
OLIVIA ENGEL-BLAIR
piiiiiiiike u dink
COLE MICHAELS
lol ded
I'm a meme.
How did they do that so fast?

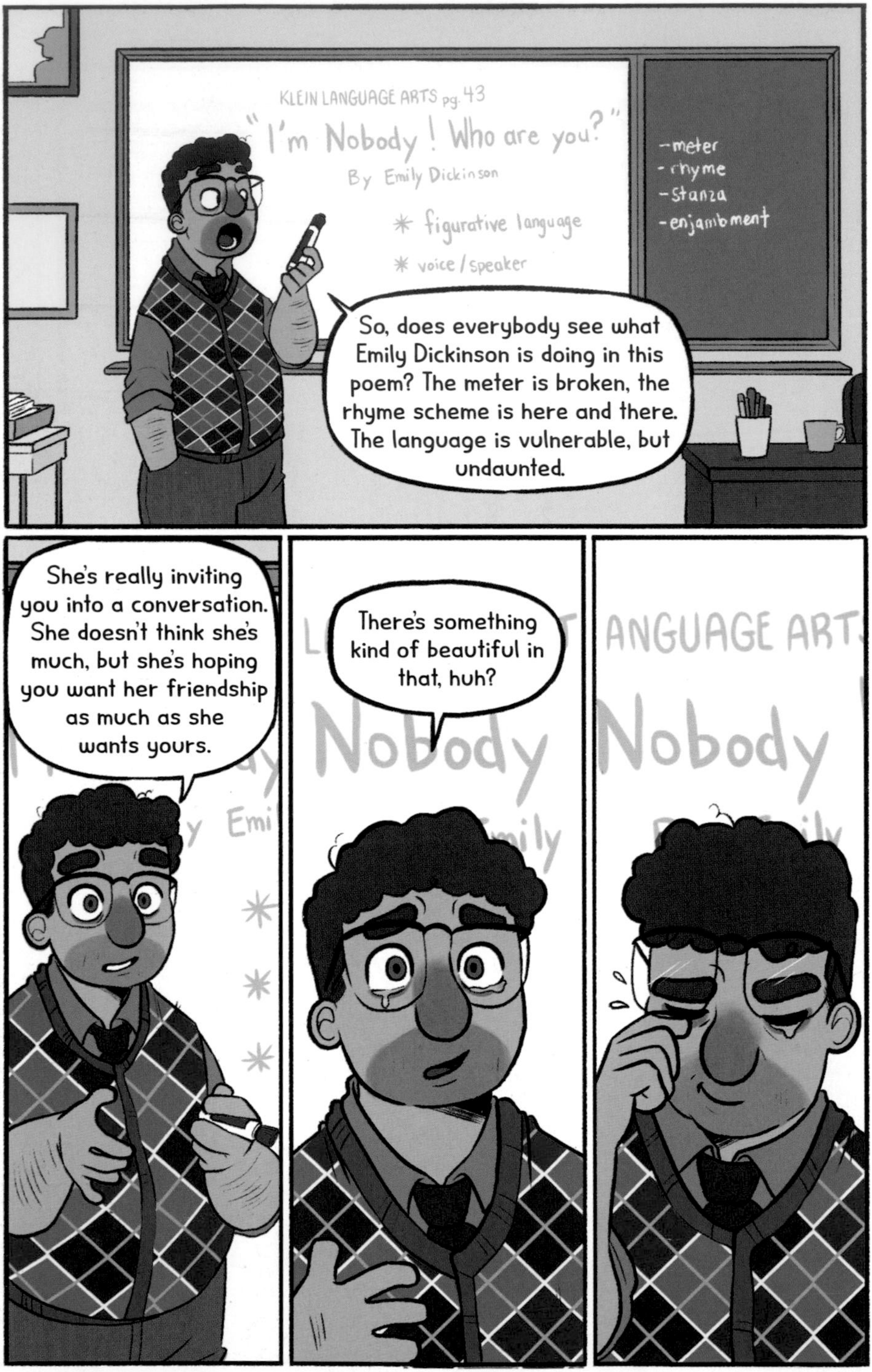

KLEIN LANGUAGE ARTS pg. 43
"I'm Nobody! Who are you?"
By Emily Dickinson
* figurative language
* voice / speaker
-meter
-rhyme
-stanza
-enjambment
So, does everybody see what Emily Dickinson is doing in this poem? The meter is broken, the rhyme scheme is here and there. The language is vulnerable, but undaunted.
She's really inviting you into a conversation. She doesn't think she's much, but she's hoping you want her friendship as much as she wants yours.
There's something kind of beautiful in that, huh?

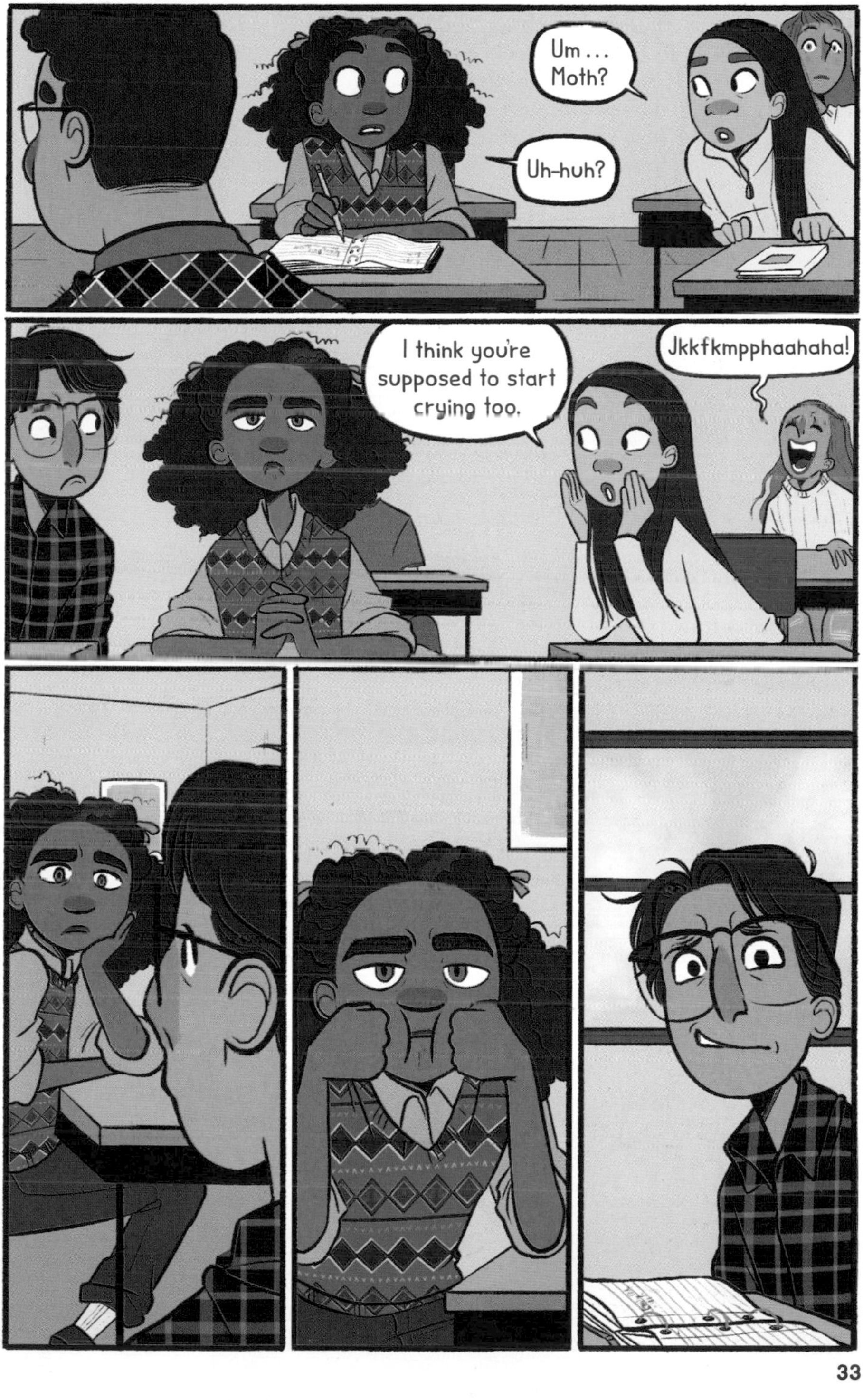
Um . . . Moth?
Uh-huh?
I think you're supposed to start crying too.
Jkkfkmpphaahaha!

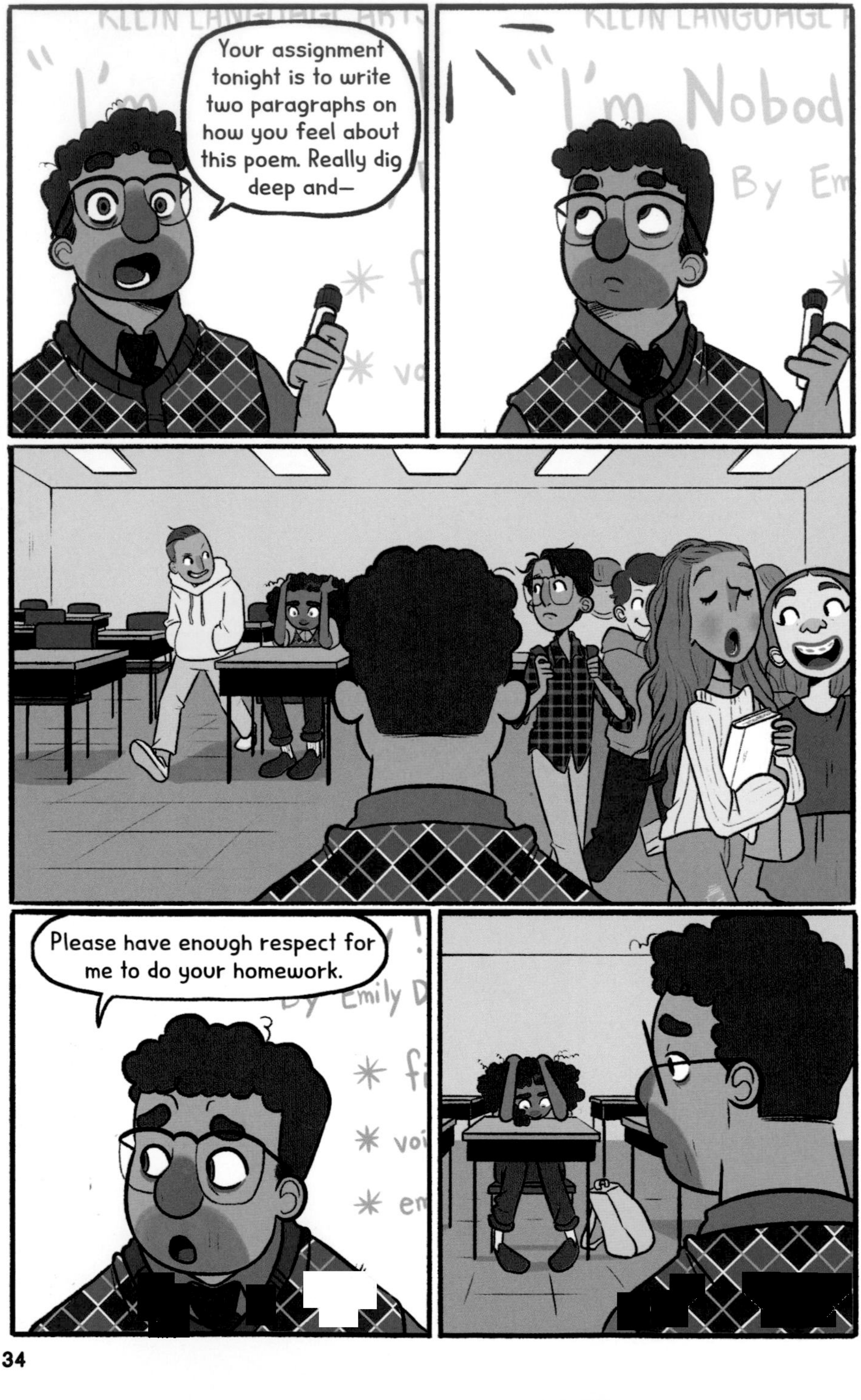
Your assignment tonight is to write two paragraphs on how you feel about this poem. Really dig deep and—
Please have enough respect for me to do your homework.

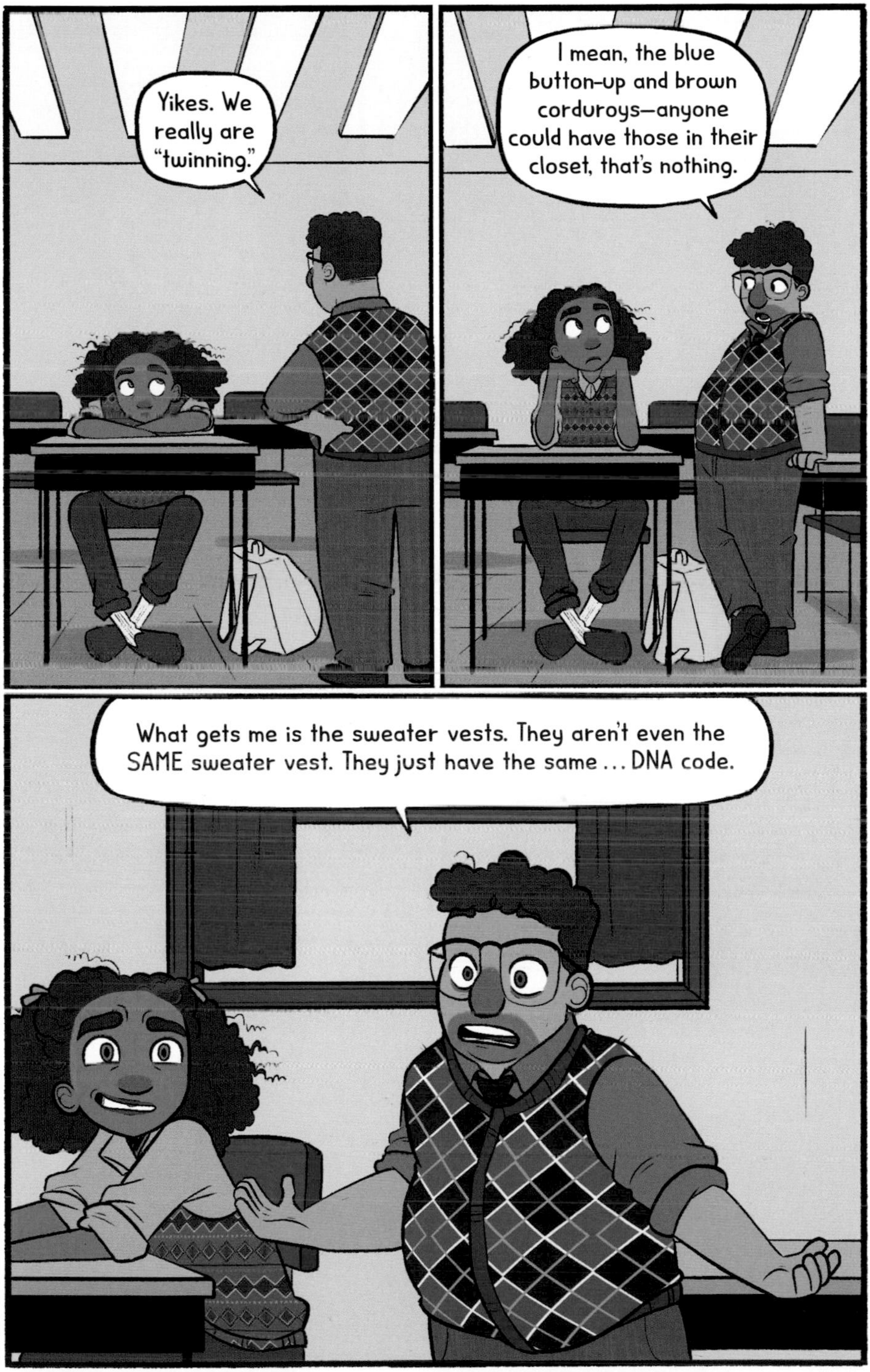
Yikes. We really are "twinning."
I mean, the blue button-up and brown corduroys—anyone could have those in their closet, that's nothing.
What gets me is the sweater vests. They aren't even the SAME sweater vest. They just have the same . . . DNA code.

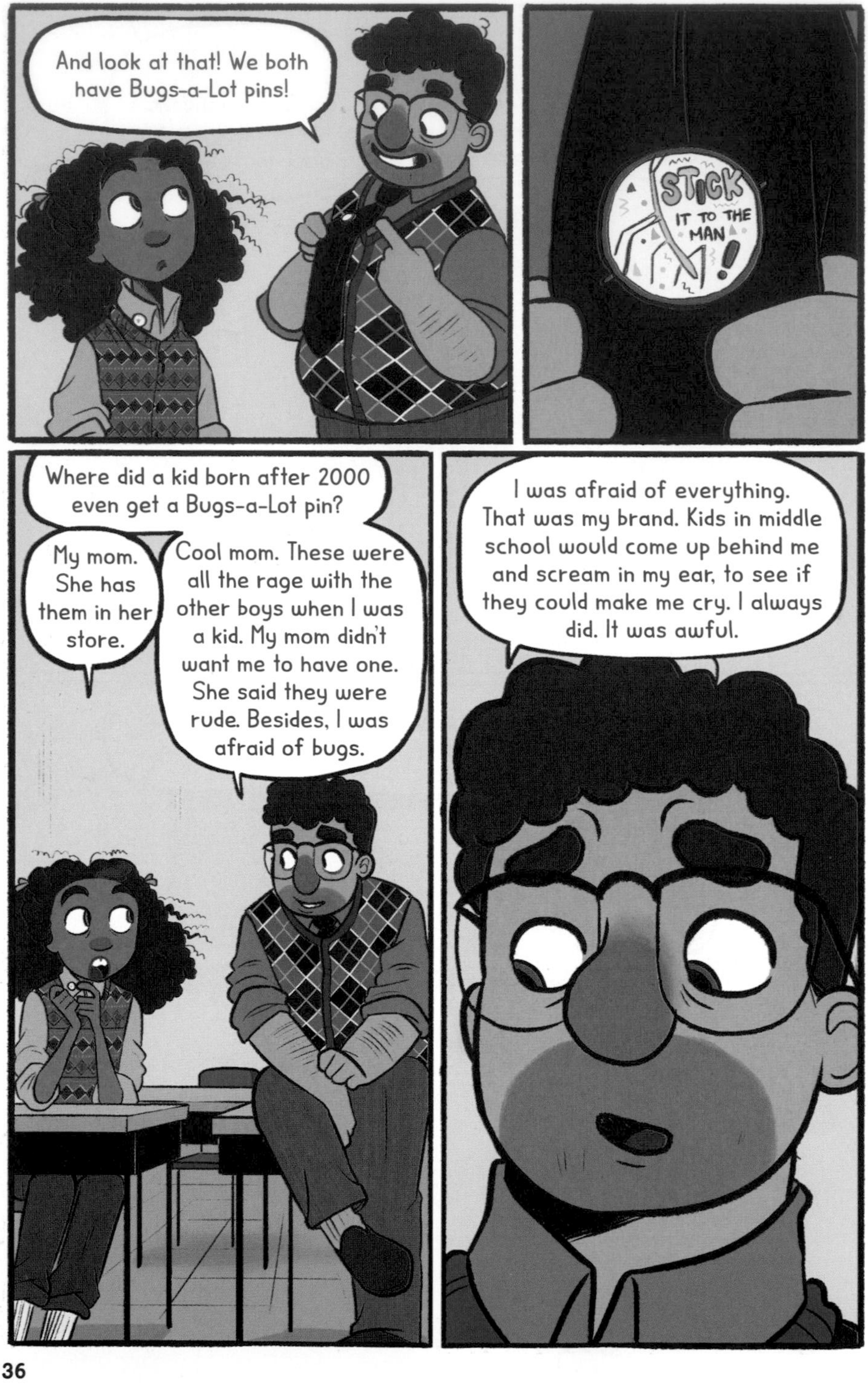
And look at that! We both have Bugs-a-Lot pins!
STICK IT TO THE MAN!
Where did a kid born after 2000 even get a Bugs-a-Lot pin?
My mom. She has them in her store.
Cool mom. These were all the rage with the other boys when I was a kid. My mom didn't want me to have one. She said they were rude. Besides, I was afraid of bugs.
I was afraid of everything. That was my brand. Kids in middle school would come up behind me and scream in my ear, to see if they could make me cry. I always did. It was awful.

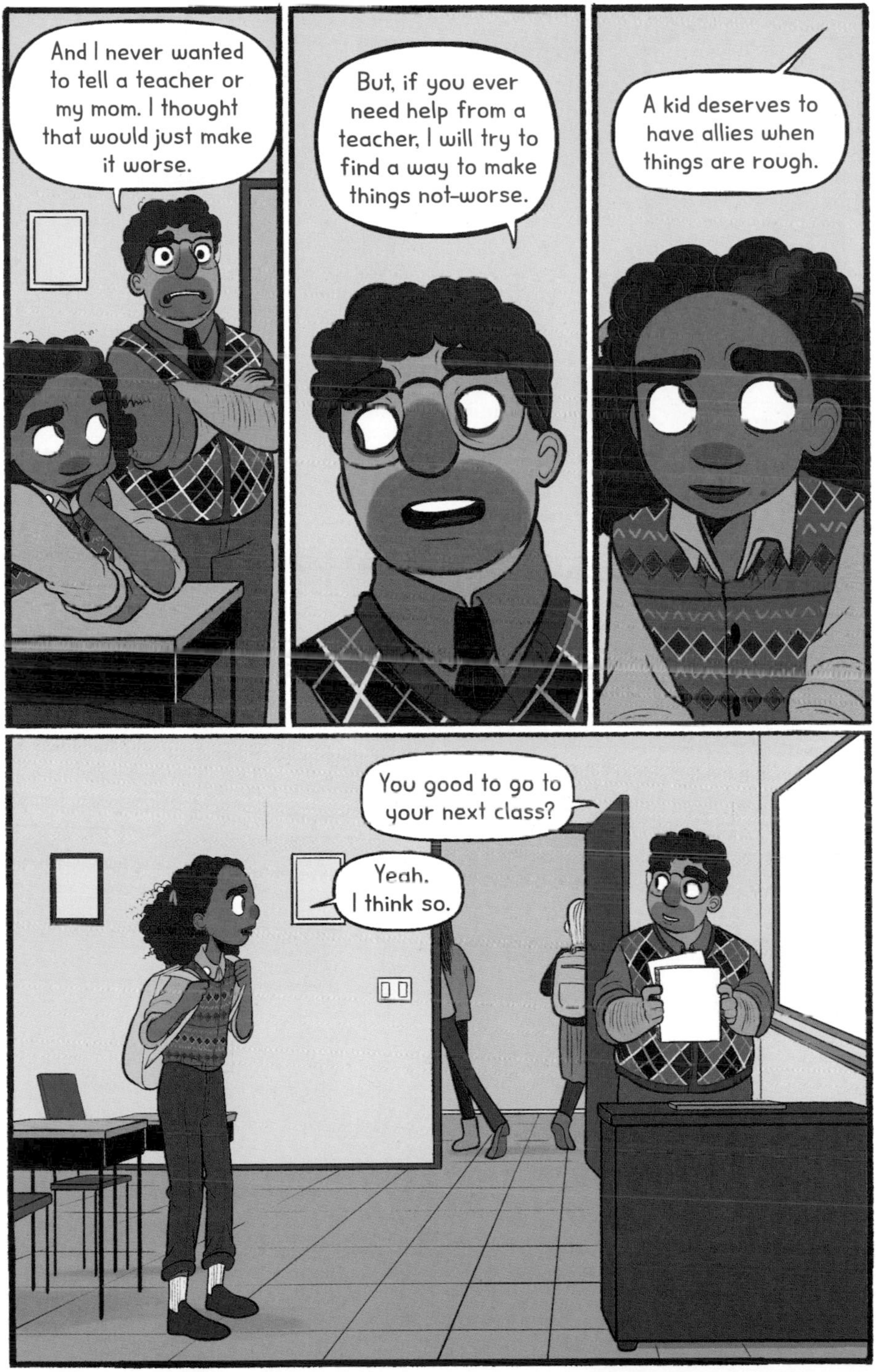
And I never wanted to tell a teacher or my mom. I thought that would just make it worse.
But, if you ever need help from a teacher, I will try to find a way to make things not-worse.
A kid deserves to have allies when things are rough.
You good to go to your next class?
Yeah. I think so.

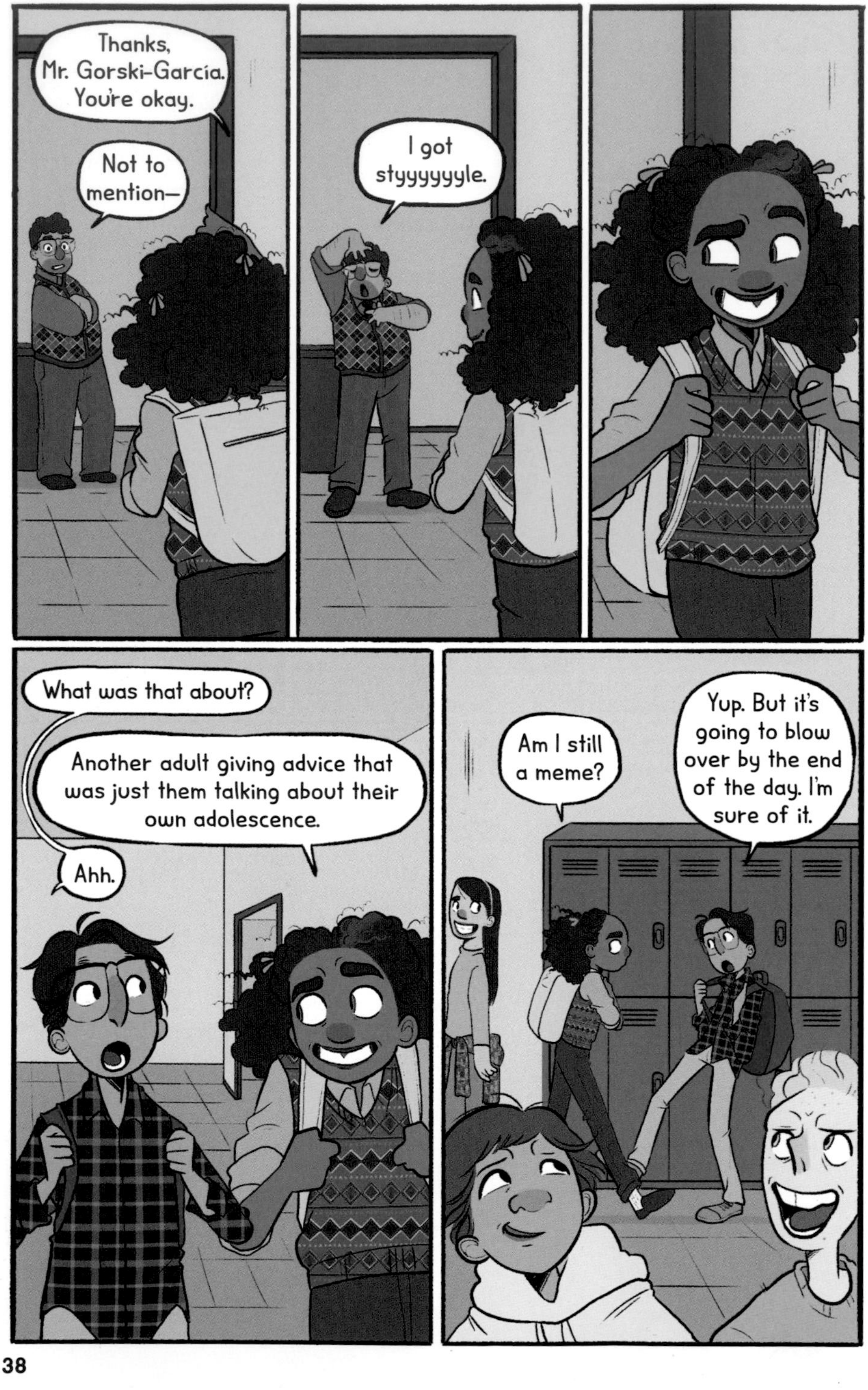
Thanks, Mr. Gorski-García. You're okay.
Not to mention—
I got styyyyyyle.
What was that about?
Another adult giving advice that was just them talking about their own adolescence.
Ahh.
Am I still a meme?
Yup. But it's going to blow over by the end of the day. I'm sure of it.

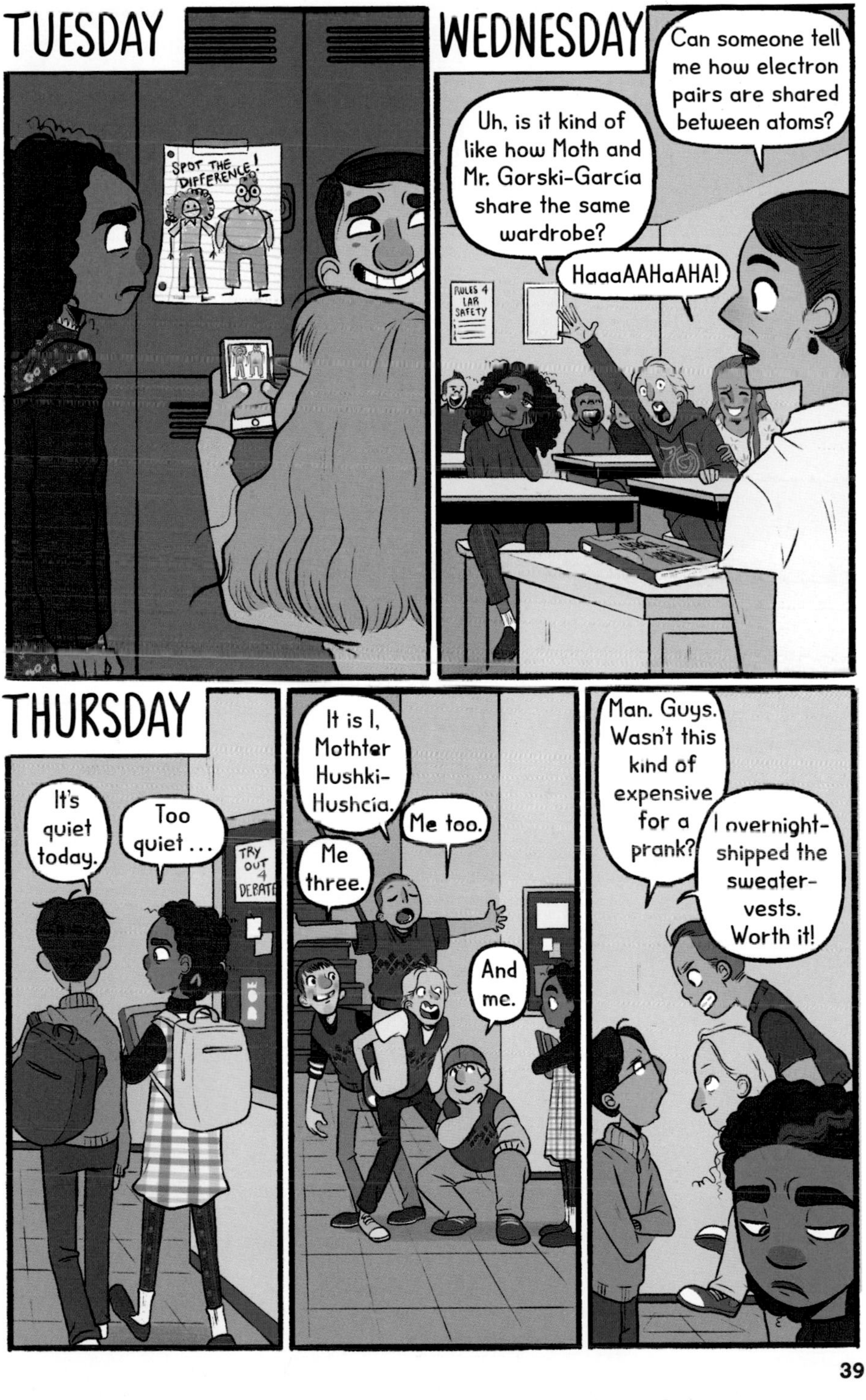
TUESDAY
SPOT THE DIFFERENCE!
WEDNESDAY
Can someone tell me how electron pairs are shared between atoms?
Uh, is it kind of like how Moth and Mr. Gorski-García share the same wardrobe?
HaaaAAHaAHA!
RULES 4 LAB SAFETY
THURSDAY
It's quiet today.
Too quiet . . .
TRY OUT 4 DEBATE
It is I, Mothter Hushki-Hushcía.
Me too.
Me three.
And me.
Man. Guys. Wasn't this kind of expensive for a prank?
I overnight-shipped the sweater-vests. Worth it!

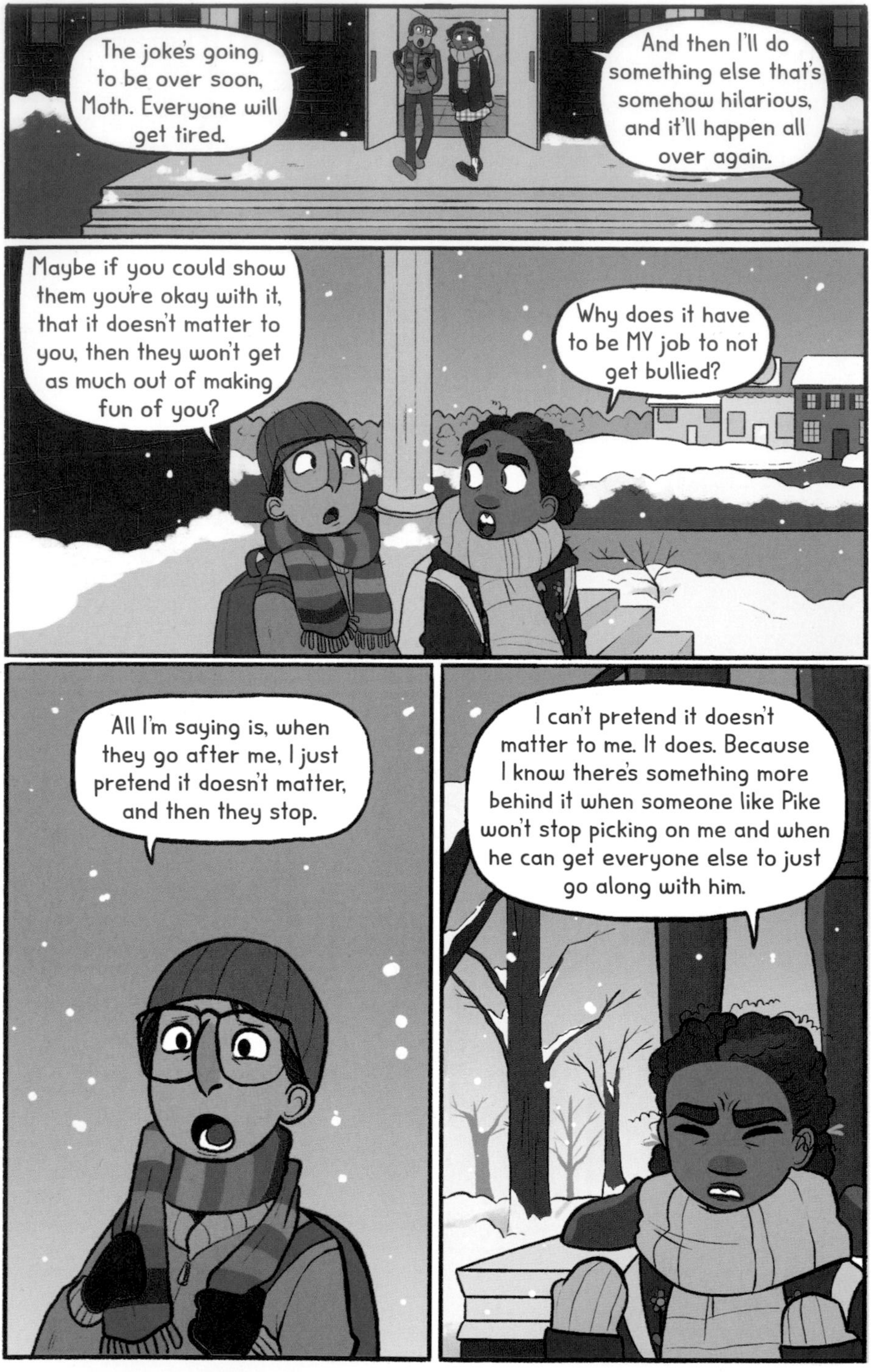
The joke's going to be over soon, Moth. Everyone will get tired.
And then I'll do something else that's somehow hilarious, and it'll happen all over again.
Maybe if you could show them you're okay with it, that it doesn't matter to you, then they won't get as much out of making fun of you?
Why does it have to be MY job to not get bullied?
All I'm saying is, when they go after me, I just pretend it doesn't matter, and then they stop.
I can't pretend it doesn't matter to me. It does. Because I know there's something more behind it when someone like Pike won't stop picking on me and when he can get everyone else to just go along with him.

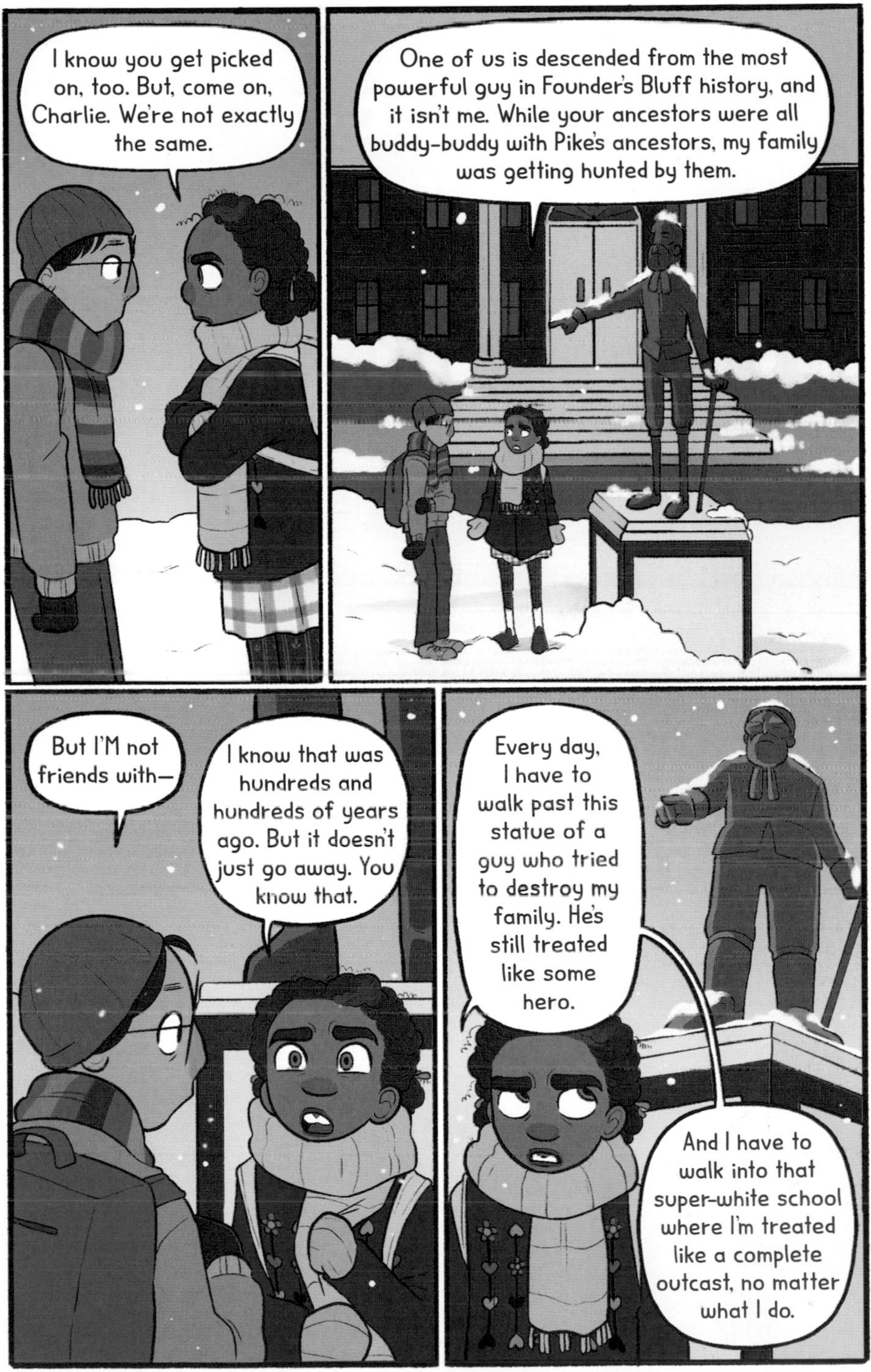
I know you get picked on, too. But, come on, Charlie. We're not exactly the same.
One of us is descended from the most powerful guy in Founder's Bluff history, and it isn't me. While your ancestors were all buddy-buddy with Pike's ancestors, my family was getting hunted by them.
But I'M not friends with—
I know that was hundreds and hundreds of years ago. But it doesn't just go away. You know that.
Every day, I have to walk past this statue of a guy who tried to destroy my family. He's still treated like some hero.
And I have to walk into that super-white school where I'm treated like a complete outcast, no matter what I do.

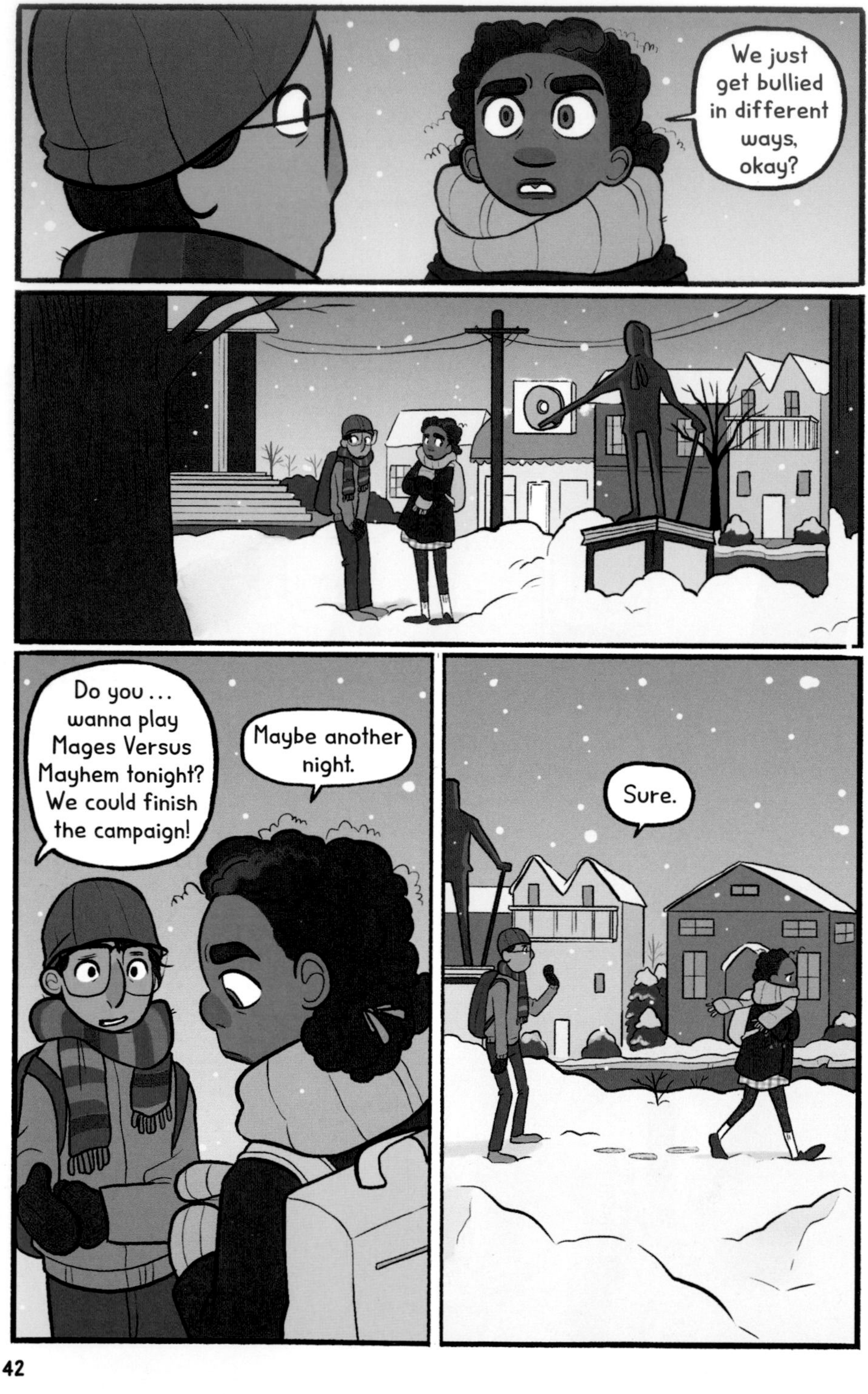
We just get bullied in different ways, okay?
Do you . . . wanna play Mages Versus Mayhem tonight? We could finish the campaign!
Maybe another night.
Sure.

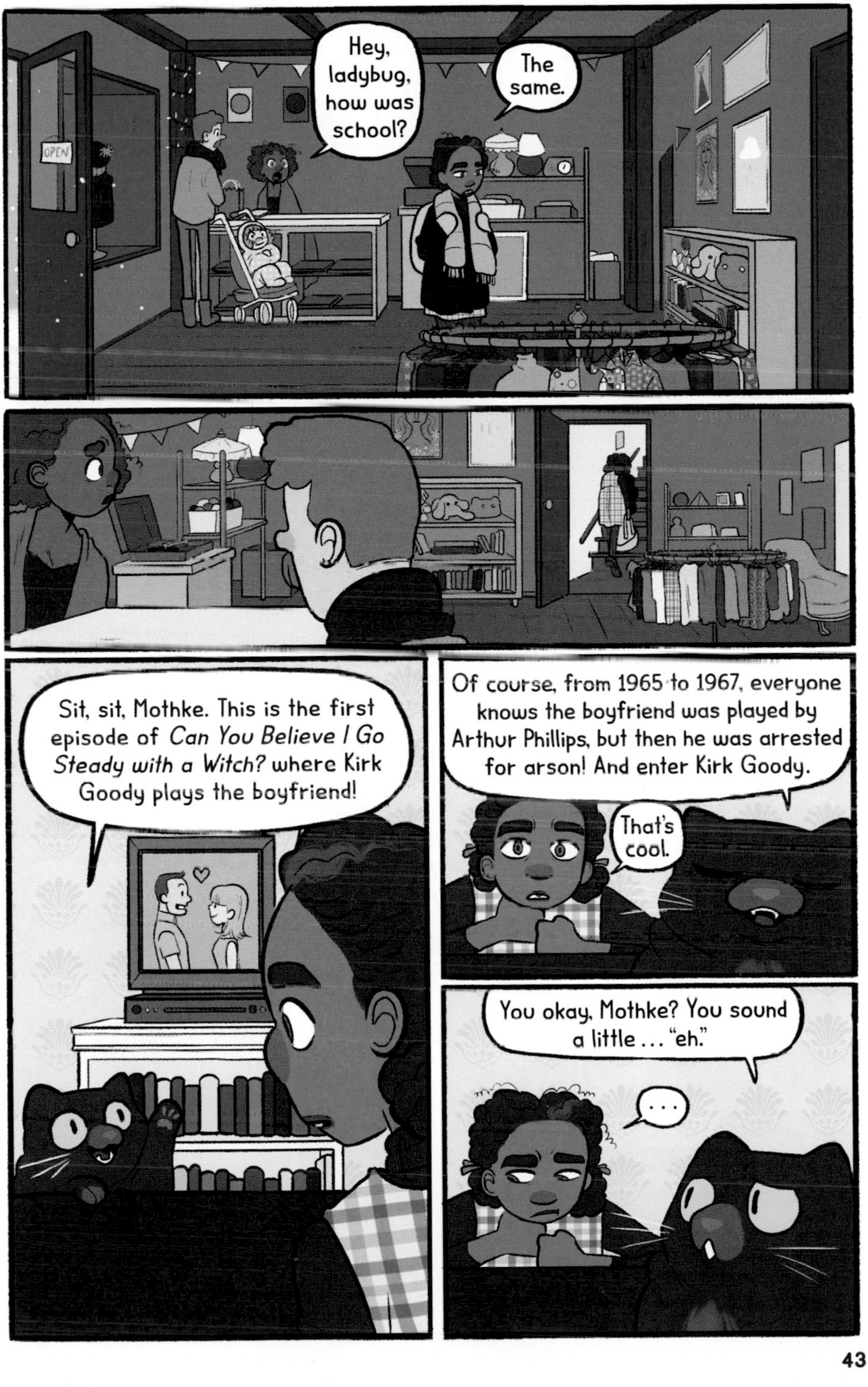
OPEN
Hey, ladybug, how was school?
The same.
Sit, sit, Mothke. This is the first episode of *Can You Believe I Go Steady with a Witch?* where Kirk Goody plays the boyfriend!
Of course, from 1965 to 1967, everyone knows the boyfriend was played by Arthur Phillips, but then he was arrested for arson! And enter Kirk Goody.
That's cool.
You okay, Mothke? You sound a little . . . "eh."
. . .

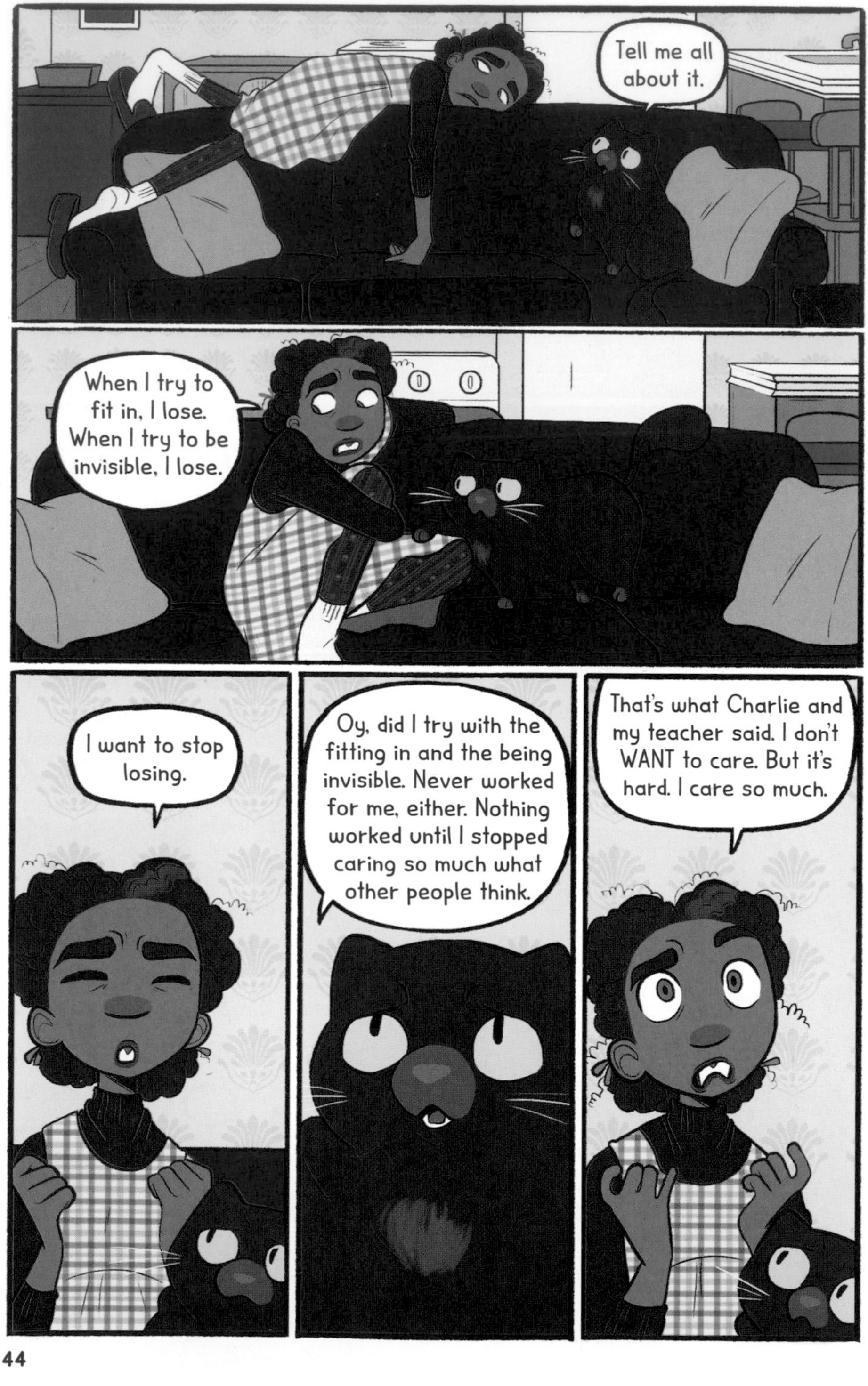
Tell me all about it.
When I try to fit in, I lose. When I try to be invisible, I lose.
I want to stop losing.
Oy, did I try with the fitting in and the being invisible. Never worked for me, either. Nothing worked until I stopped caring so much what other people think.
That's what Charlie and my teacher said. I don't WANT to care. But it's hard. I care so much.

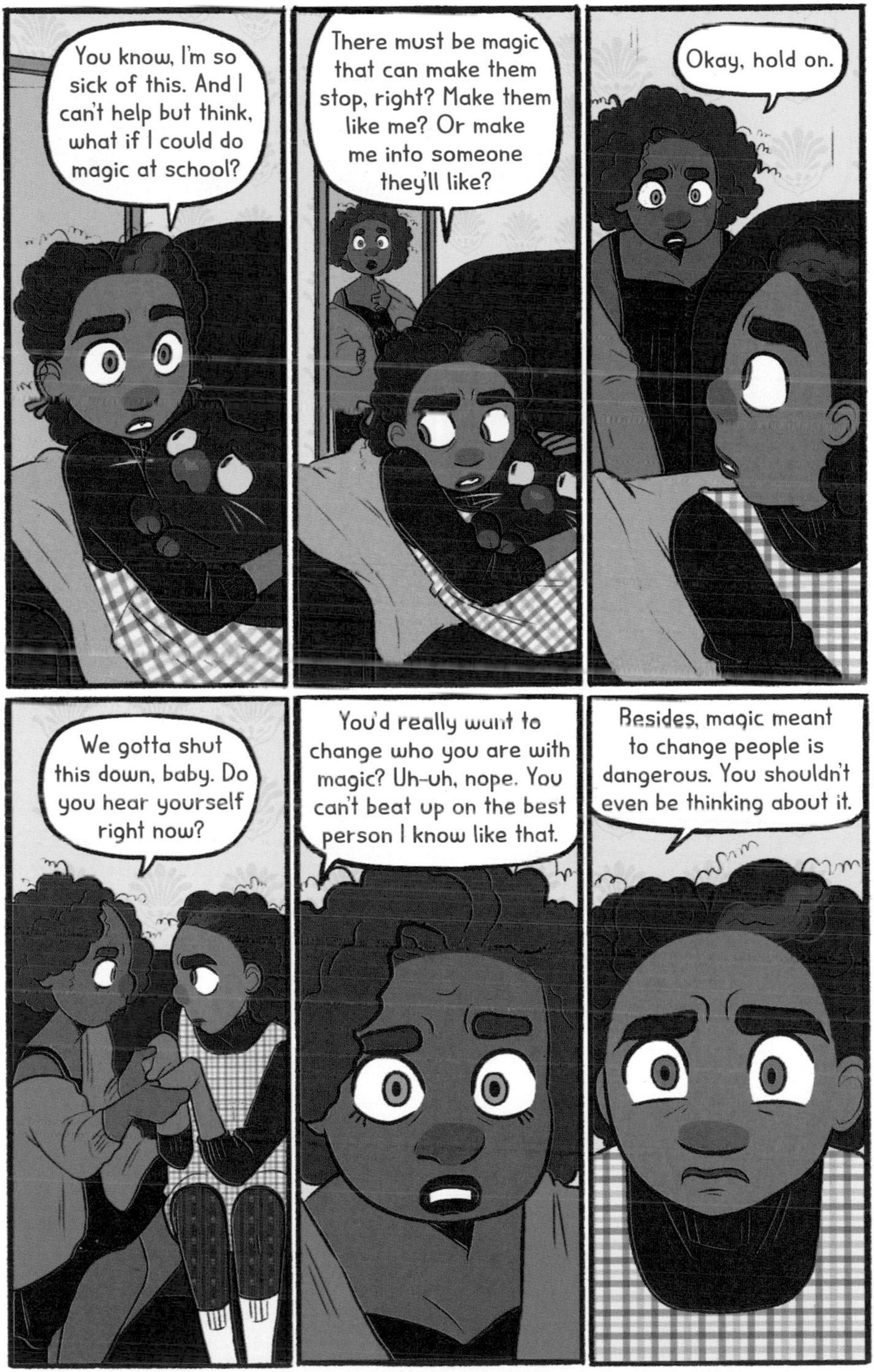
You know, I'm so sick of this. And I can't help but think, what if I could do magic at school?
There must be magic that can make them stop, right? Make them like me? Or make me into someone they'll like?
Okay, hold on.
We gotta shut this down, baby. Do you hear yourself right now?
You'd really want to change who you are with magic? Uh-uh, nope. You can't beat up on the best person I know like that.
Besides, magic meant to change people is dangerous. You shouldn't even be thinking about it.

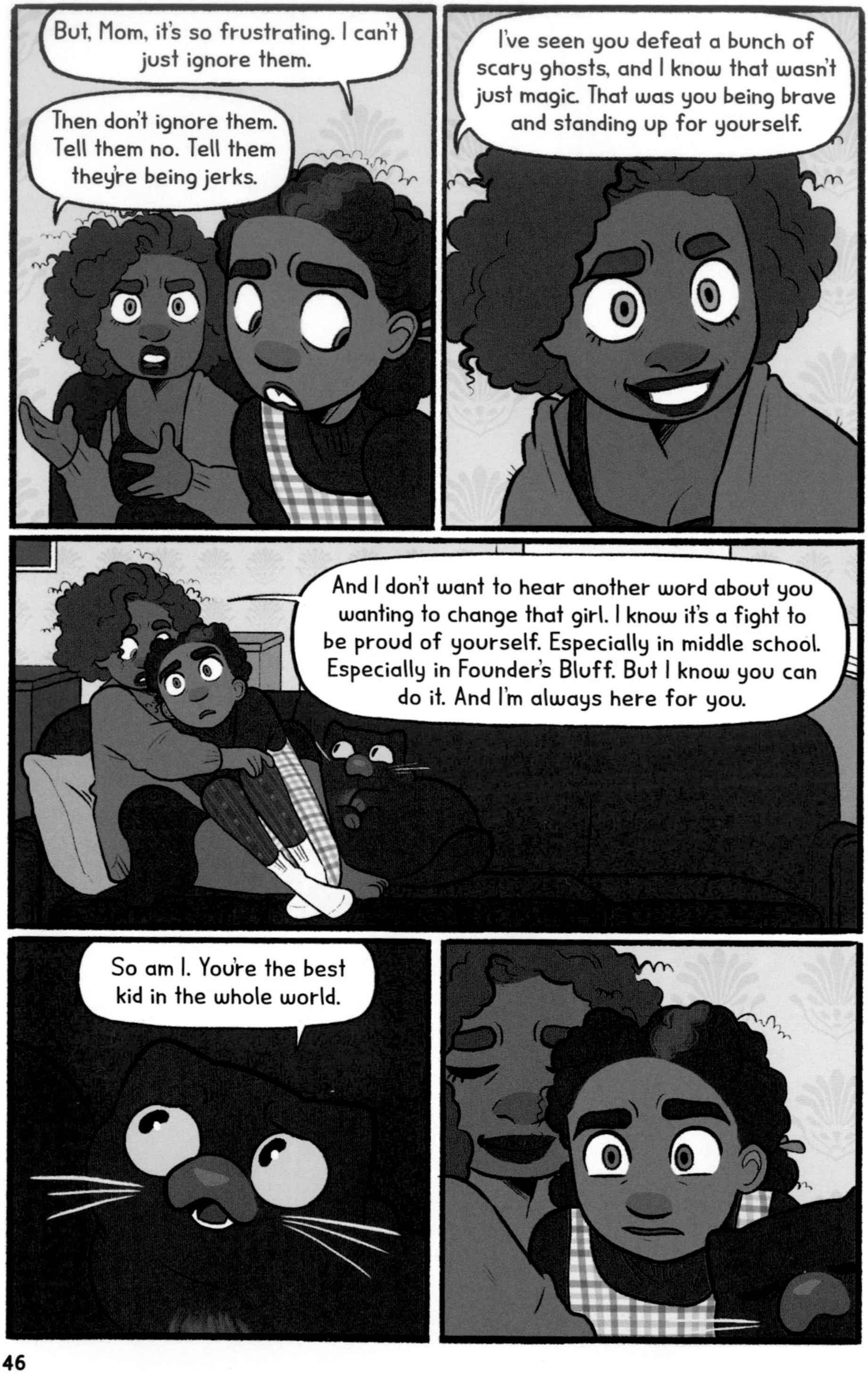
But, Mom, it's so frustrating. I can't just ignore them.
Then don't ignore them. Tell them no. Tell them they're being jerks.
I've seen you defeat a bunch of scary ghosts, and I know that wasn't just magic. That was you being brave and standing up for yourself.
And I don't want to hear another word about you wanting to change that girl. I know it's a fight to be proud of yourself. Especially in middle school. Especially in Founder's Bluff. But I know you can do it. And I'm always here for you.
So am I. You're the best kid in the whole world.

CHAPTER 3
Sarah's Bask

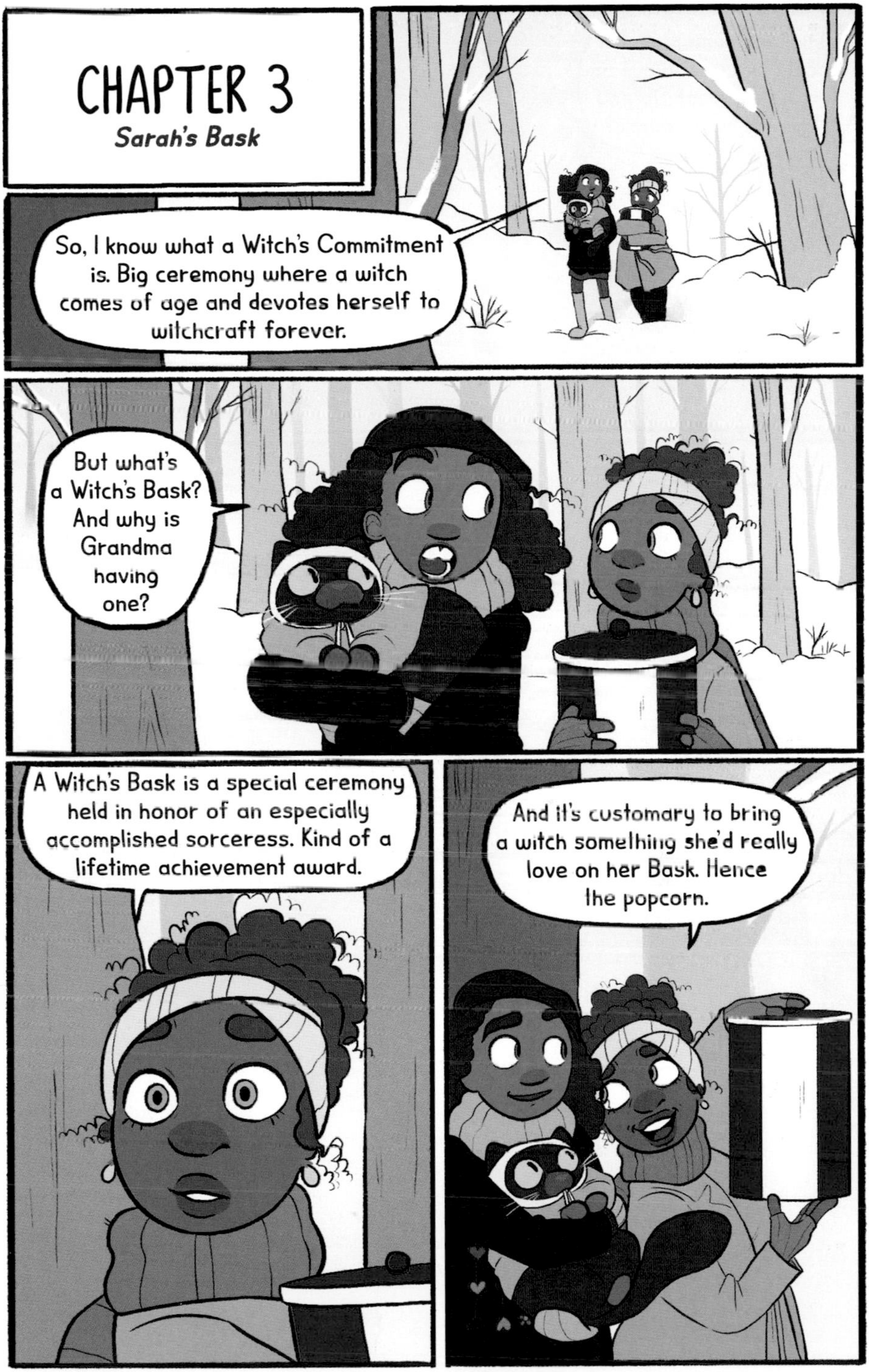
So, I know what a Witch's Commitment is. Big ceremony where a witch comes of age and devotes herself to witchcraft forever.
But what's a Witch's Bask? And why is Grandma having one?
A Witch's Bask is a special ceremony held in honor of an especially accomplished sorceress. Kind of a lifetime achievement award.
And it's customary to bring a witch something she'd really love on her Bask. Hence the popcorn.

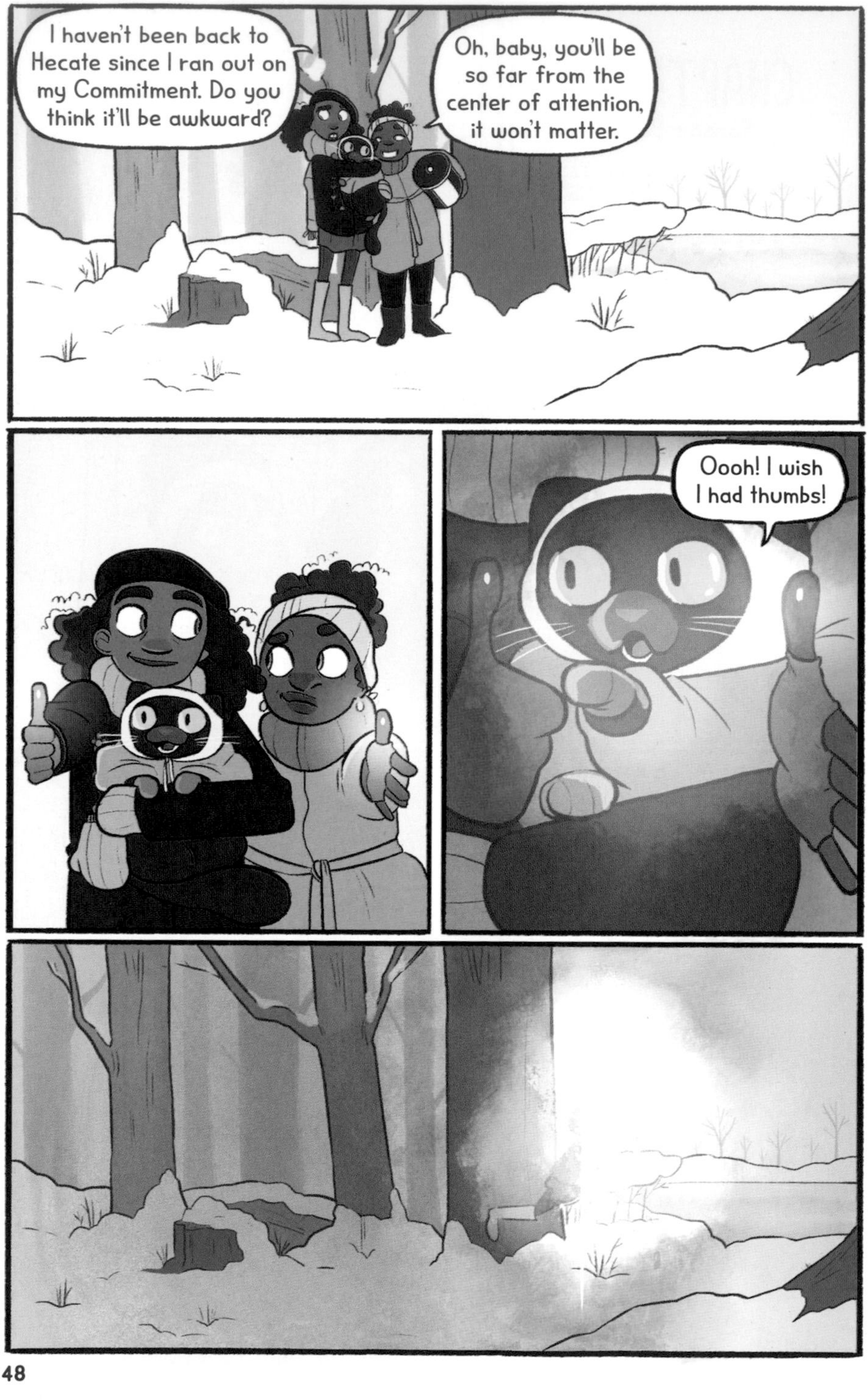
I haven't been back to Hecate since I ran out on my Commitment. Do you think it'll be awkward?
Oh, baby, you'll be so far from the center of attention, it won't matter.
Oooh! I wish I had thumbs!

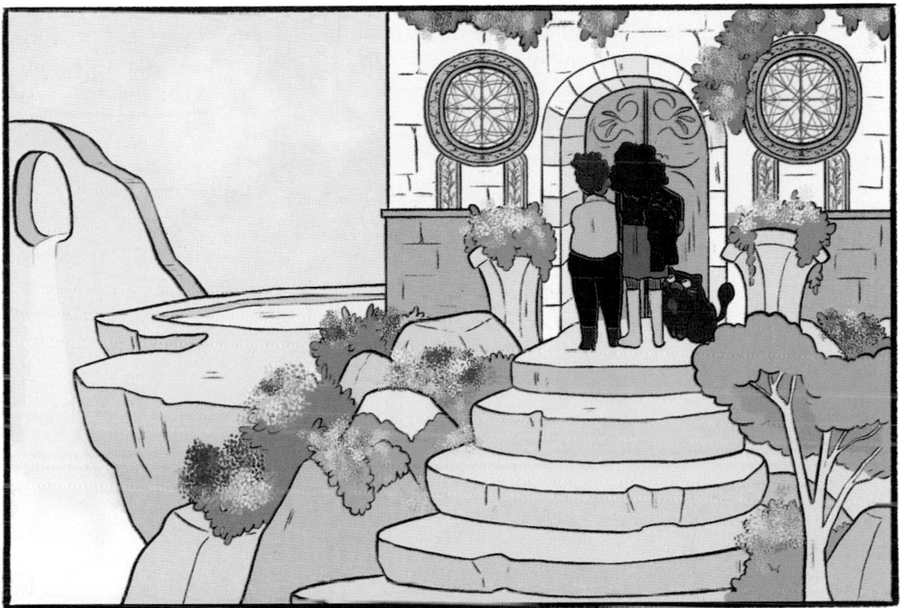

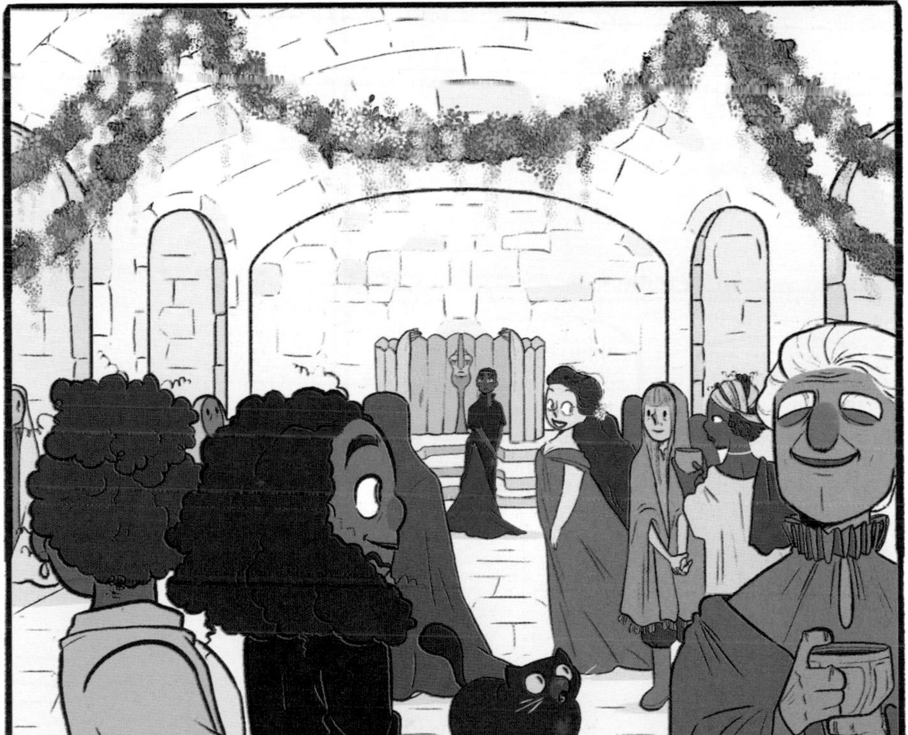

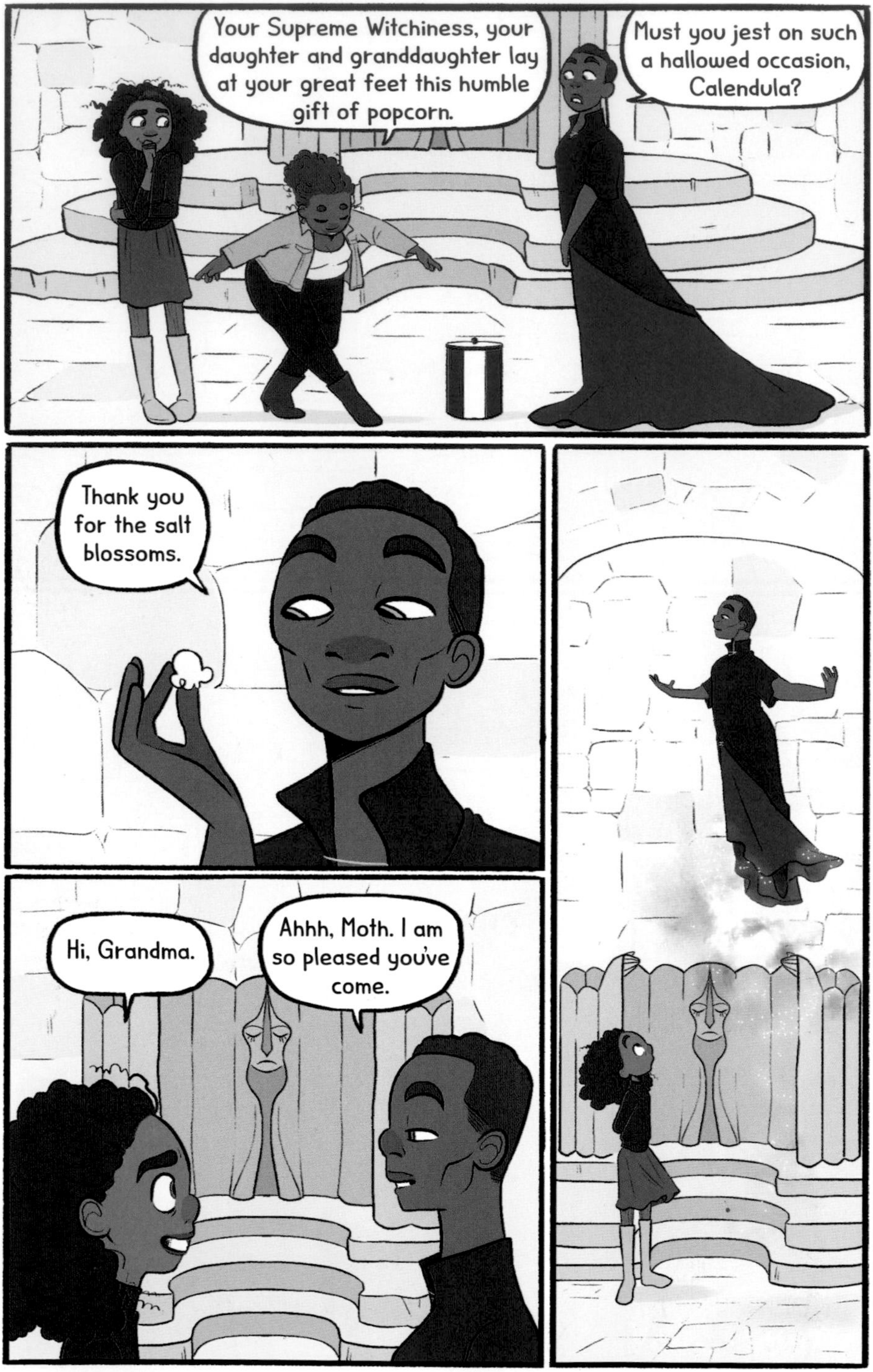

Your Supreme Witchiness, your daughter and granddaughter lay at your great feet this humble gift of popcorn.
Must you jest on such a hallowed occasion, Calendula?
Thank you for the salt blossoms.
Hi, Grandma.
Ahhh, Moth. I am so pleased you've come.

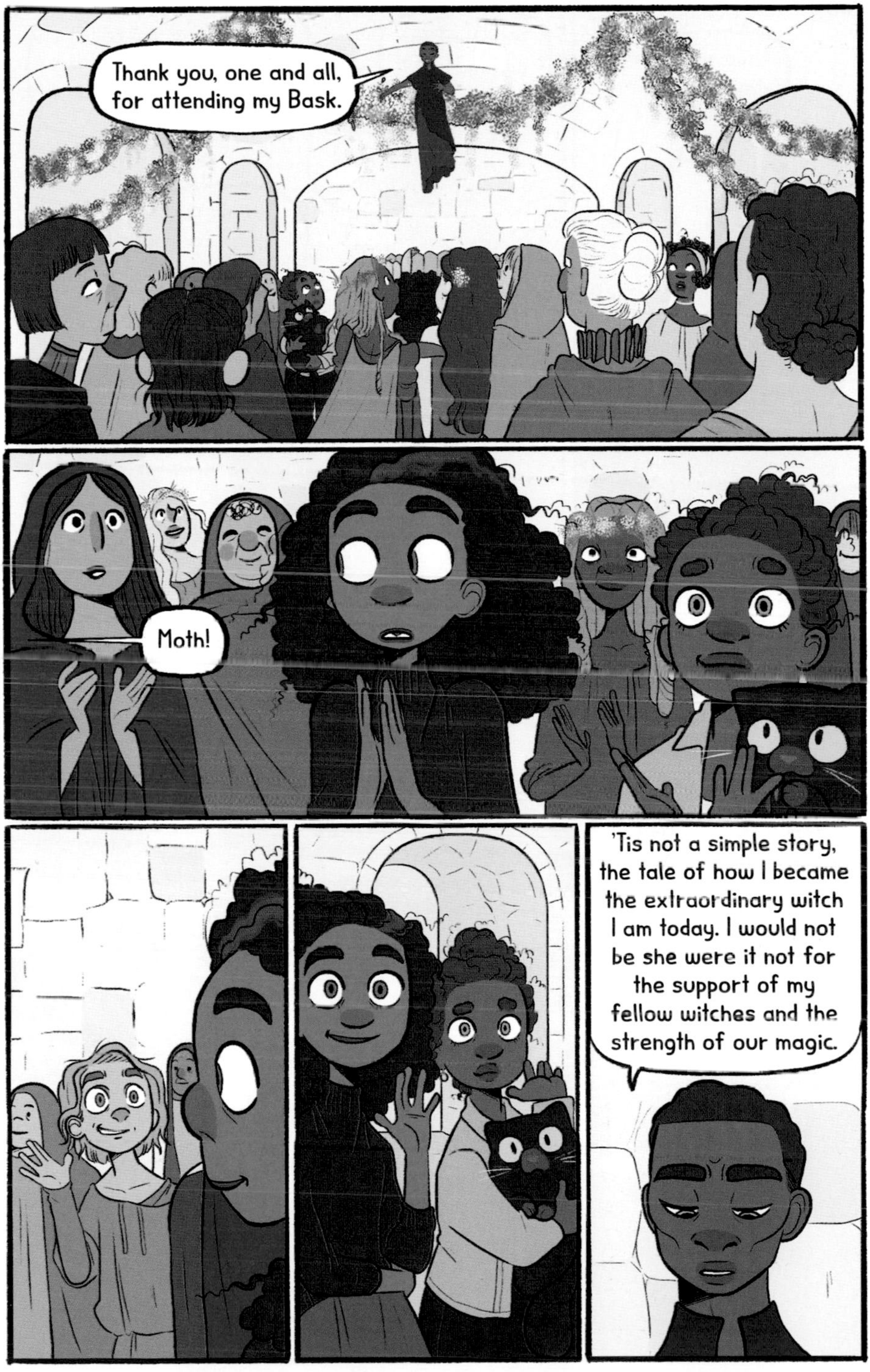
Thank you, one and all, for attending my Bask.
Moth!
'Tis not a simple story, the tale of how I became the extraordinary witch I am today. I would not be she were it not for the support of my fellow witches and the strength of our magic.

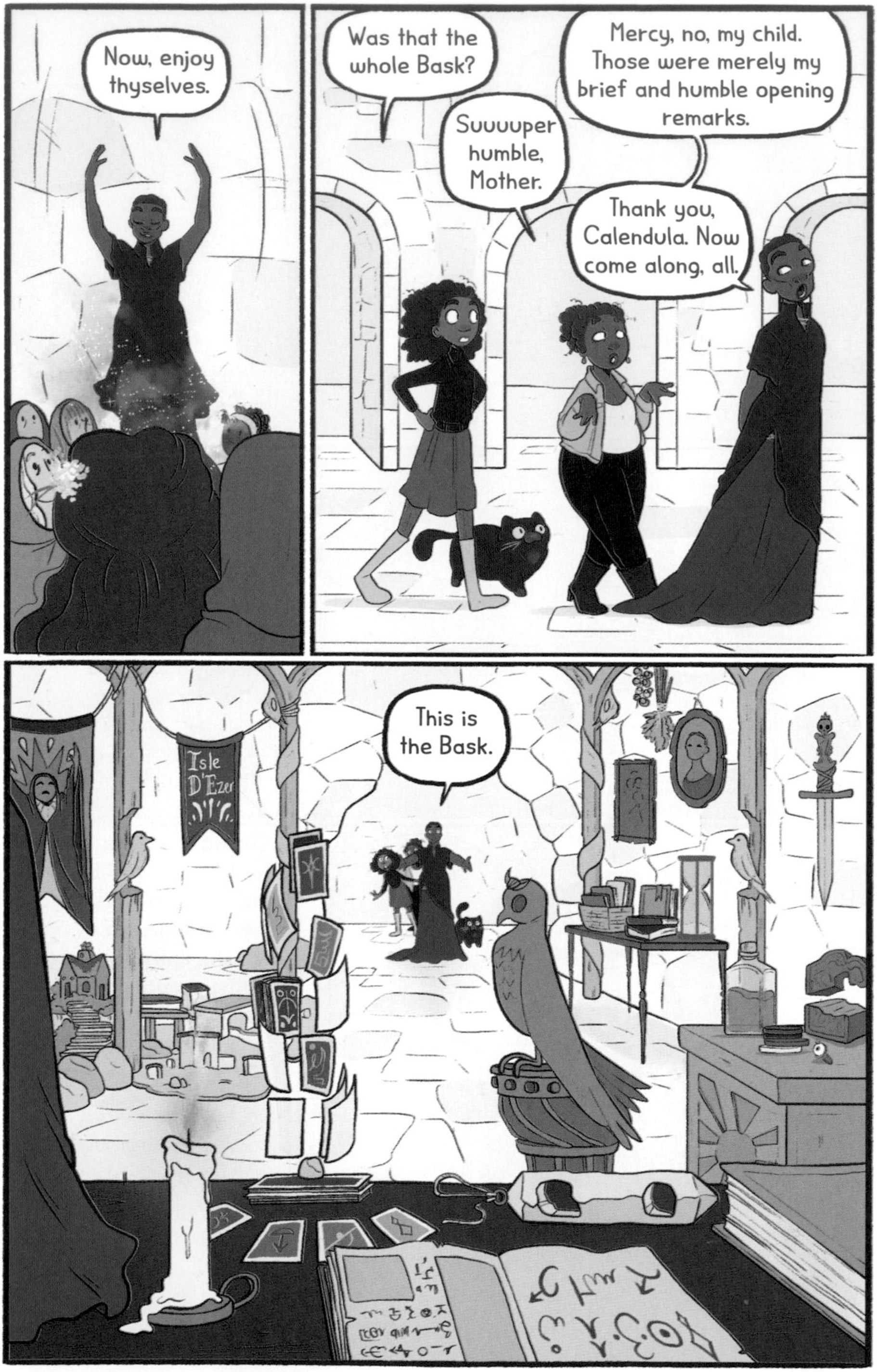
Now, enjoy thyselves.
Was that the whole Bask?
Mercy, no, my child. Those were merely my brief and humble opening remarks.
Suuuuper humble, Mother.
Thank you, Calendula. Now come along, all.
Isle D'Ezer
This is the Bask.

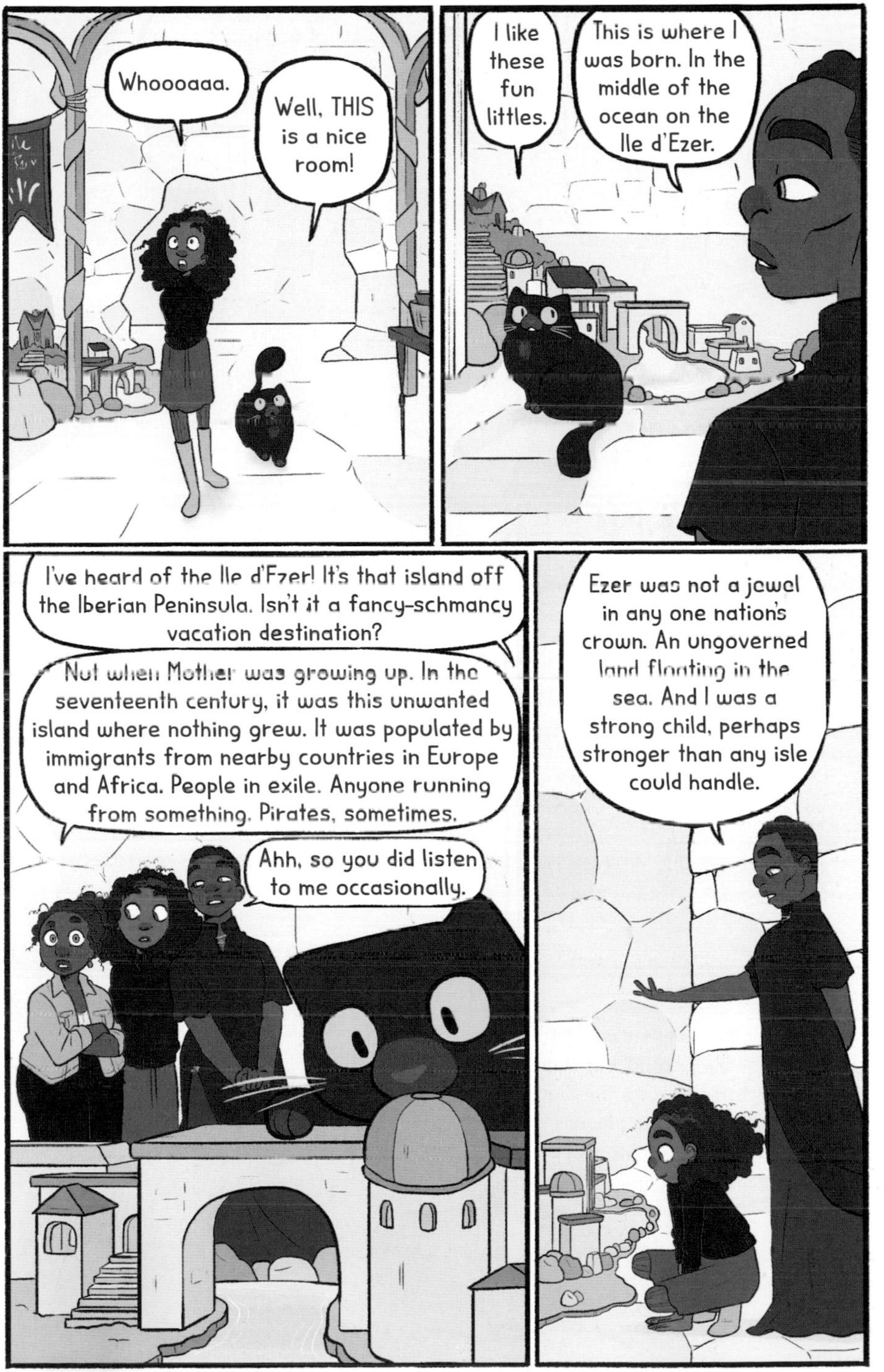
Whoooaaa.
Well, THIS is a nice room!
I like these fun littles.
This is where I was born. In the middle of the ocean on the Ile d'Ezer.
I've heard of the Ile d'Ezer! It's that island off the Iberian Peninsula. Isn't it a fancy-schmancy vacation destination?
Not when Mother was growing up. In the seventeenth century, it was this unwanted island where nothing grew. It was populated by immigrants from nearby countries in Europe and Africa. People in exile. Anyone running from something. Pirates, sometimes.
Ahh, so you did listen to me occasionally.
Ezer was not a jewel in any one nation's crown. An ungoverned land floating in the sea. And I was a strong child, perhaps stronger than any isle could handle.

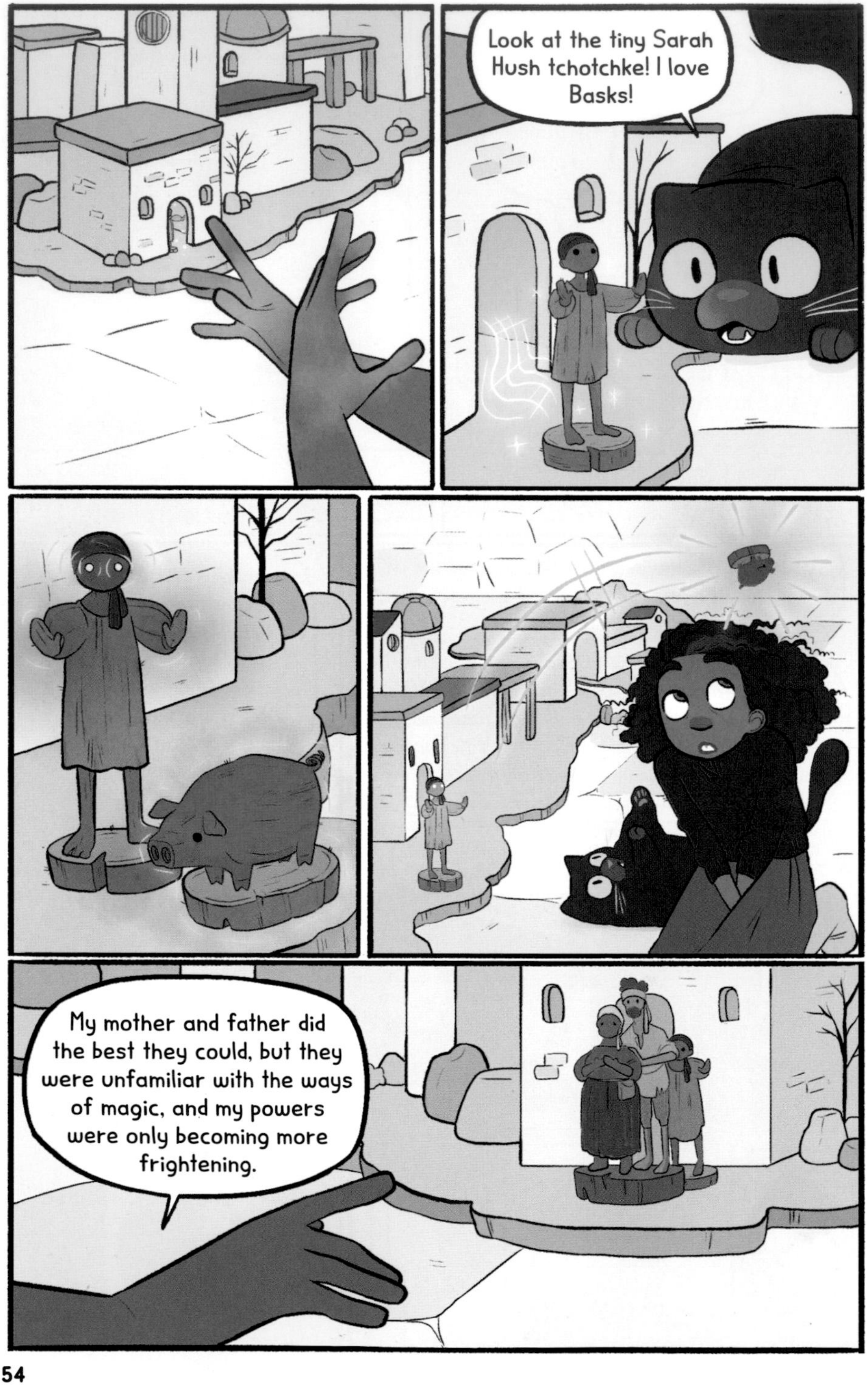
Look at the tiny Sarah Hush tchotchke! I love Basks!
My mother and father did the best they could, but they were unfamiliar with the ways of magic, and my powers were only becoming more frightening.

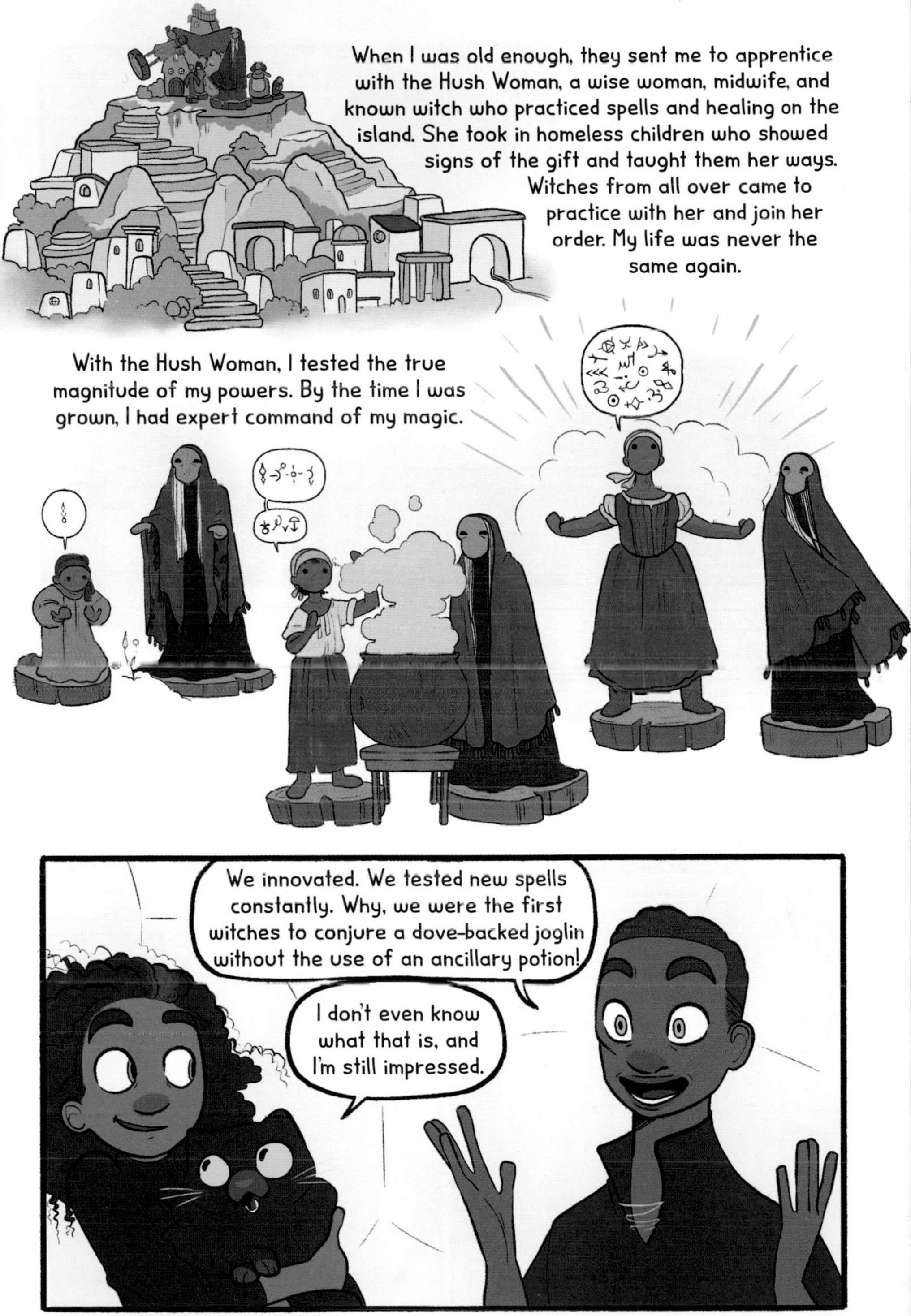
When I was old enough, they sent me to apprentice with the Hush Woman, a wise woman, midwife, and known witch who practiced spells and healing on the island. She took in homeless children who showed signs of the gift and taught them her ways. Witches from all over came to practice with her and join her order. My life was never the same again.
With the Hush Woman, I tested the true magnitude of my powers. By the time I was grown, I had expert command of my magic.
We innovated. We tested new spells constantly. Why, we were the first witches to conjure a dove-backed joglin without the use of an ancillary potion!
I don't even know what that is, and I'm still impressed.

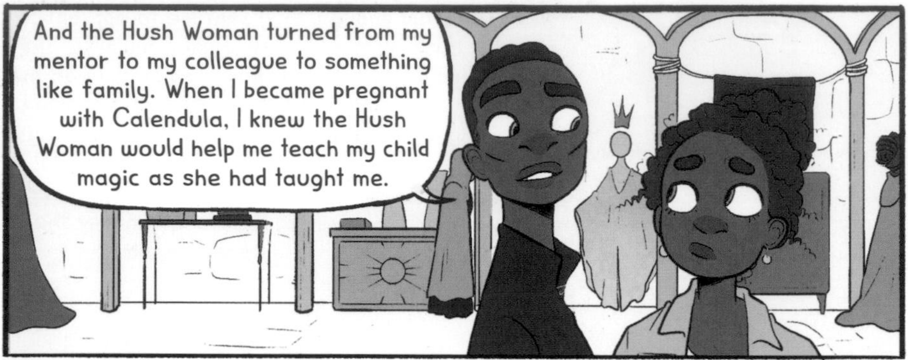

And the Hush Woman turned from my mentor to my colleague to something like family. When I became pregnant with Calendula, I knew the Hush Woman would help me teach my child magic as she had taught me.

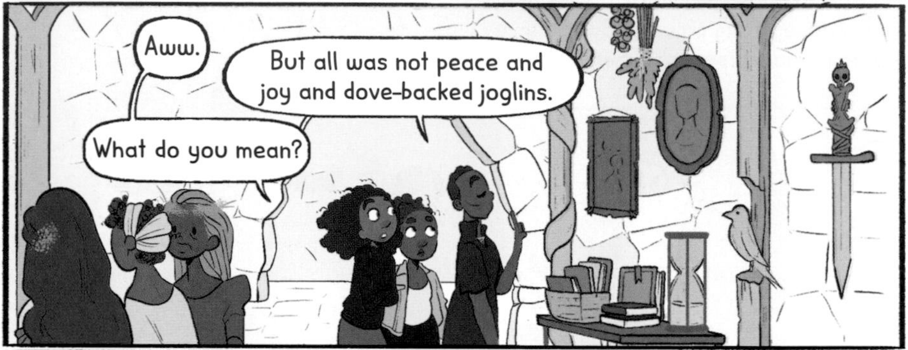

Aww.
What do you mean?
But all was not peace and joy and dove-backed joglins.

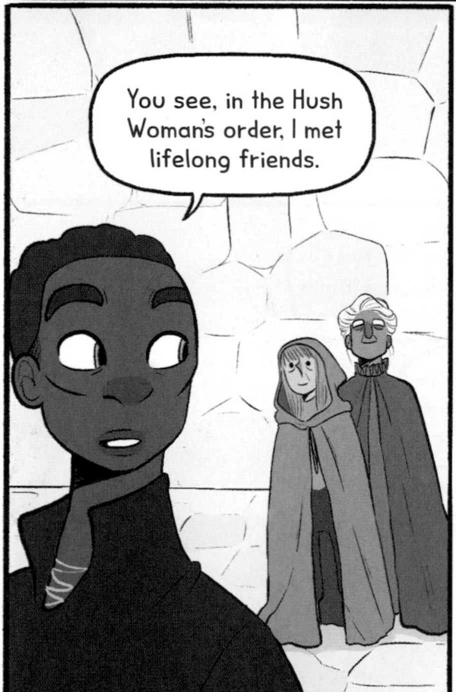

You see, in the Hush Woman's order, I met lifelong friends.

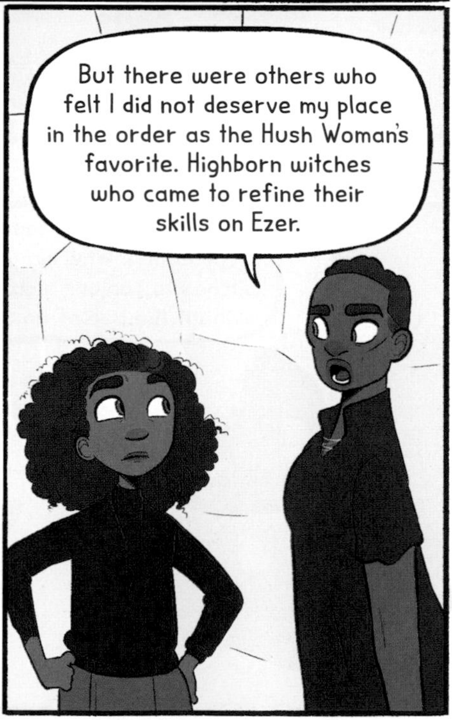

But there were others who felt I did not deserve my place in the order as the Hush Woman's favorite. Highborn witches who came to refine their skills on Ezer.

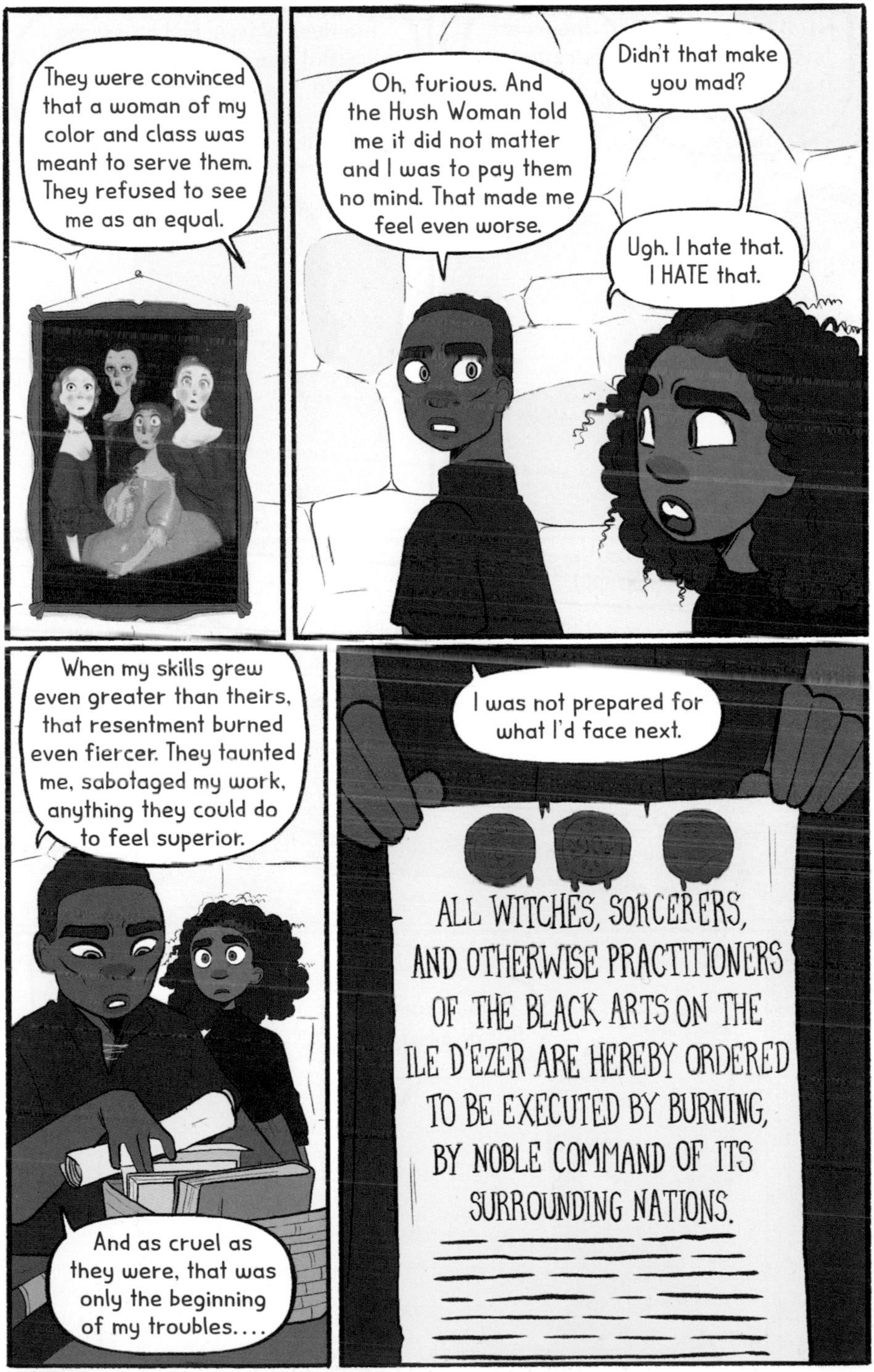
They were convinced that a woman of my color and class was meant to serve them. They refused to see me as an equal.
Oh, furious. And the Hush Woman told me it did not matter and I was to pay them no mind. That made me feel even worse.
Didn't that make you mad?
Ugh. I hate that. I HATE that.
When my skills grew even greater than theirs, that resentment burned even fiercer. They taunted me, sabotaged my work, anything they could do to feel superior.
And as cruel as they were, that was only the beginning of my troubles....
I was not prepared for what I'd face next.
ALL WITCHES, SORCERERS, AND OTHERWISE PRACTITIONERS OF THE BLACK ARTS ON THE ILE D'EZER ARE HEREBY ORDERED TO BE EXECUTED BY BURNING, BY NOBLE COMMAND OF ITS SURROUNDING NATIONS.

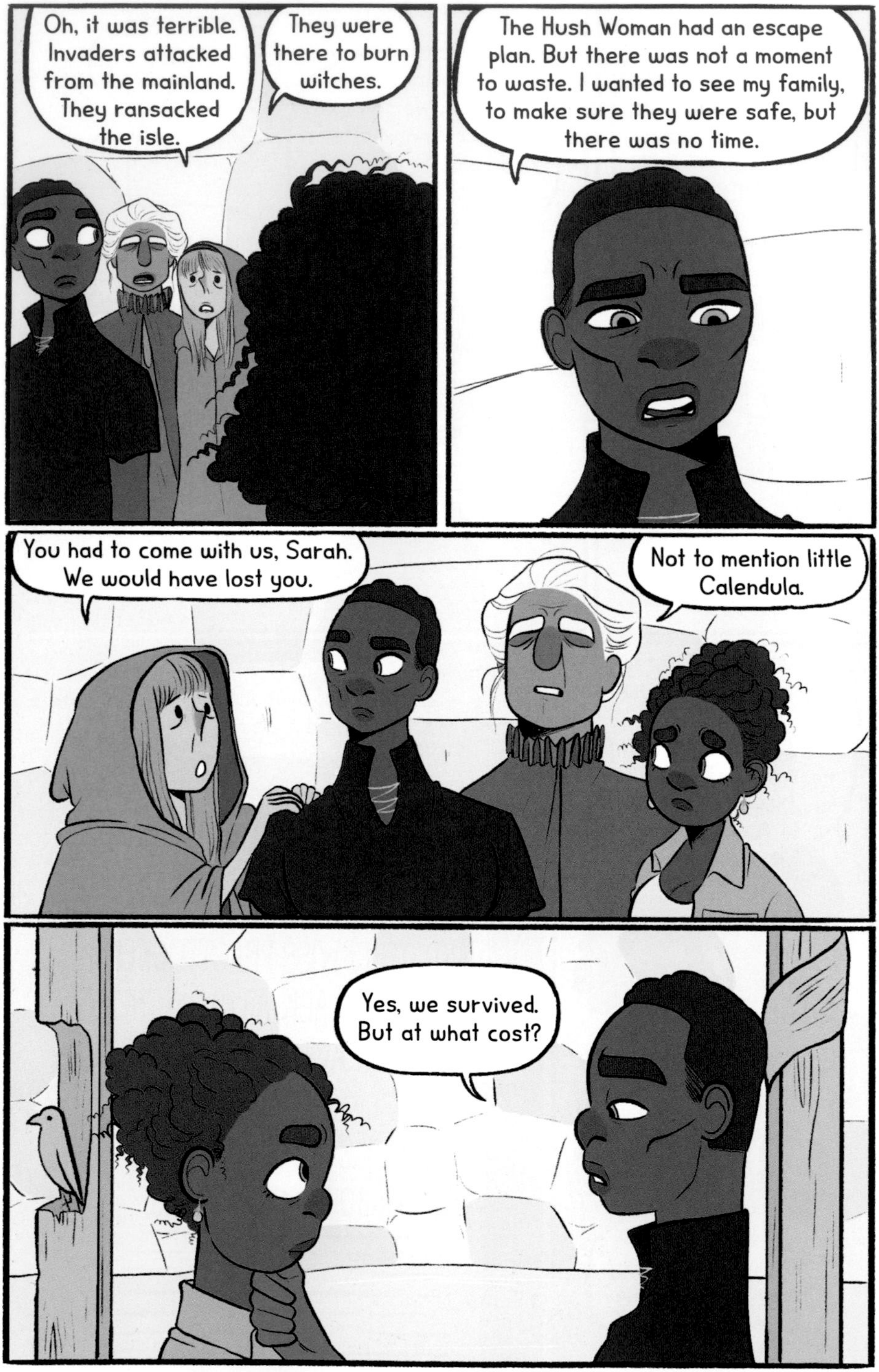
Oh, it was terrible. Invaders attacked from the mainland. They ransacked the isle.
They were there to burn witches.
The Hush Woman had an escape plan. But there was not a moment to waste. I wanted to see my family, to make sure they were safe, but there was no time.
You had to come with us, Sarah. We would have lost you.
Not to mention little Calendula.
Yes, we survived. But at what cost?

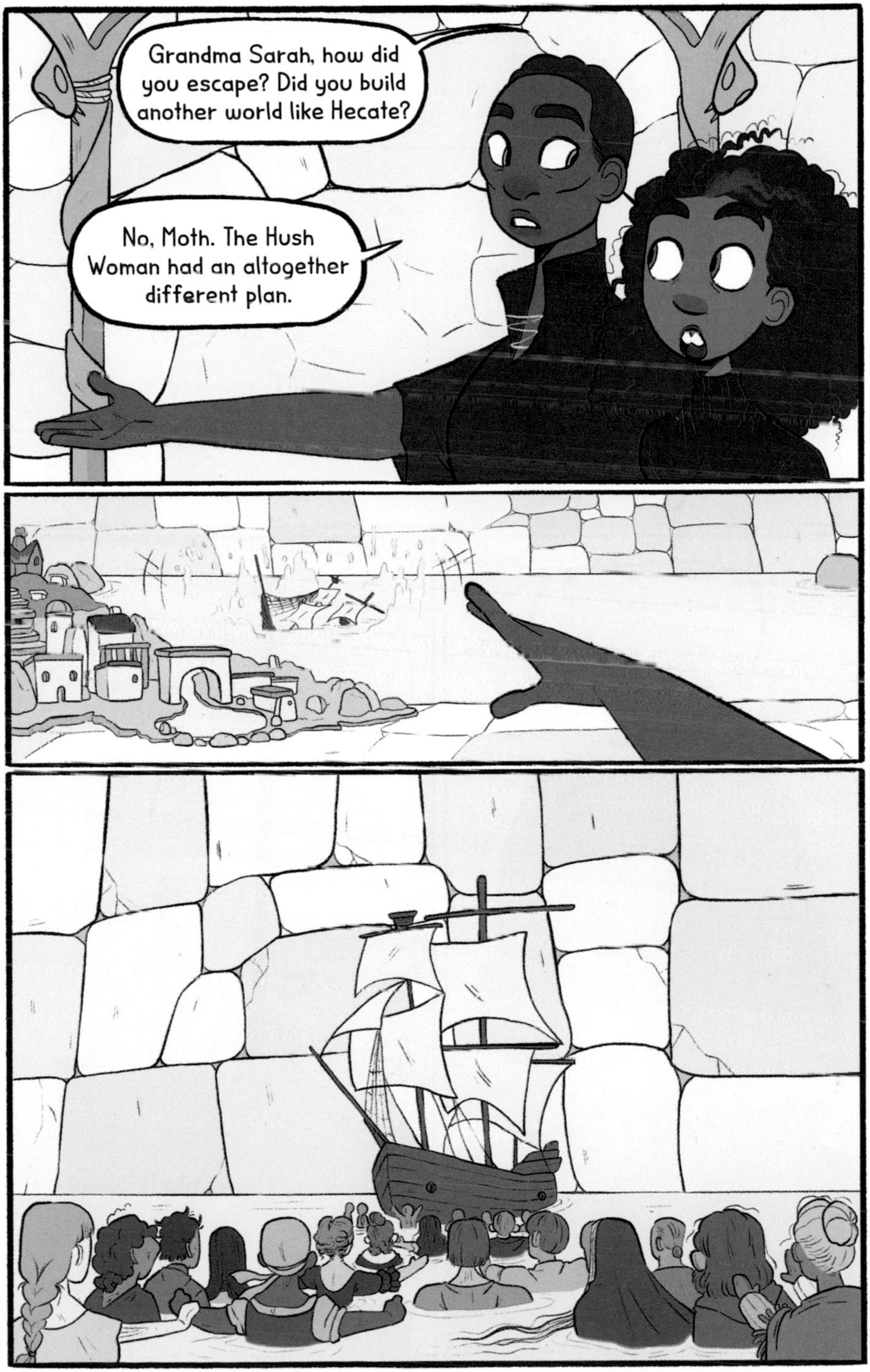
Grandma Sarah, how did you escape? Did you build another world like Hecate?
No, Moth. The Hush Woman had an altogether different plan.

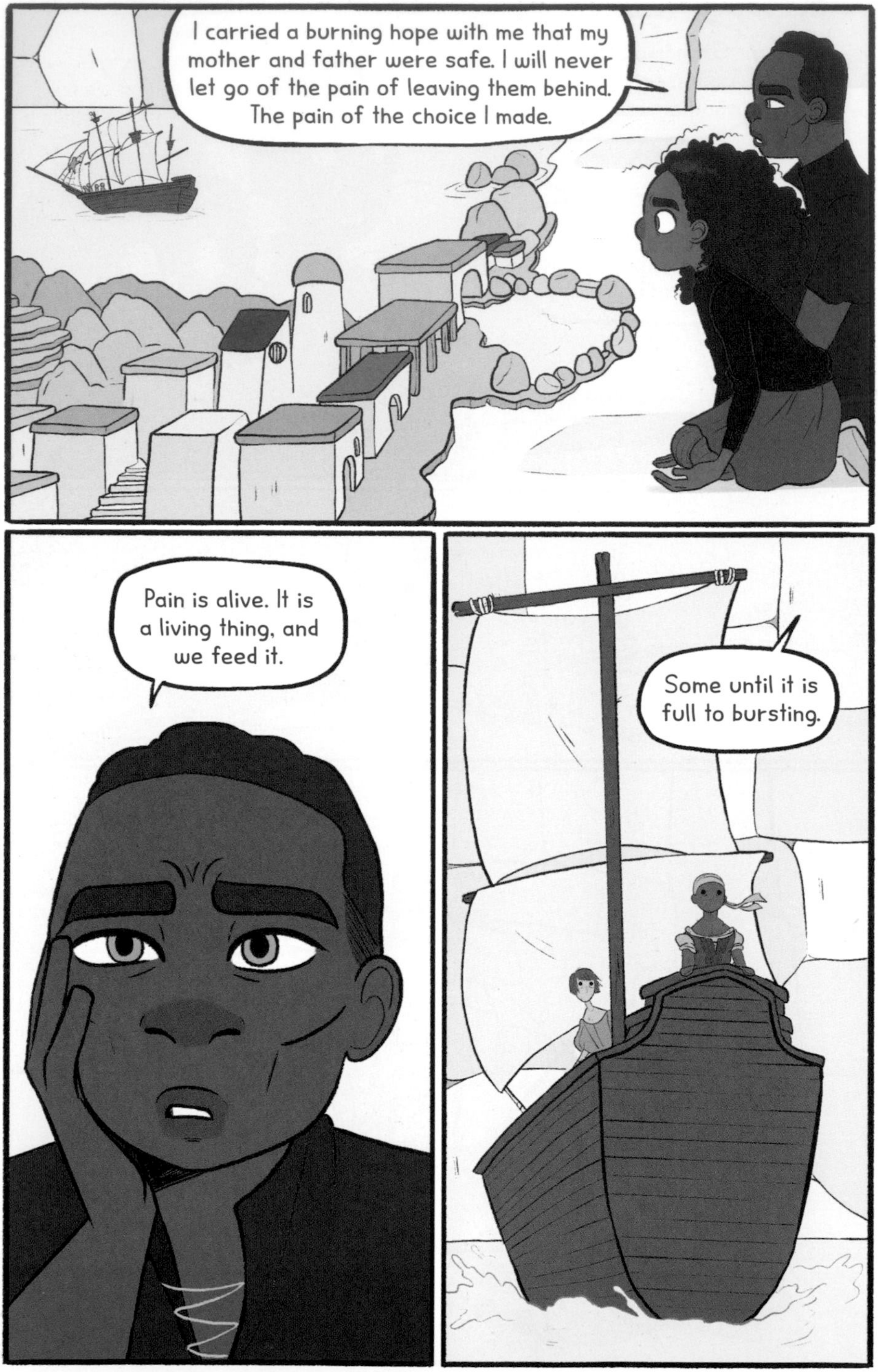
I carried a burning hope with me that my mother and father were safe. I will never let go of the pain of leaving them behind. The pain of the choice I made.
Pain is alive. It is a living thing, and we feed it.
Some until it is full to bursting.

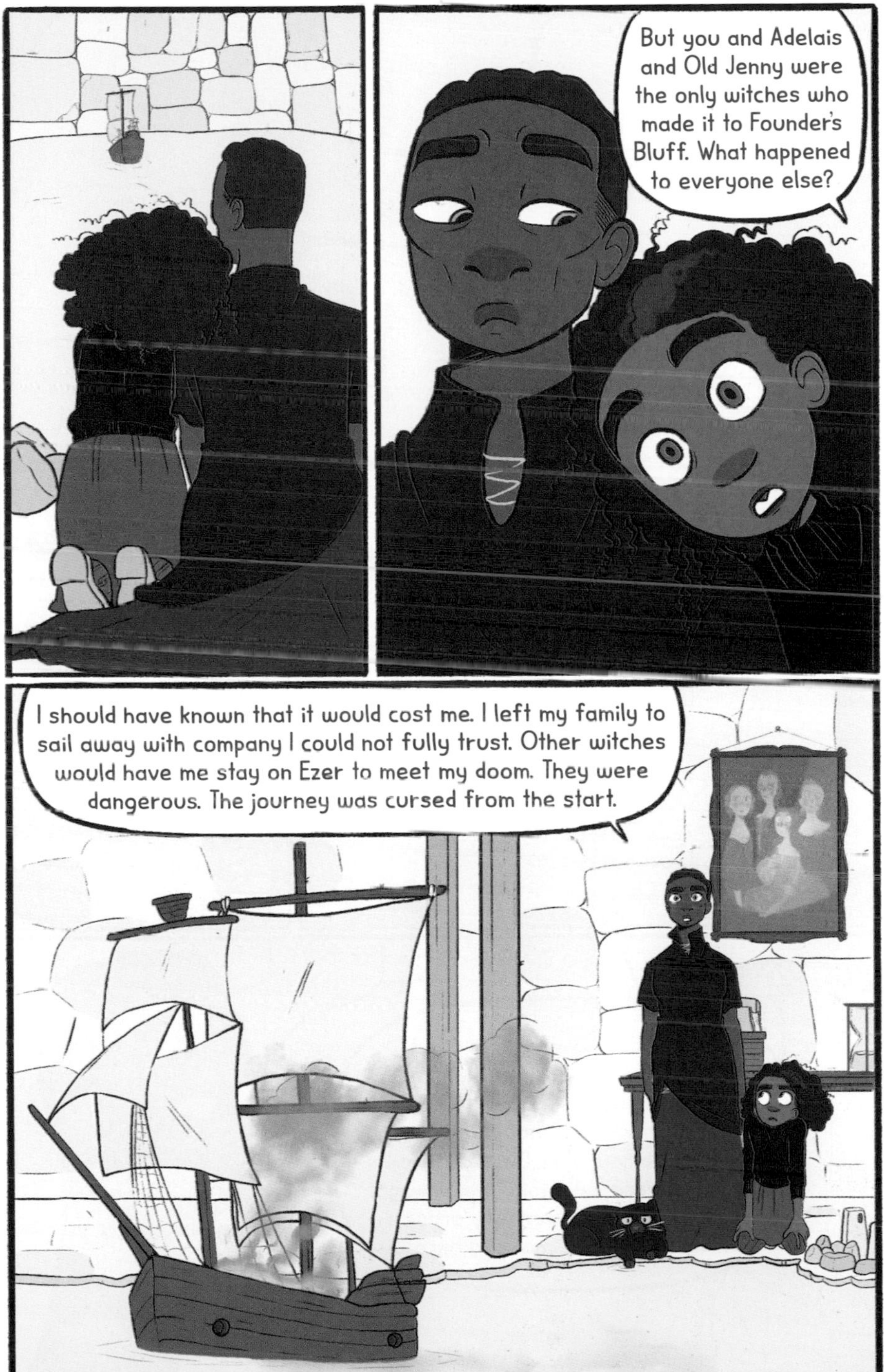
But you and Adelais and Old Jenny were the only witches who made it to Founder's Bluff. What happened to everyone else?
I should have known that it would cost me. I left my family to sail away with company I could not fully trust. Other witches would have me stay on Ezer to meet my doom. They were dangerous. The journey was cursed from the start.

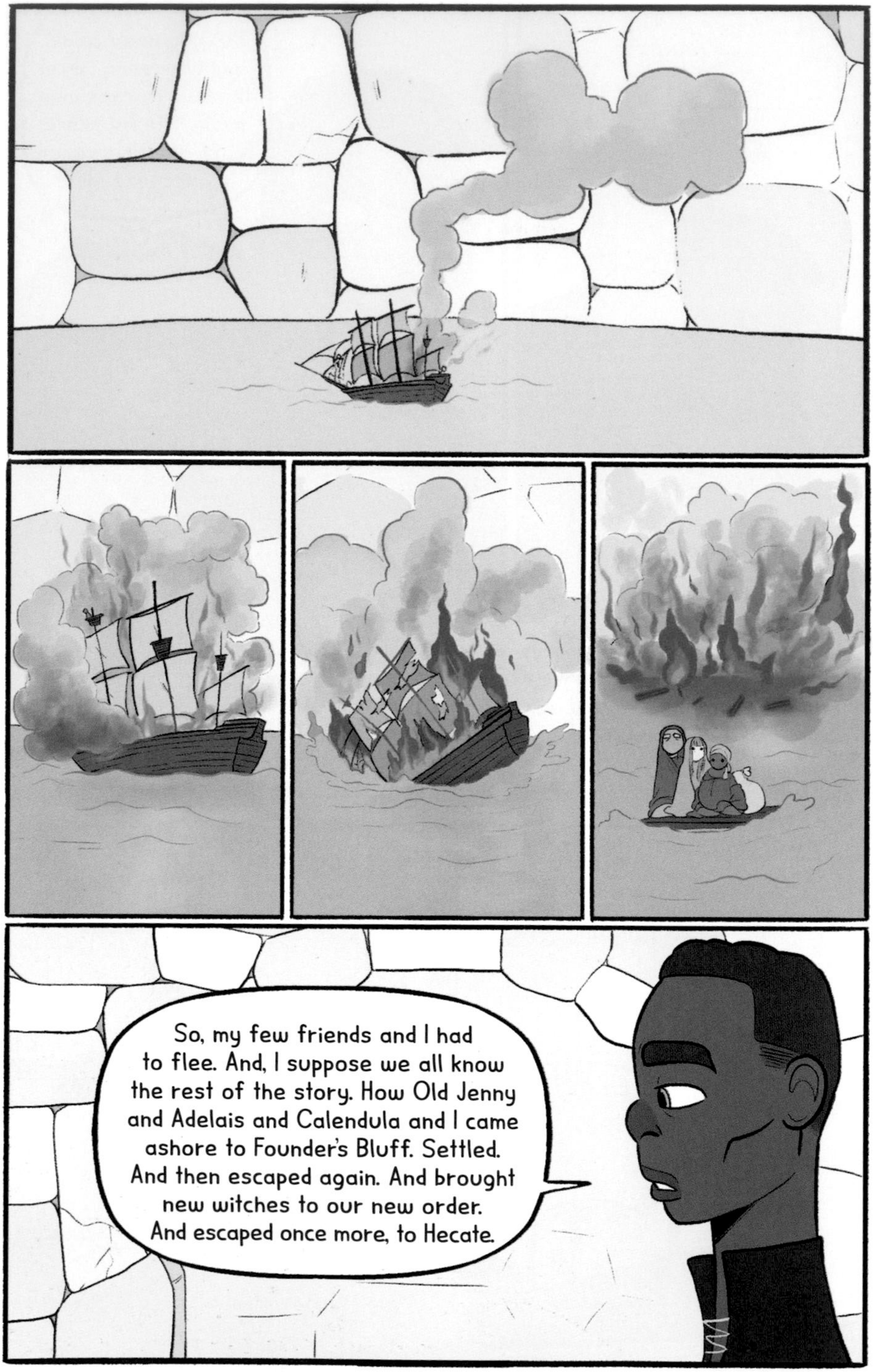
So, my few friends and I had to flee. And, I suppose we all know the rest of the story. How Old Jenny and Adelais and Calendula and I came ashore to Founder's Bluff. Settled. And then escaped again. And brought new witches to our new order. And escaped once more, to Hecate.

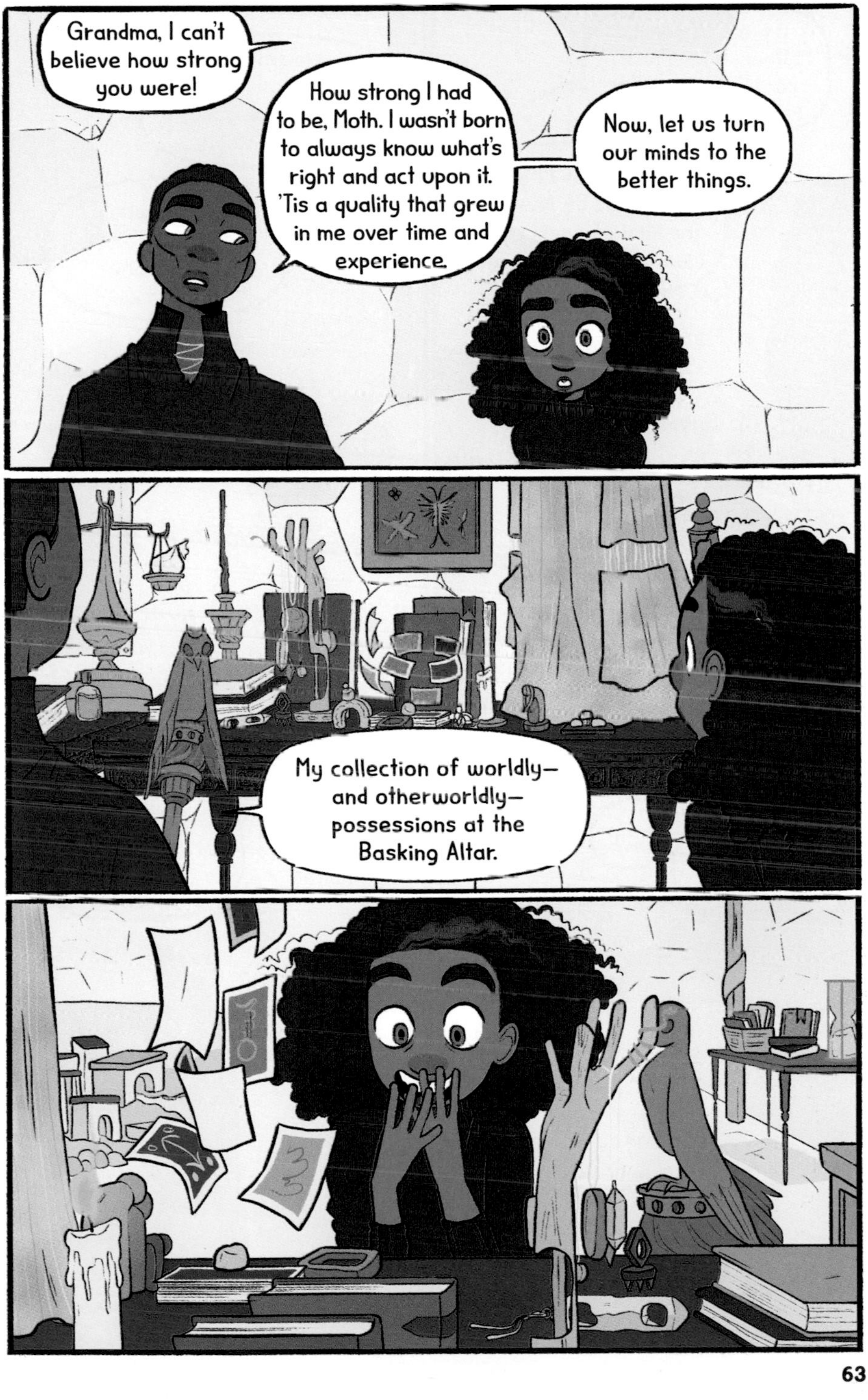

Grandma, I can't believe how strong you were!
How strong I had to be, Moth. I wasn't born to always know what's right and act upon it. 'Tis a quality that grew in me over time and experience.
Now, let us turn our minds to the better things.
My collection of worldly— and otherworldly— possessions at the Basking Altar.

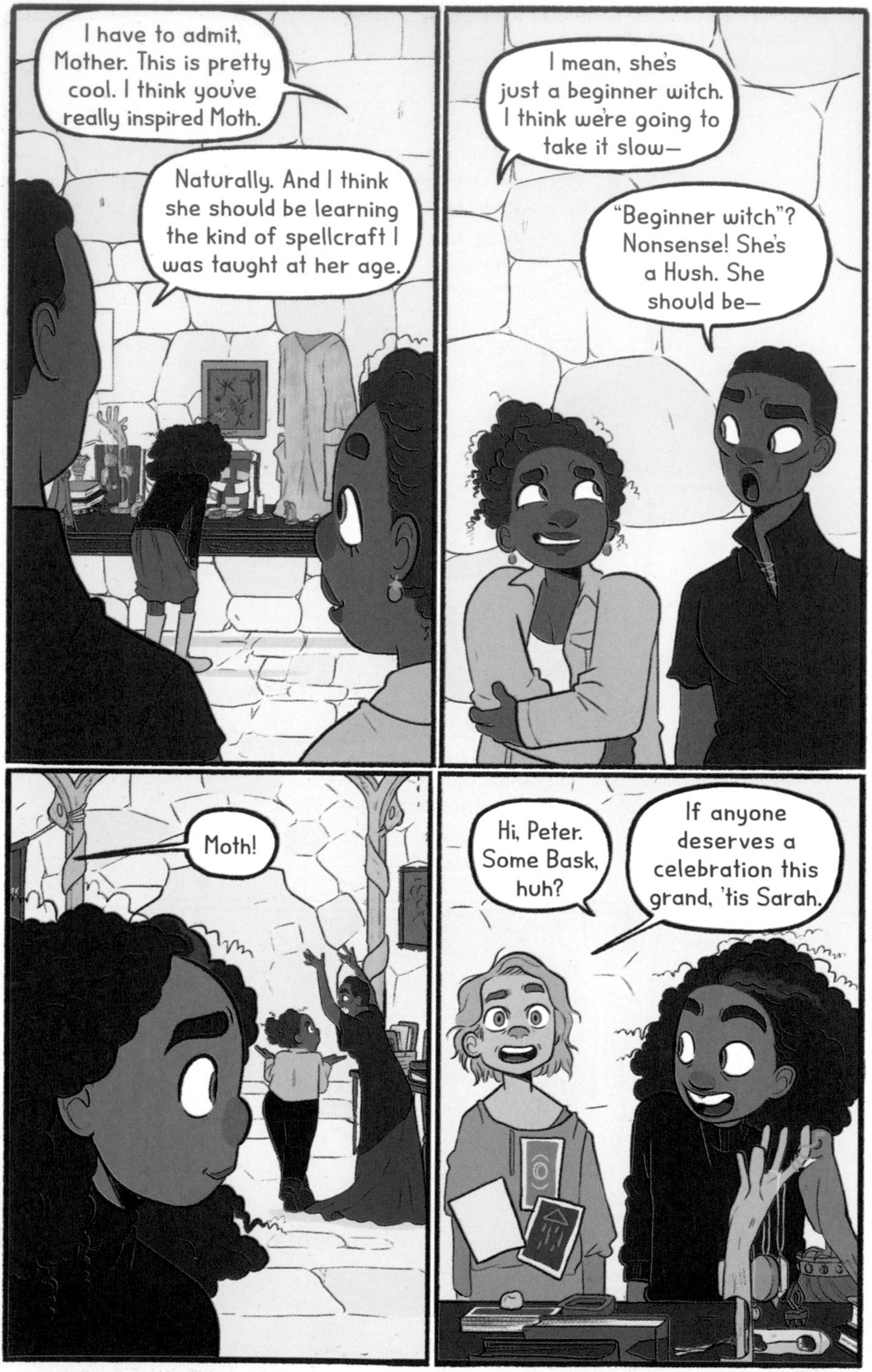
I have to admit, Mother. This is pretty cool. I think you've really inspired Moth.
Naturally. And I think she should be learning the kind of spellcraft I was taught at her age.
I mean, she's just a beginner witch. I think we're going to take it slow—
"Beginner witch"? Nonsense! She's a Hush. She should be—
Moth!
Hi, Peter. Some Bask, huh?
If anyone deserves a celebration this grand, 'tis Sarah.

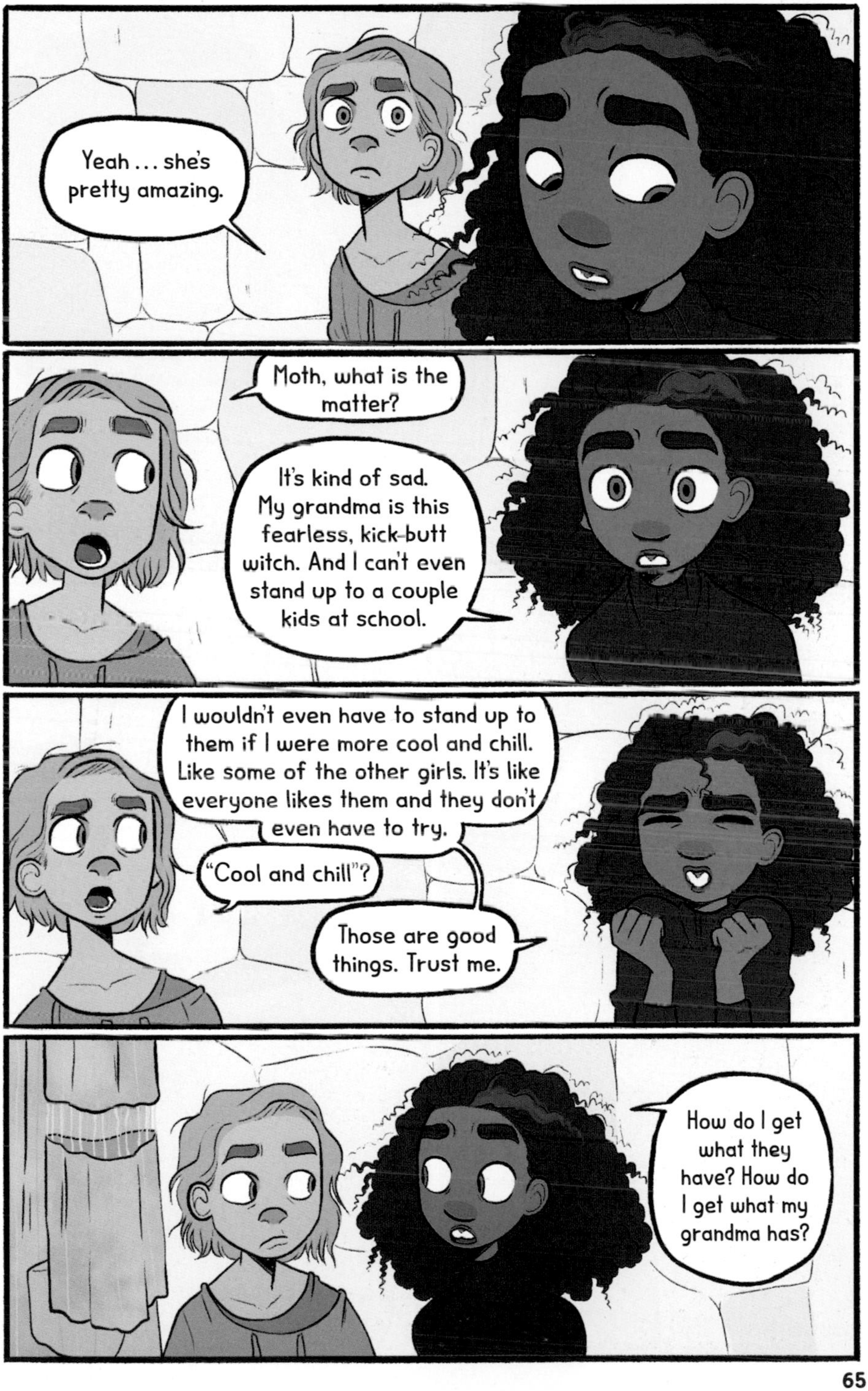
Yeah . . . she's pretty amazing.
Moth, what is the matter?
It's kind of sad. My grandma is this fearless, kick-butt witch. And I can't even stand up to a couple kids at school.
I wouldn't even have to stand up to them if I were more cool and chill. Like some of the other girls. It's like everyone likes them and they don't even have to try.
"Cool and chill"?
Those are good things. Trust me.
How do I get what they have? How do I get what my grandma has?

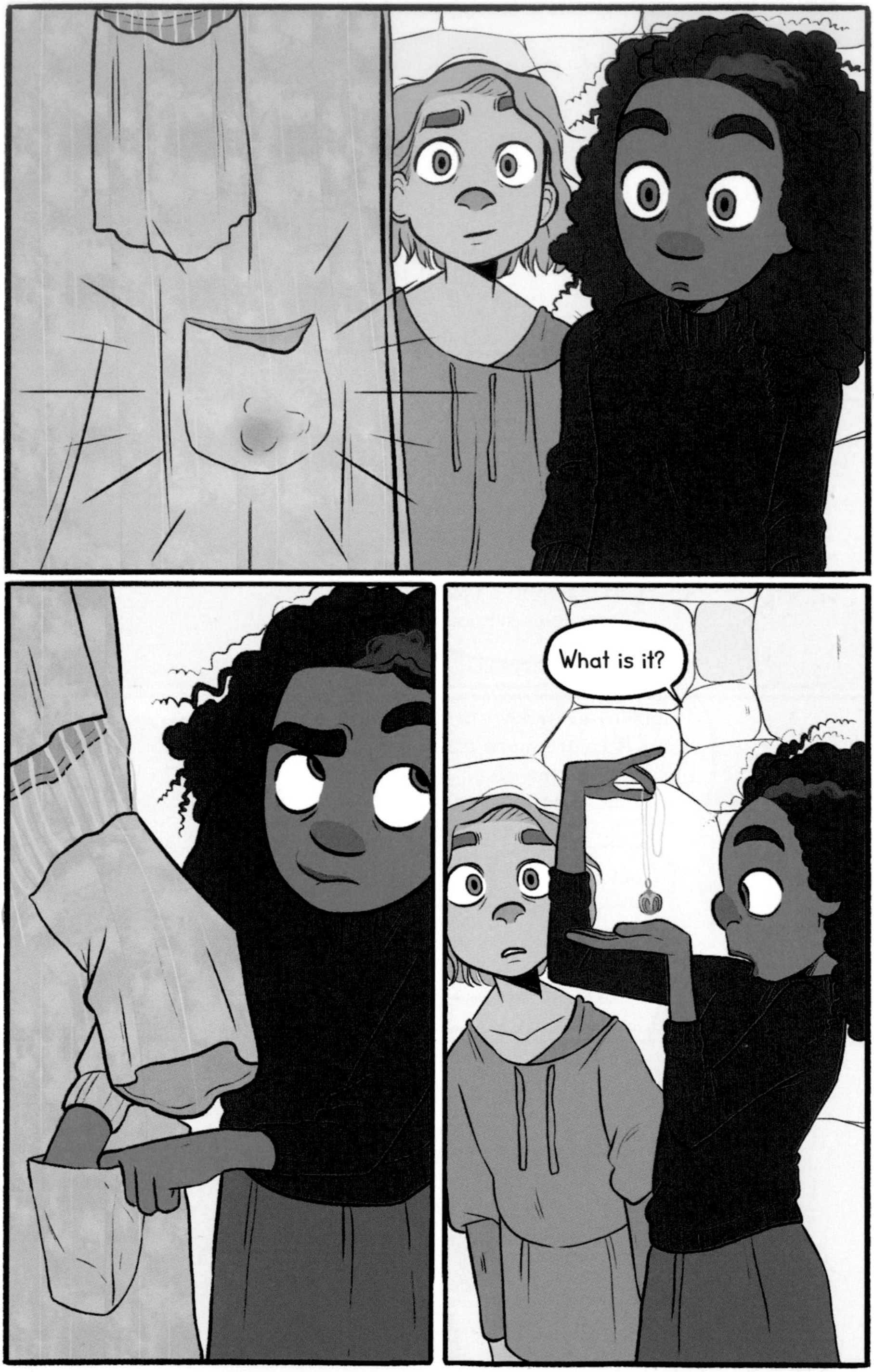
What is it?

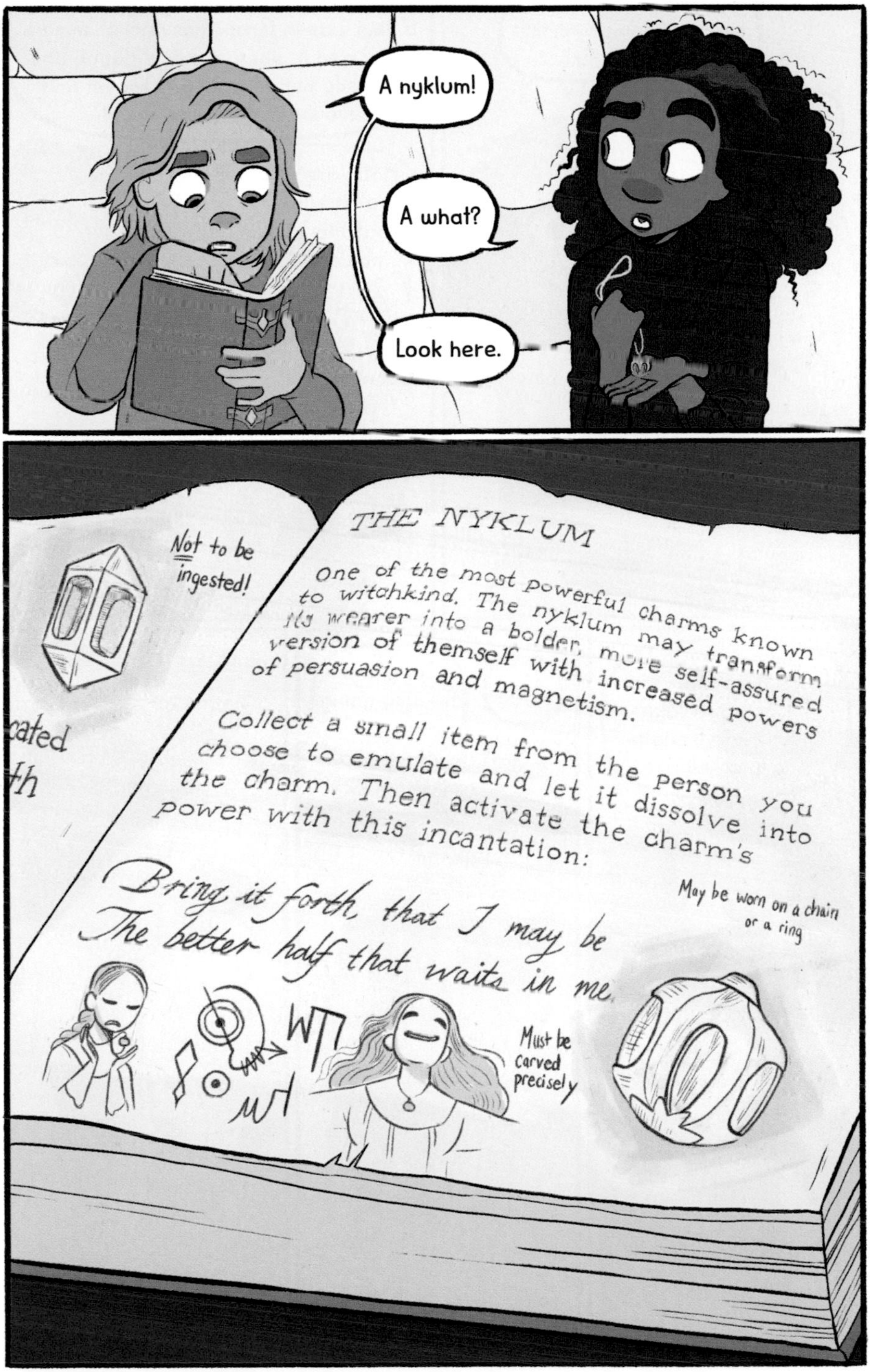
A nyklum!
A what?
Look here.
Not to be ingested!
cated
th
THE NYKLUM
One of the most powerful charms known to witchkind. The nyklum may transform its wearer into a bolder, more self-assured version of themself with increased powers of persuasion and magnetism.
Collect a small item from the person you choose to emulate and let it dissolve into the charm. Then activate the charm's power with this incantation:
Bring it forth that I may be
The better half that waits in me.
May be worn on a chain or a ring
Must be carved precisely

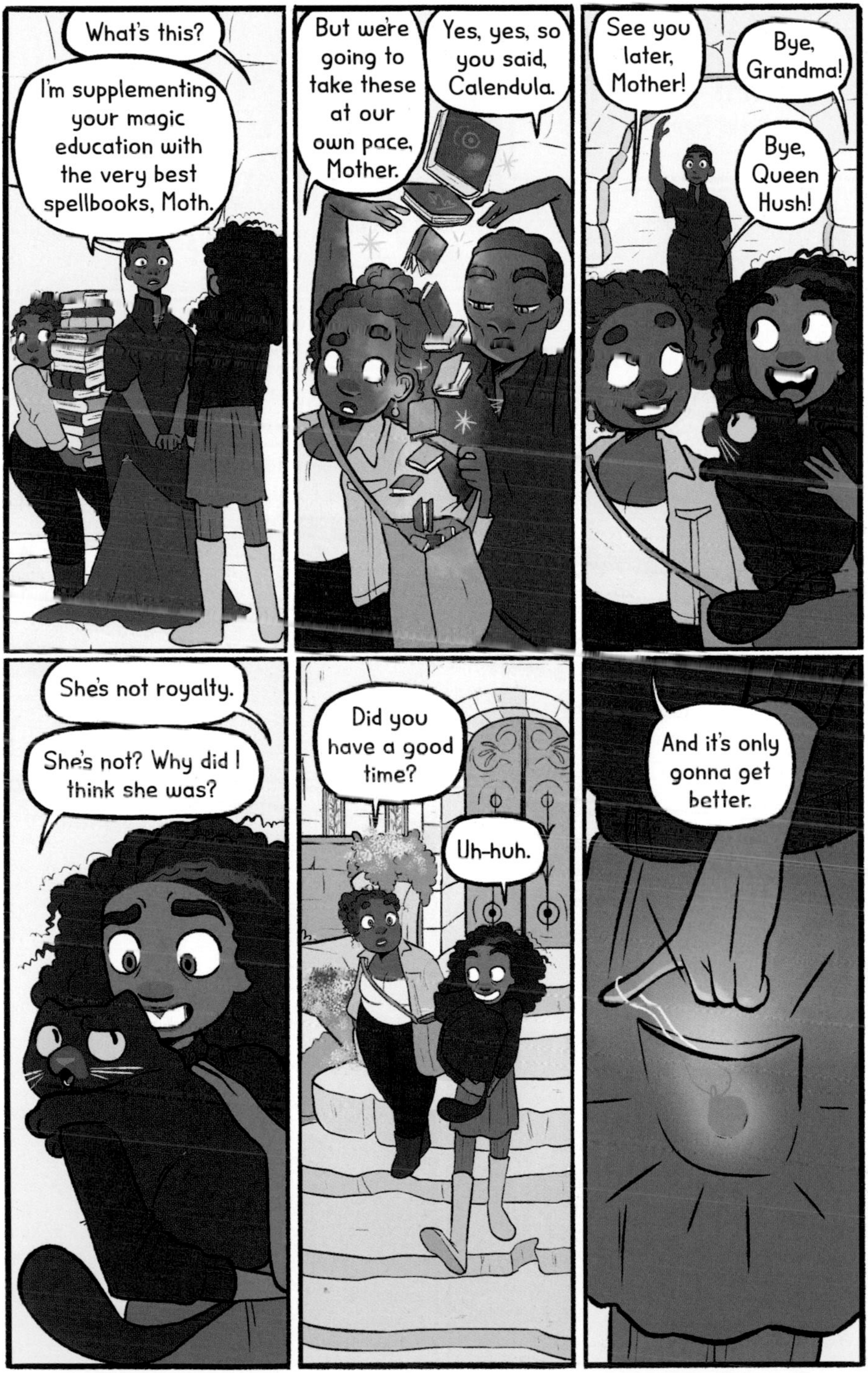
What's this?
I'm supplementing your magic education with the very best spellbooks, Moth.
But we're going to take these at our own pace, Mother.
Yes, yes, so you said, Calendula.
See you later, Mother!
Bye, Grandma!
Bye, Queen Hush!
She's not royalty.
She's not? Why did I think she was?
Did you have a good time?
Uh-huh.
And it's only gonna get better.

CHAPTER 4

The Most Popular Girls

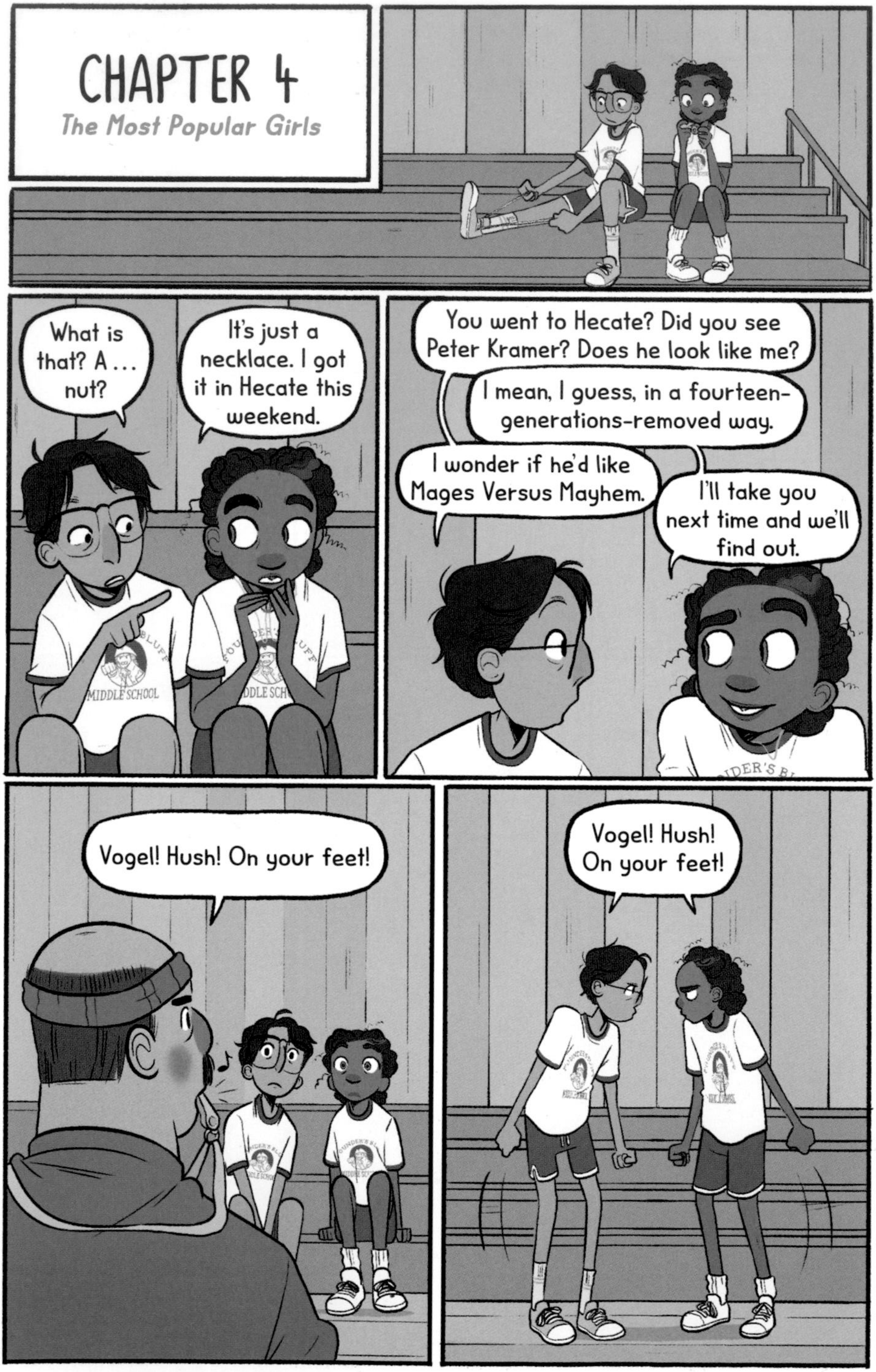
What is that? A . . . nut?
It's just a necklace. I got it in Hecate this weekend.
You went to Hecate? Did you see Peter Kramer? Does he look like me?
I mean, I guess, in a fourteen-generations-removed way.
I wonder if he'd like Mages Versus Mayhem.
I'll take you next time and we'll find out.
Vogel! Hush! On your feet!
Vogel! Hush! On your feet!

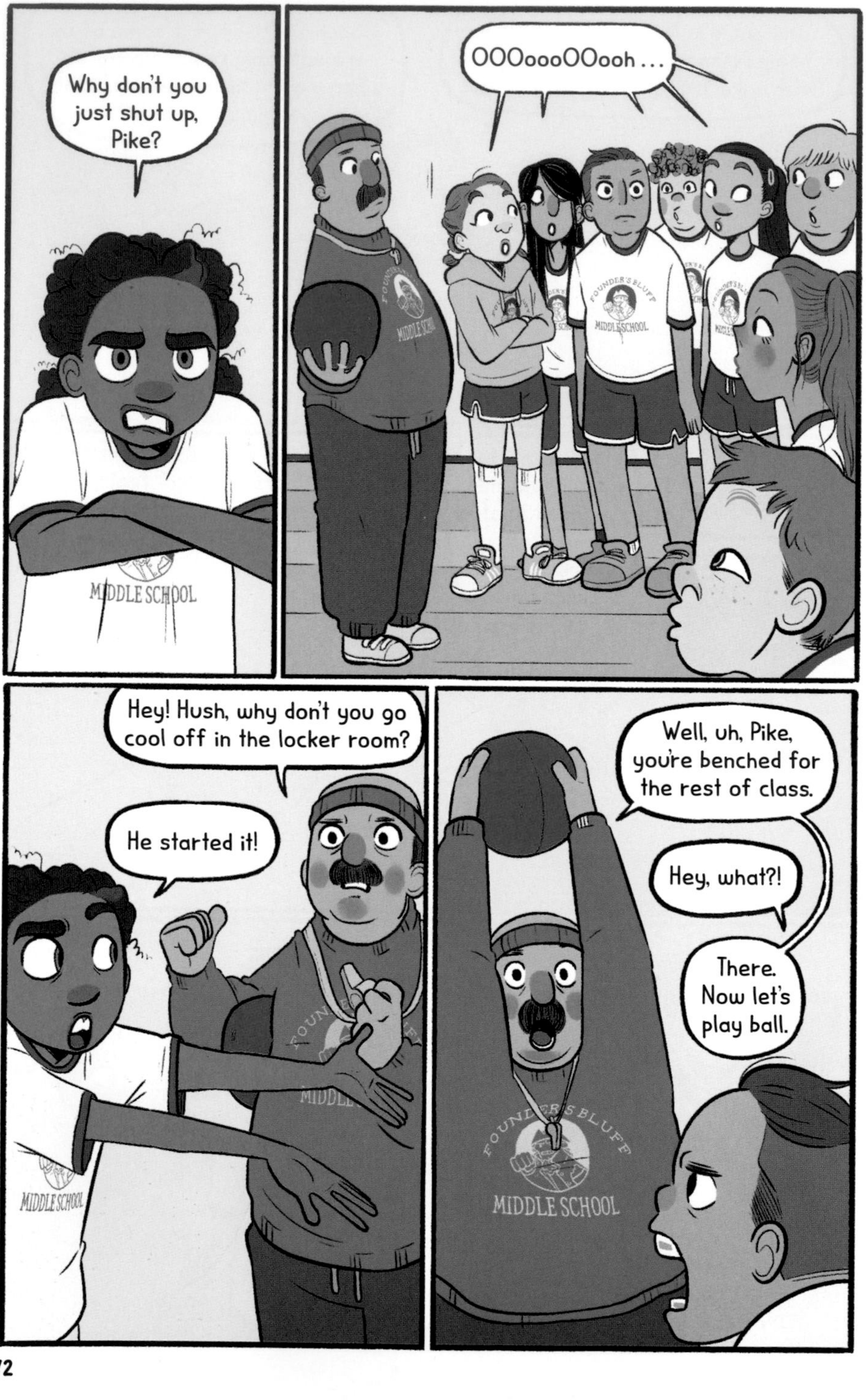
Why don't you just shut up, Pike?
OOOoooOOooh . . .
FOUNDER'S BLUFF MIDDLE SCHOOL
MIDDLE SCHOOL
Hey! Hush, why don't you go cool off in the locker room?
He started it!
MIDDLE SCHOOL
Well, uh, Pike, you're benched for the rest of class.
Hey, what?!
There. Now let's play ball.
FOUNDER'S BLUFF MIDDLE SCHOOL

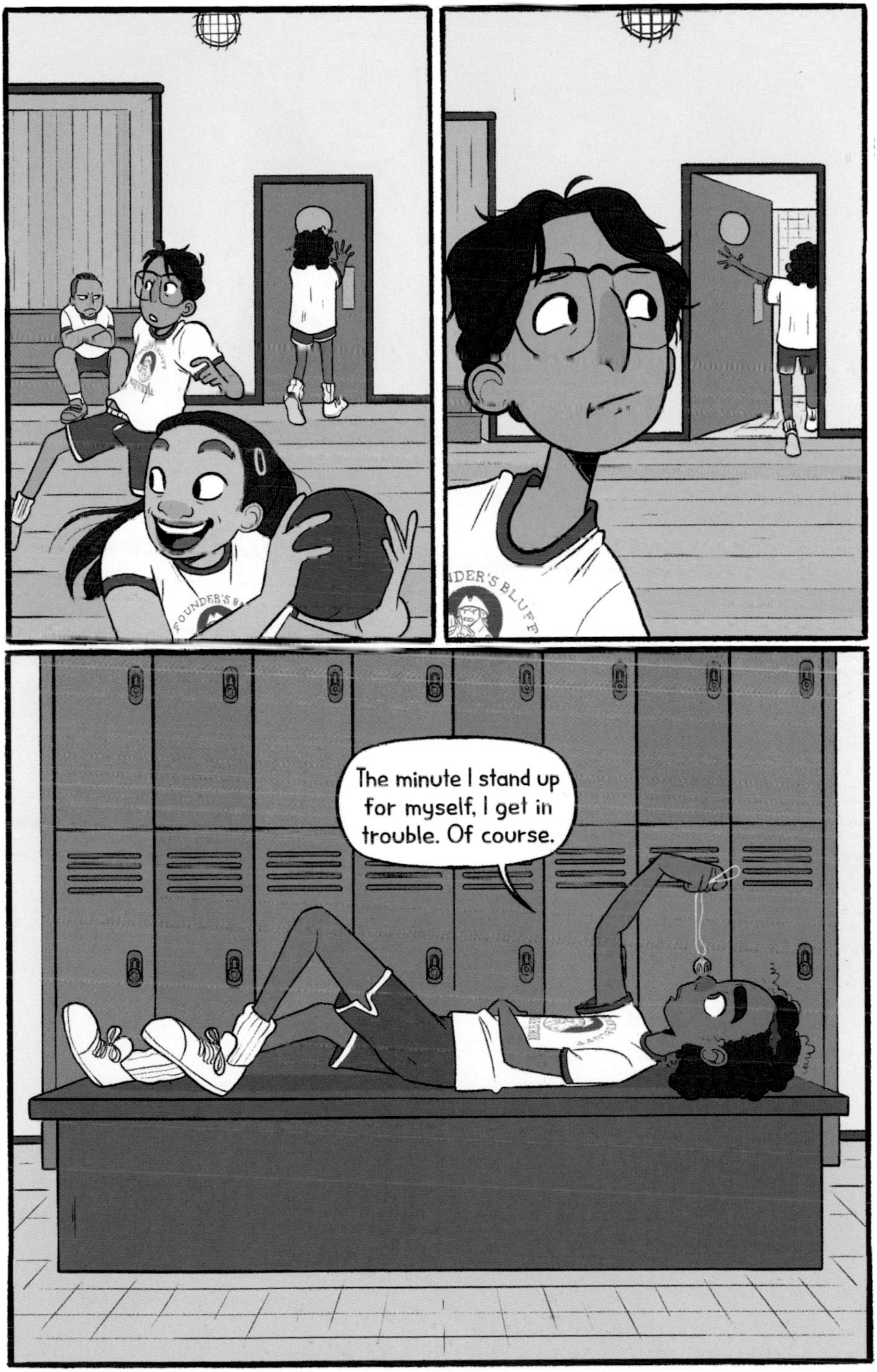
FOUNDER'S BLUFF
The minute I stand up for myself, I get in trouble. Of course.

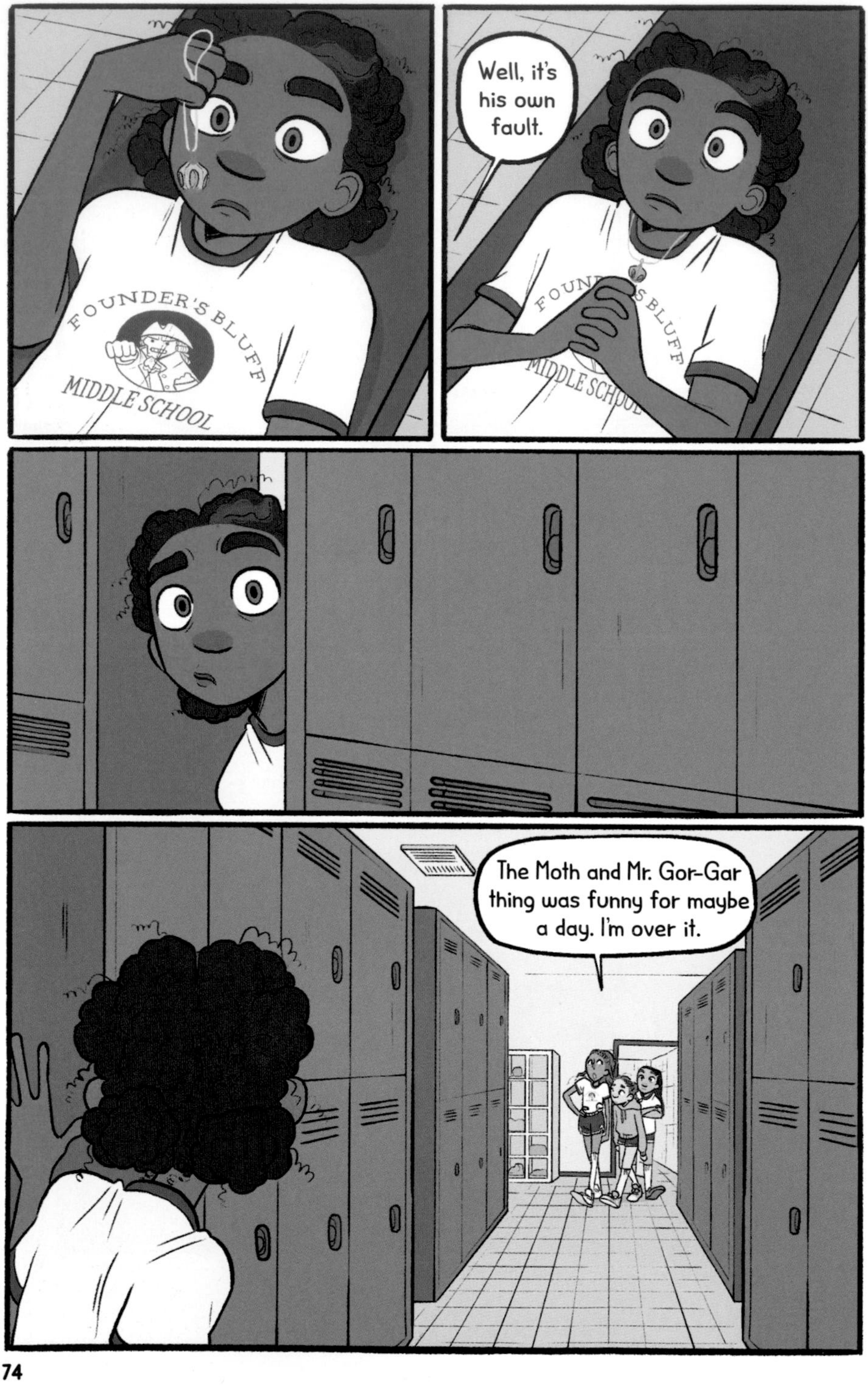
FOUNDER'S BLUFF
MIDDLE SCHOOL
Well, it's his own fault.
FOUNDER'S BLUFF
MIDDLE SCHOOL
The Moth and Mr. Gor-Gar thing was funny for maybe a day. I'm over it.

75

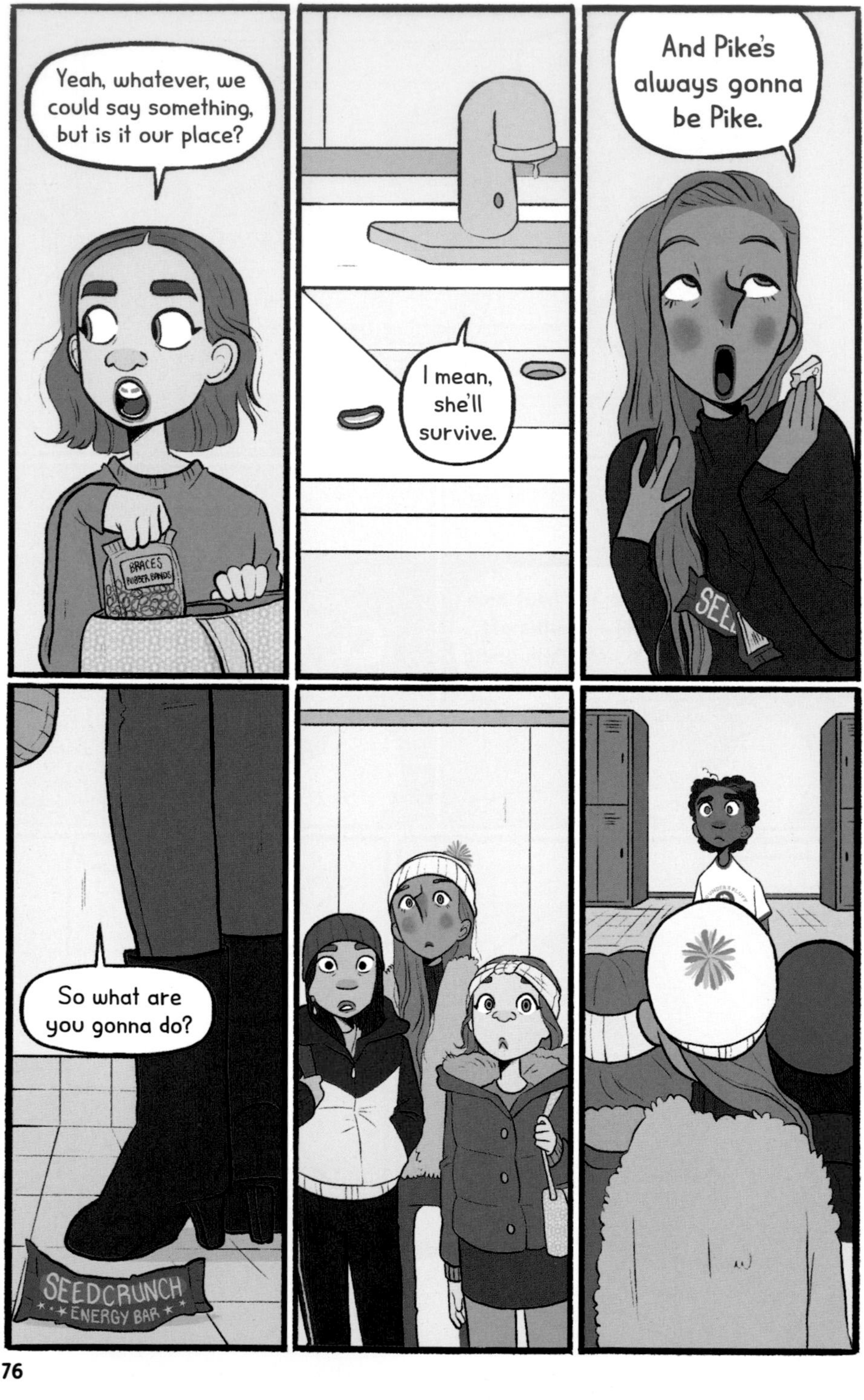
Yeah, whatever, we could say something, but is it our place?
BRACES RUBBER BANDS
I mean, she'll survive.
And Pike's always gonna be Pike.
So what are you gonna do?
SEEDCRUNCH ENERGY BAR

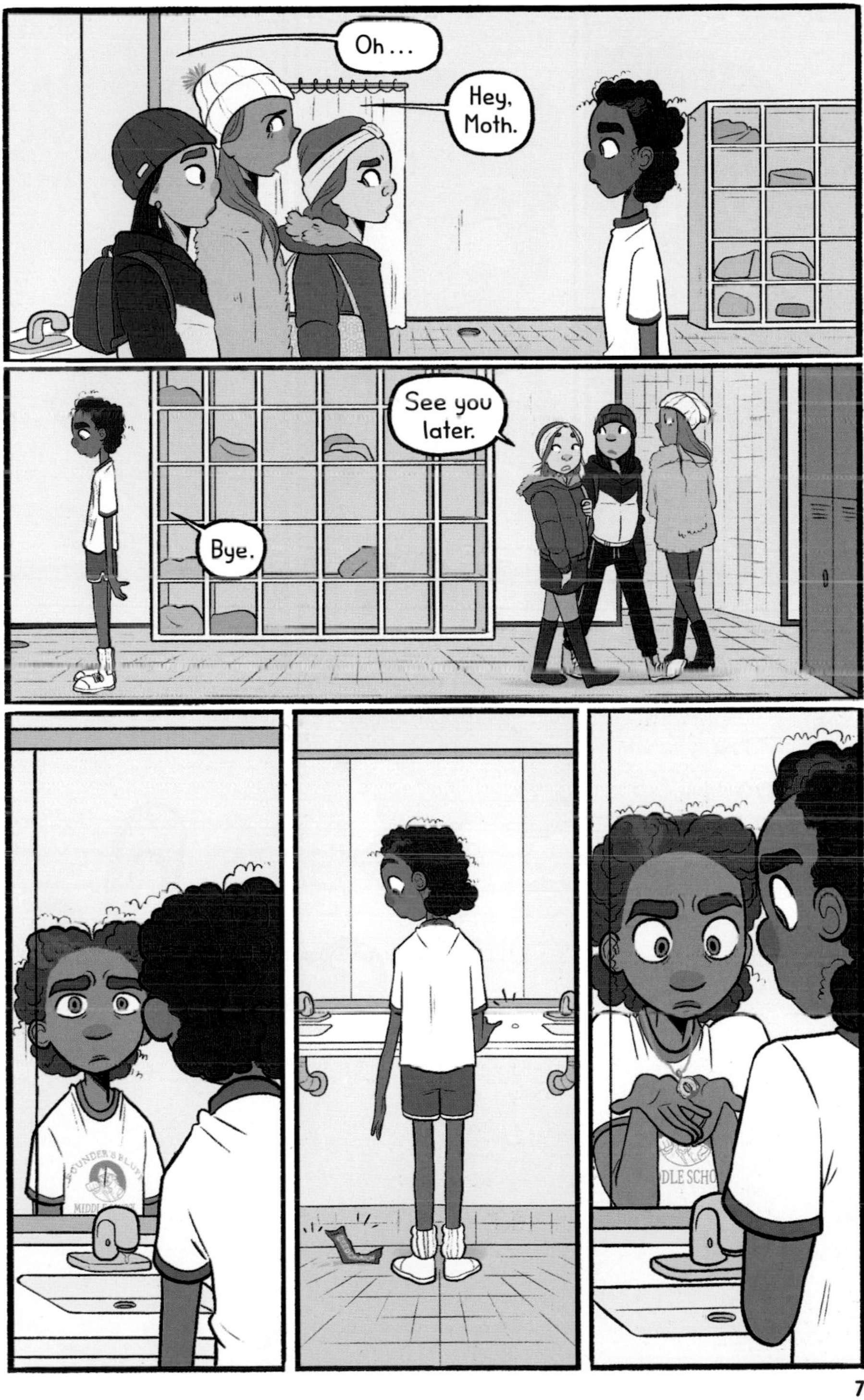
Oh...
Hey, Moth.
See you later.
Bye.
FOUNDER'S BLUFF MIDDLE SCHOOL

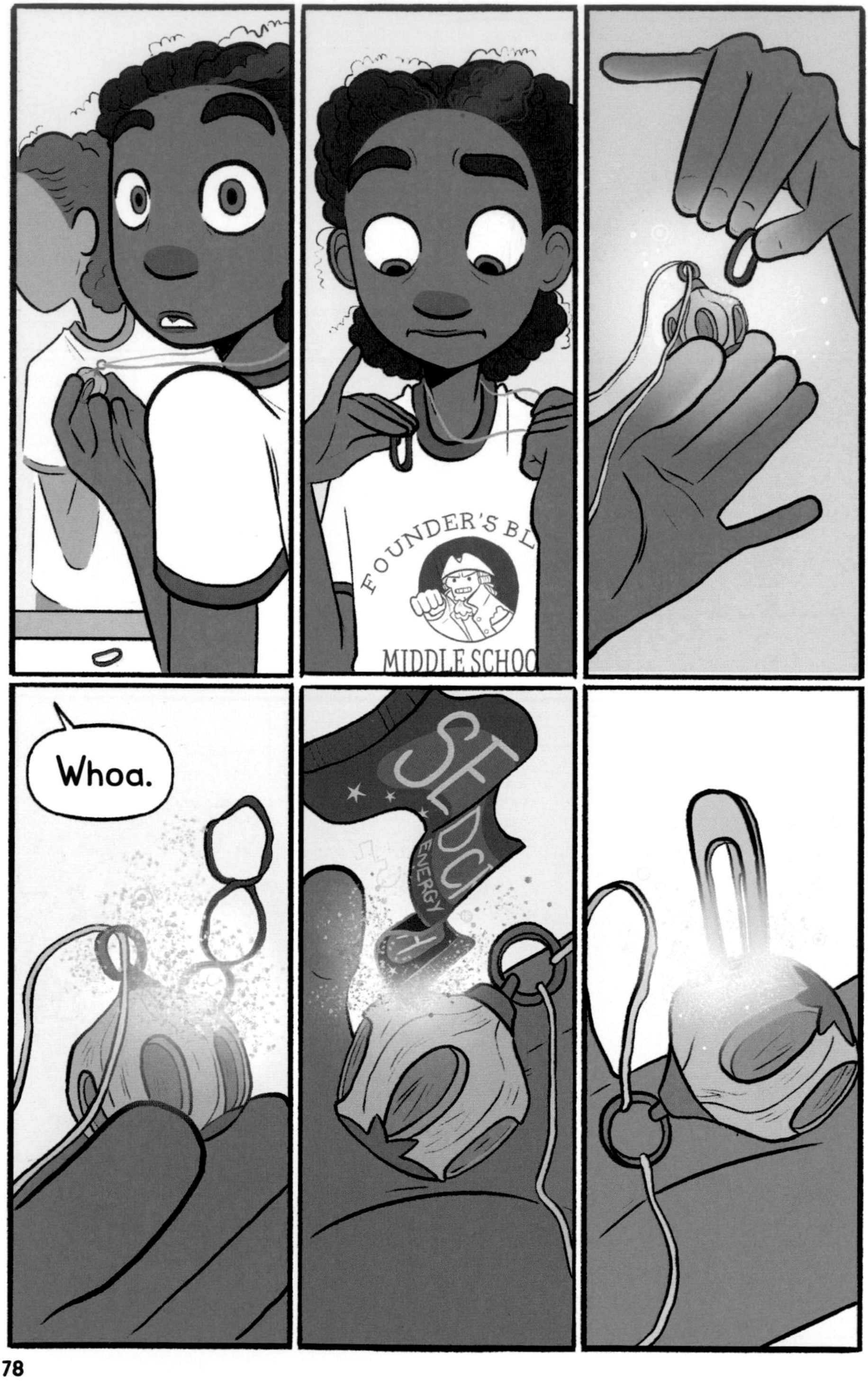
FOUNDER'S BL
MIDDLE SCHOO
Whoa.
ENERGY

81

CHAPTER 5

Founderella

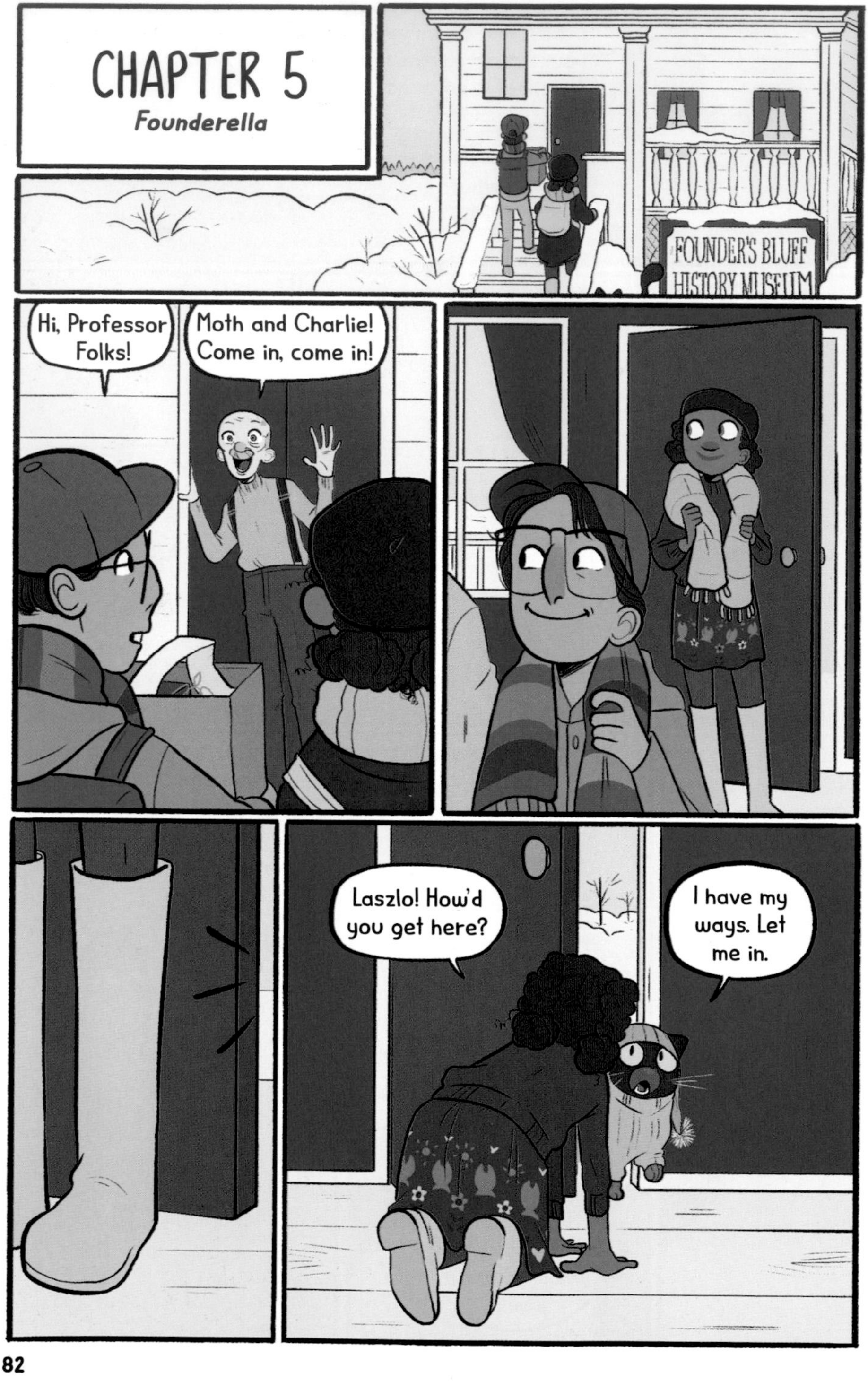
FOUNDER'S BLUFF HISTORY MUSEUM
Hi, Professor Folks!
Moth and Charlie! Come in, come in!
Laszlo! How'd you get here?
I have my ways. Let me in.

83

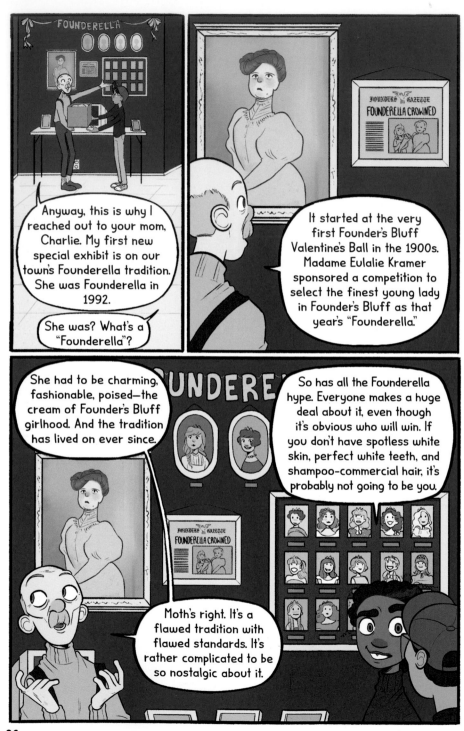

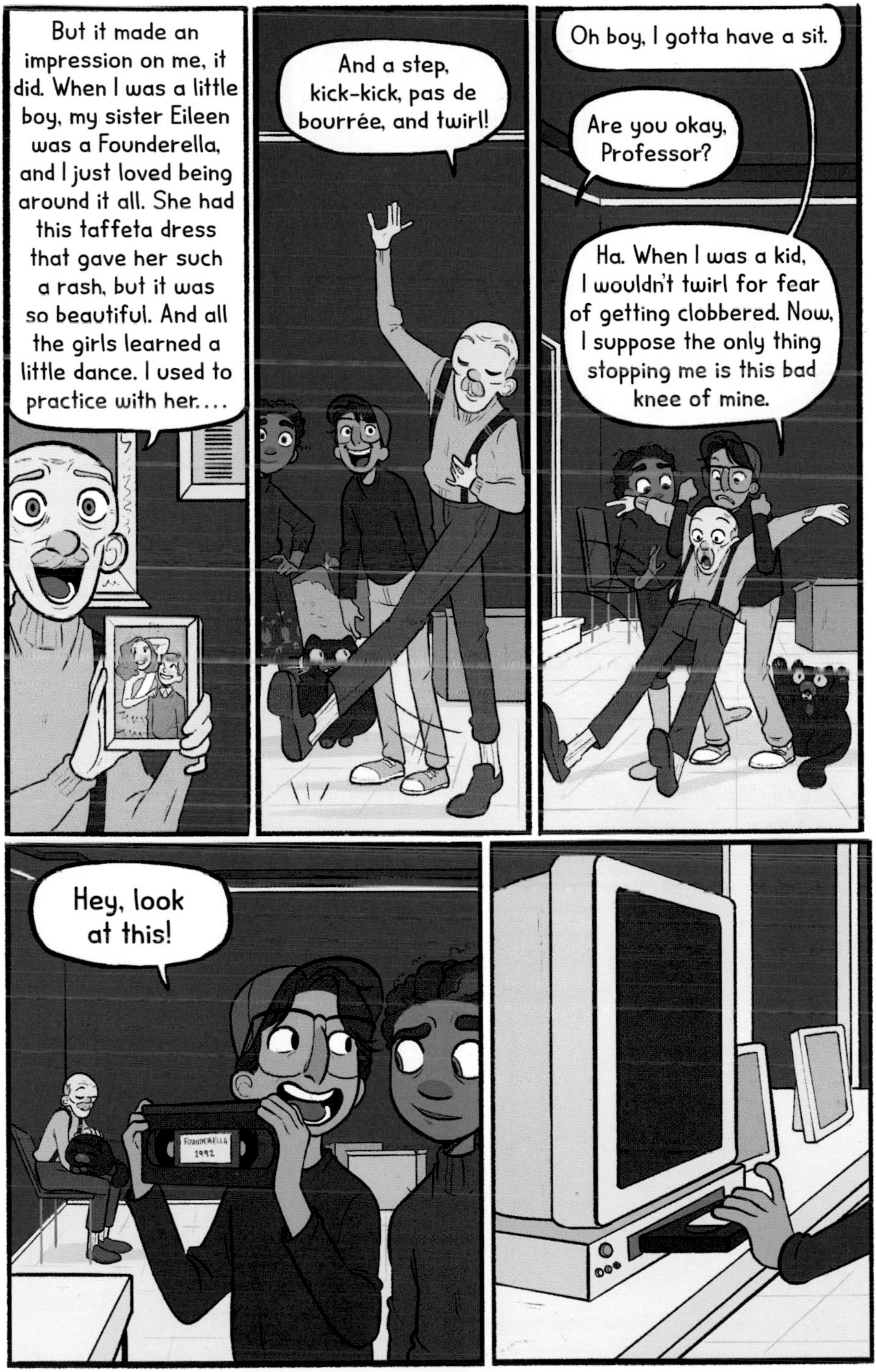

But it made an impression on me, it did. When I was a little boy, my sister Eileen was a Founderella, and I just loved being around it all. She had this taffeta dress that gave her such a rash, but it was so beautiful. And all the girls learned a little dance. I used to practice with her. . . .
And a step, kick-kick, pas de bourrée, and twirl!
Oh boy, I gotta have a sit.
Are you okay, Professor?
Ha. When I was a kid, I wouldn't twirl for fear of getting clobbered. Now, I suppose the only thing stopping me is this bad knee of mine.
Hey, look at this!
FOUNDERELLA
1992

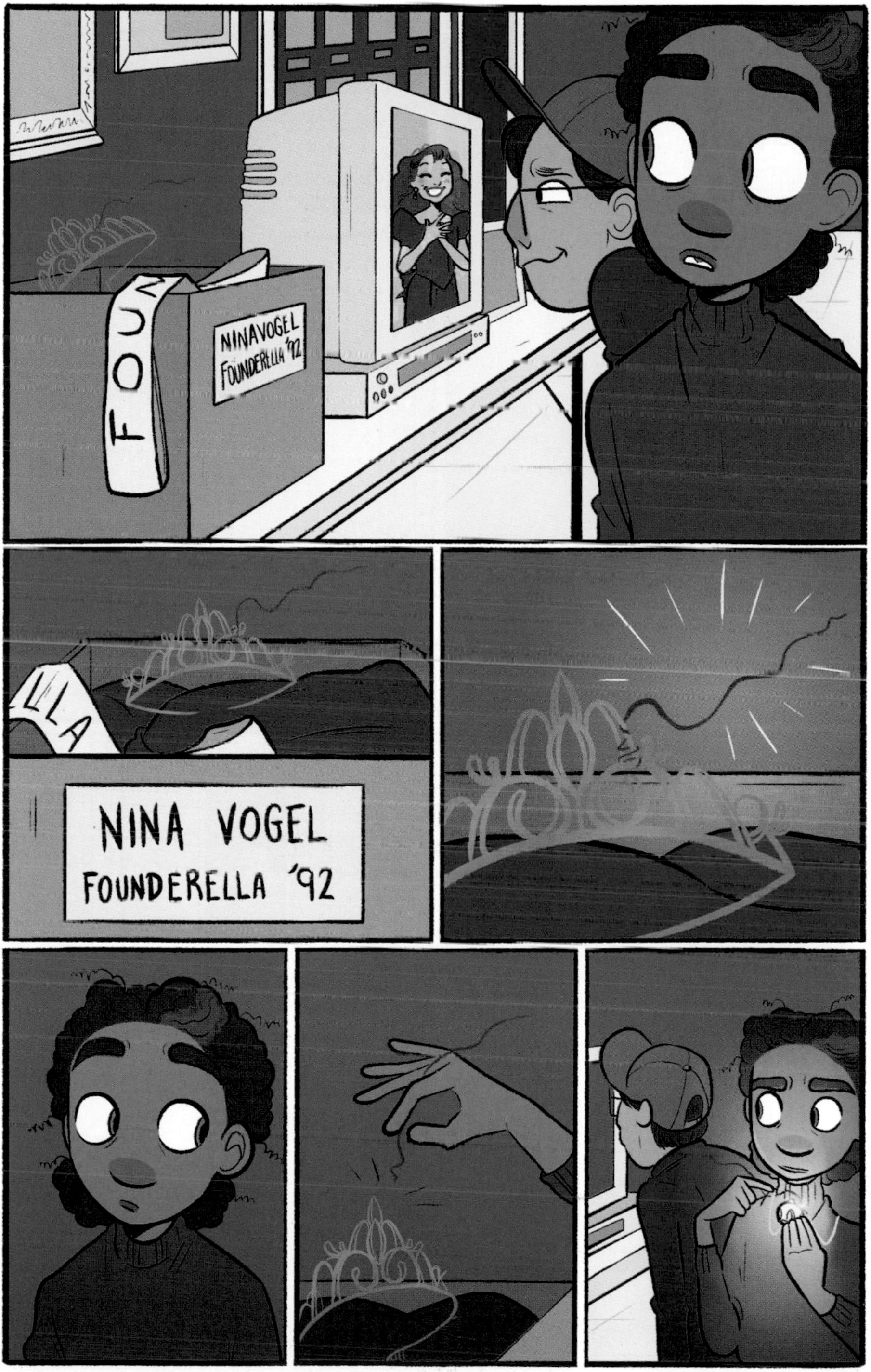
FOUN
NINA VOGEL
FOUNDERELLA '92
LLA
NINA VOGEL
FOUNDERELLA '92

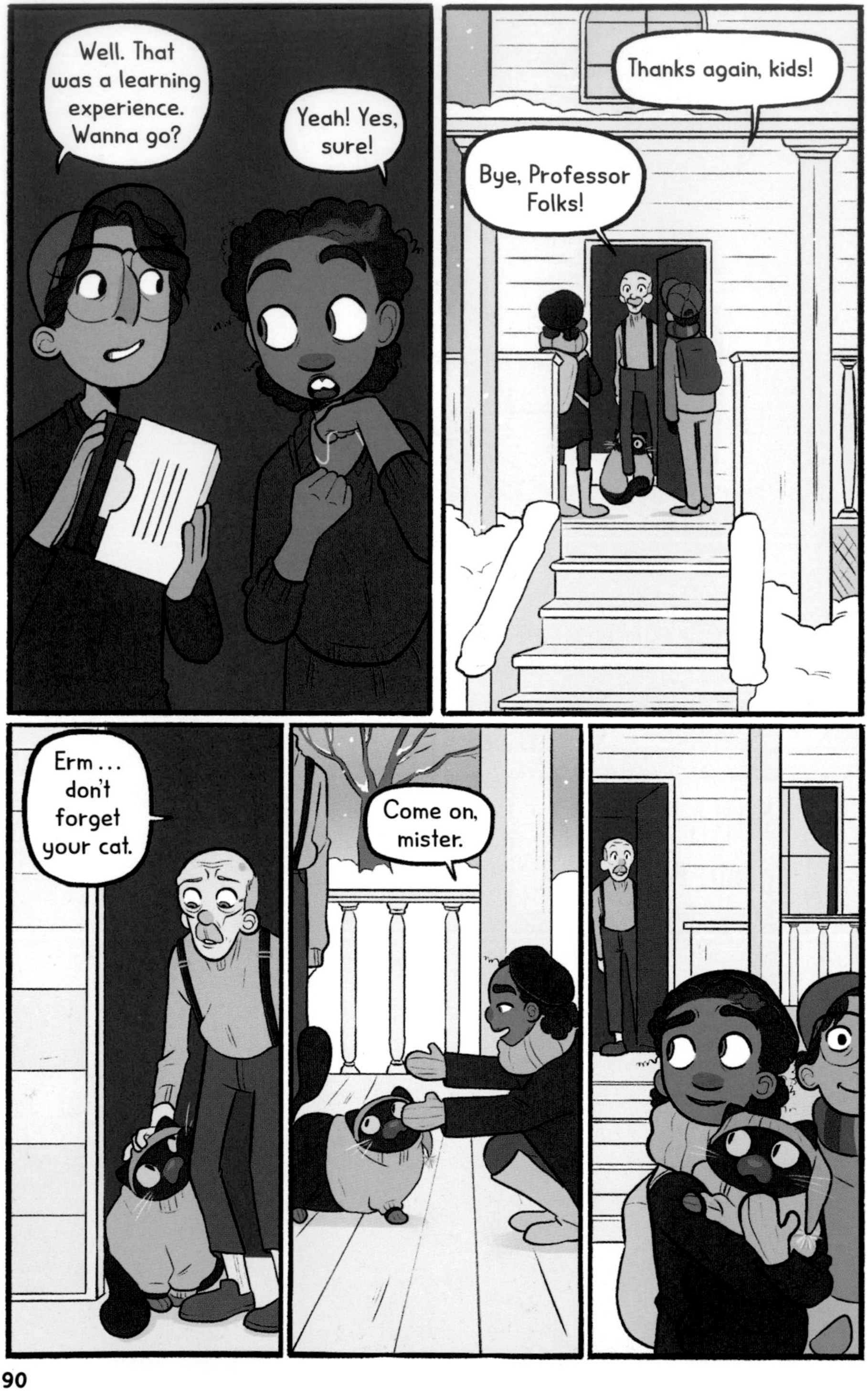
Well. That was a learning experience. Wanna go?
Yeah! Yes, sure!
Thanks again, kids!
Bye, Professor Folks!
Erm . . . don't forget your cat.
Come on, mister.

It's so strange to see Mom that young. Does it feel like that when you go into your mom's diary?

My mom never got her eyelids that blue.

You wanna know how it really feels to be Founderella?

FaaaaanTASTIC!

Ha ha ha ha ha ha ha ha ha ha ha ha!

What if it really is fantastic?

Maybe it was for my mom. But you really think you'd like it?

I mean, remember when you called out the Founder's Fest pageant as a trash town event that we should all forget about? Isn't this basically the same thing?

I know it hasn't been the best.

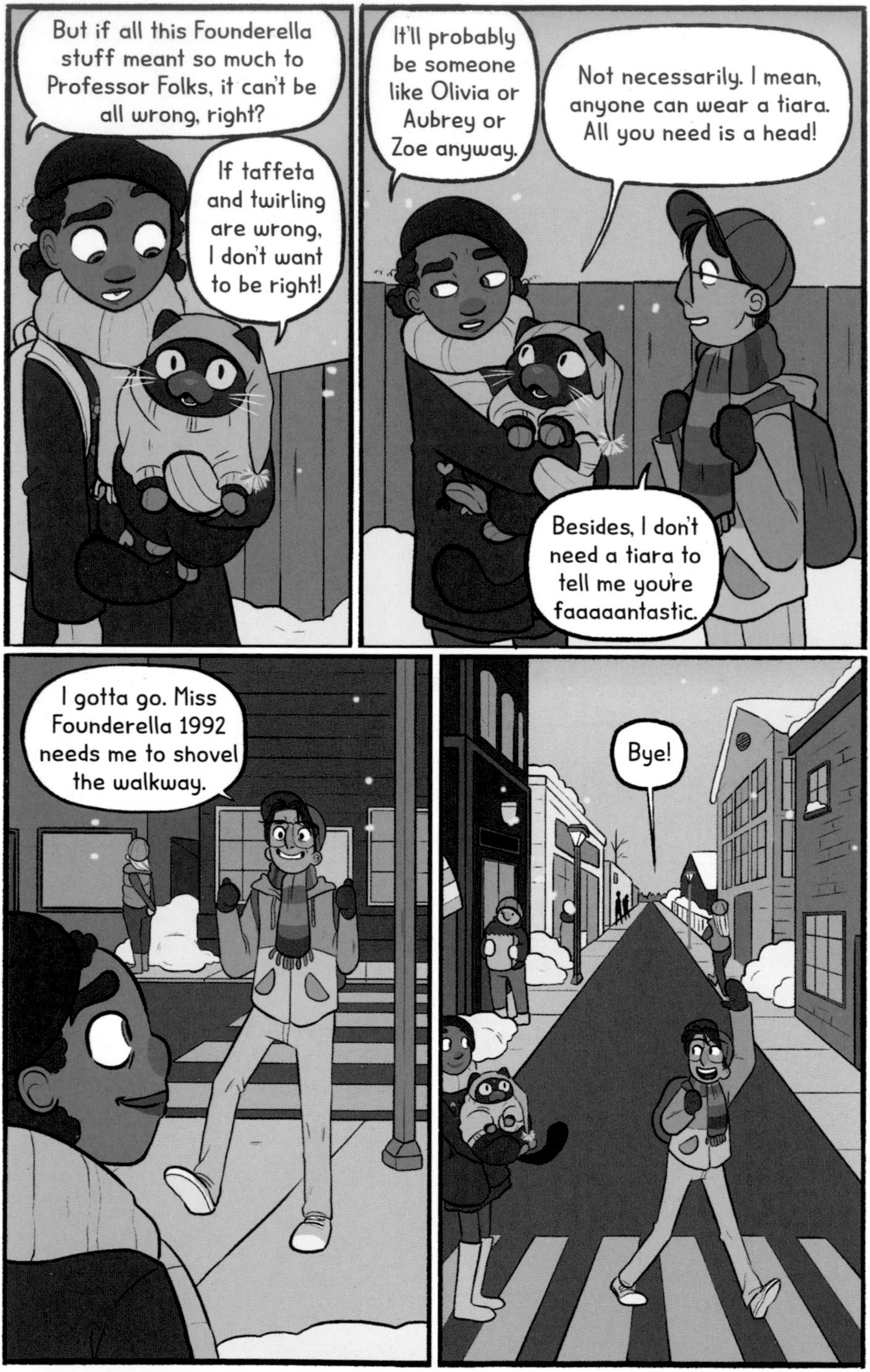
But if all this Founderella stuff meant so much to Professor Folks, it can't be all wrong, right?
If taffeta and twirling are wrong, I don't want to be right!
It'll probably be someone like Olivia or Aubrey or Zoe anyway.
Not necessarily. I mean, anyone can wear a tiara. All you need is a head!
Besides, I don't need a tiara to tell me you're faaaaantastic.
I gotta go. Miss Founderella 1992 needs me to shovel the walkway.
Bye!

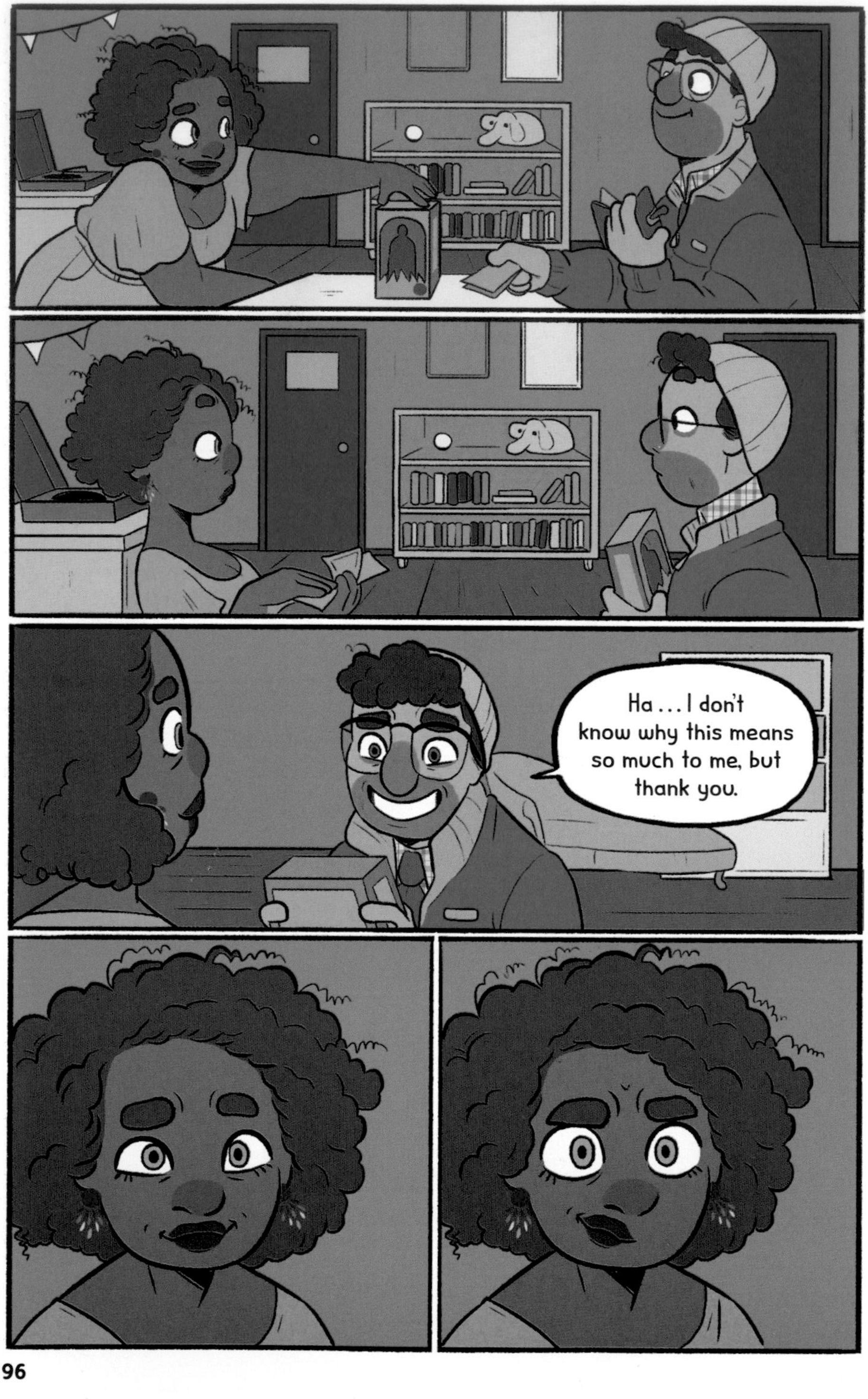
Ha . . . I don't know why this means so much to me, but thank you.

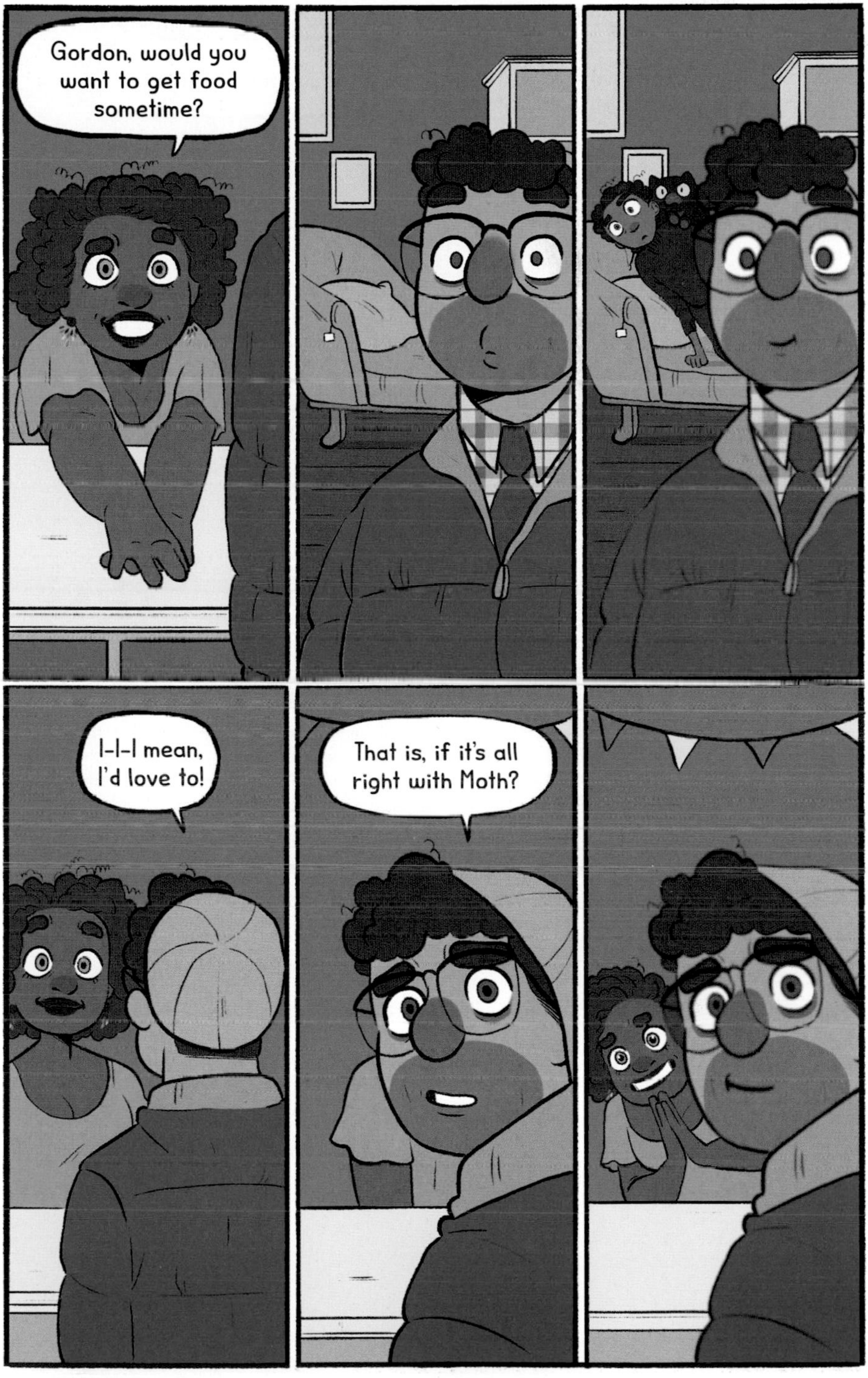
Gordon, would you want to get food sometime?
I-I-I mean, I'd love to!
That is, if it's all right with Moth?

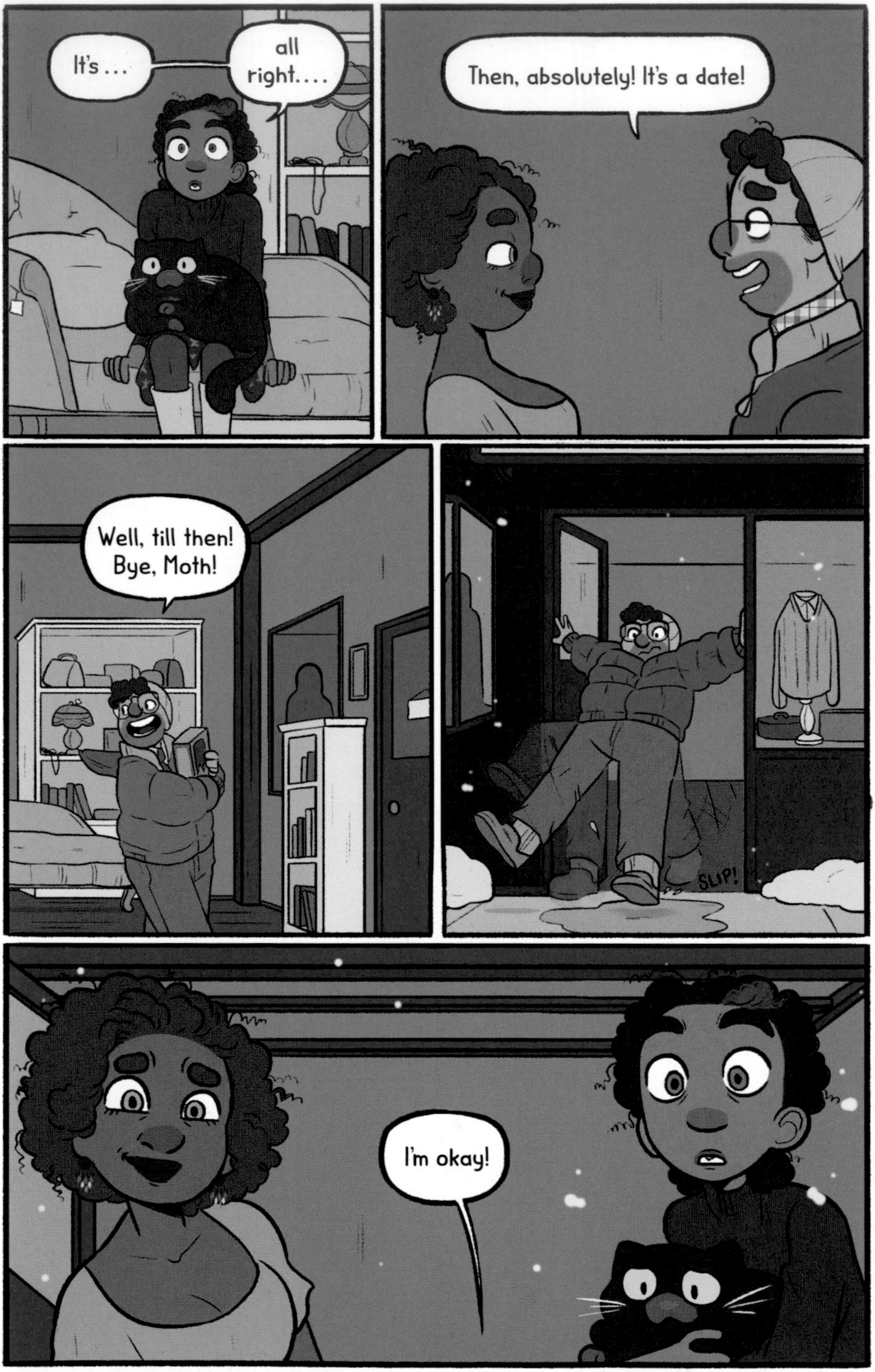
It's . . .
all right. . . .
Then, absolutely! It's a date!
Well, till then! Bye, Moth!
SLIP!
I'm okay!

100

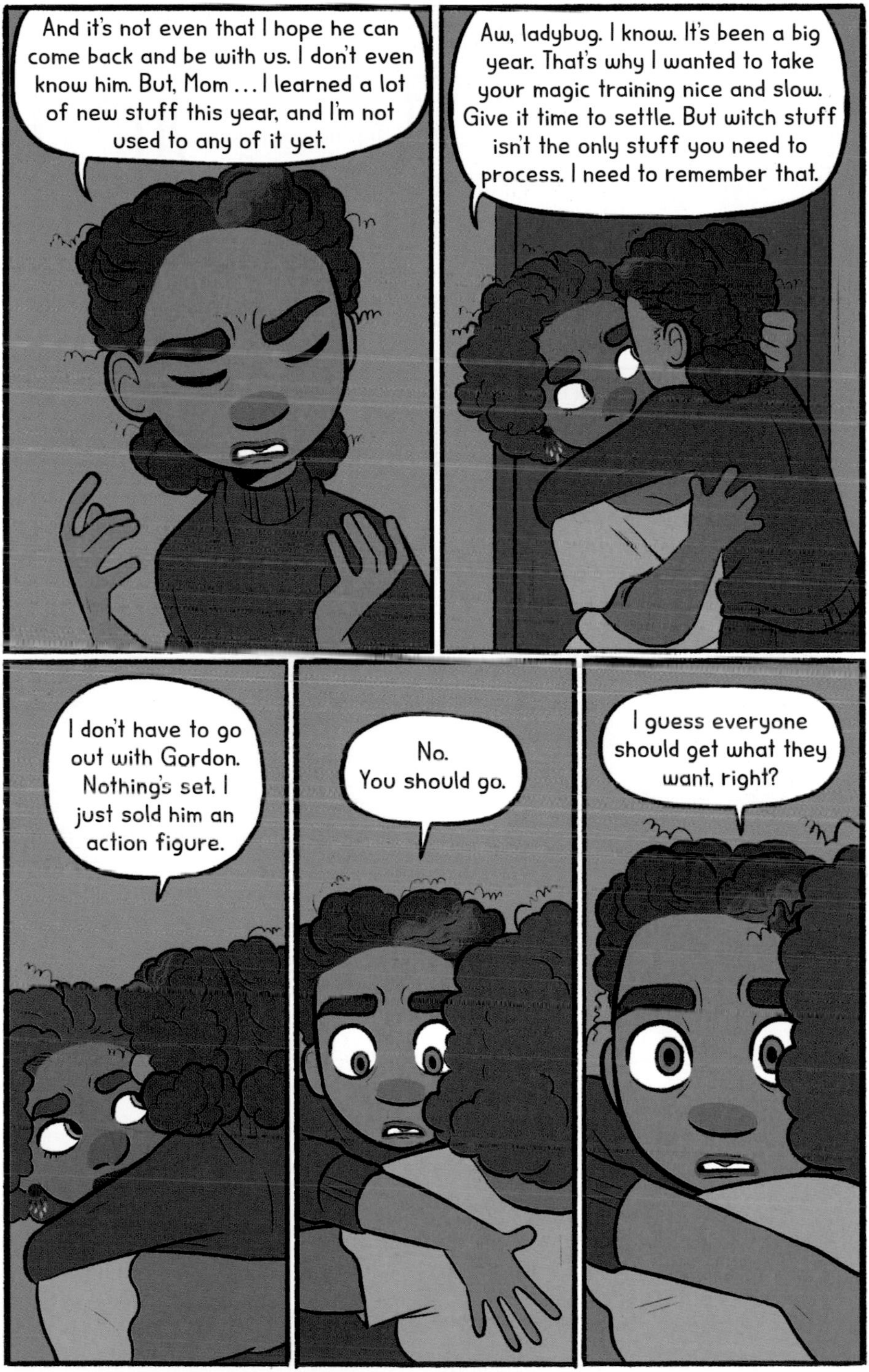
And it's not even that I hope he can come back and be with us. I don't even know him. But, Mom . . . I learned a lot of new stuff this year, and I'm not used to any of it yet.
Aw, ladybug. I know. It's been a big year. That's why I wanted to take your magic training nice and slow. Give it time to settle. But witch stuff isn't the only stuff you need to process. I need to remember that.
I don't have to go out with Gordon. Nothing's set. I just sold him an action figure.
No. You should go.
I guess everyone should get what they want, right?

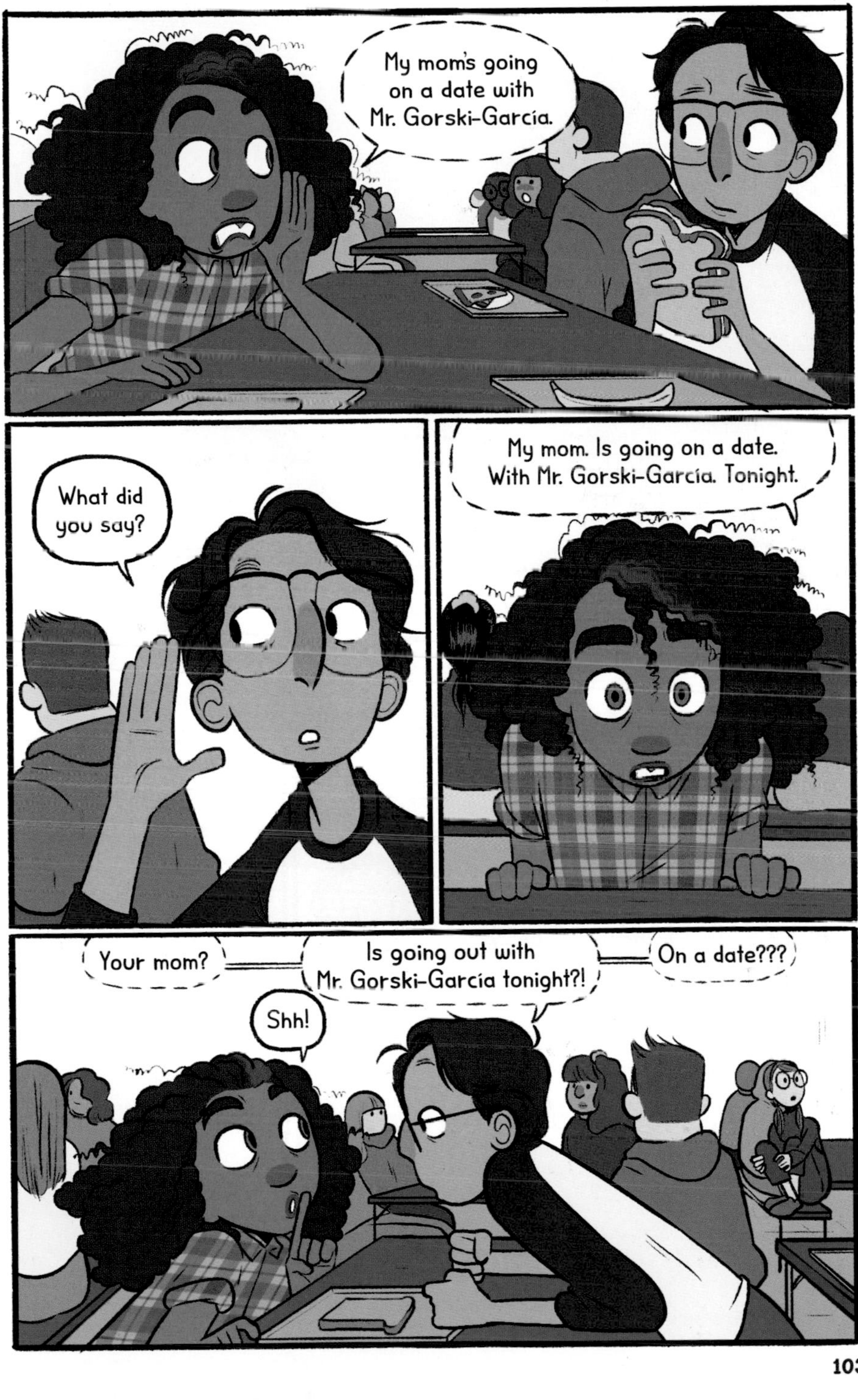

My mom's going on a date with Mr. Gorski-García.
What did you say?
My mom. Is going on a date. With Mr. Gorski-García. Tonight.
Your mom?
Is going out with Mr. Gorski-García tonight?!
On a date???
Shh!

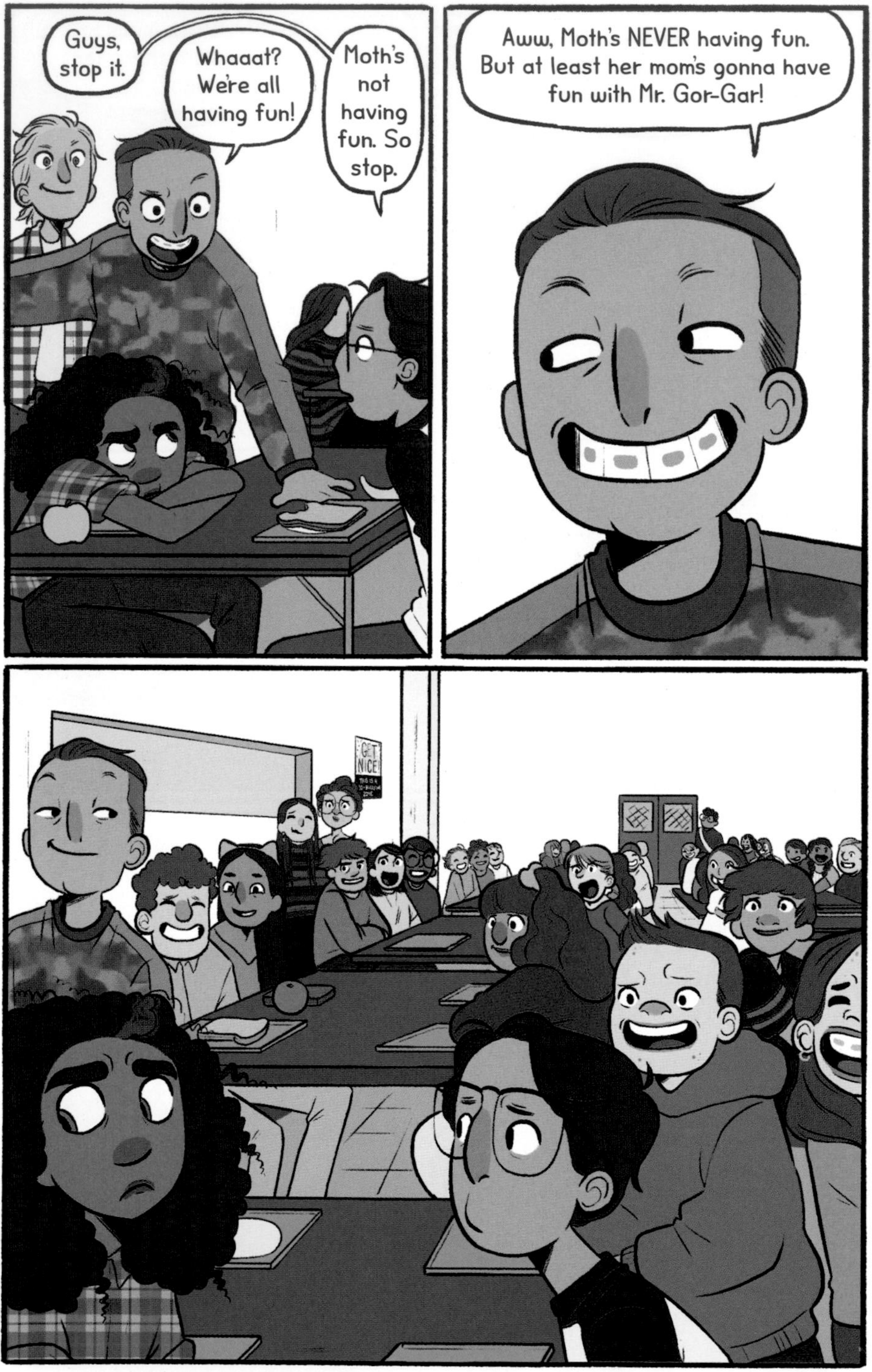
Guys, stop it.
Whaaat? We're all having fun!
Moth's not having fun. So stop.
Aww, Moth's NEVER having fun. But at least her mom's gonna have fun with Mr. Gor-Gar!
GET NICE!

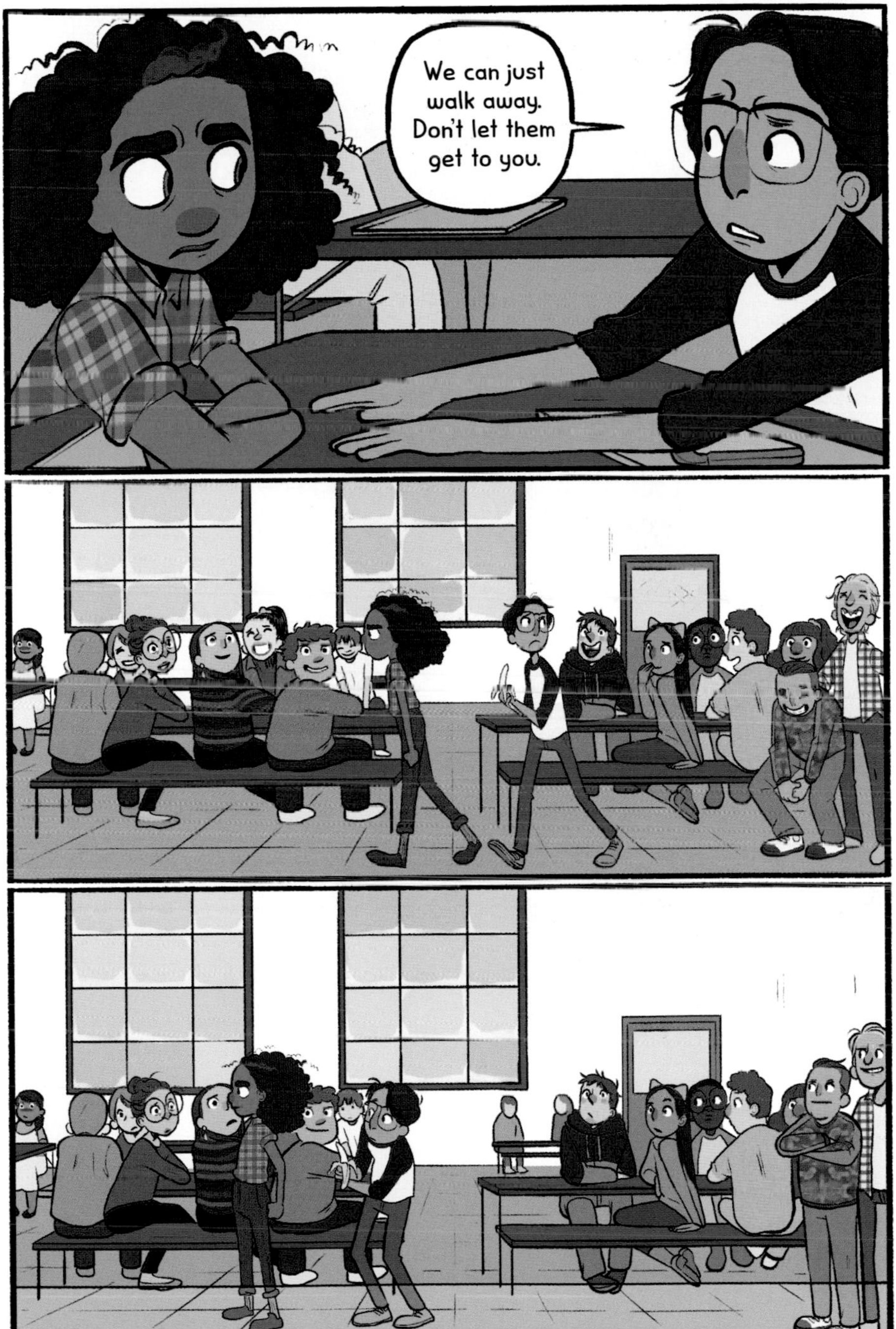
We can just walk away. Don't let them get to you.

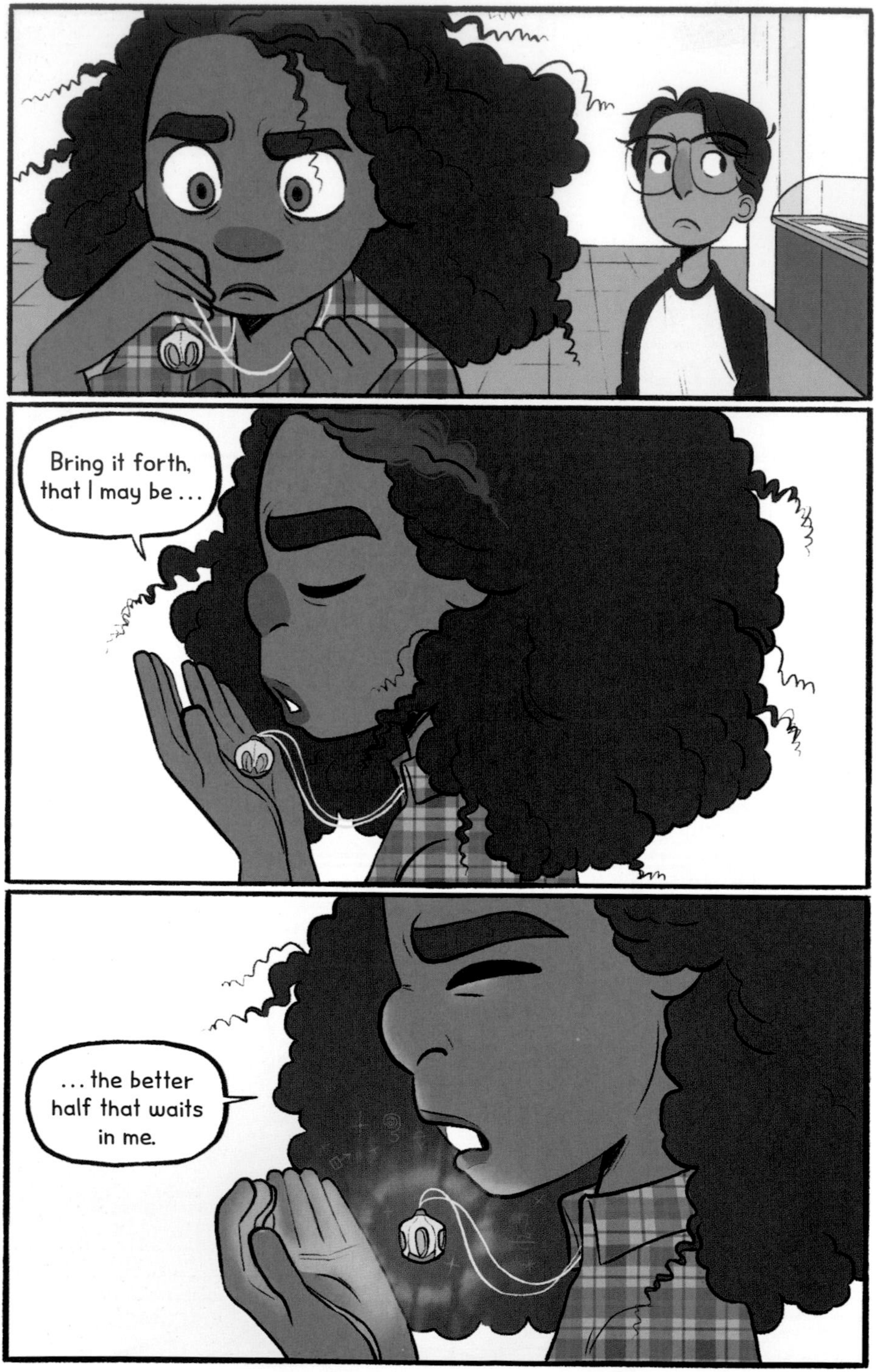
Bring it forth, that I may be . . .
. . . the better half that waits in me.

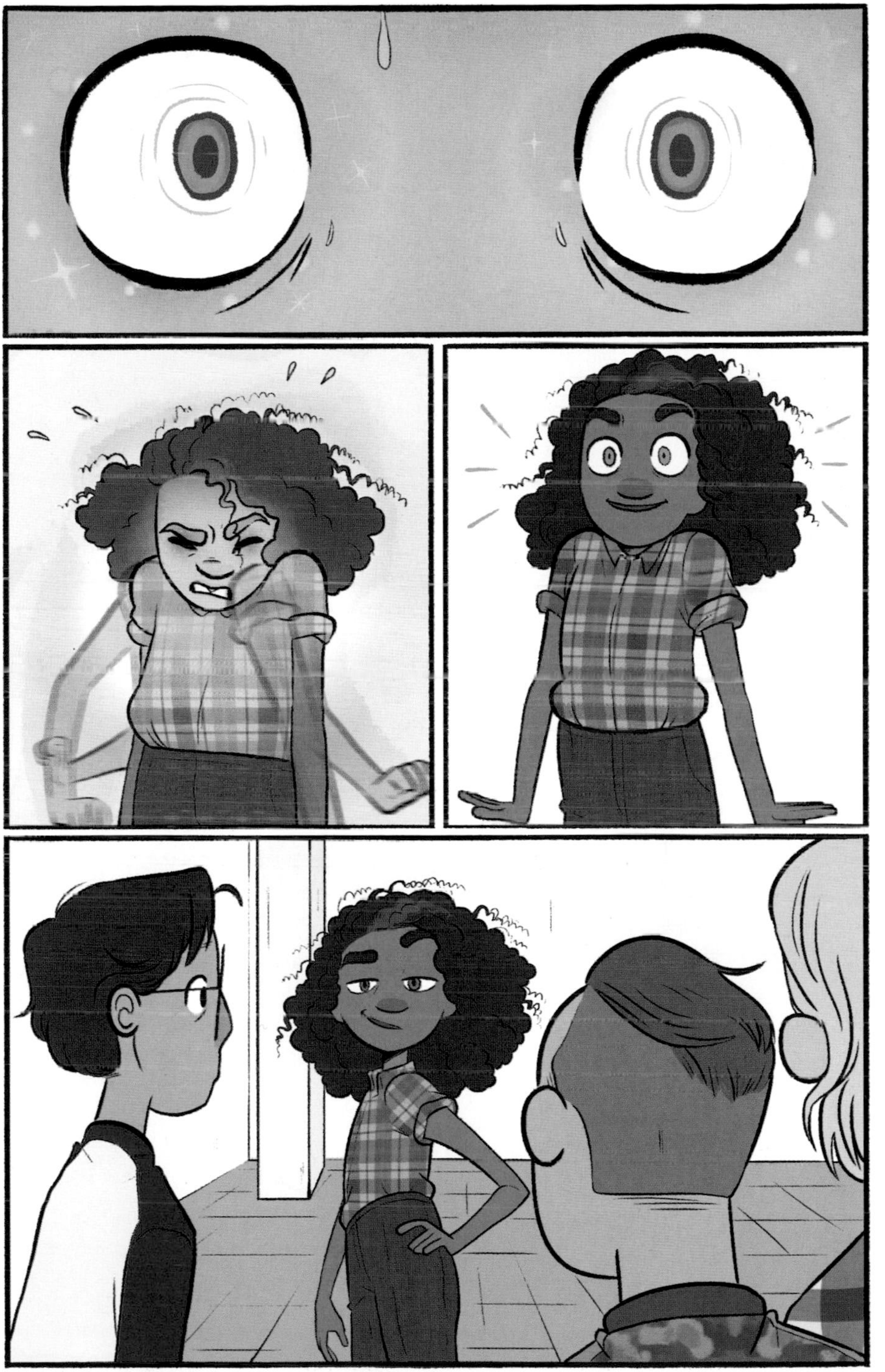

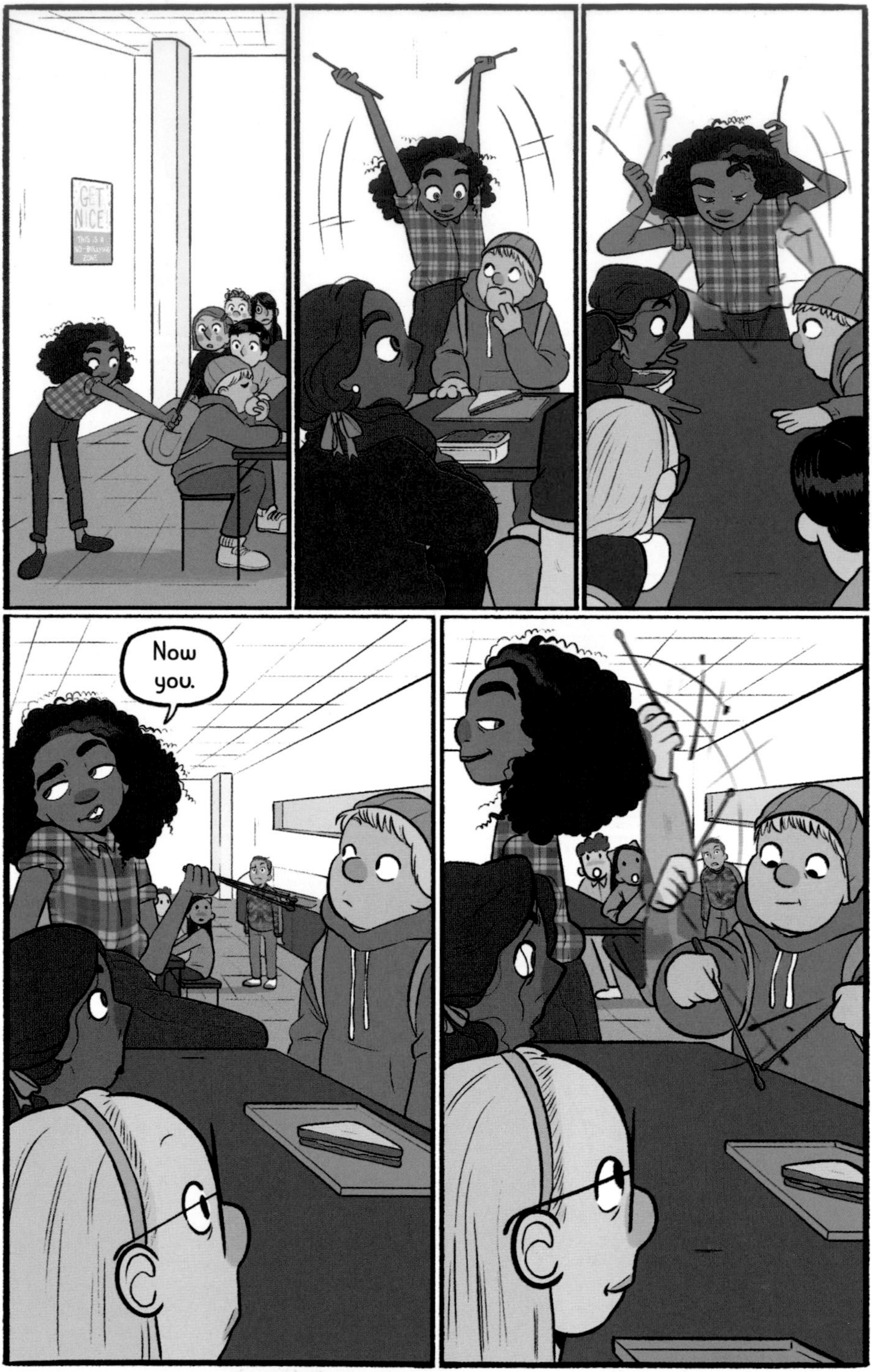
GET NICE!
Now you.

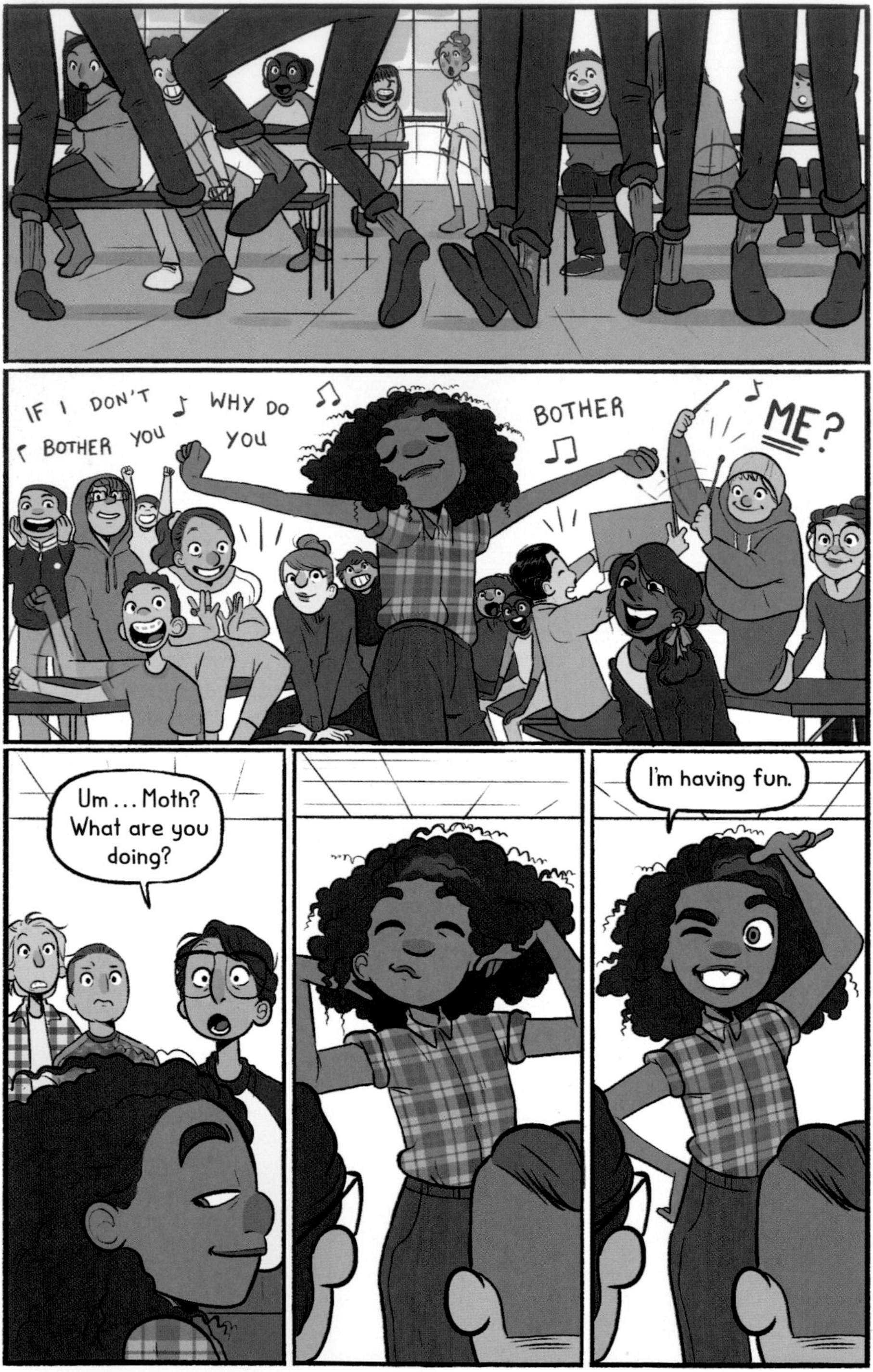

IF I DON'T BOTHER YOU
WHY DO YOU
BOTHER
ME?
Um . . . Moth? What are you doing?
I'm having fun.

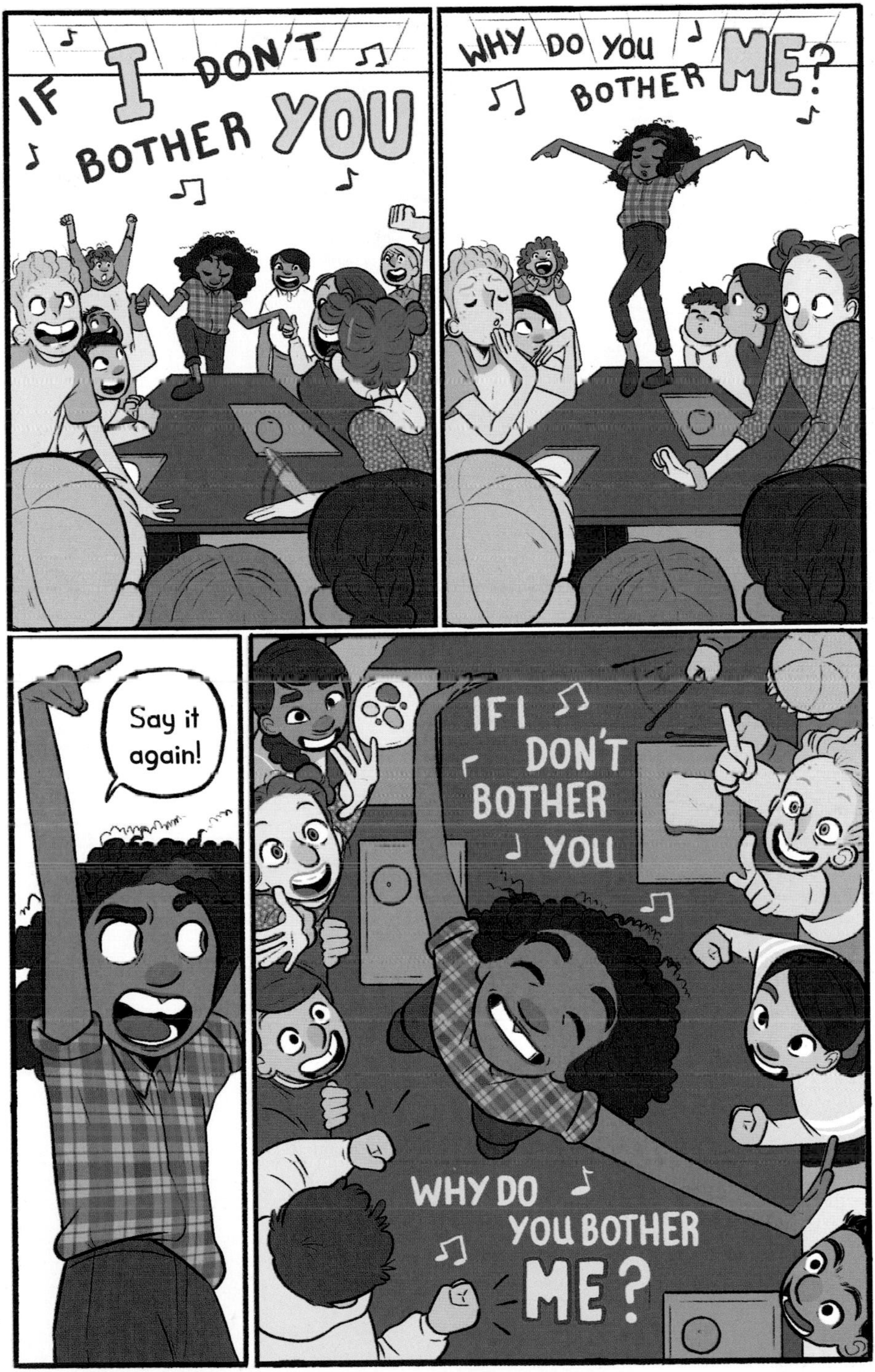
IF I DON'T BOTHER YOU
WHY DO YOU BOTHER ME?
Say it again!
IF I DON'T BOTHER YOU
WHY DO YOU BOTHER ME?

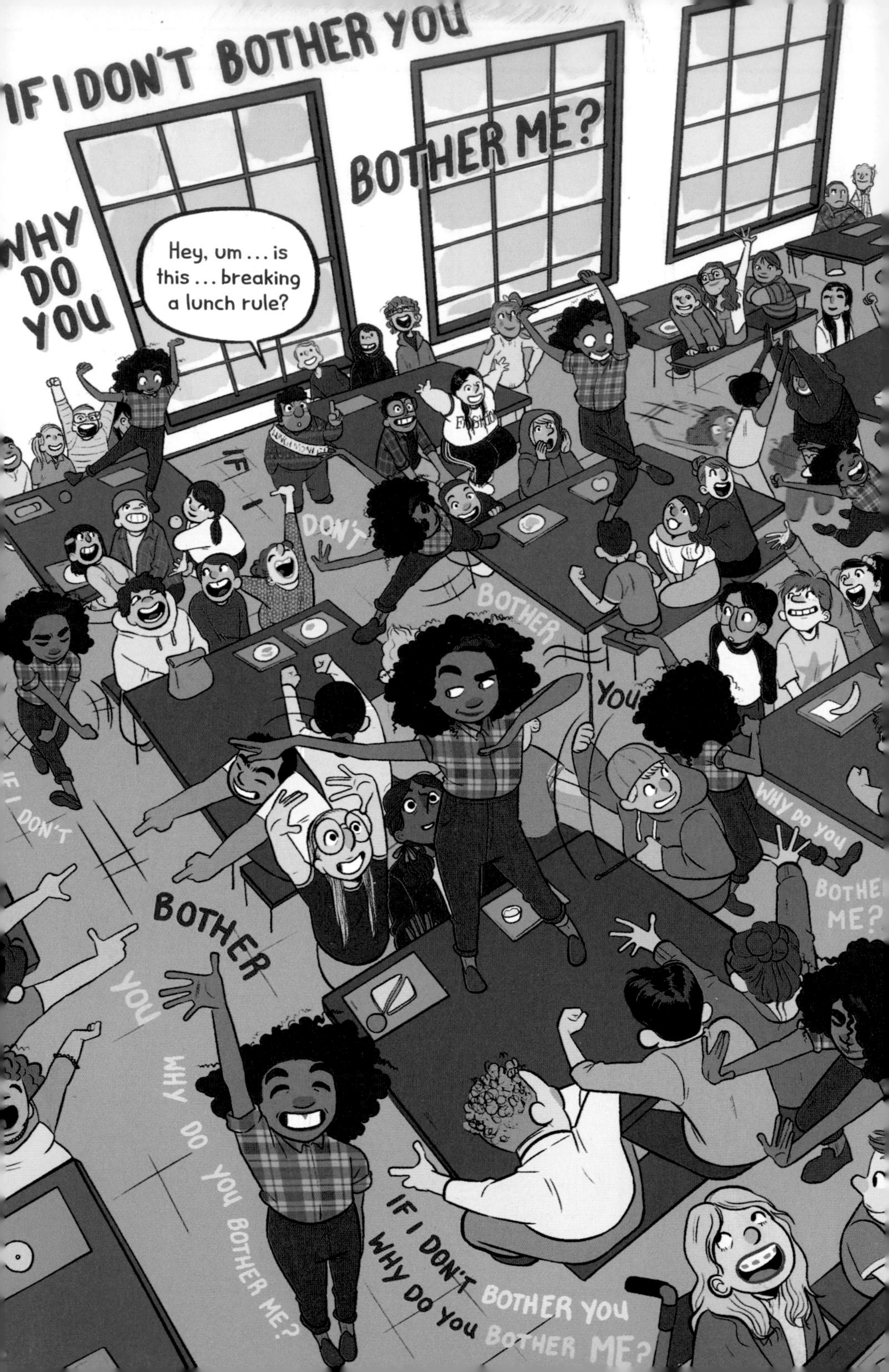
IF I DON'T BOTHER YOU
WHY DO YOU
BOTHER ME?
Hey, um . . . is this . . . breaking a lunch rule?
FASHION
IF
I
DON'T
BOTHER
YOU
IF I DON'T
BOTHER
YOU
WHY DO YOU
BOTHER
ME?
WHY DO YOU BOTHER ME?
IF I DON'T BOTHER YOU
WHY DO YOU BOTHER ME?

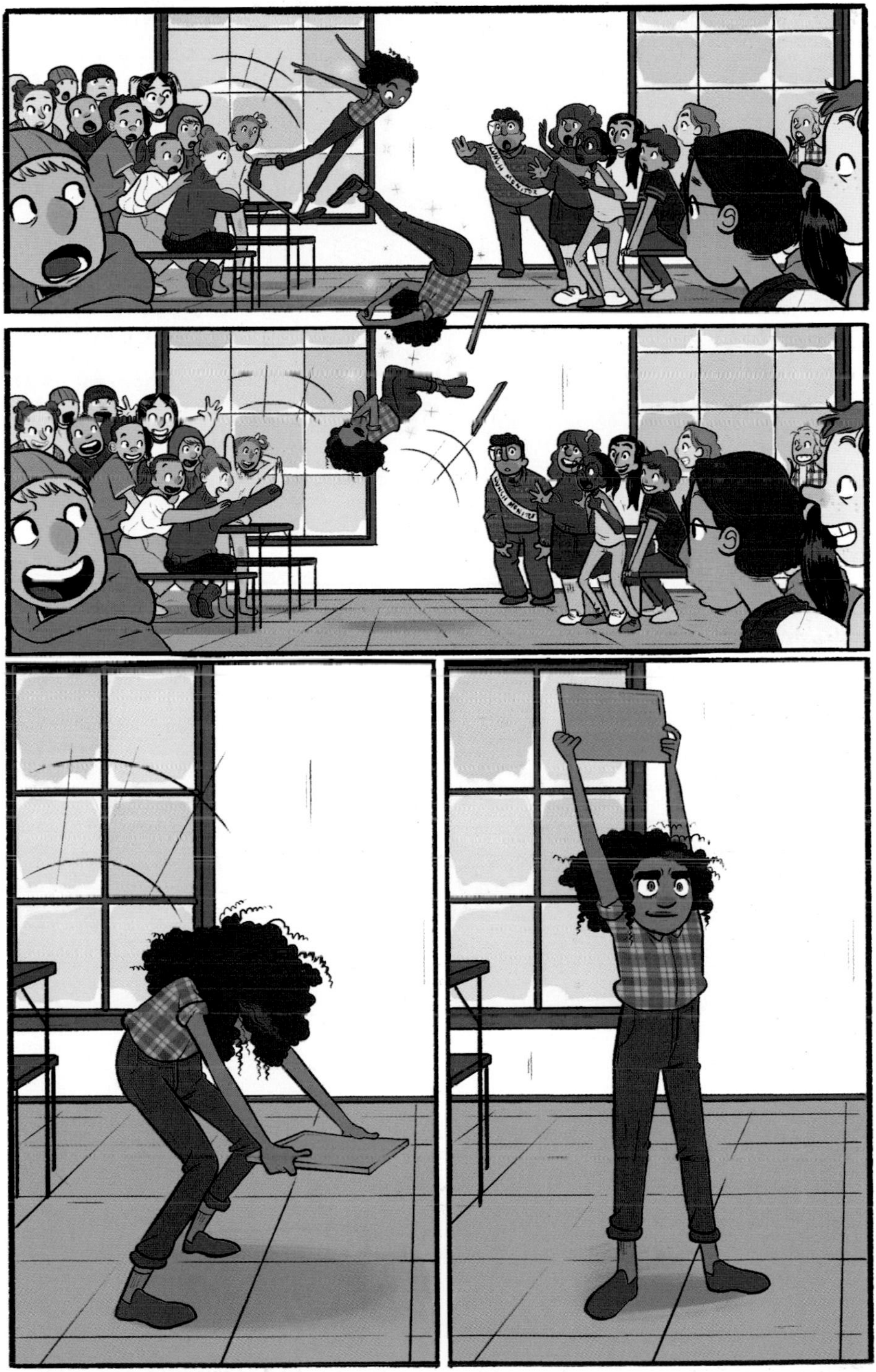
LUNCH MONITOR
LUNCH MONITOR

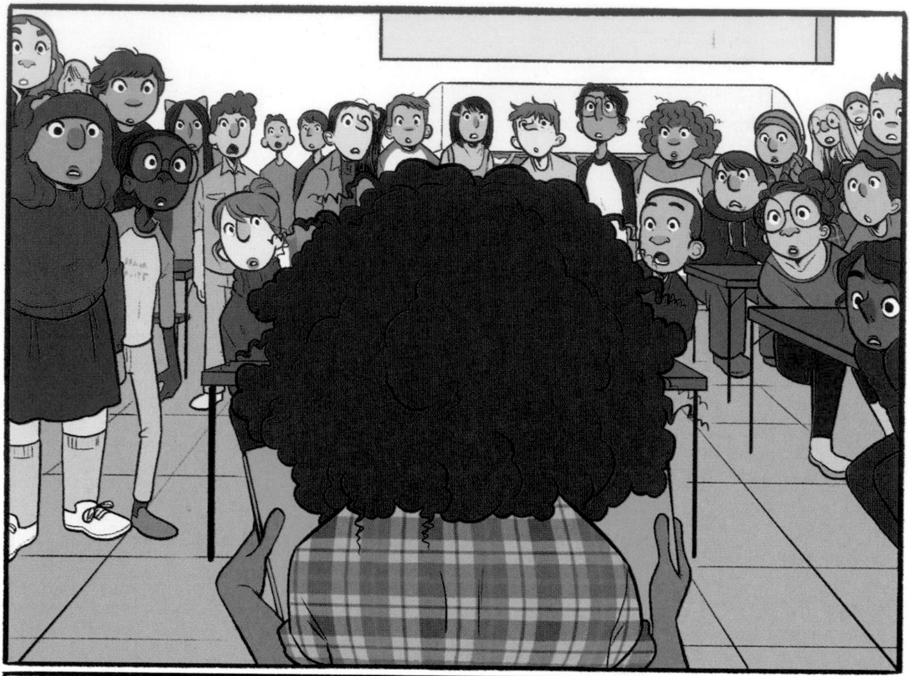

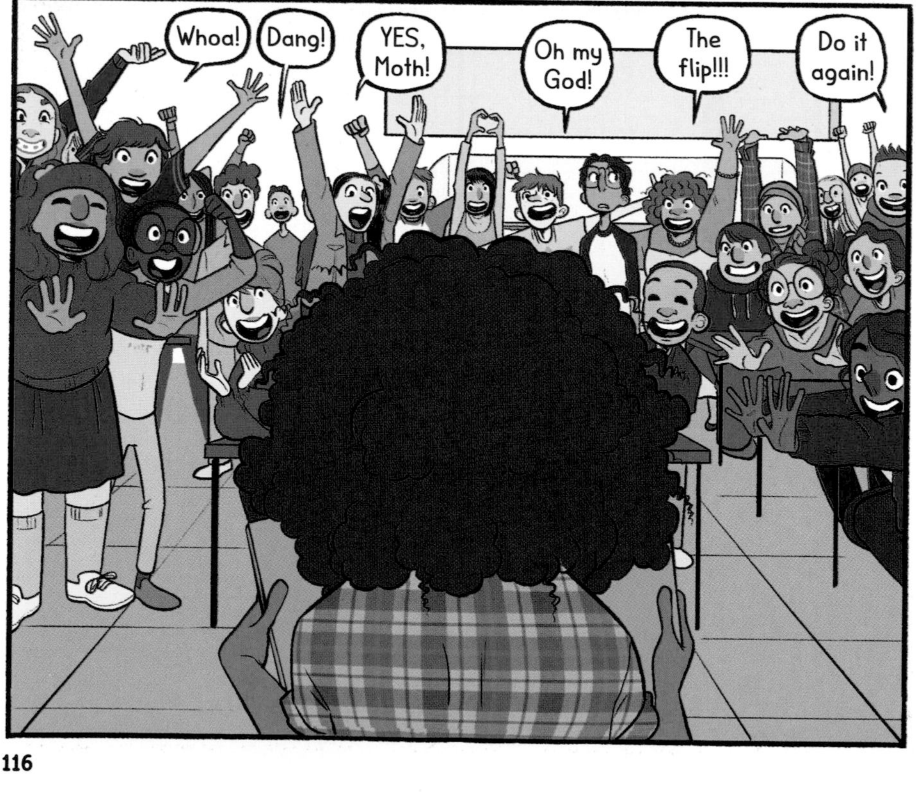
Whoa!
Dang!
YES, Moth!
Oh my God!
The flip!!!
Do it again!

117

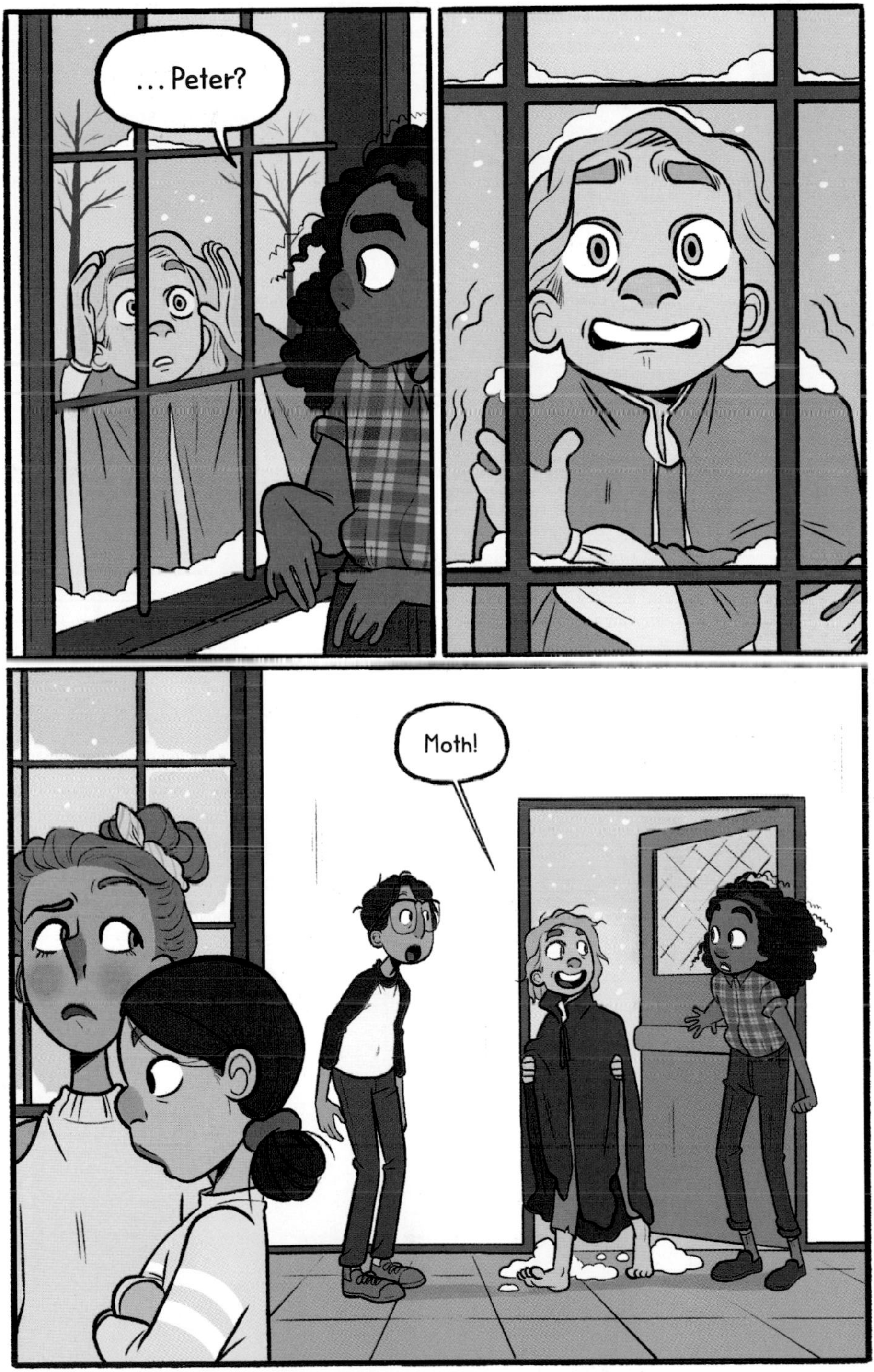
...Peter?
Moth!

121

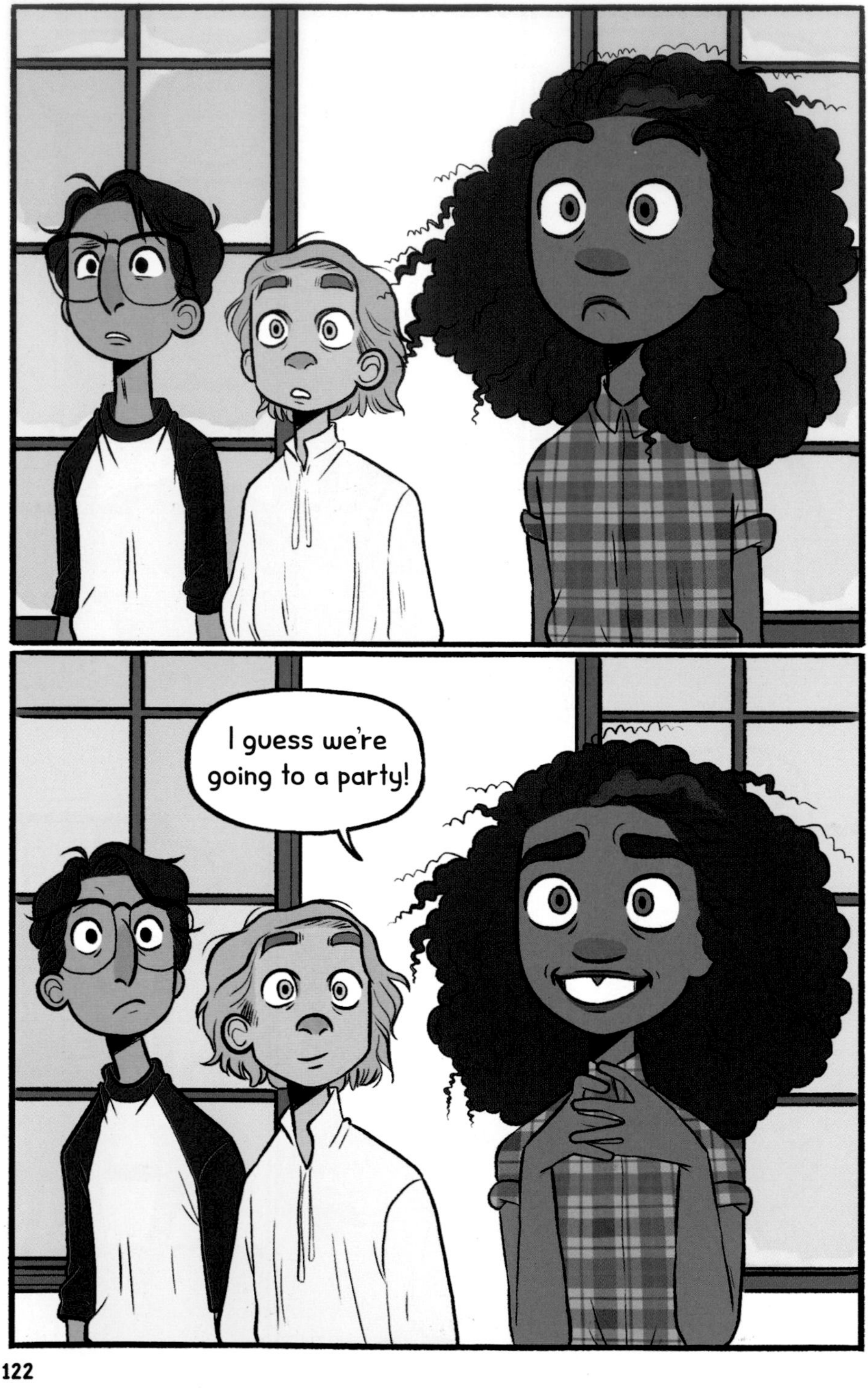
I guess we're going to a party!

CHAPTER 7

Mass Pike

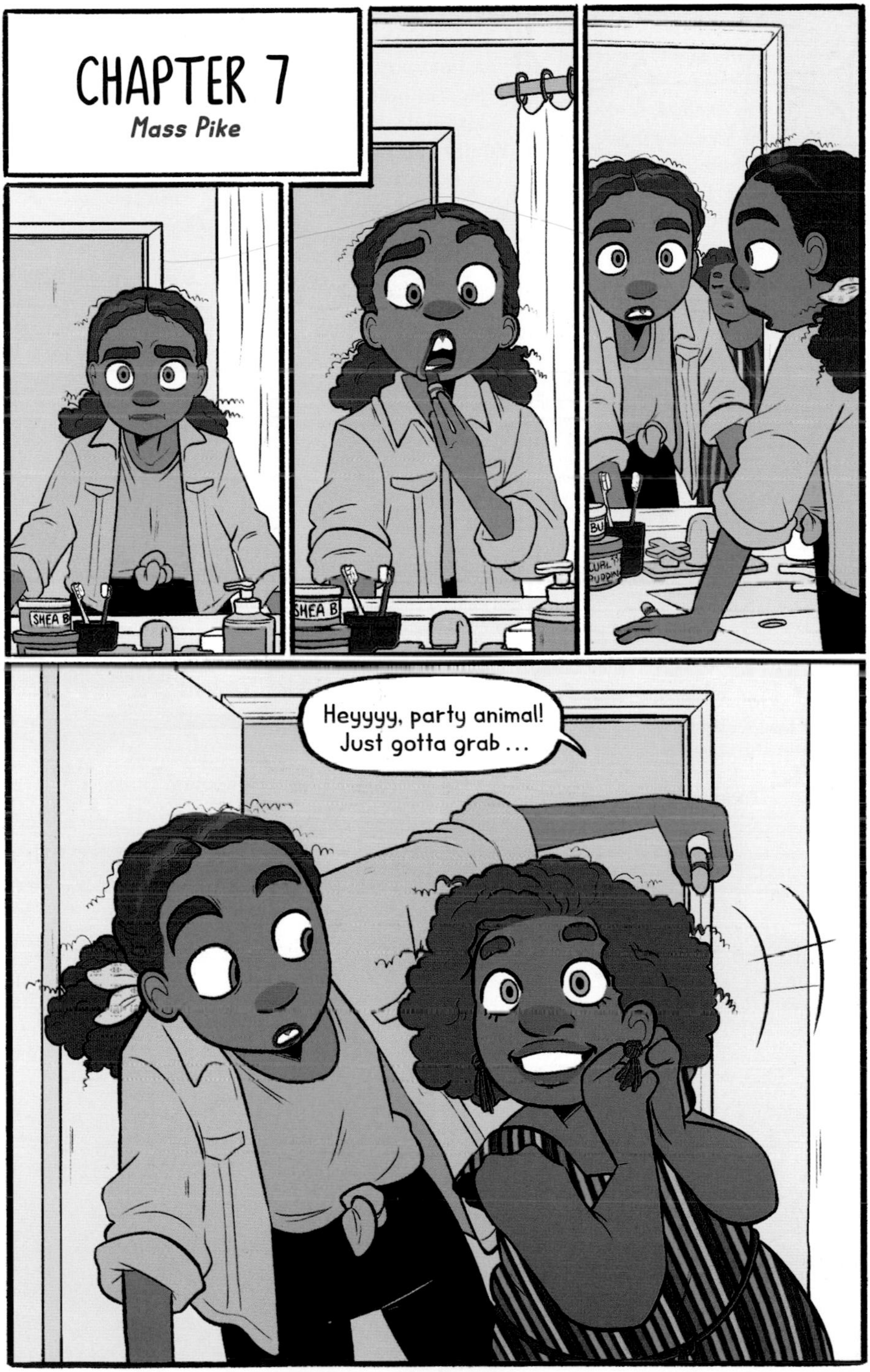
Heyyyy, party animal! Just gotta grab . . .

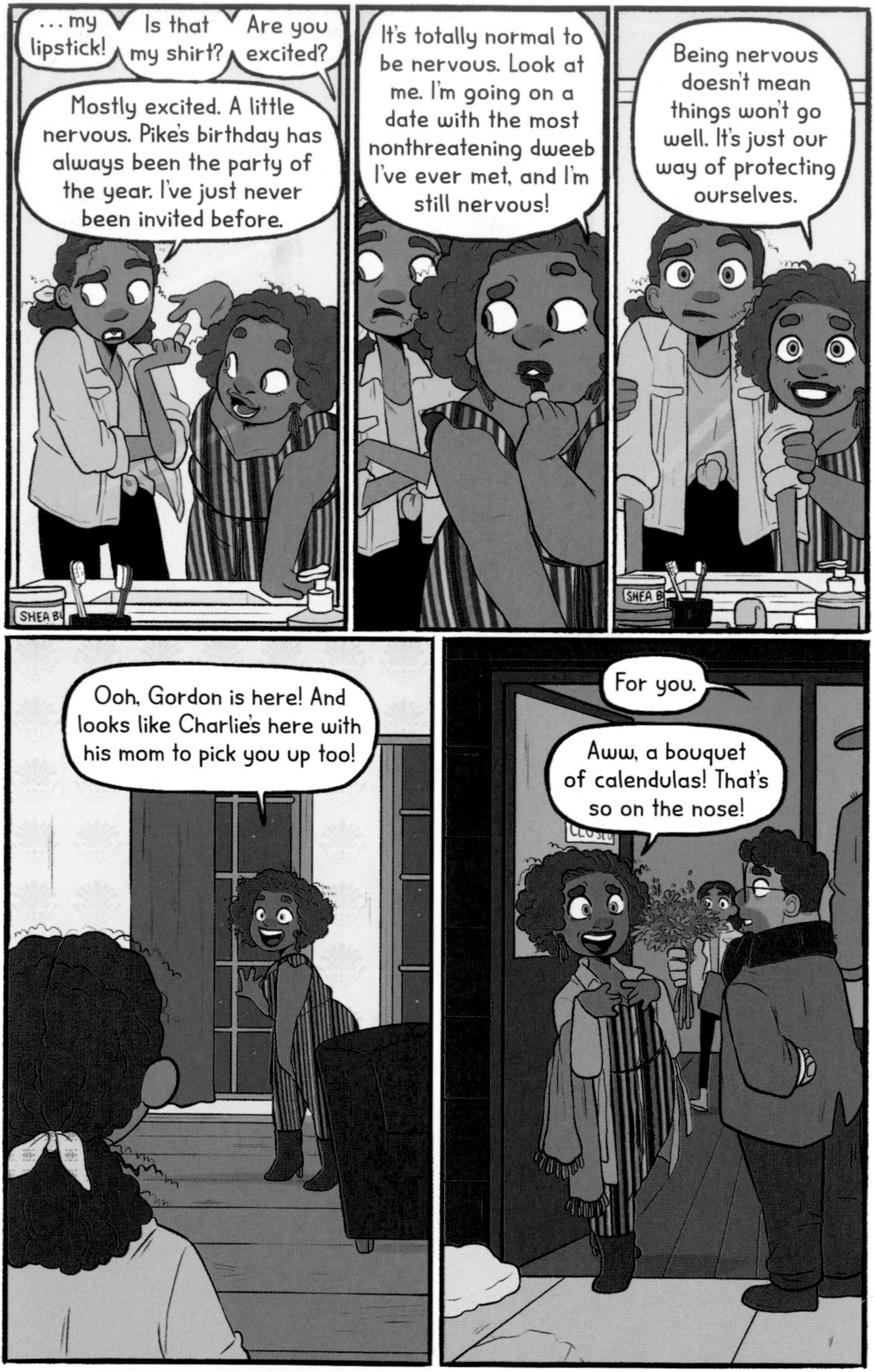

... my lipstick!
Is that my shirt?
Are you excited?
Mostly excited. A little nervous. Pike's birthday has always been the party of the year. I've just never been invited before.
It's totally normal to be nervous. Look at me. I'm going on a date with the most nonthreatening dweeb I've ever met, and I'm still nervous!
Being nervous doesn't mean things won't go well. It's just our way of protecting ourselves.
Ooh, Gordon is here! And looks like Charlie's here with his mom to pick you up too!
For you.
Aww, a bouquet of calendulas! That's so on the nose!

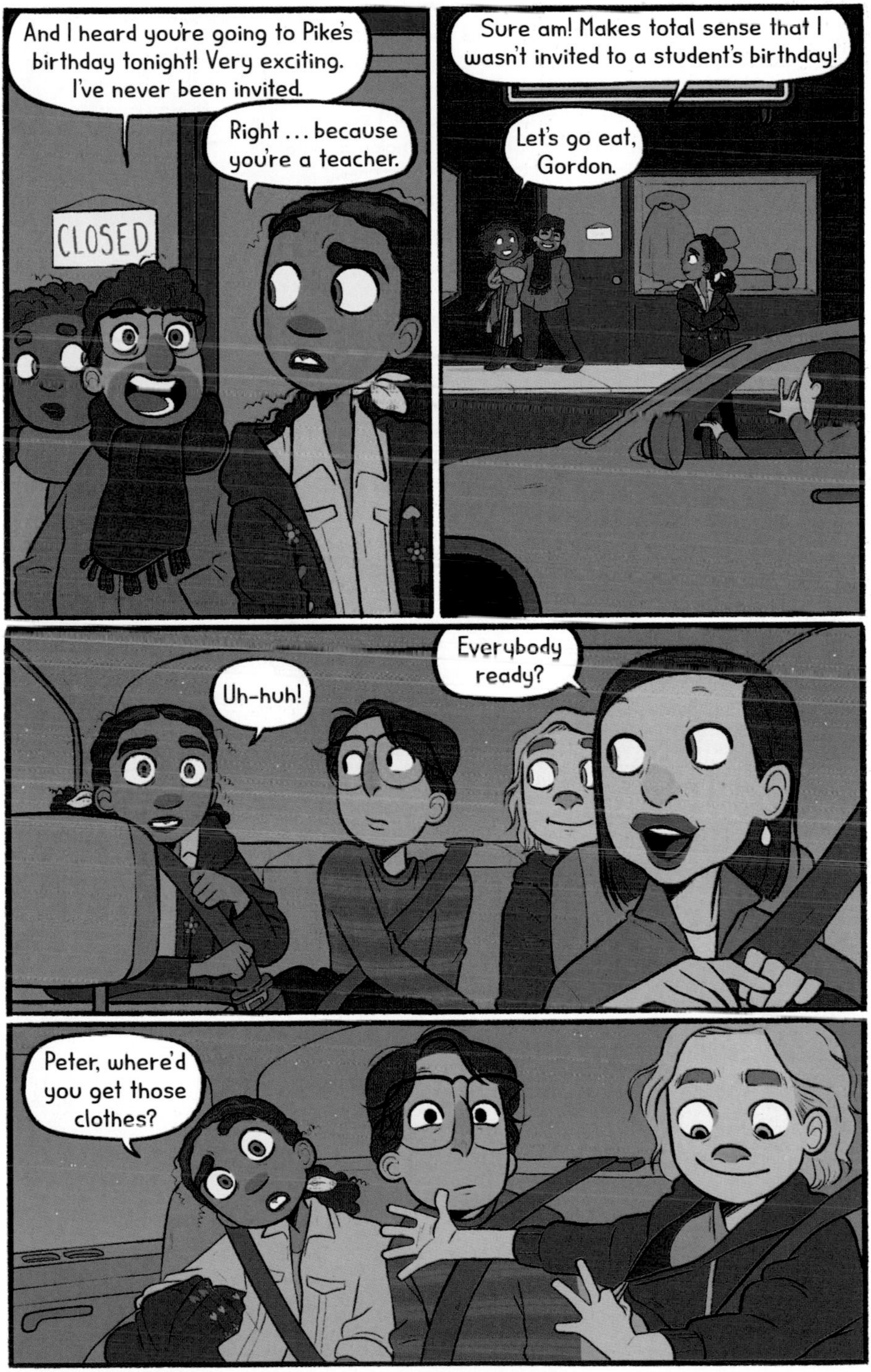
And I heard you're going to Pike's birthday tonight! Very exciting. I've never been invited.
Right . . . because you're a teacher.
CLOSED
Sure am! Makes total sense that I wasn't invited to a student's birthday!
Let's go eat, Gordon.
Uh-huh!
Everybody ready?
Peter, where'd you get those clothes?

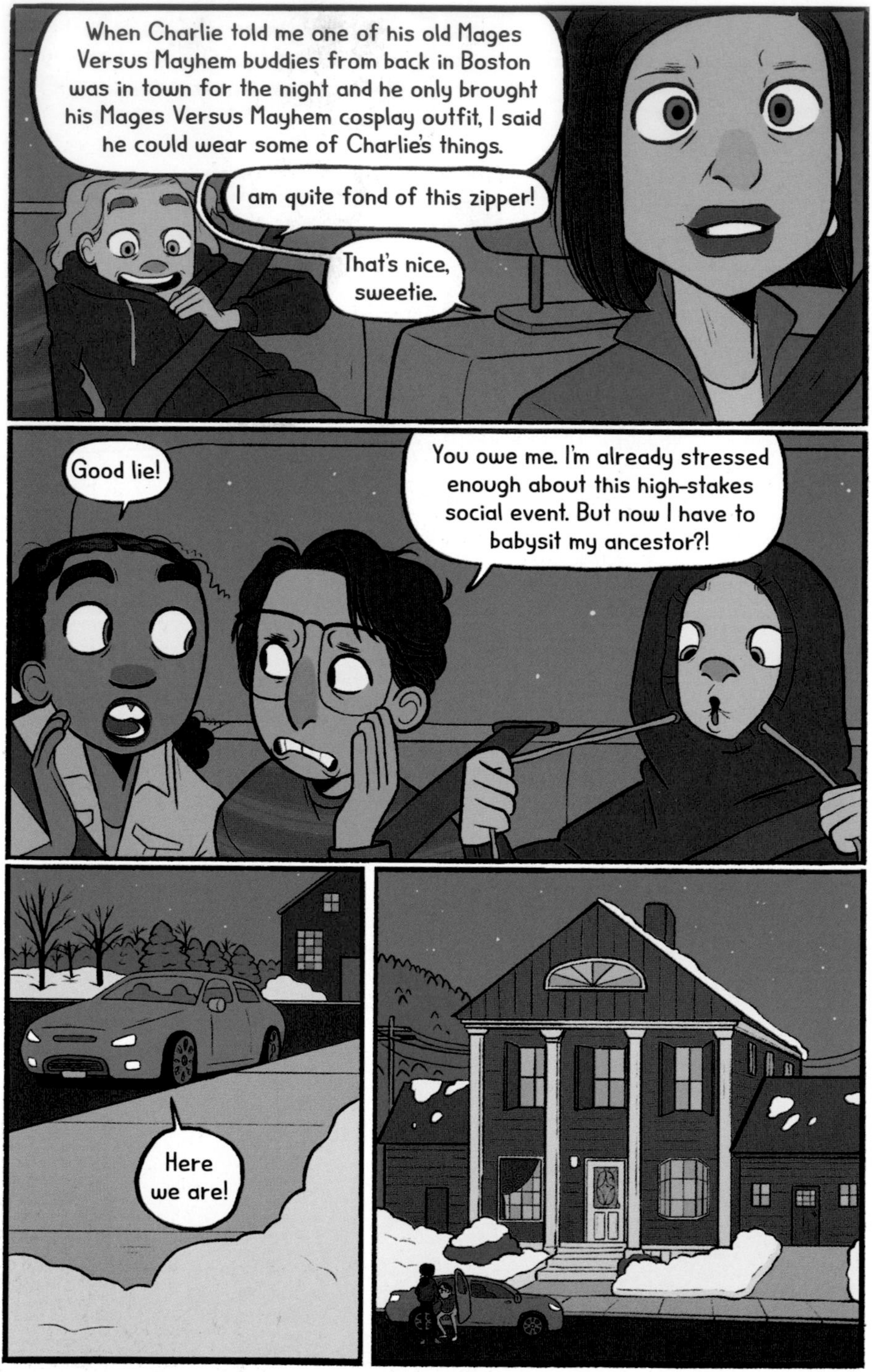
When Charlie told me one of his old Mages Versus Mayhem buddies from back in Boston was in town for the night and he only brought his Mages Versus Mayhem cosplay outfit, I said he could wear some of Charlie's things.
I am quite fond of this zipper!
That's nice, sweetie.
Good lie!
You owe me. I'm already stressed enough about this high-stakes social event. But now I have to babysit my ancestor?!
Here we are!

127

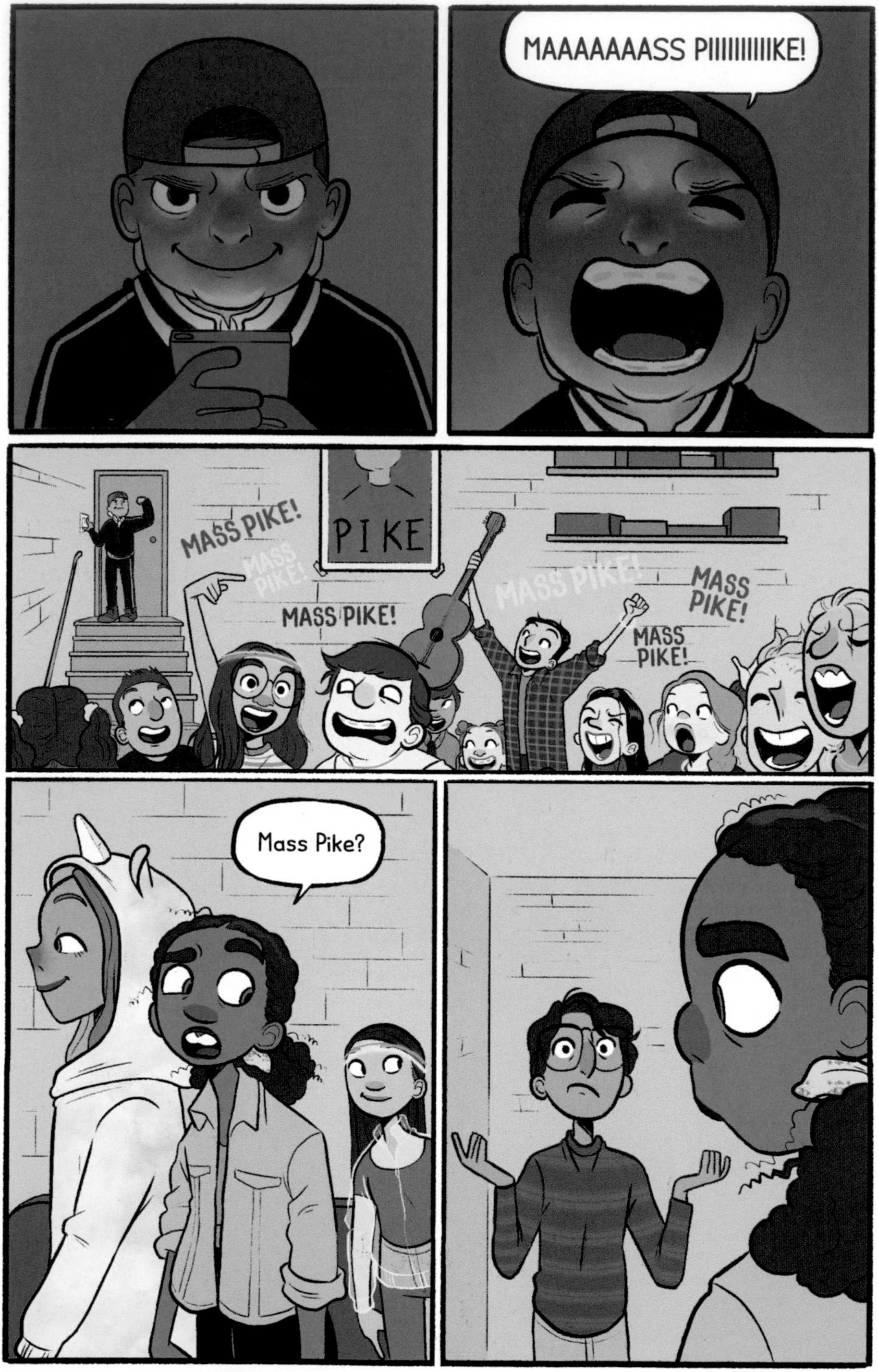
MAAAAAAASS PIIIIIIIIIKE!
MASS PIKE!
PIKE
MASS PIKE!
MASS PIKE!
MASS PIKE!
MASS PIKE!
MASS PIKE!
MASS PIKE!
Mass Pike?

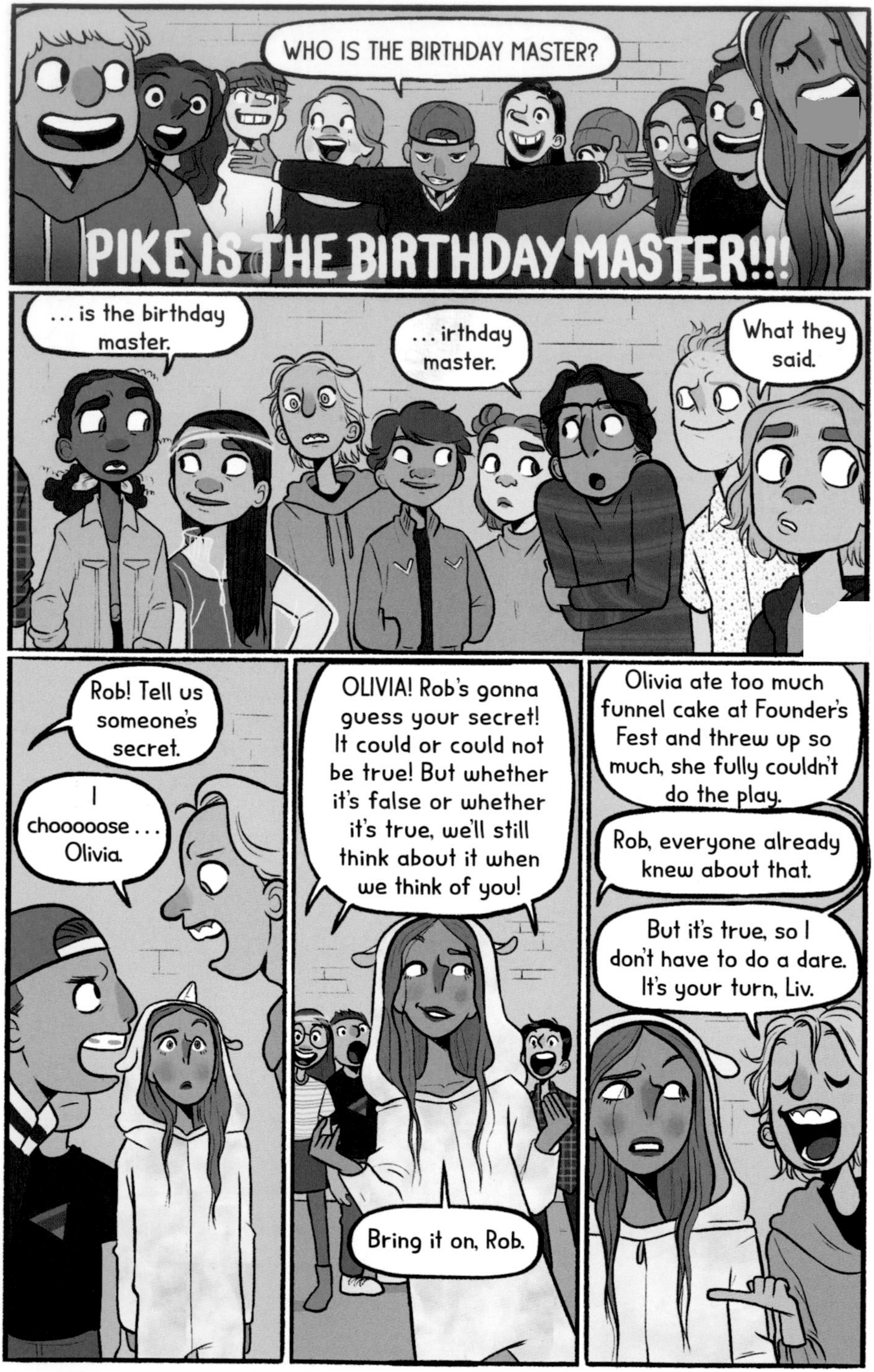
WHO IS THE BIRTHDAY MASTER?
PIKE IS THE BIRTHDAY MASTER!!!
. . . is the birthday master.
. . . irthday master.
What they said.
Rob! Tell us someone's secret.
I chooooose . . . Olivia.
OLIVIA! Rob's gonna guess your secret! It could or could not be true! But whether it's false or whether it's true, we'll still think about it when we think of you!
Bring it on, Rob.
Olivia ate too much funnel cake at Founder's Fest and threw up so much, she fully couldn't do the play.
Rob, everyone already knew about that.
But it's true, so I don't have to do a dare. It's your turn, Liv.

138

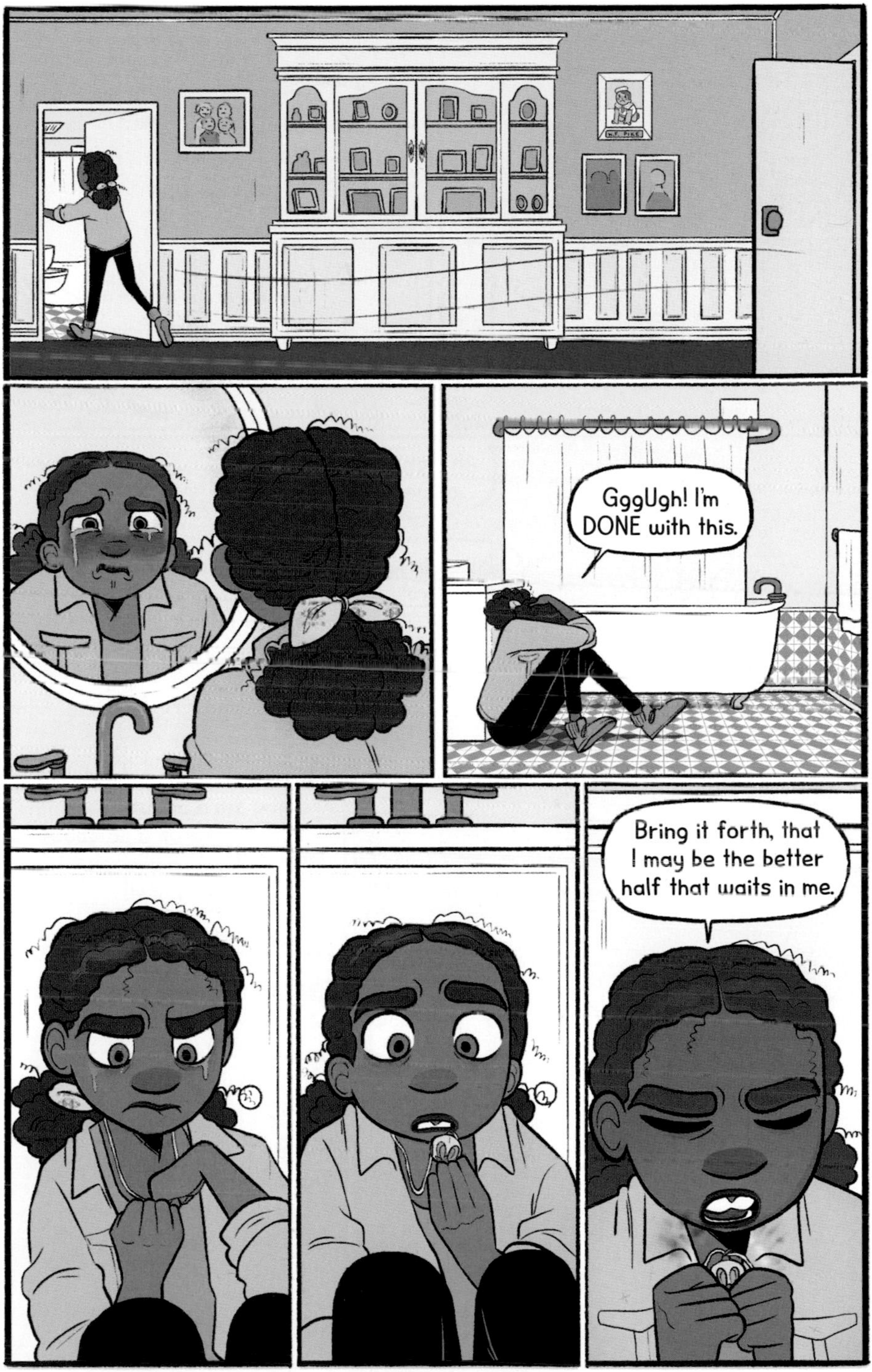
GggUgh! I'm DONE with this.
Bring it forth, that I may be the better half that waits in me.

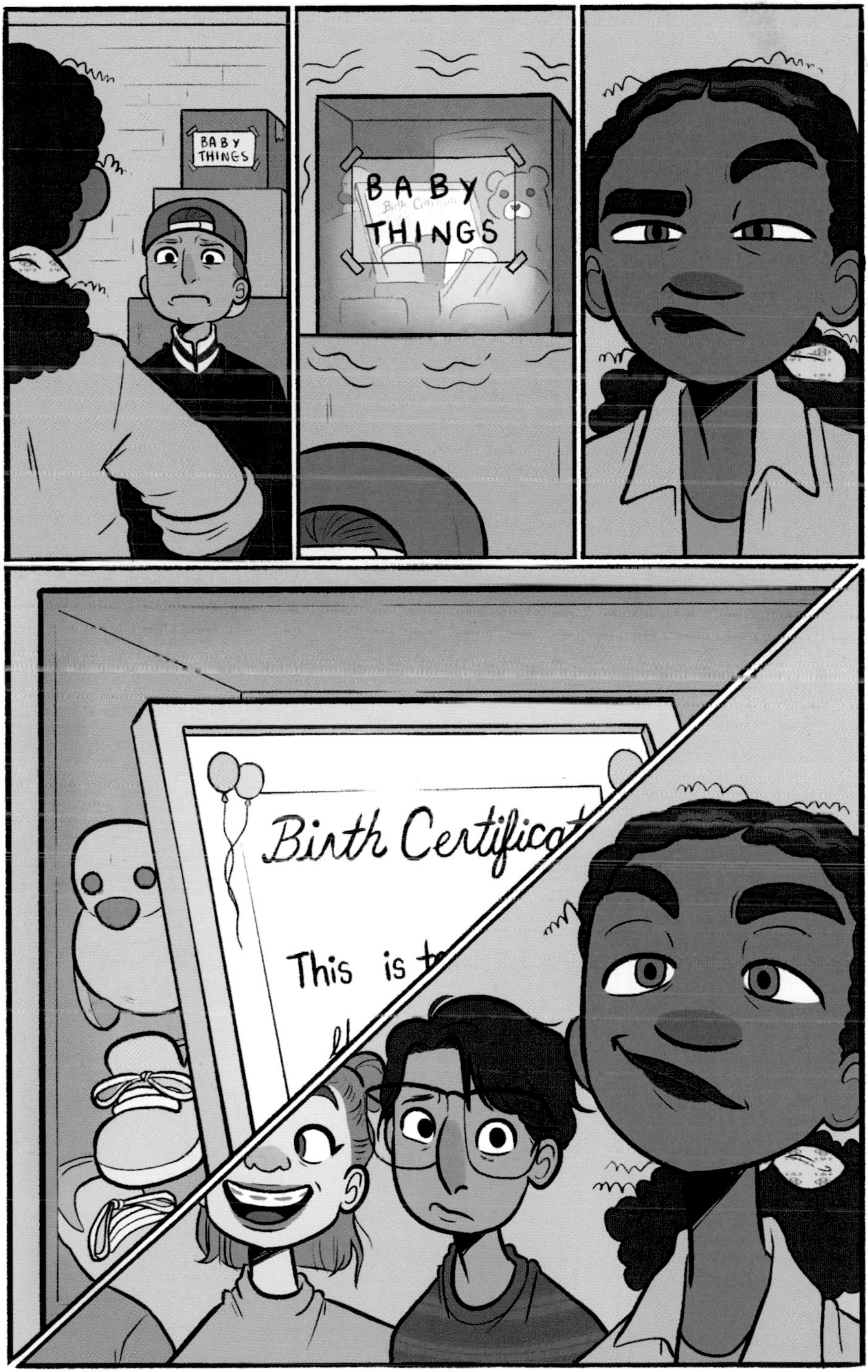
BABY THINGS
BABY THINGS
Birth Certificat
This is t

145

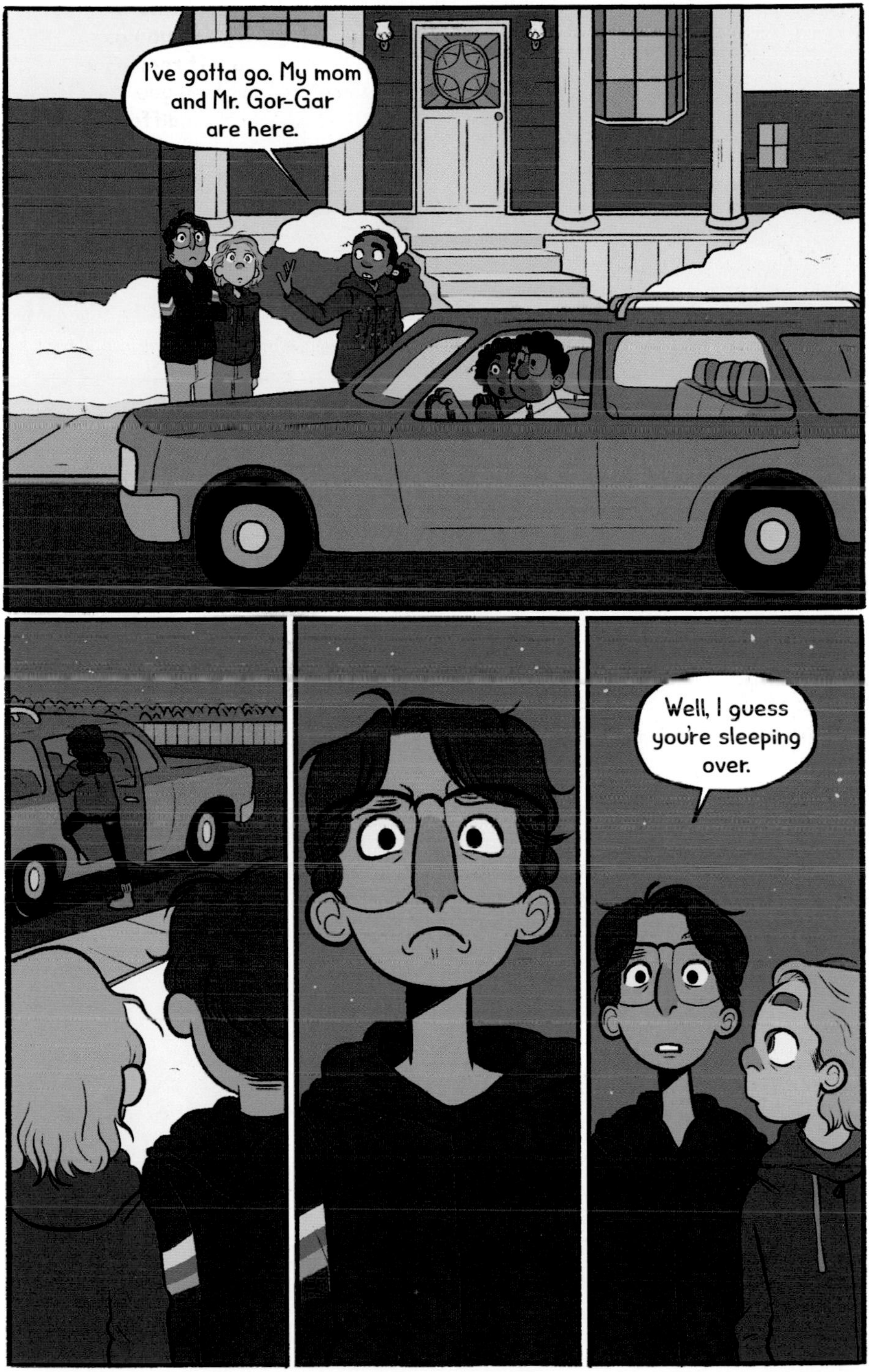

I've gotta go. My mom and Mr. Gor-Gar are here.
Well, I guess you're sleeping over.

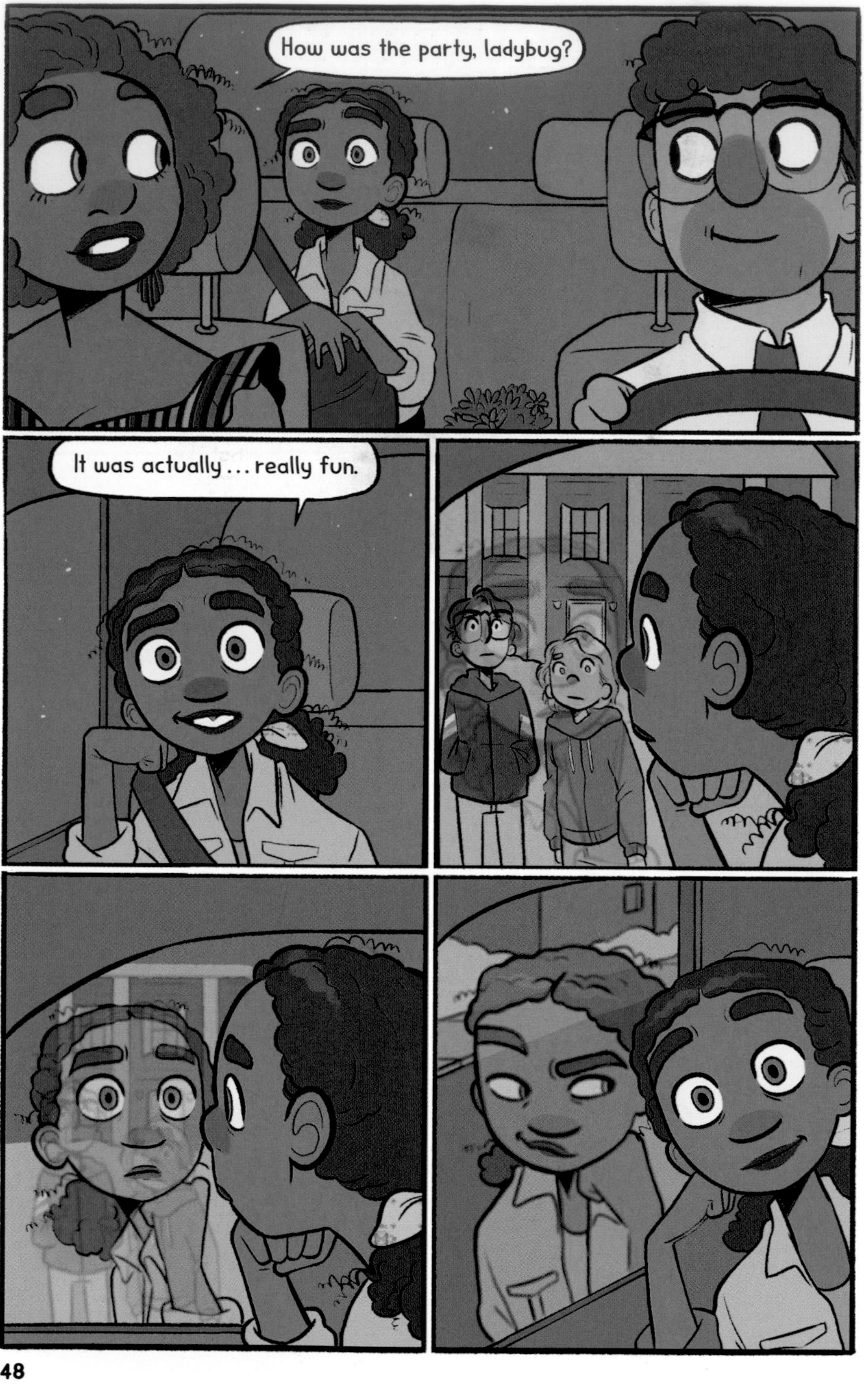
How was the party, ladybug?
It was actually... really fun.

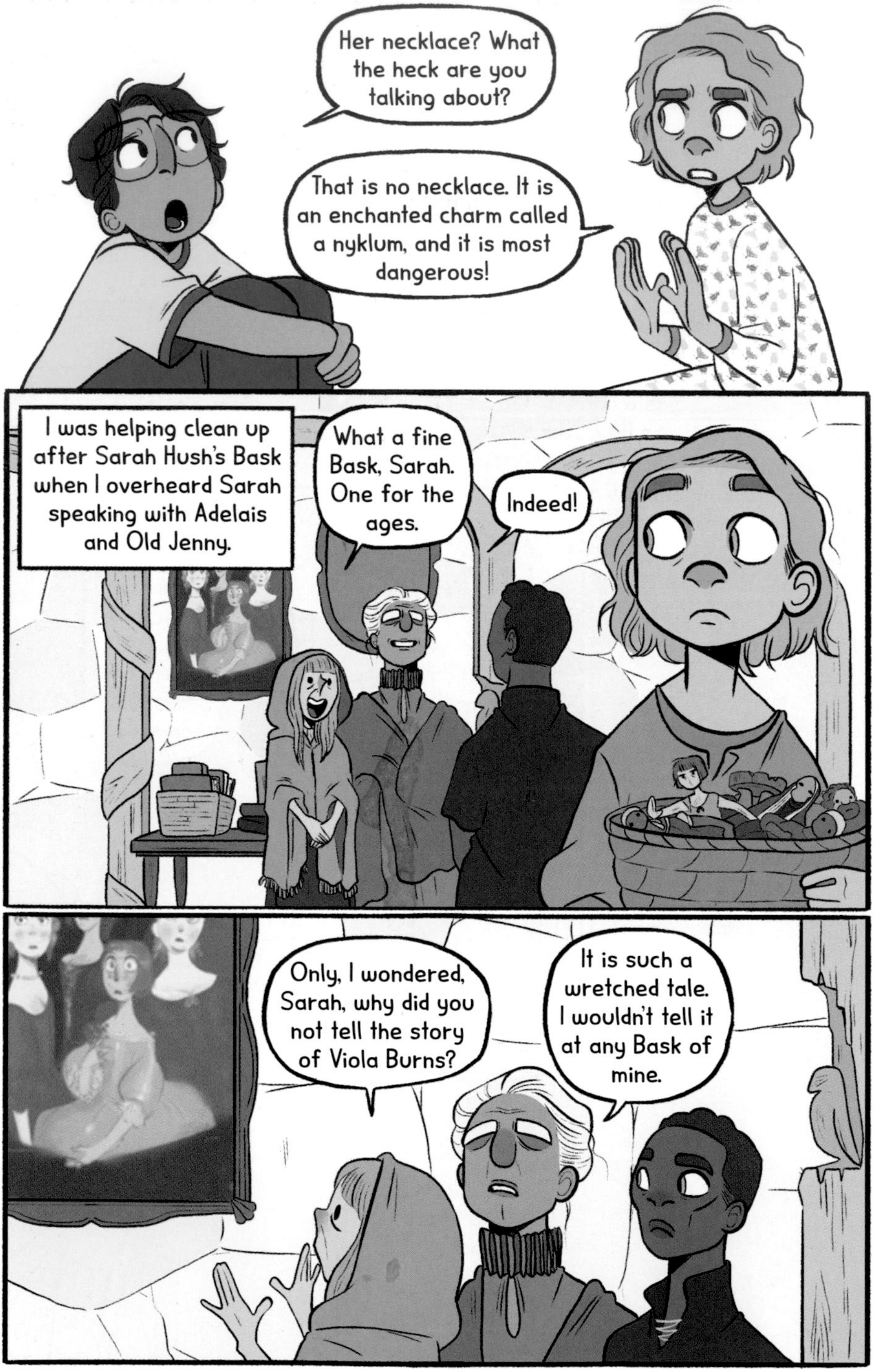
Her necklace? What the heck are you talking about?
That is no necklace. It is an enchanted charm called a nyklum, and it is most dangerous!
I was helping clean up after Sarah Hush's Bask when I overheard Sarah speaking with Adelais and Old Jenny.
What a fine Bask, Sarah. One for the ages.
Indeed!
Only, I wondered, Sarah, why did you not tell the story of Viola Burns?
It is such a wretched tale. I wouldn't tell it at any Bask of mine.

Pardon. What about Viola Burns?

Oh, Peter, Old Jenny is right. It is not a pleasant tale, but I do think there is value in hearing it.

Viola Burns was a witch in the order back on the Île d'Ezer. Born into a legacy of English nobility who secretly practiced magic. She came to the isle to study with the Hush Woman.

She was hardworking and very studious. But she did not have much of a natural grasp of her power.

January the thirteenth

A new witch joined the order. The Hush Woman says she is of noble blood.

Viola Burns

For as you know, Peter, when a witch is afraid, her magic can be weak and unpredictable. And when a witch forces herself into magic she is not yet prepared to do, the results may be catastrophic.

155

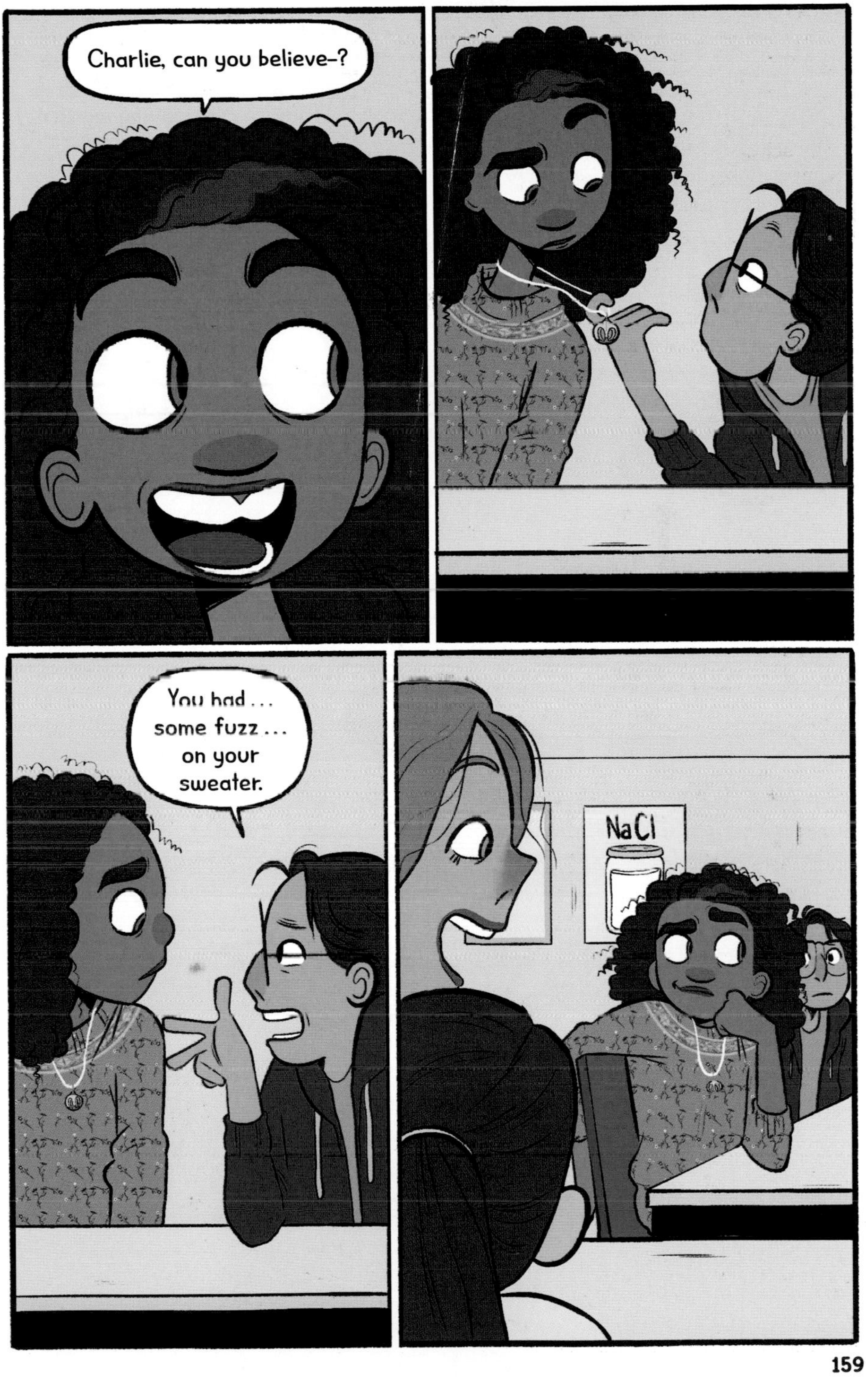
Charlie, can you believe–?
You had . . . some fuzz . . . on your sweater.
NaCl

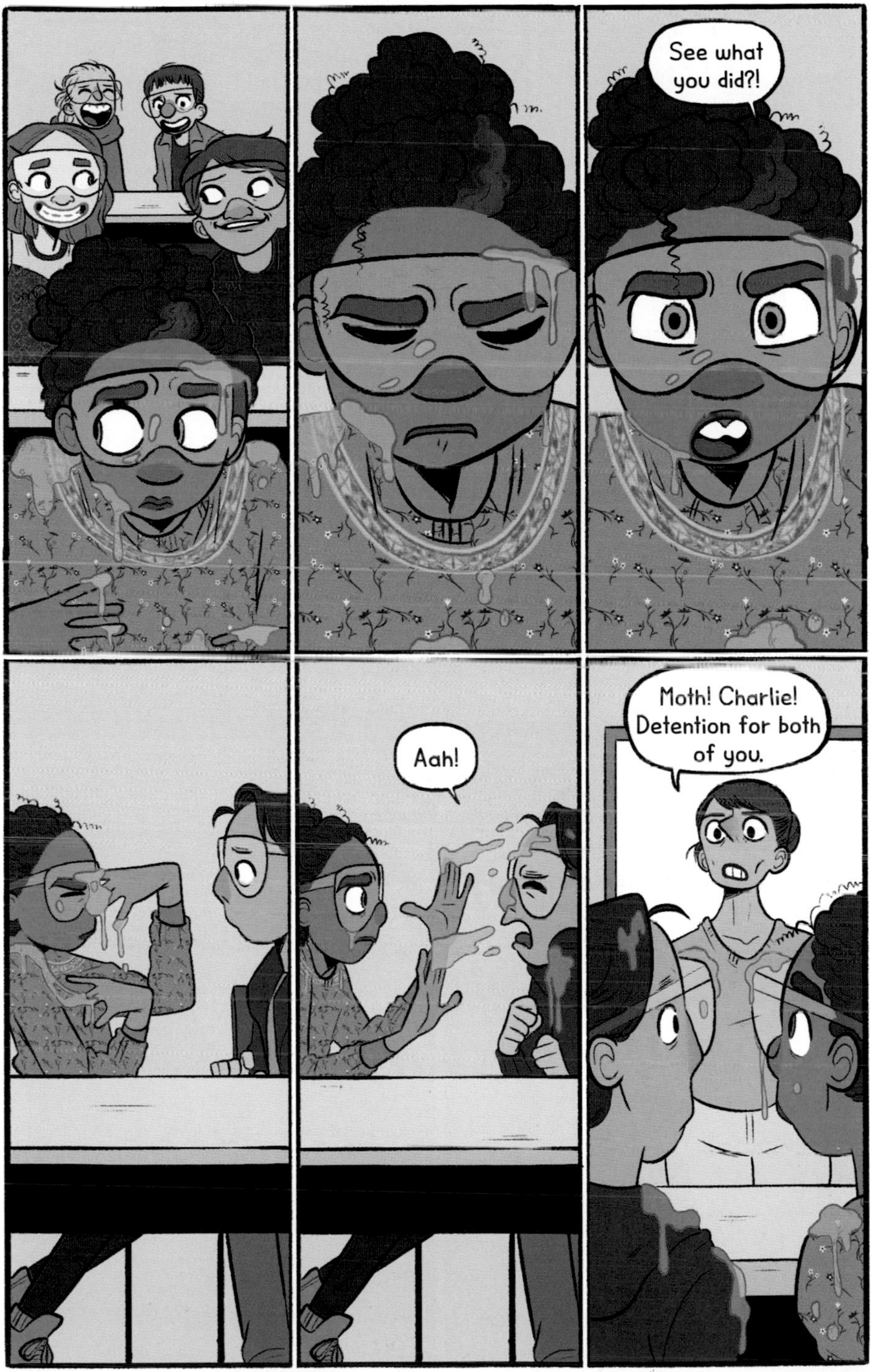
See what you did?!
Aah!
Moth! Charlie! Detention for both of you.

165

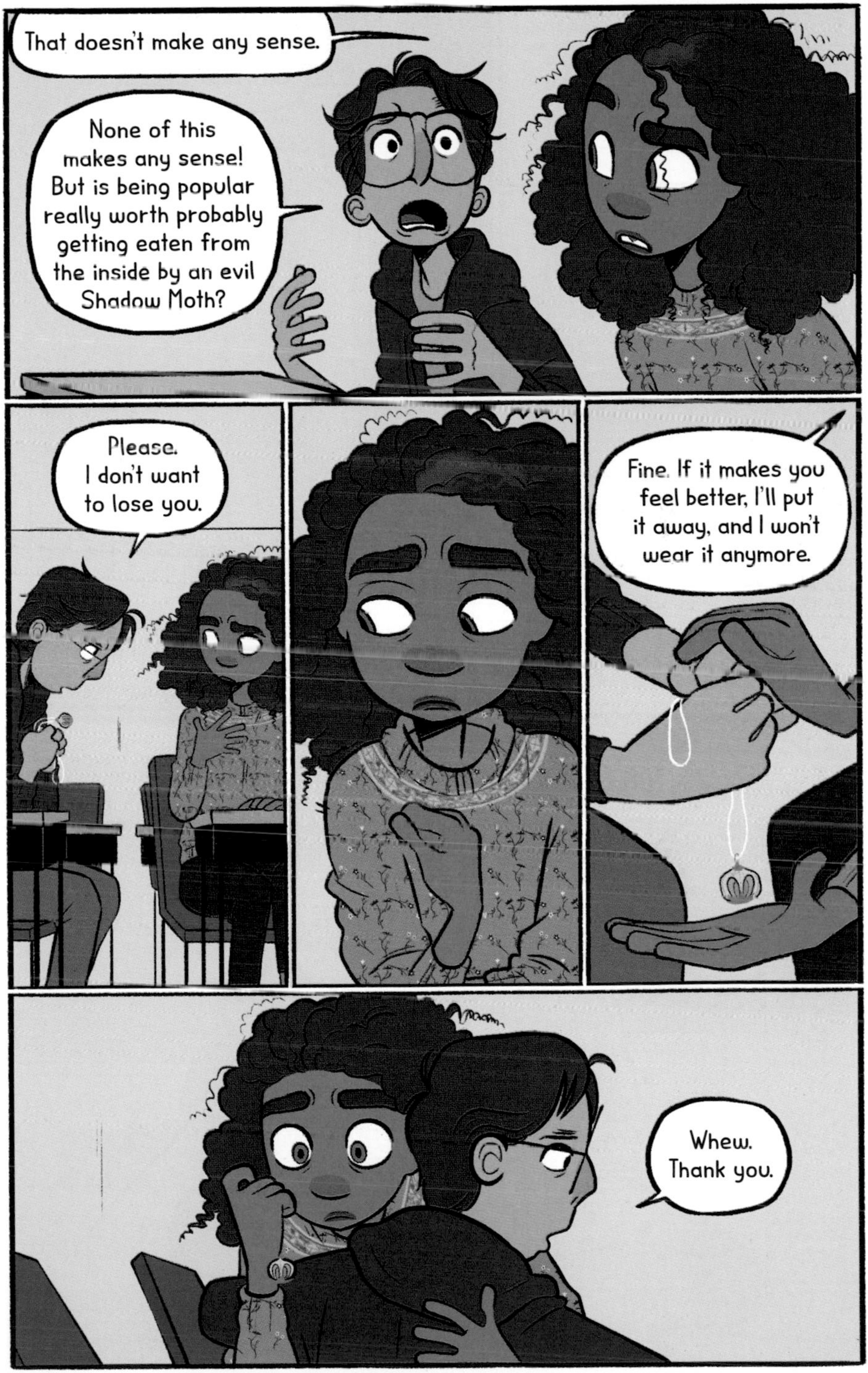
That doesn't make any sense.
None of this makes any sense! But is being popular really worth probably getting eaten from the inside by an evil Shadow Moth?
Please. I don't want to lose you.
Fine. If it makes you feel better, I'll put it away, and I won't wear it anymore.
Whew. Thank you.

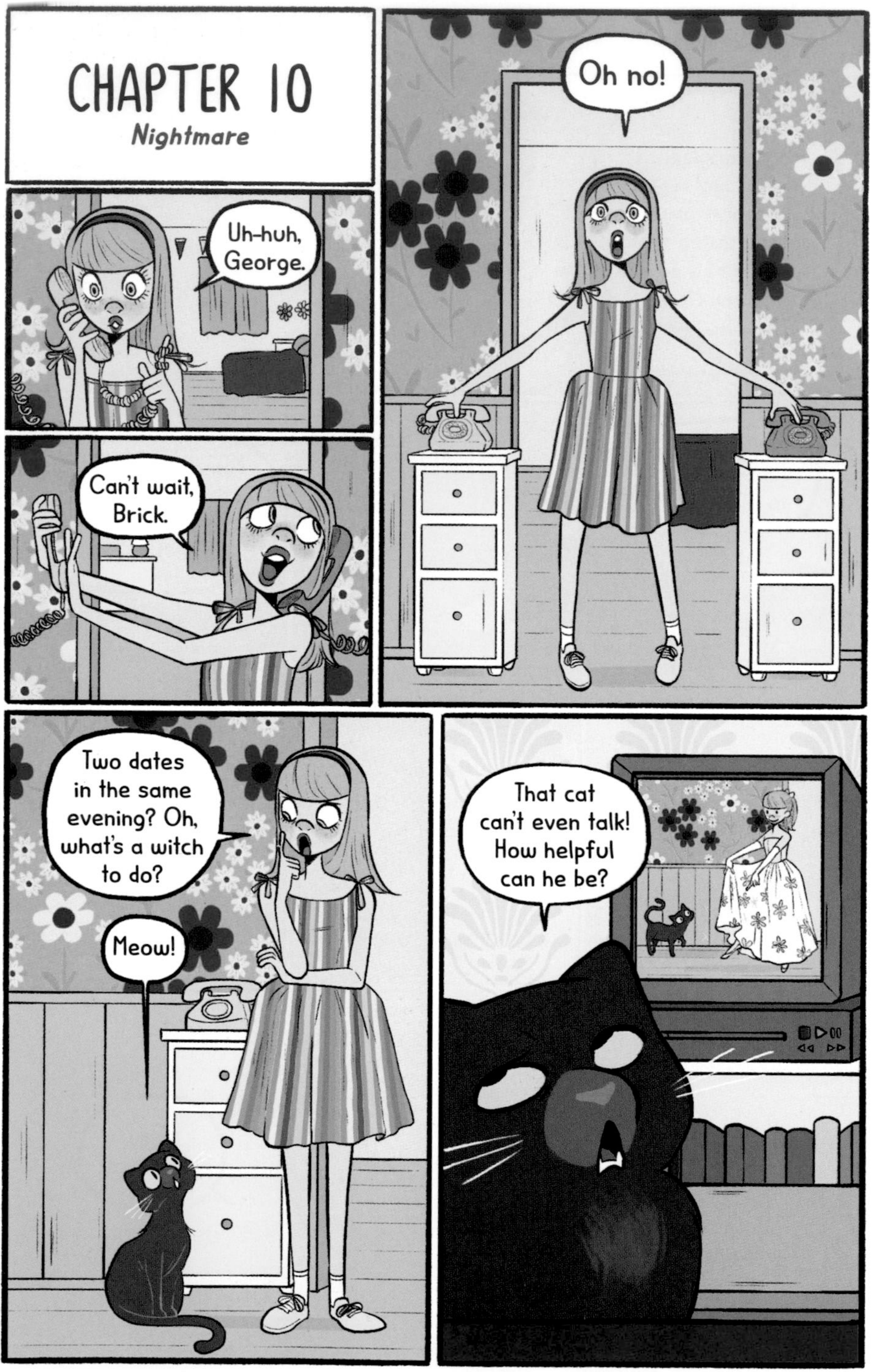
CHAPTER 10
Nightmare
Oh no!
Uh-huh, George.
Can't wait, Brick.
Two dates in the same evening? Oh, what's a witch to do?
Meow!
That cat can't even talk! How helpful can he be?

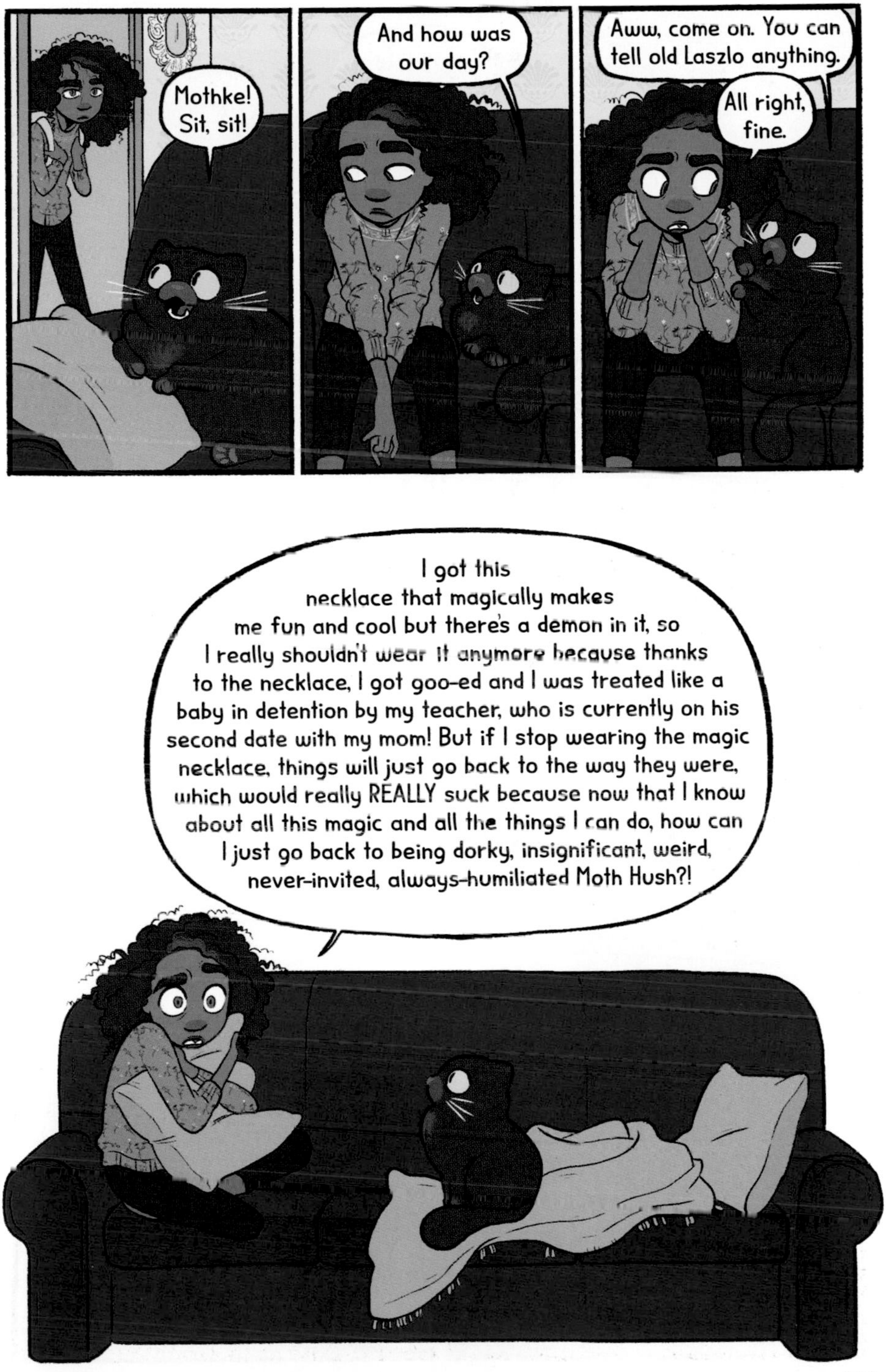
Mothke! Sit, sit!
And how was our day?
Aww, come on. You can tell old Laszlo anything.
All right, fine.
I got this necklace that magically makes me fun and cool but there's a demon in it, so I really shouldn't wear it anymore because thanks to the necklace, I got goo-ed and I was treated like a baby in detention by my teacher, who is currently on his second date with my mom! But if I stop wearing the magic necklace, things will just go back to the way they were, which would really REALLY suck because now that I know about all this magic and all the things I can do, how can I just go back to being dorky, insignificant, weird, never-invited, always-humiliated Moth Hush?!

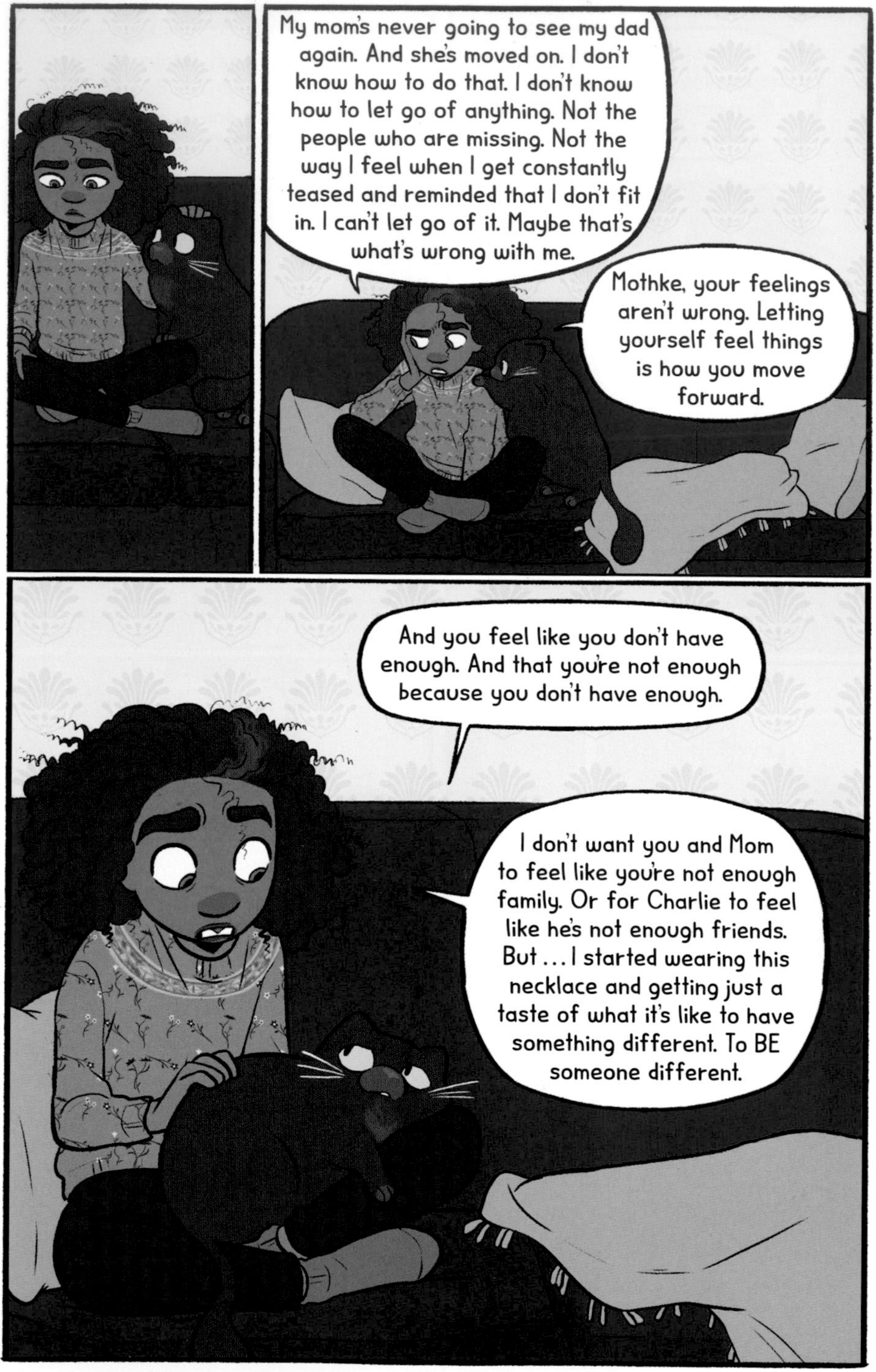
My mom's never going to see my dad again. And she's moved on. I don't know how to do that. I don't know how to let go of anything. Not the people who are missing. Not the way I feel when I get constantly teased and reminded that I don't fit in. I can't let go of it. Maybe that's what's wrong with me.
Mothke, your feelings aren't wrong. Letting yourself feel things is how you move forward.
And you feel like you don't have enough. And that you're not enough because you don't have enough.
I don't want you and Mom to feel like you're not enough family. Or for Charlie to feel like he's not enough friends. But . . . I started wearing this necklace and getting just a taste of what it's like to have something different. To BE someone different.

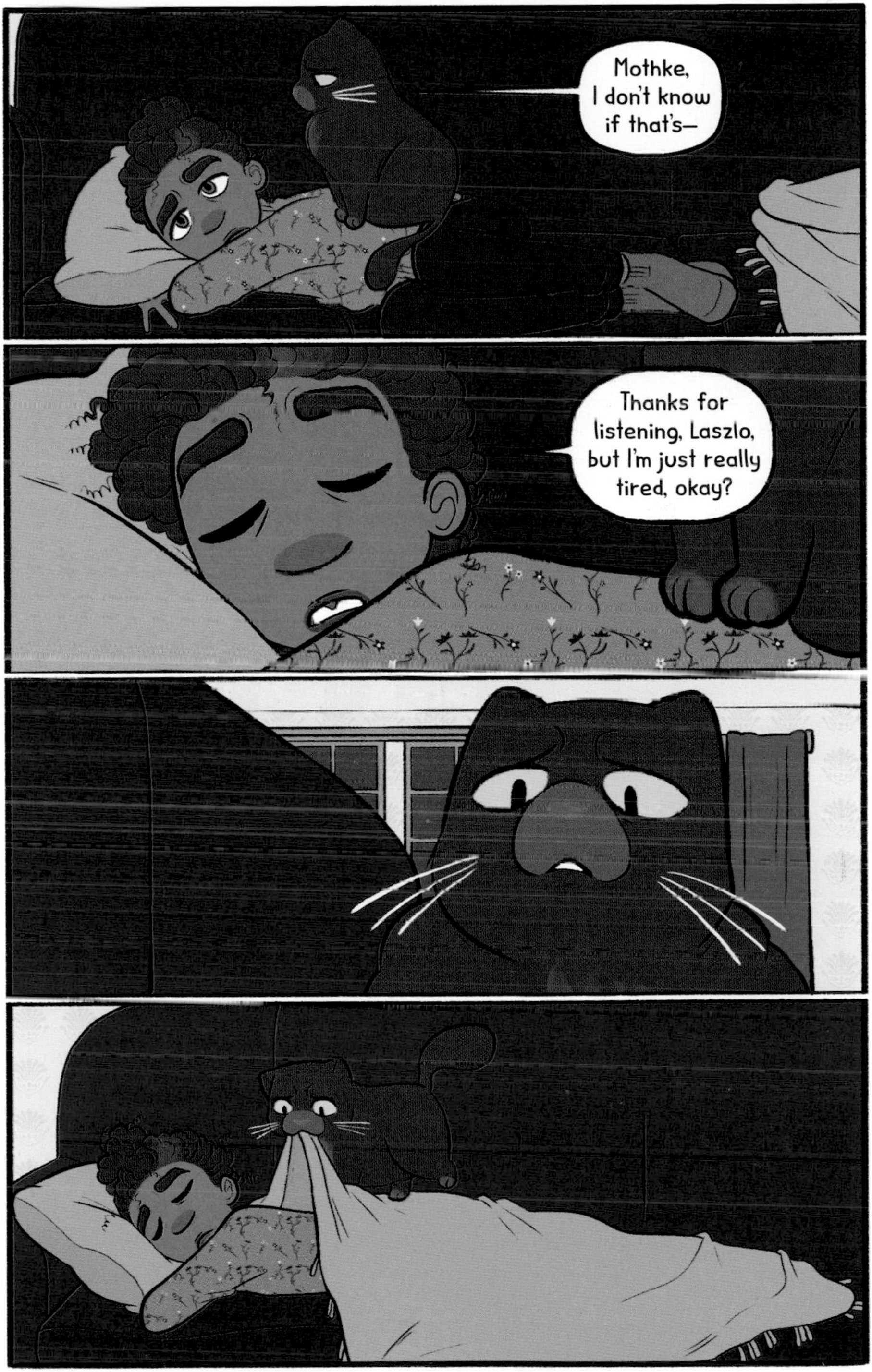
Mothke, I don't know if that's—
Thanks for listening, Laszlo, but I'm just really tired, okay?

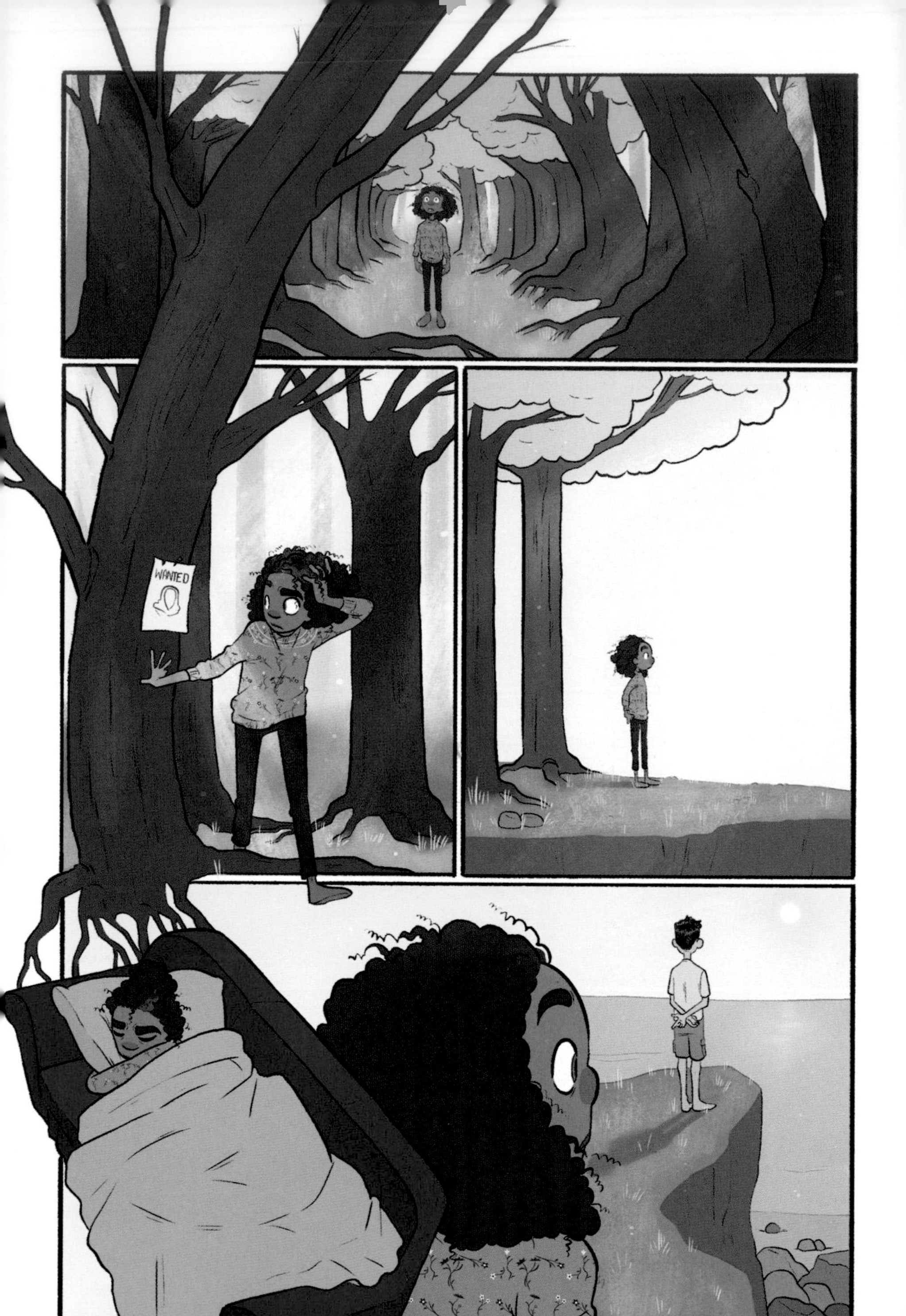
WANTED

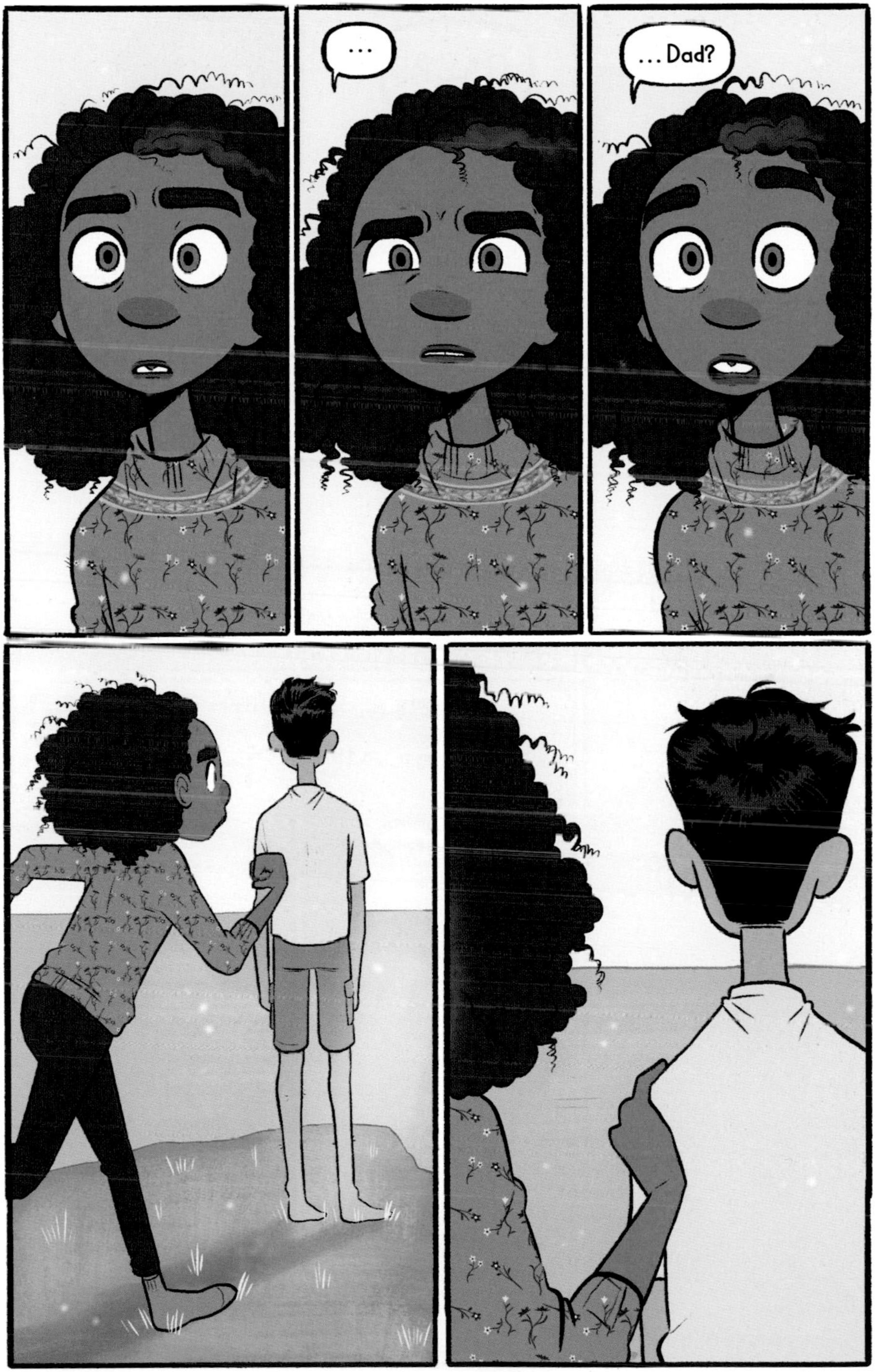
...
...Dad?

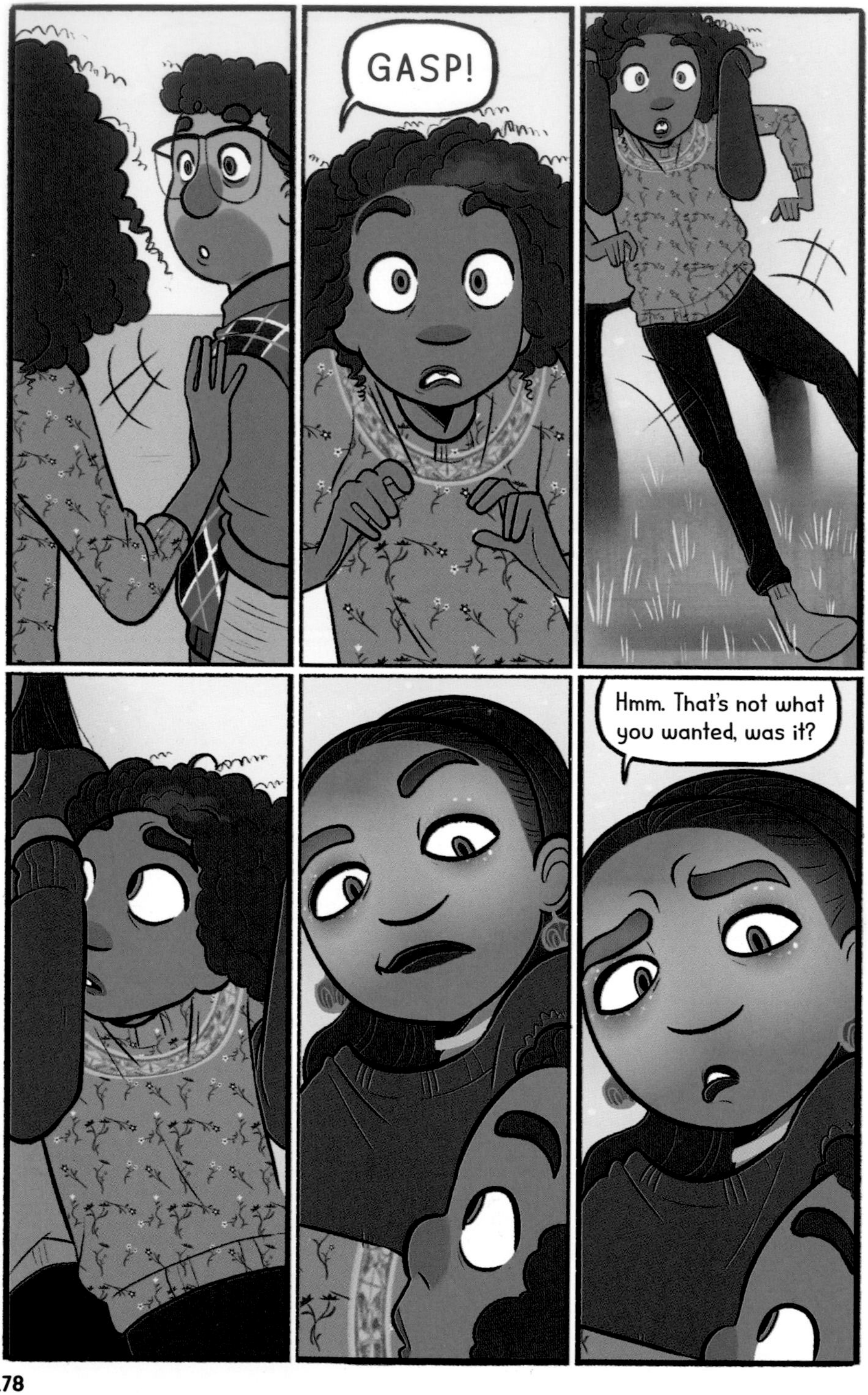
GASP!
Hmm. That's not what you wanted, was it?

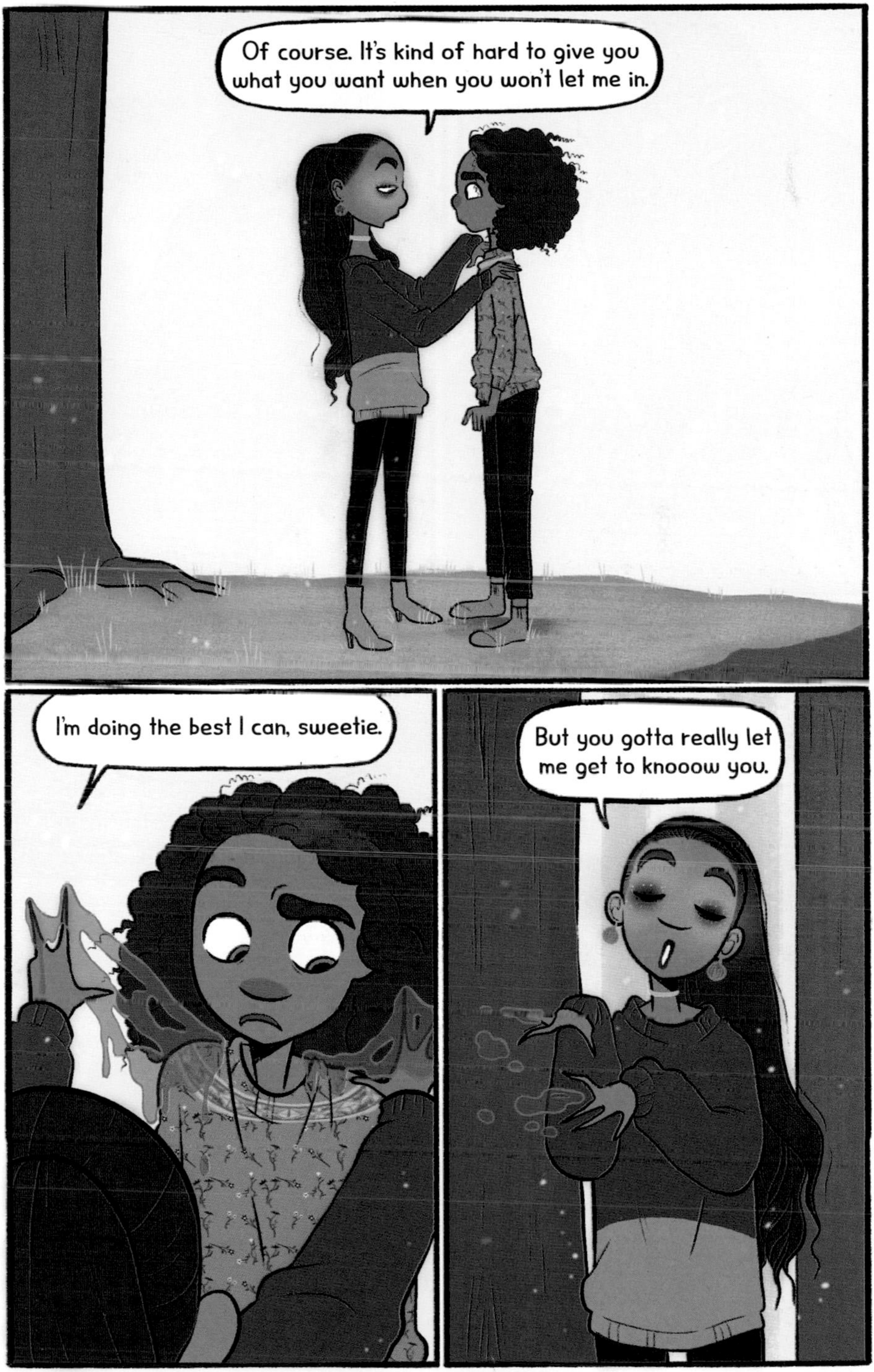
Of course. It's kind of hard to give you what you want when you won't let me in.
I'm doing the best I can, sweetie.
But you gotta really let me get to knooow you.

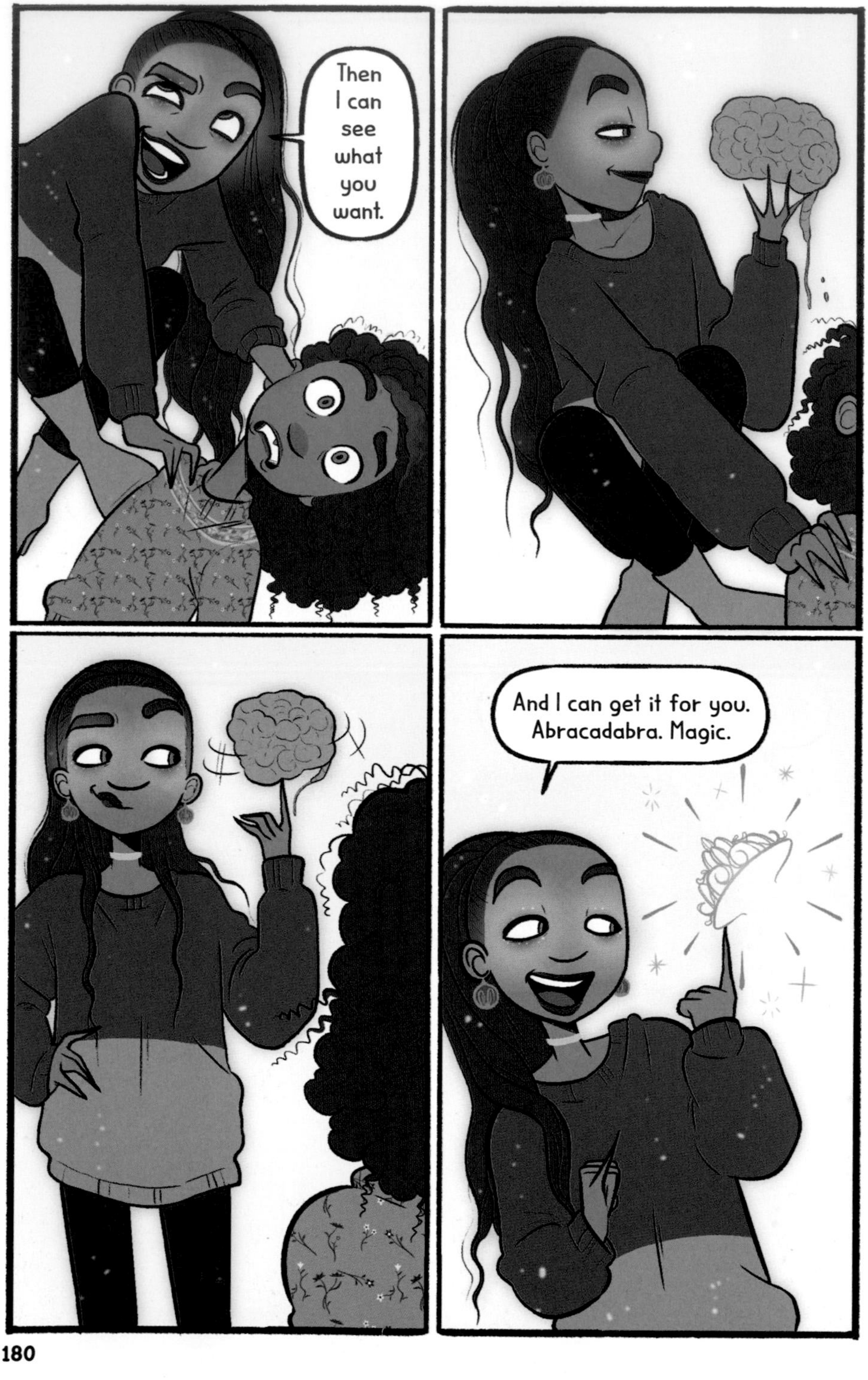
Then I can see what you want.
And I can get it for you. Abracadabra. Magic.

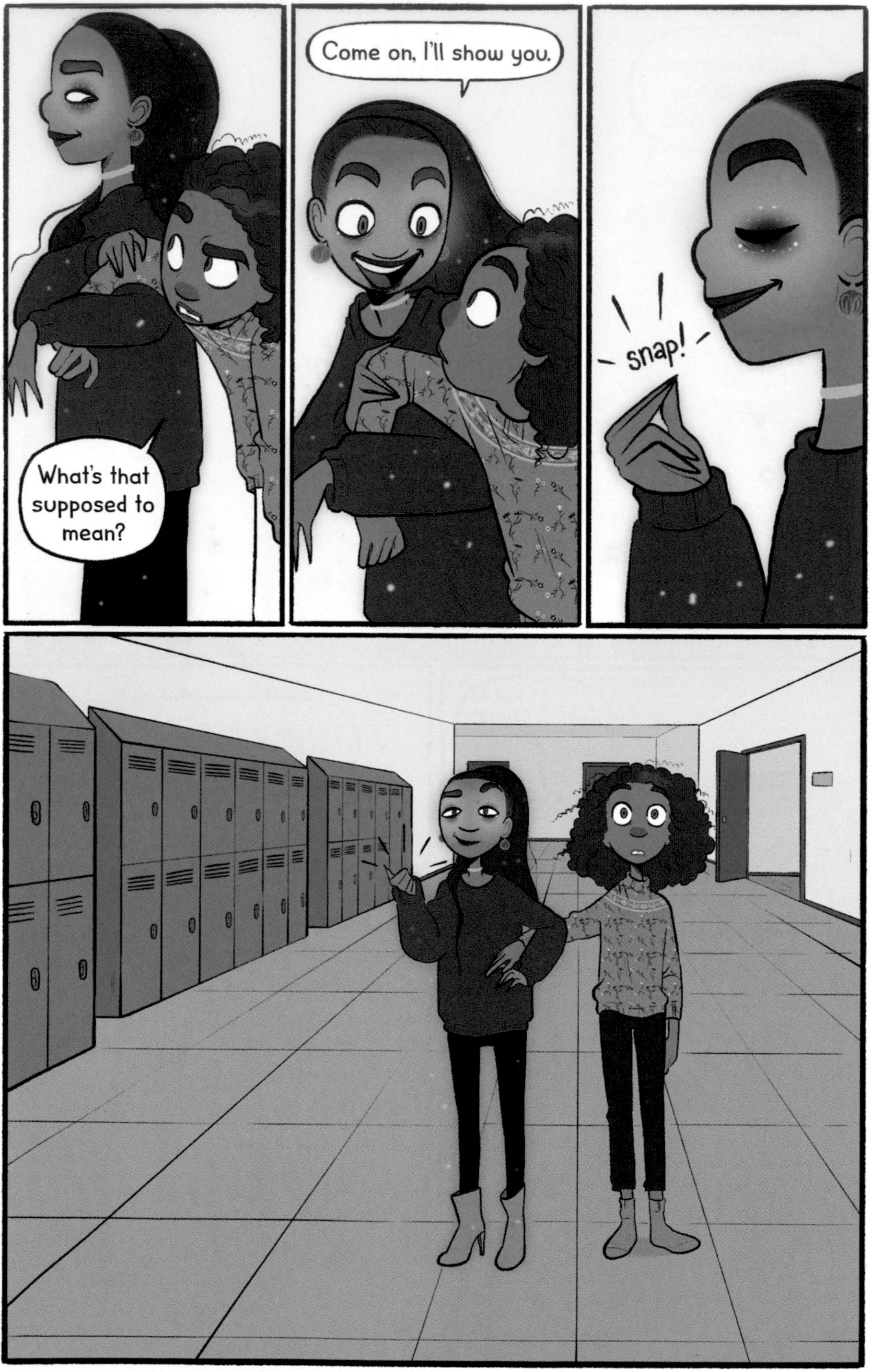
What's that supposed to mean?
Come on, I'll show you.
snap!

183

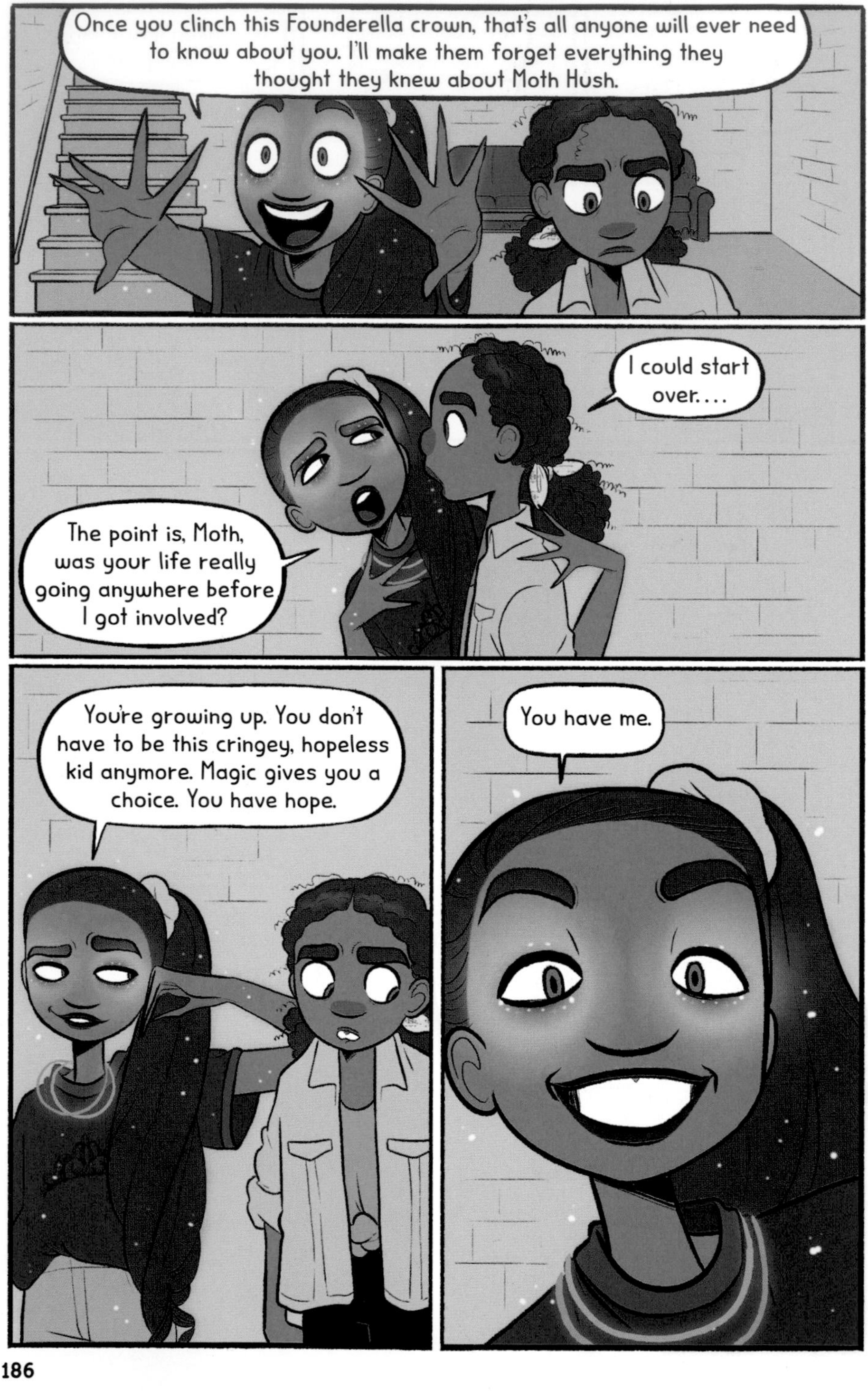
Once you clinch this Founderella crown, that's all anyone will ever need to know about you. I'll make them forget everything they thought they knew about Moth Hush.
I could start over. . . .
The point is, Moth, was your life really going anywhere before I got involved?
You're growing up. You don't have to be this cringey, hopeless kid anymore. Magic gives you a choice. You have hope.
You have me.

CHAPTER 11

The Valentine's Ball

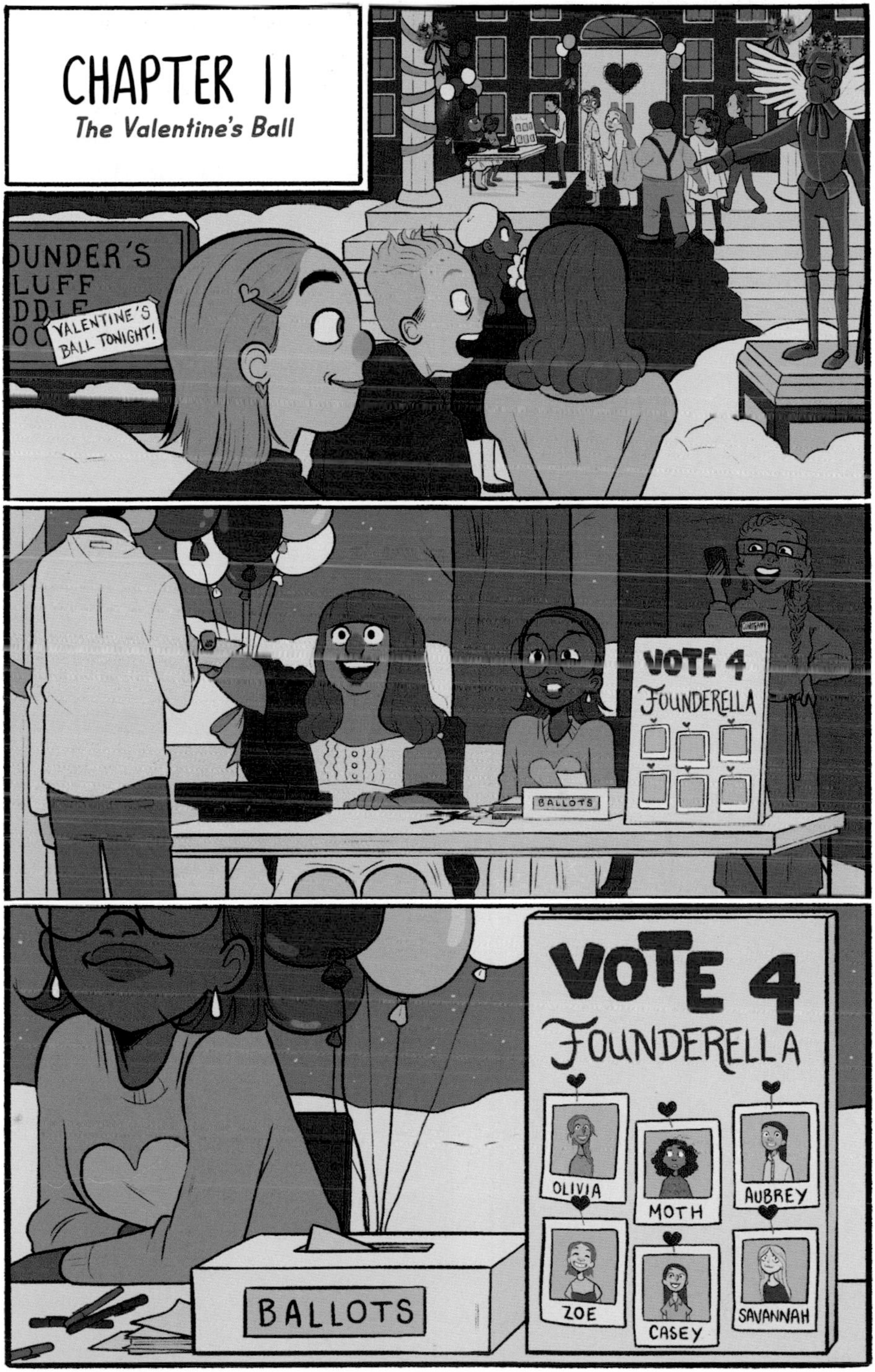

VALENTINE'S BALL TONIGHT!
VOTE 4 FOUNDERELLA
BALLOTS
VOTE 4 FOUNDERELLA
OLIVIA
MOTH
AUBREY
ZOE
CASEY
SAVANNAH
BALLOTS

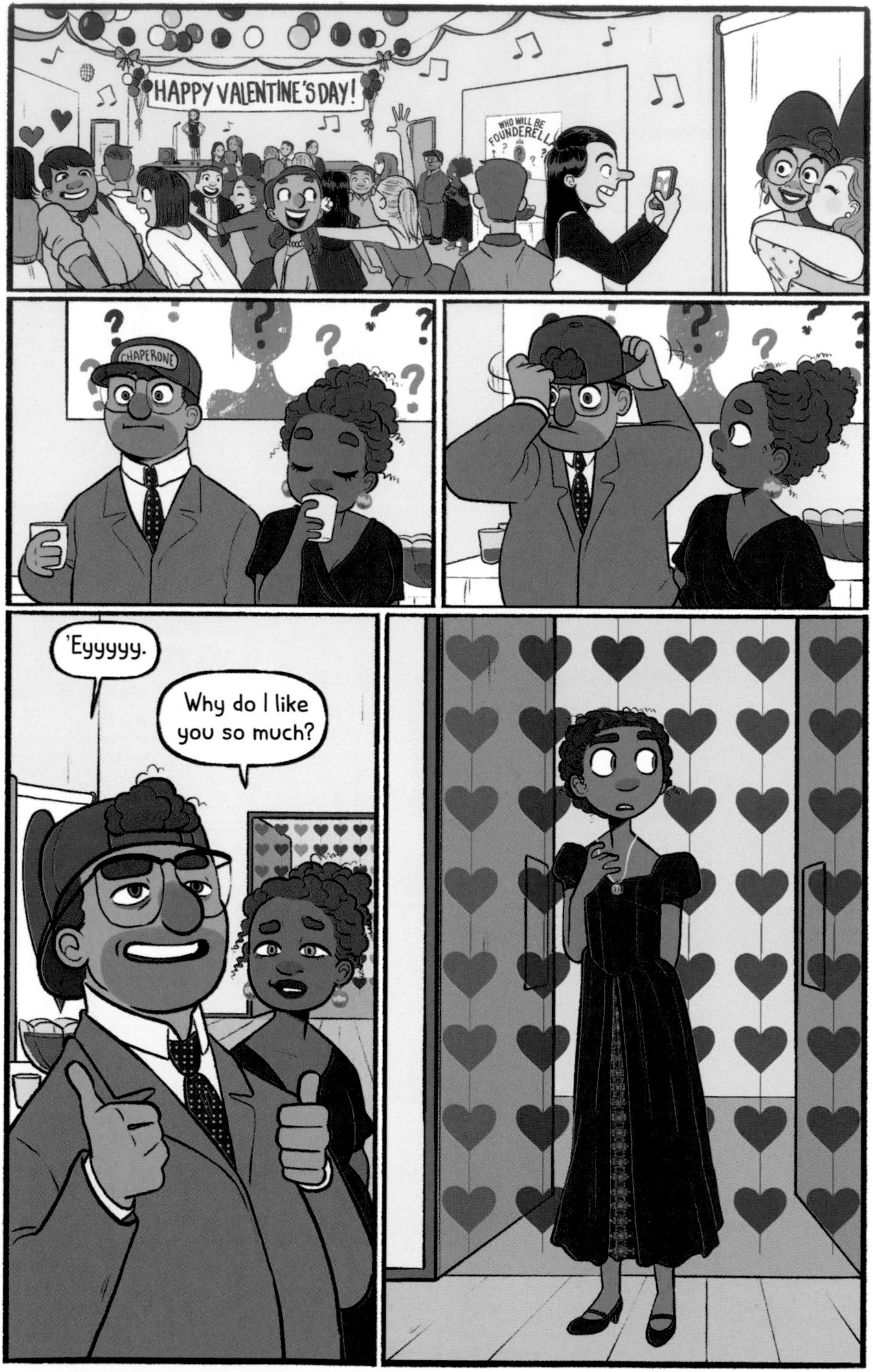
HAPPY VALENTINE'S DAY!
WHO WILL BE FOUNDERELLA
CHAPERONE
'Eyyyyy.
Why do I like you so much?

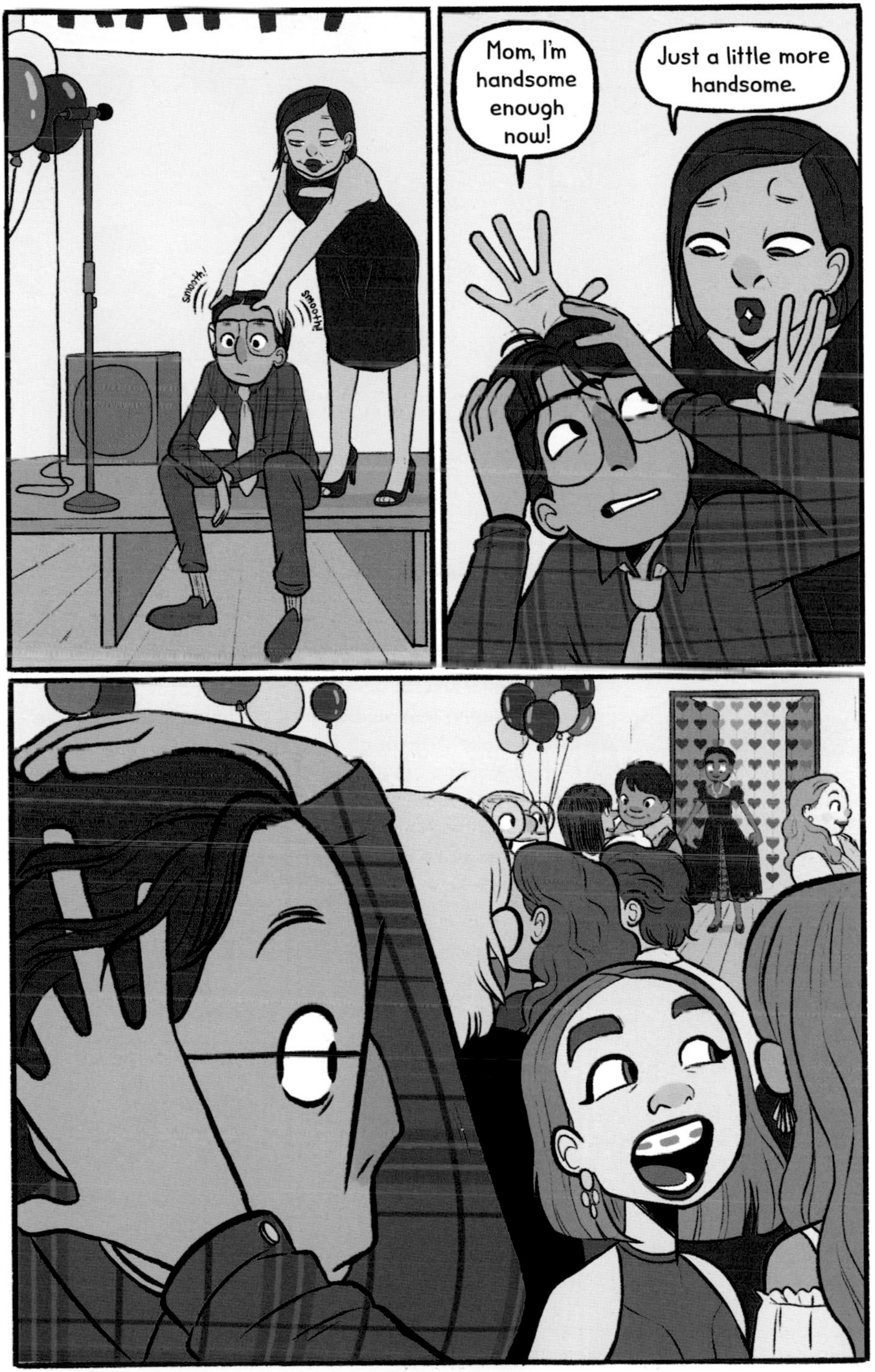
smooth!
smooth!
Mom, I'm handsome enough now!
Just a little more handsome.

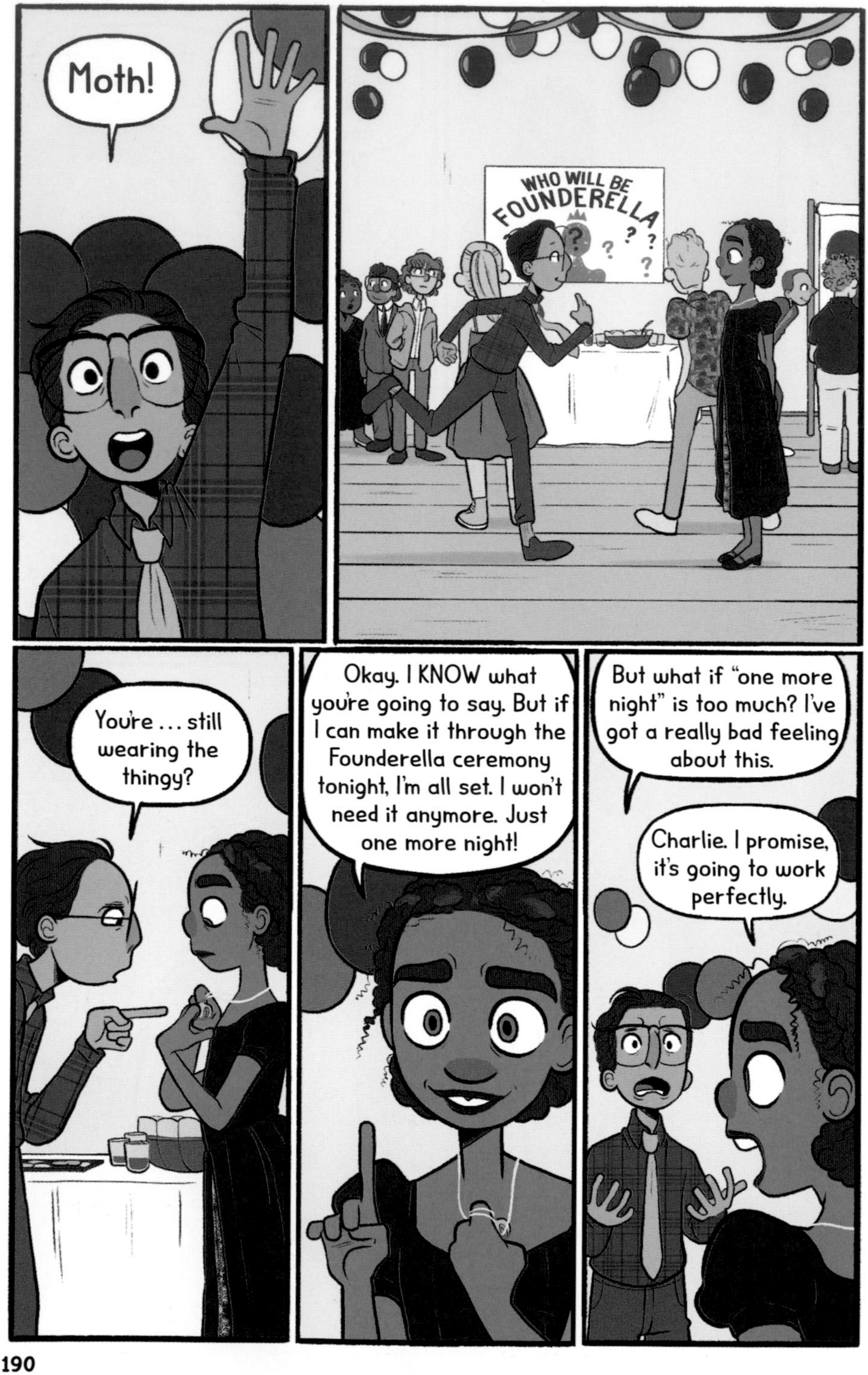
Moth!
WHO WILL BE FOUNDERELLA
You're . . . still wearing the thingy?
Okay. I KNOW what you're going to say. But if I can make it through the Founderella ceremony tonight, I'm all set. I won't need it anymore. Just one more night!
But what if "one more night" is too much? I've got a really bad feeling about this.
Charlie. I promise, it's going to work perfectly.

191

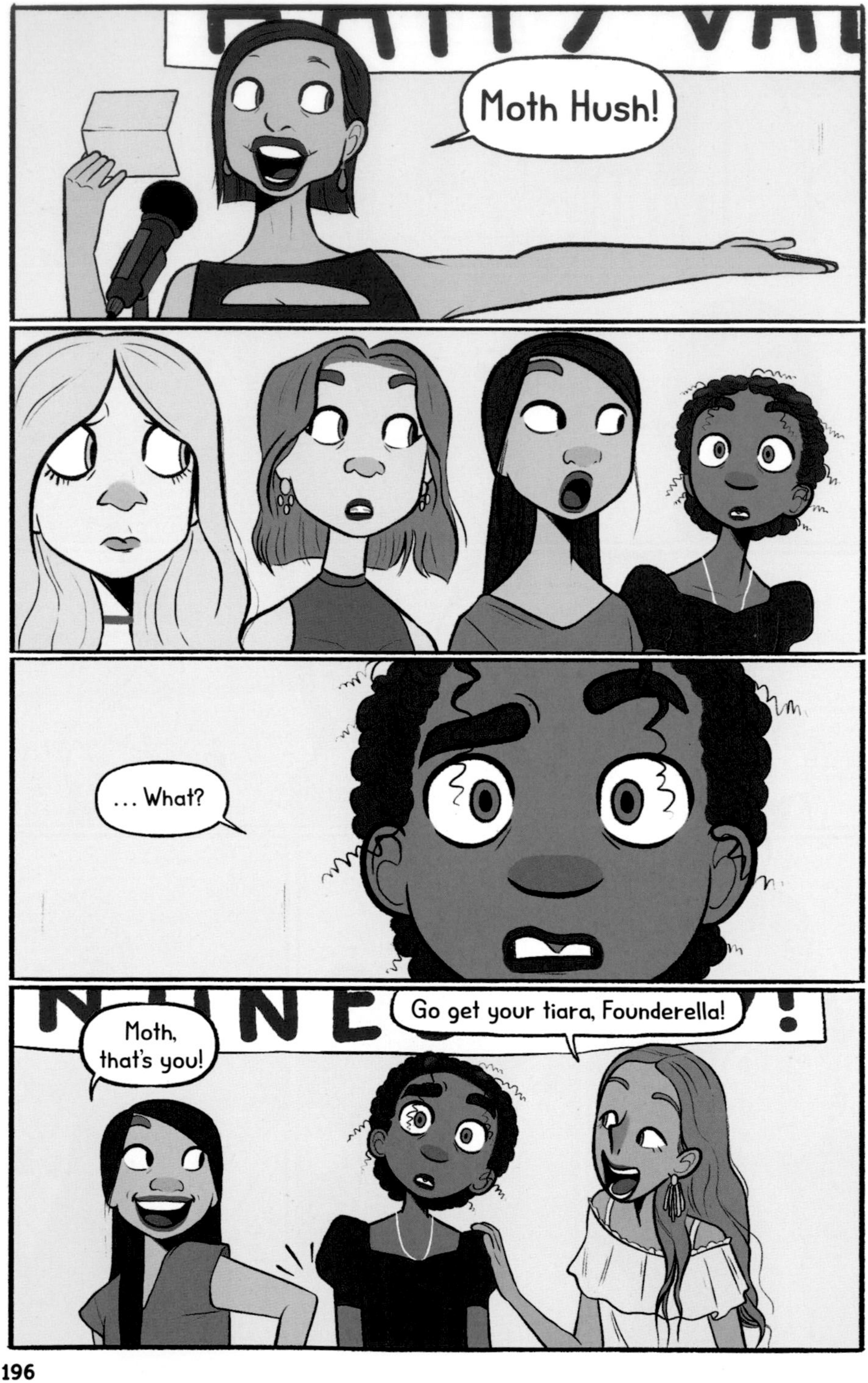
Moth Hush!
... What?
Moth,
that's you!
Go get your tiara, Founderella!

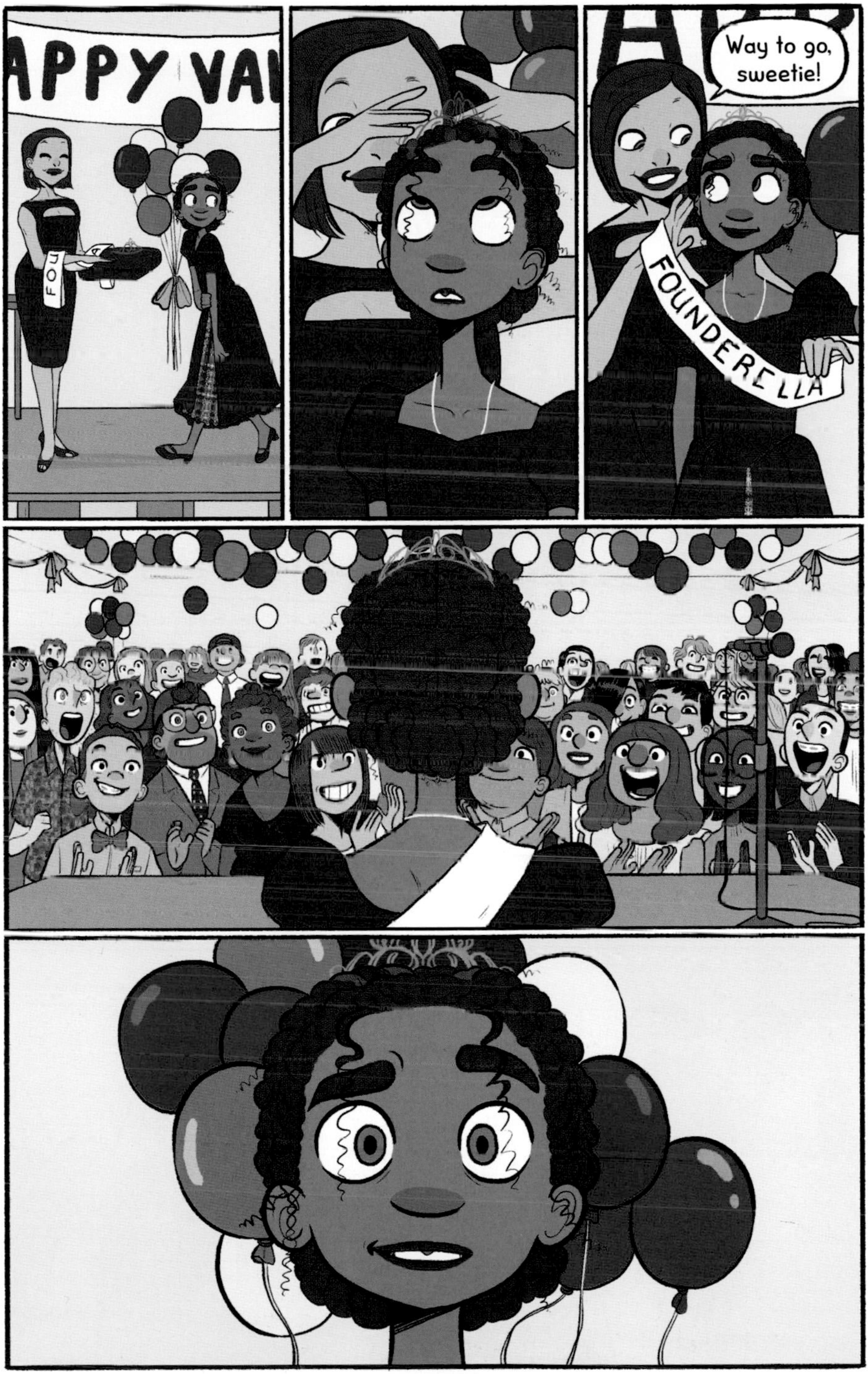
APPY VAL
FOU
Way to go, sweetie!
FOUNDERELLA

199

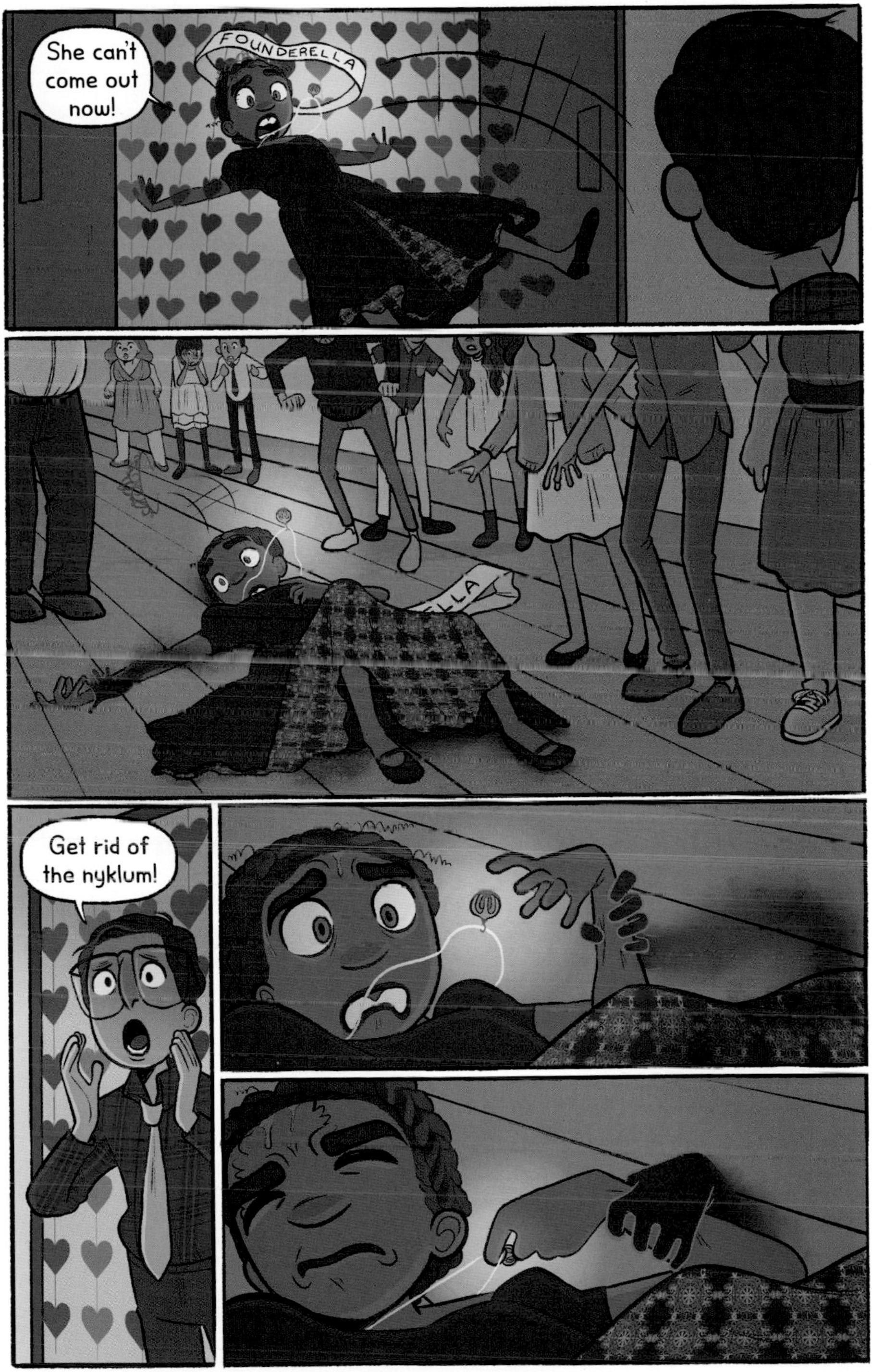
She can't come out now!
FOUNDERELLA
Get rid of the nyklum!

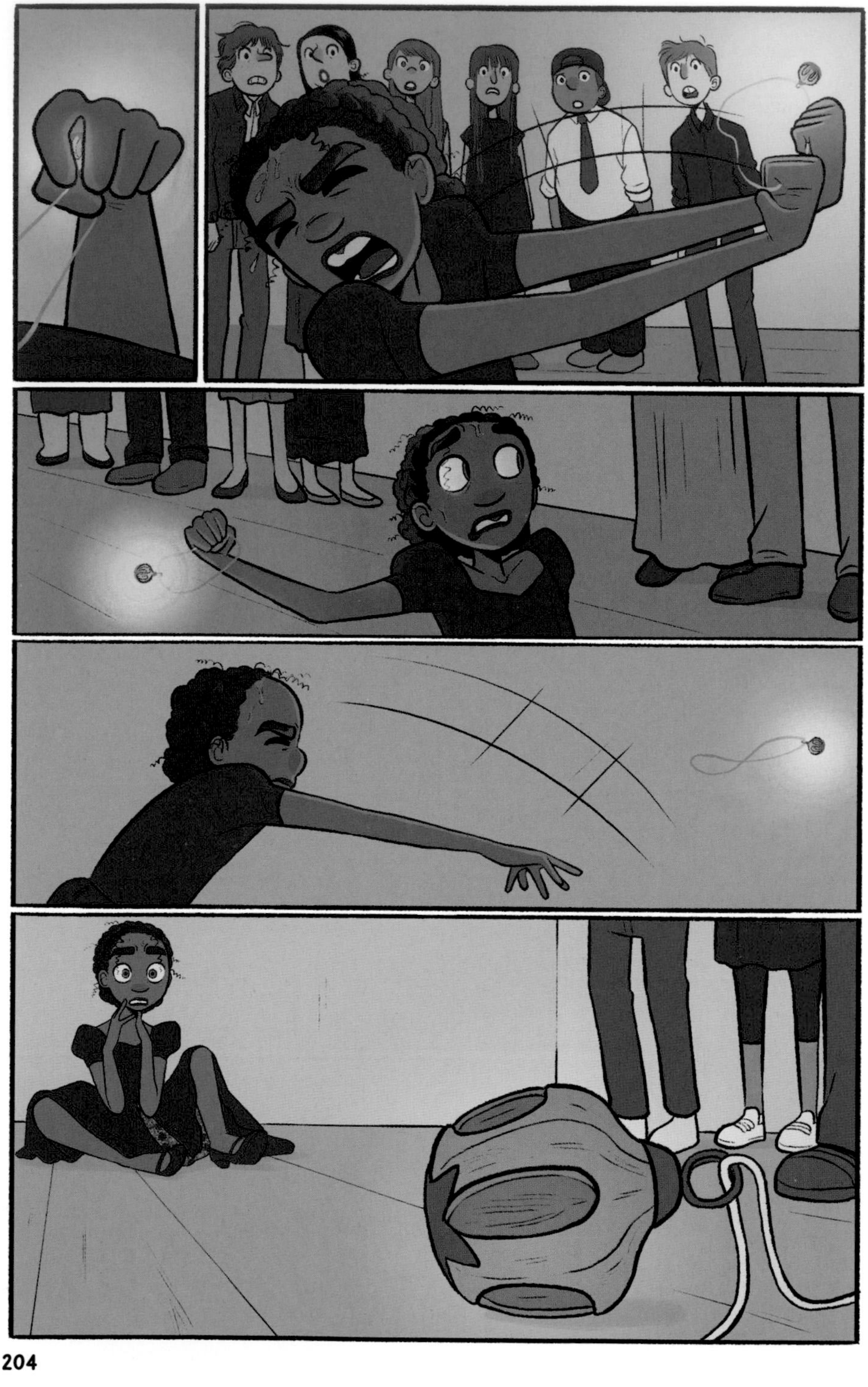

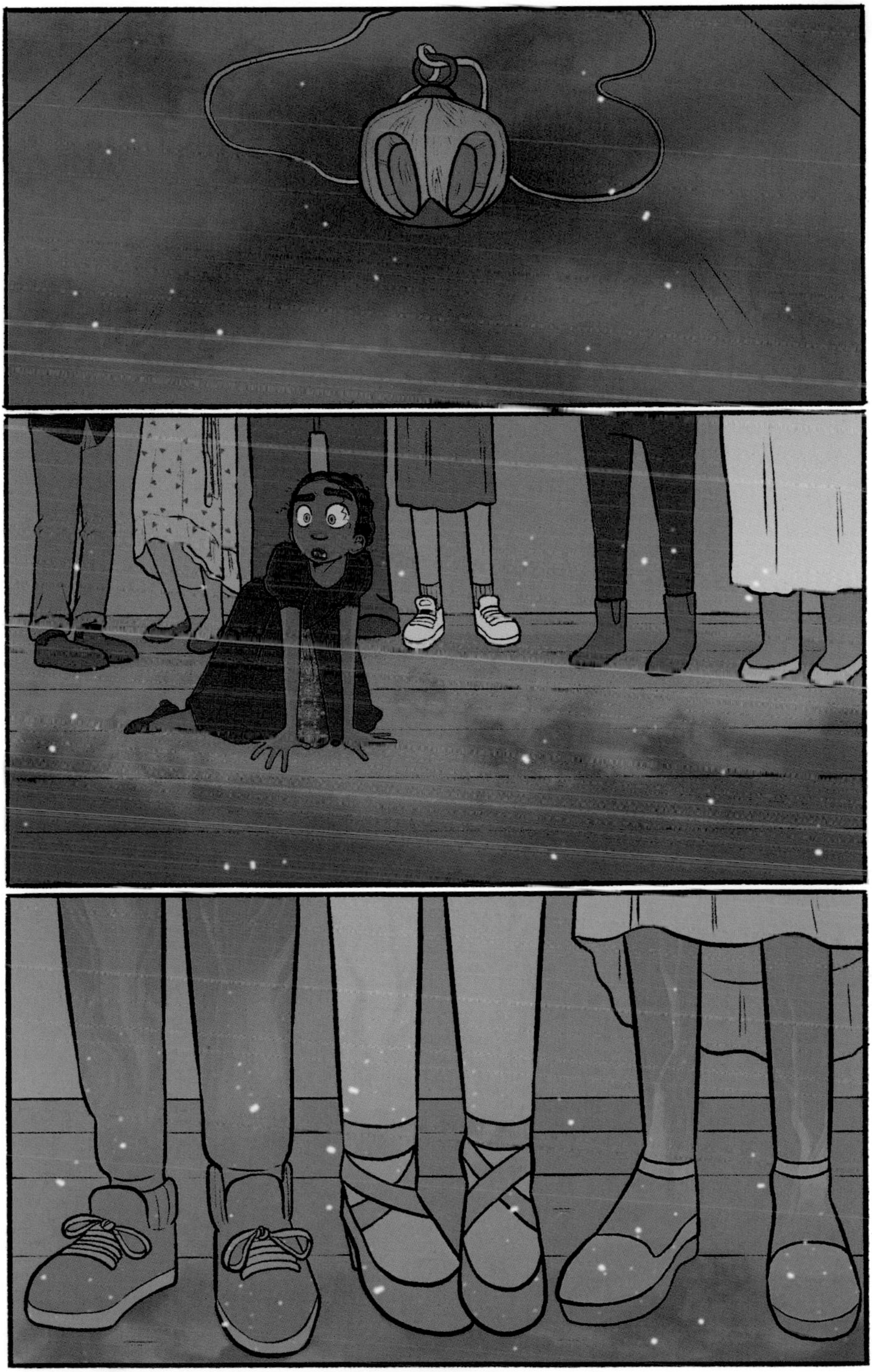

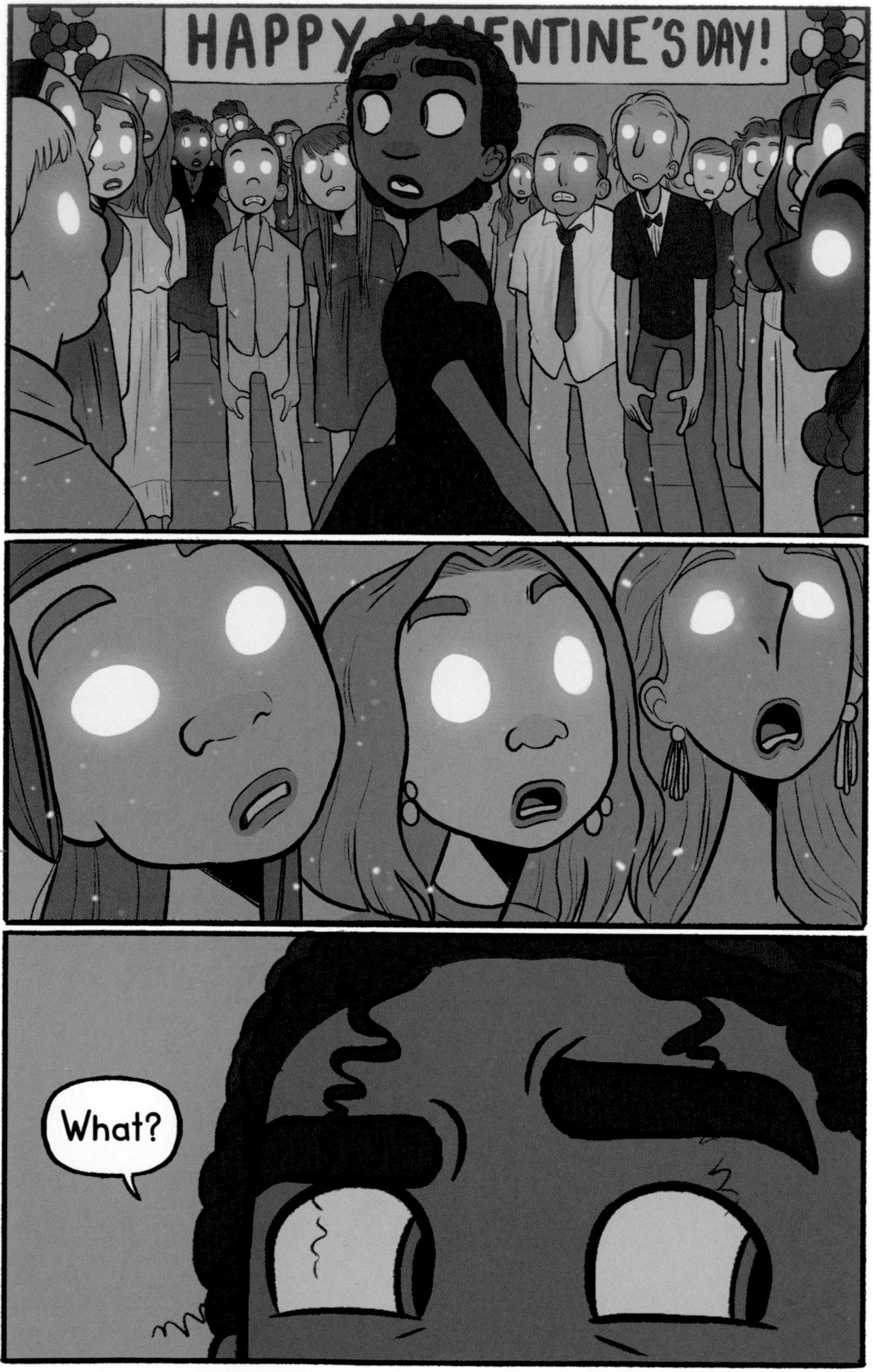
HAPPY
ENTINE'S DAY!
What?

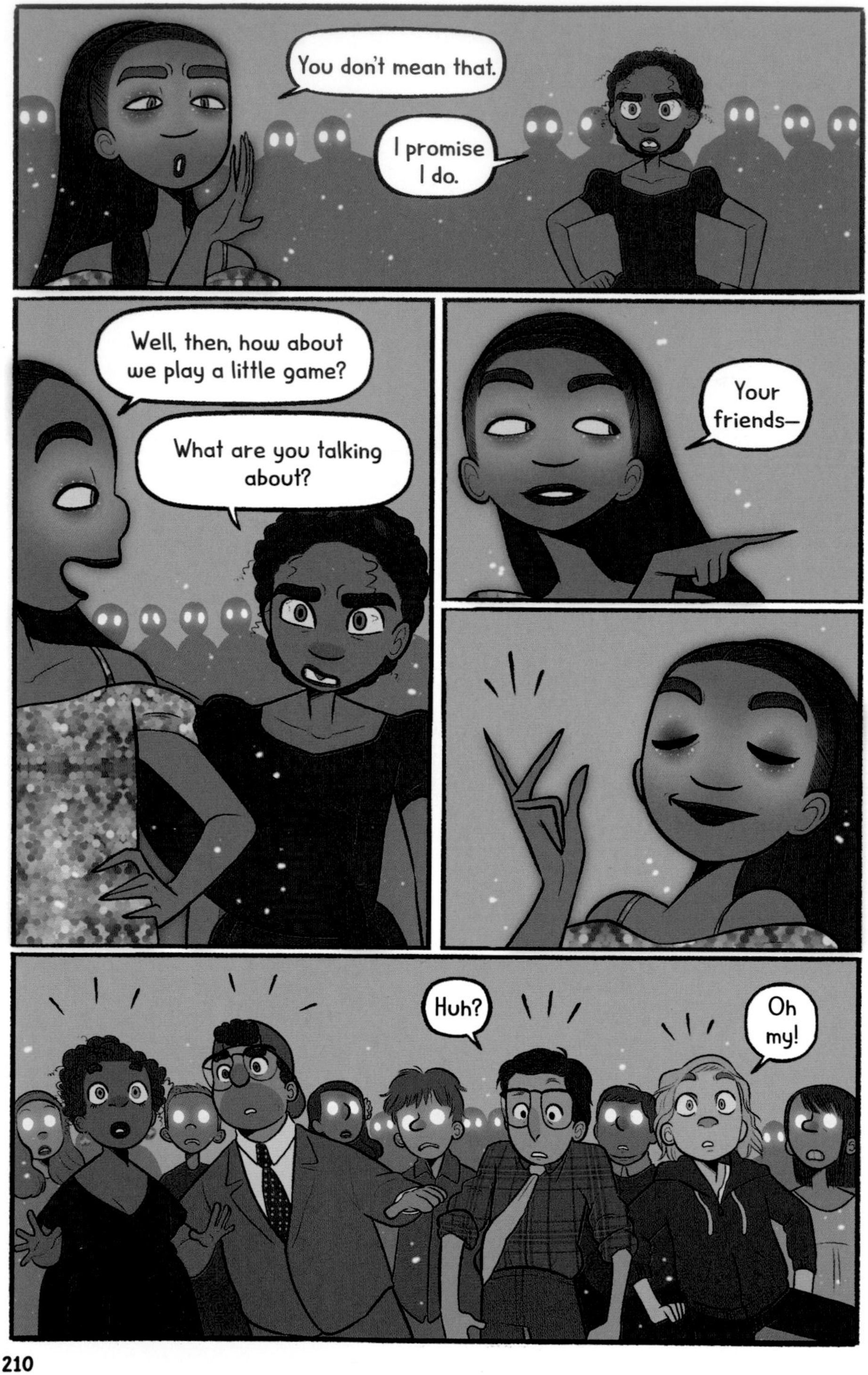
You don't mean that.
I promise I do.
Well, then, how about we play a little game?
What are you talking about?
Your friends—
Huh?
Oh my!

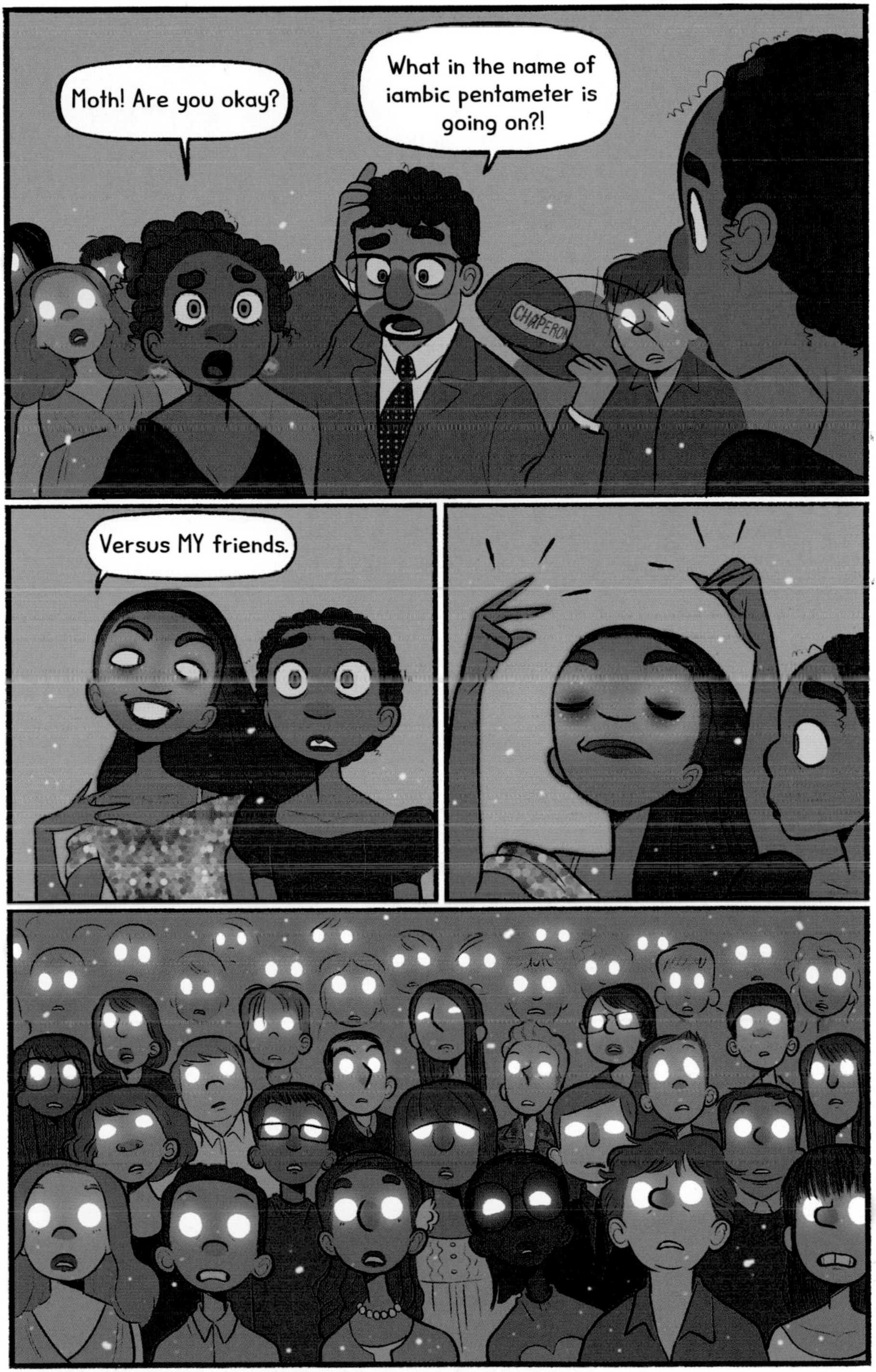
Moth! Are you okay?
What in the name of iambic pentameter is going on?!
CHAPERON
Versus MY friends.

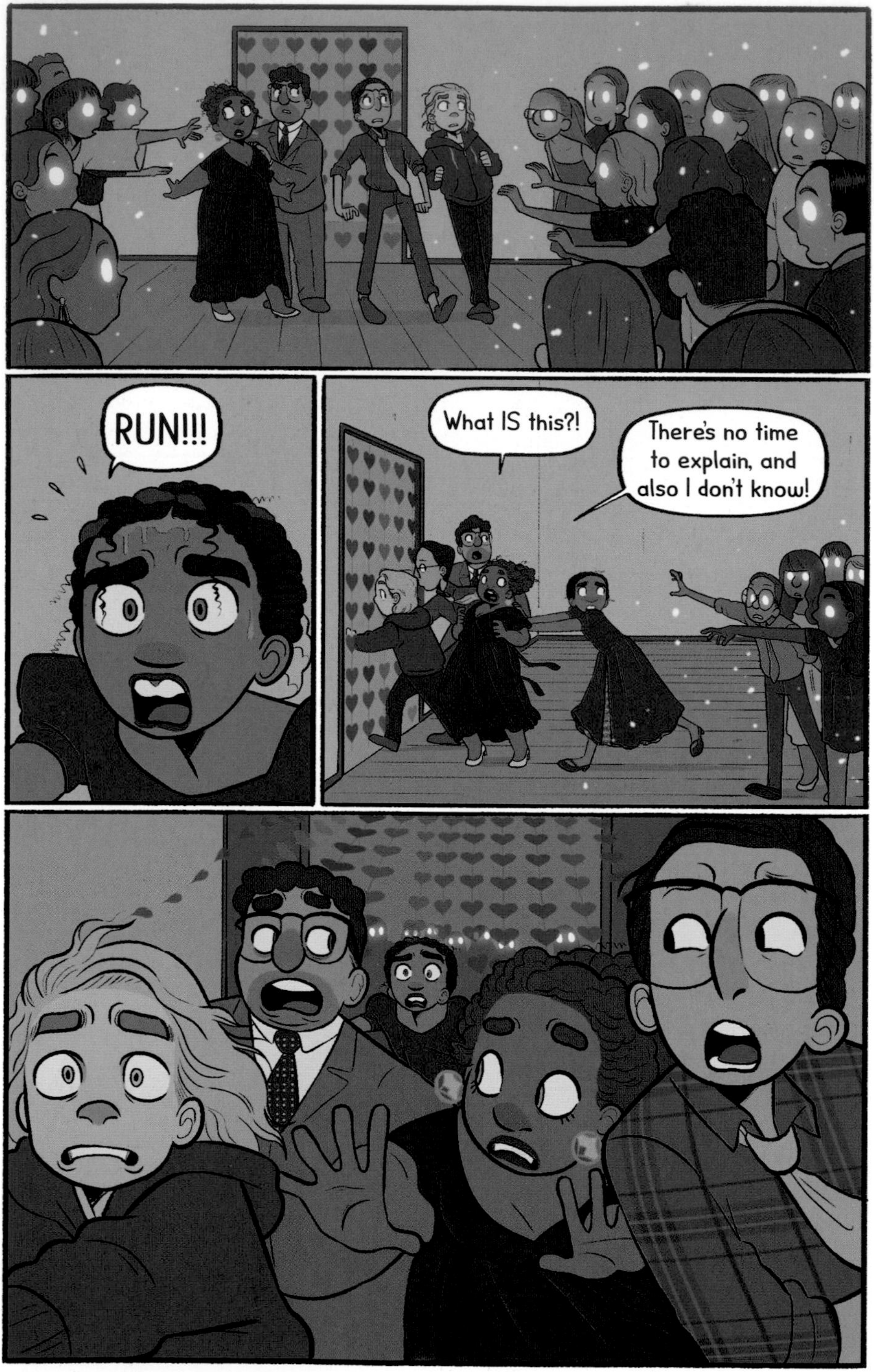
RUN!!!
What IS this?!
There's no time to explain, and also I don't know!

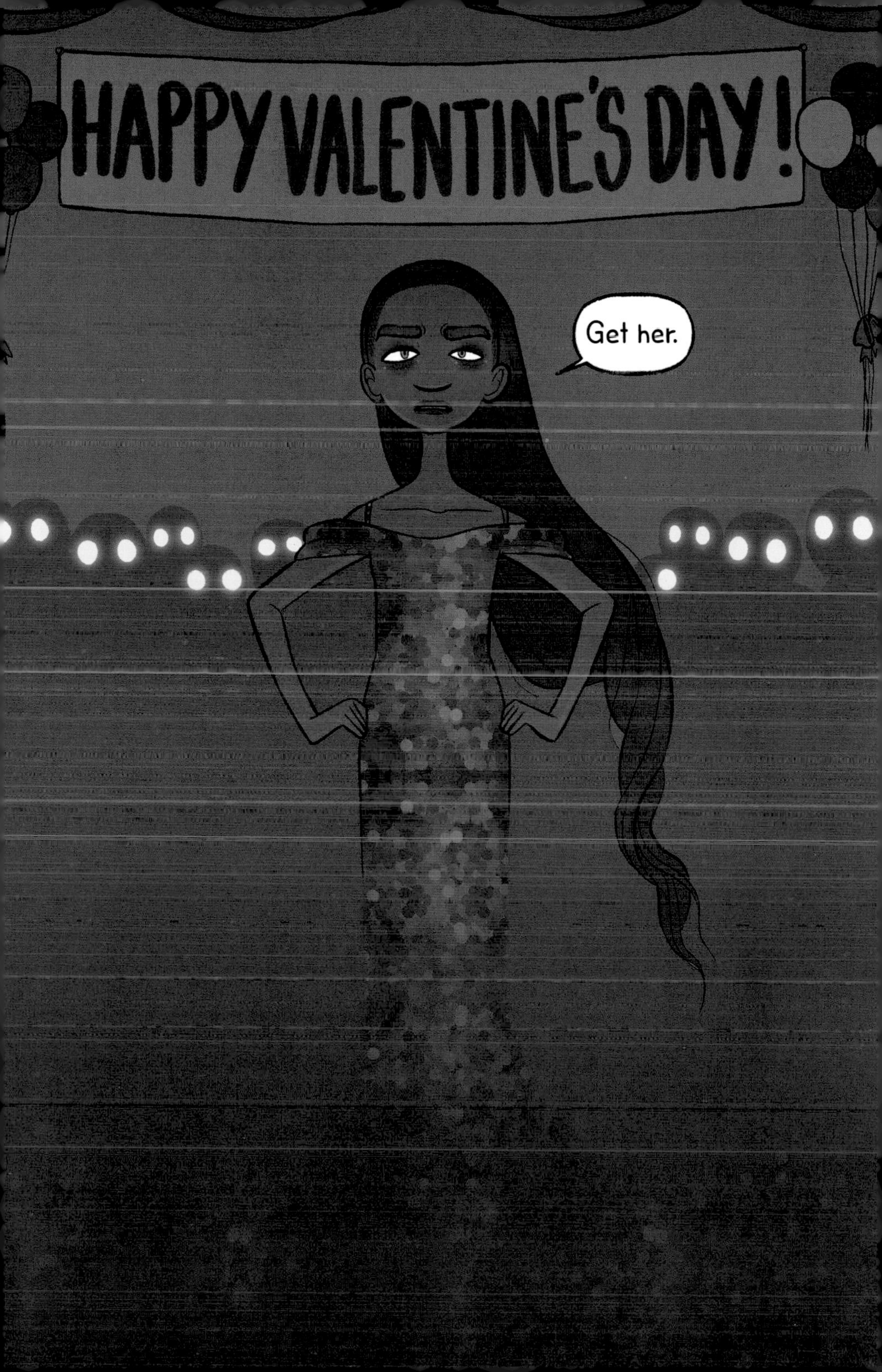
HAPPY VALENTINE'S DAY!
Get her.

CHAPTER 12
Moth and Her Shadow

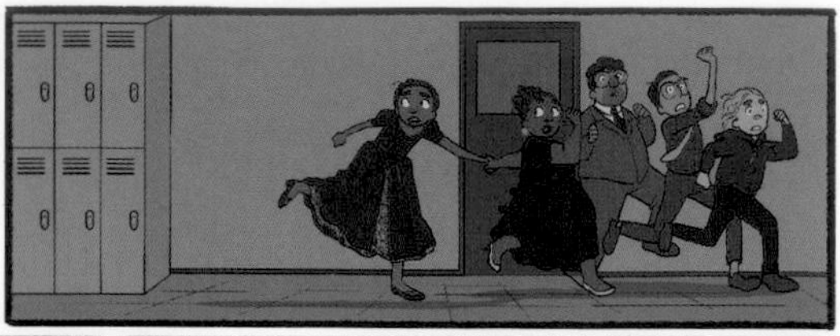

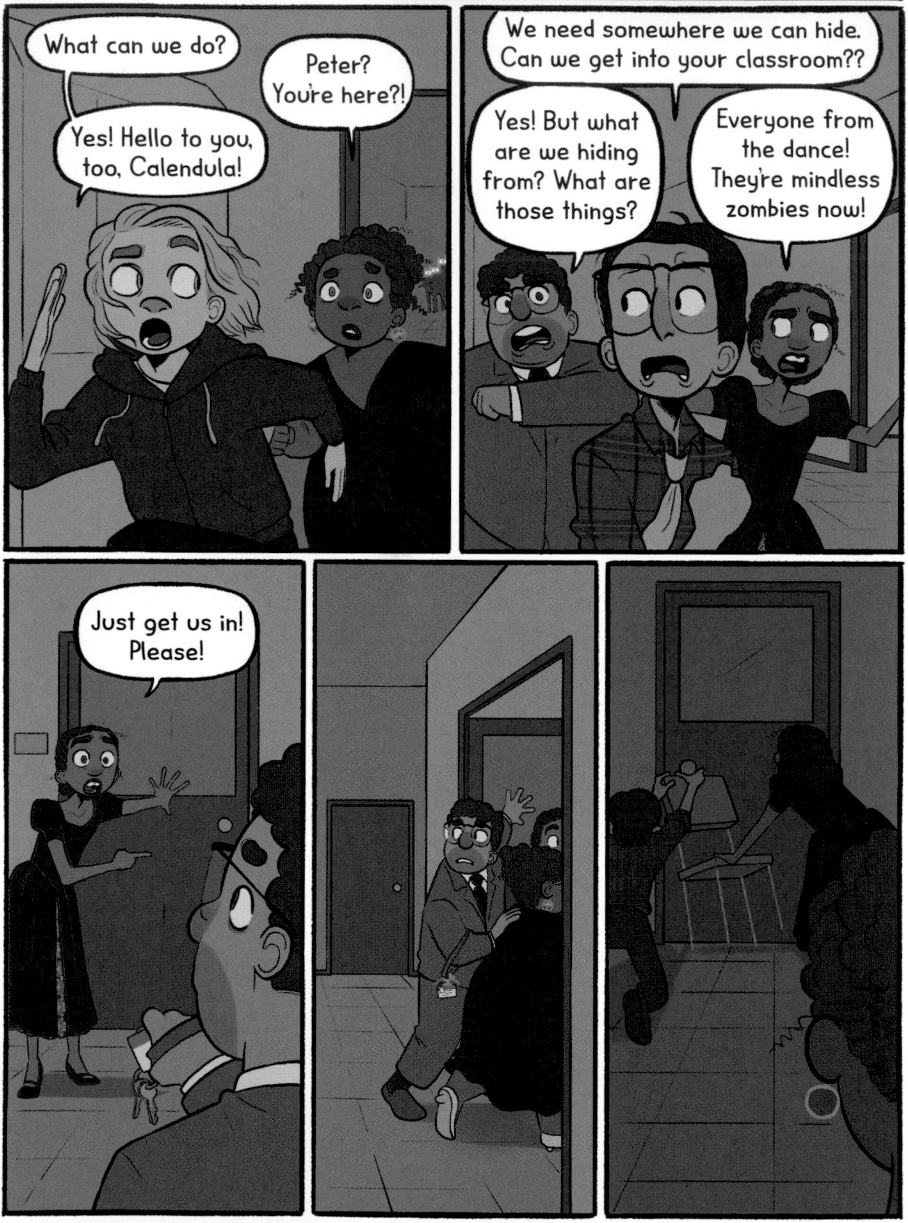

What can we do?
Peter? You're here?!
Yes! Hello to you, too, Calendula!
We need somewhere we can hide. Can we get into your classroom??
Yes! But what are we hiding from? What are those things?
Everyone from the dance! They're mindless zombies now!
Just get us in! Please!

216

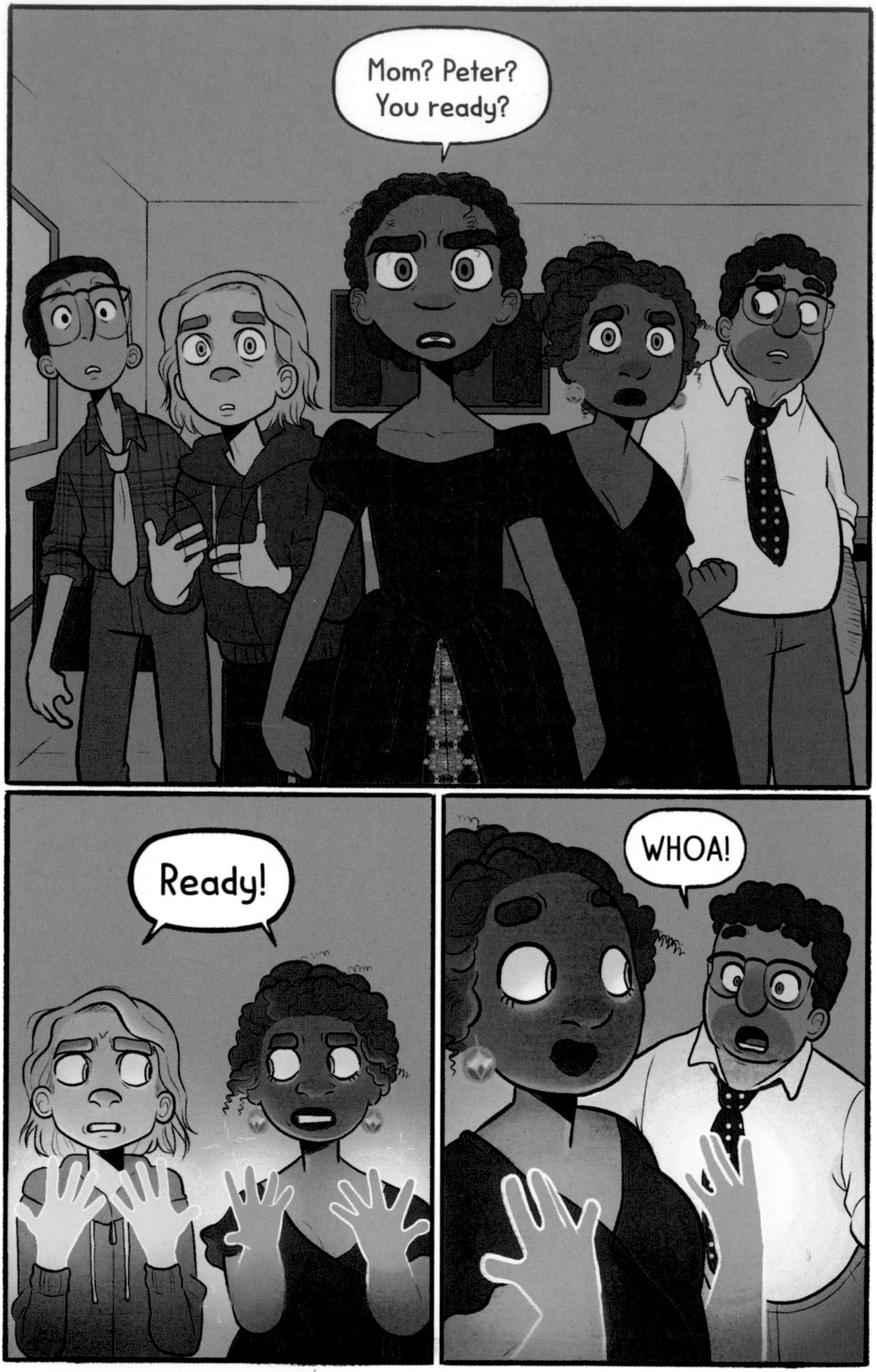
Mom? Peter?
You ready?
Ready!
WHOA!

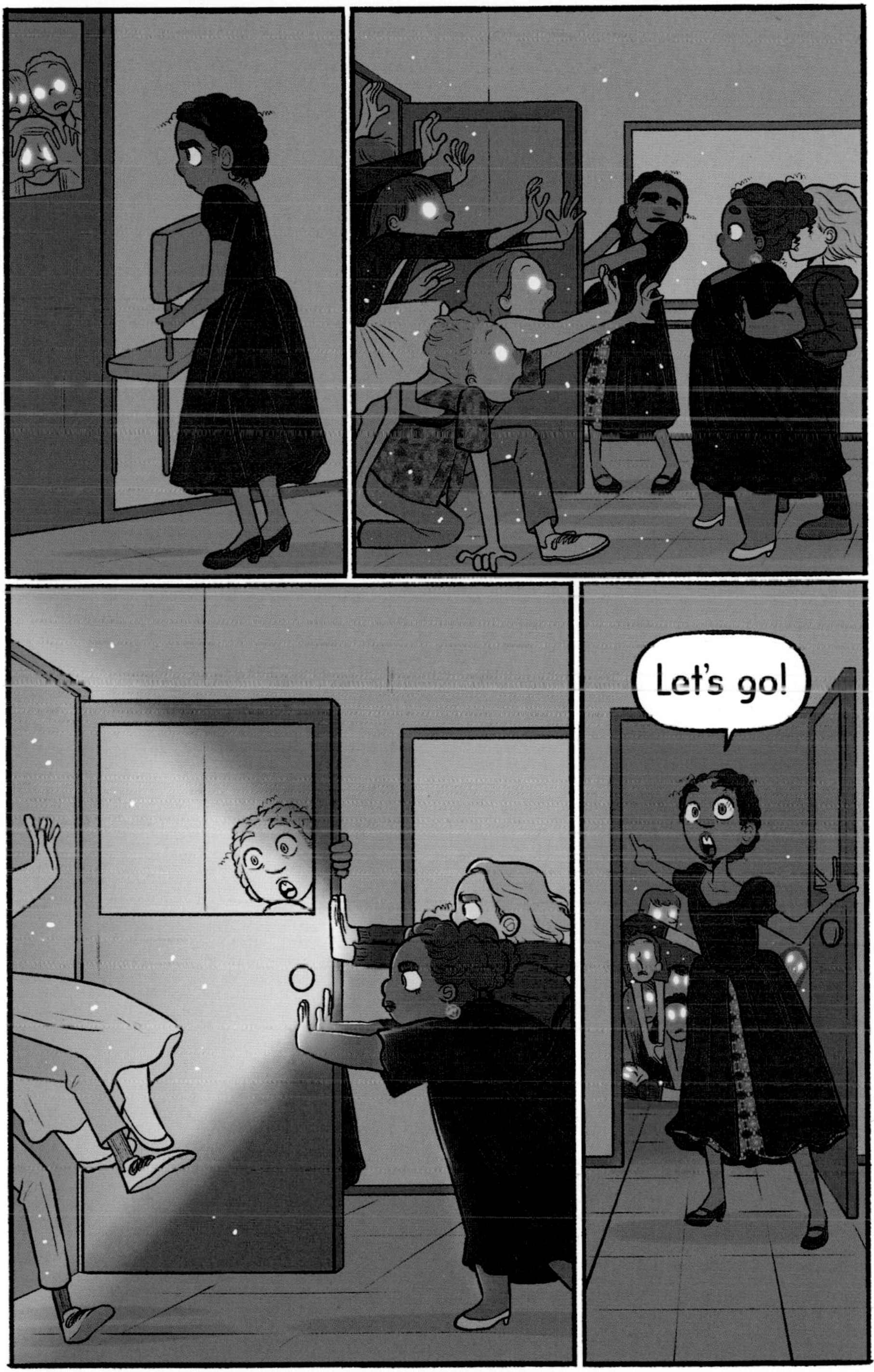
Let's go!

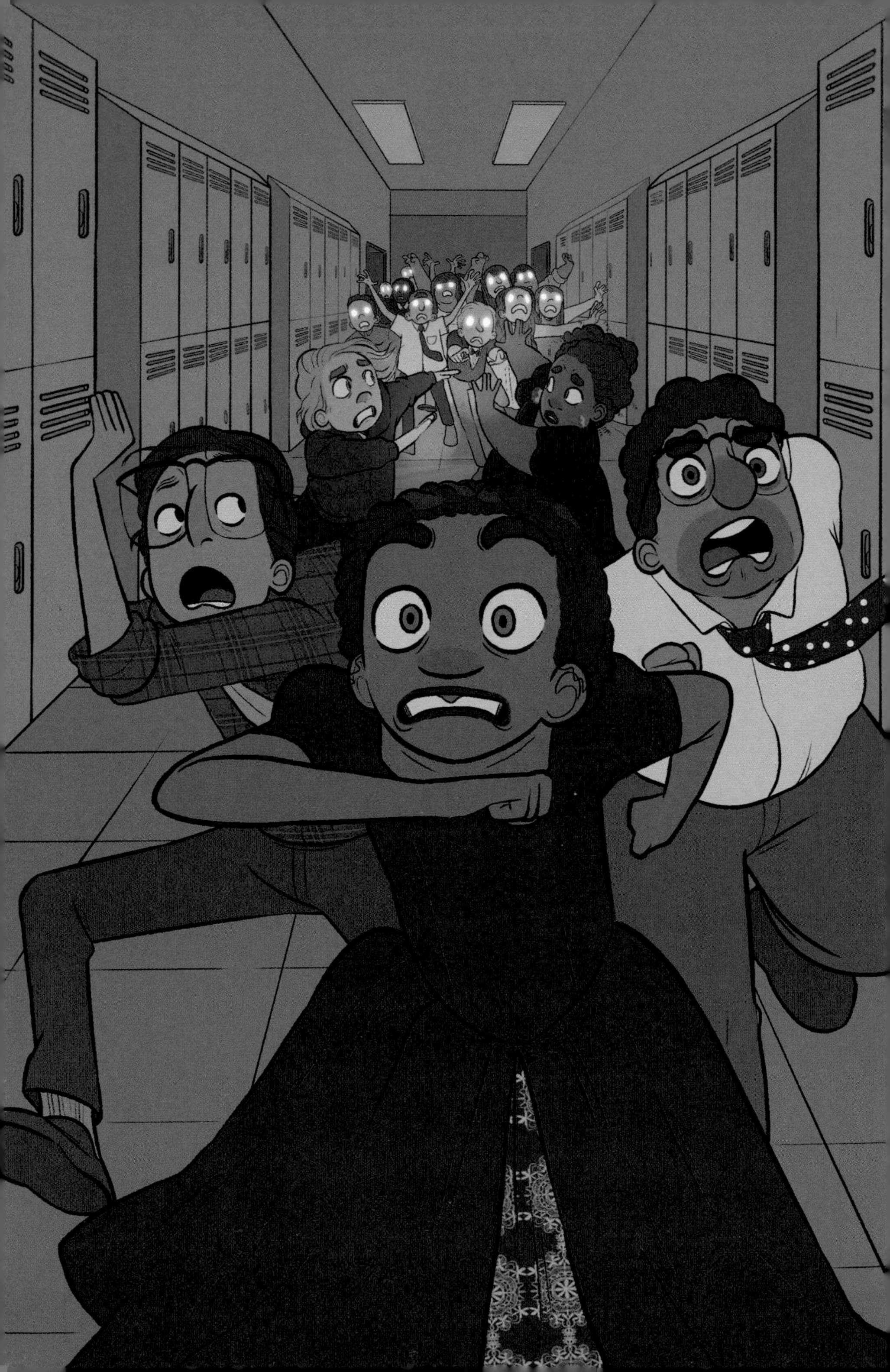

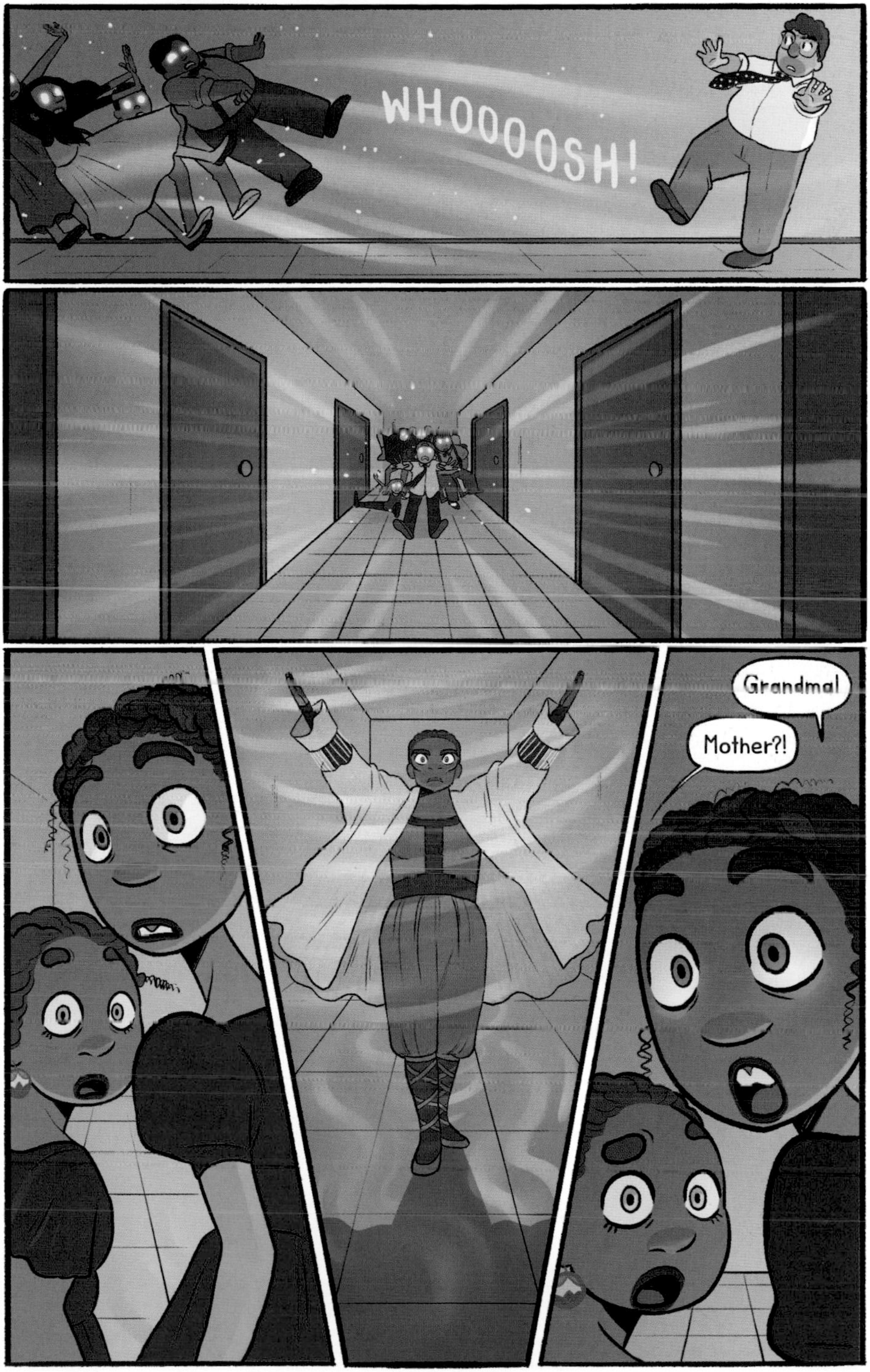
WHOOOOSH!
Grandma!
Mother?!

226

227

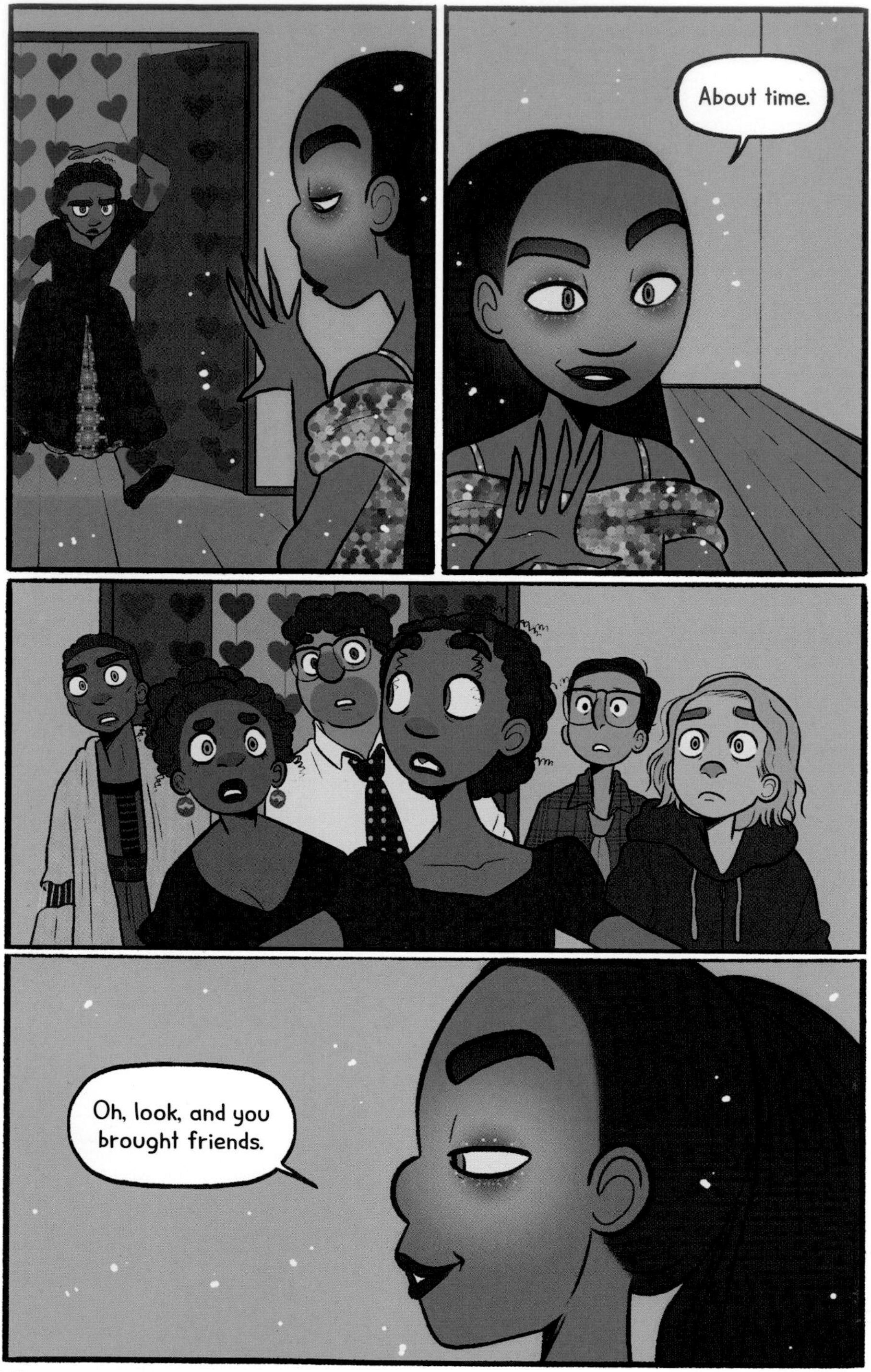
About time.
Oh, look, and you brought friends.

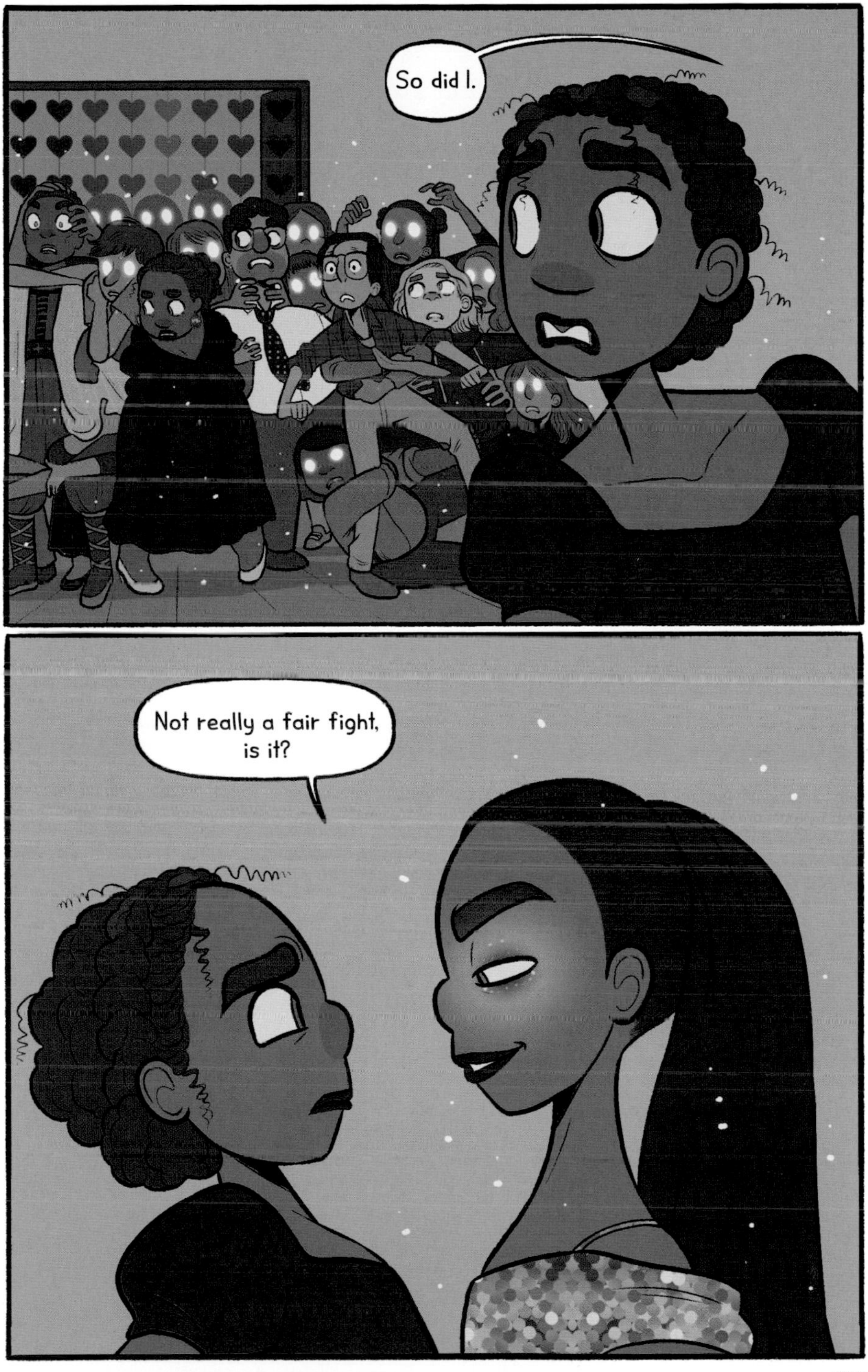
So did I.
Not really a fair fight, is it?

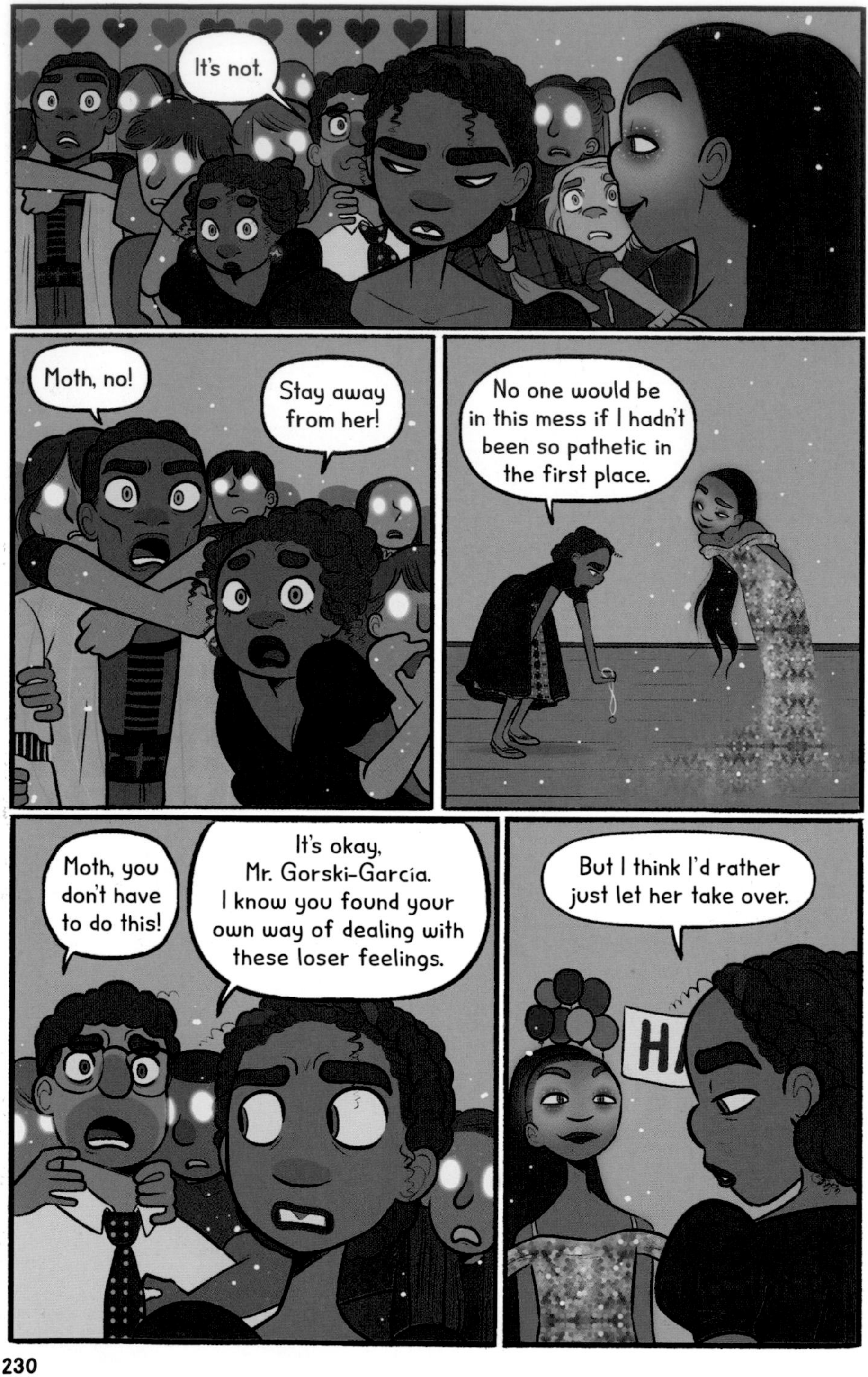
It's not.
Moth, no!
Stay away from her!
No one would be in this mess if I hadn't been so pathetic in the first place.
Moth, you don't have to do this!
It's okay, Mr. Gorski-García. I know you found your own way of dealing with these loser feelings.
But I think I'd rather just let her take over.
HA

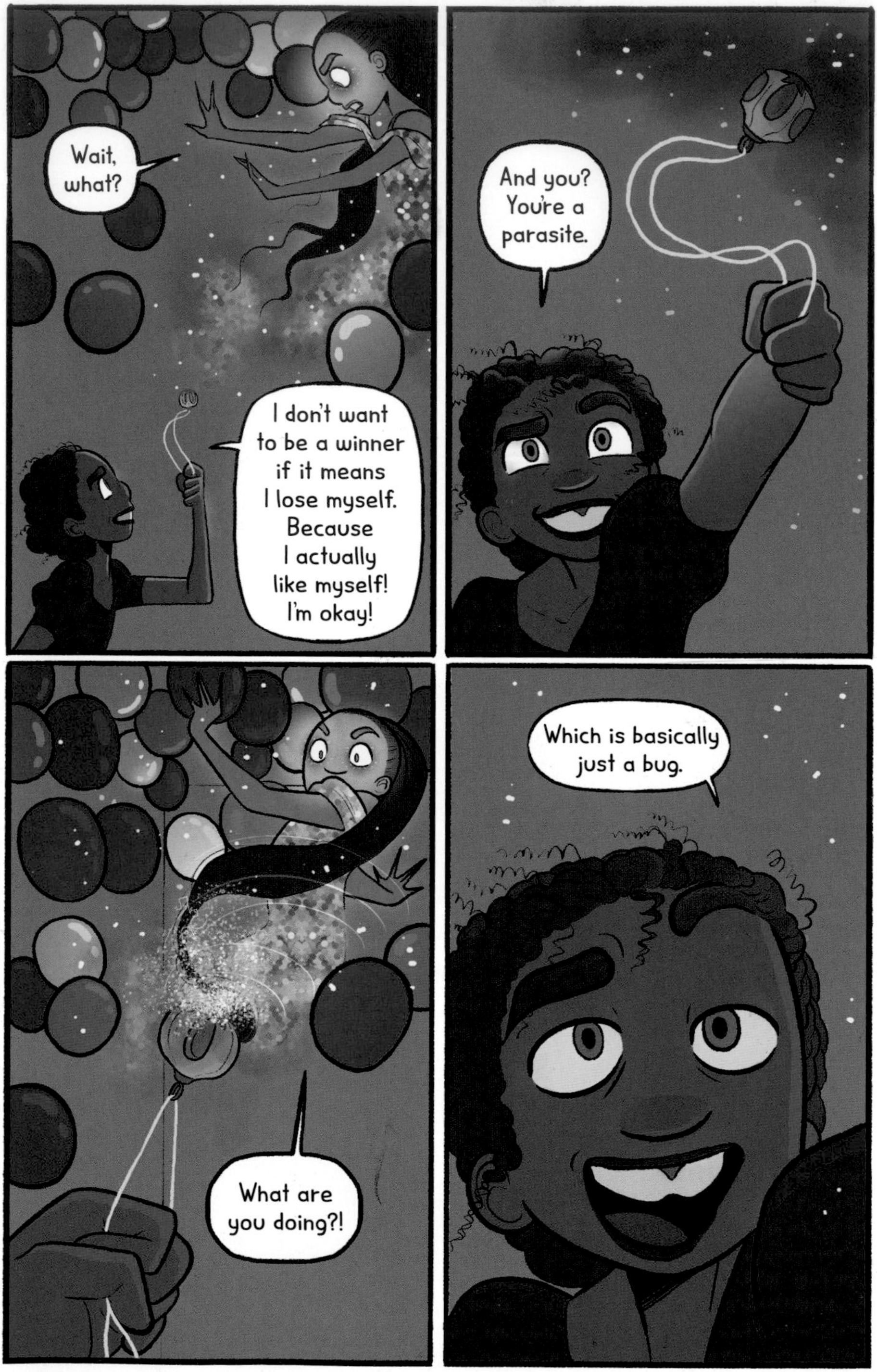
Wait, what?
I don't want to be a winner if it means I lose myself. Because I actually like myself! I'm okay!
And you? You're a parasite.
What are you doing?!
Which is basically just a bug.

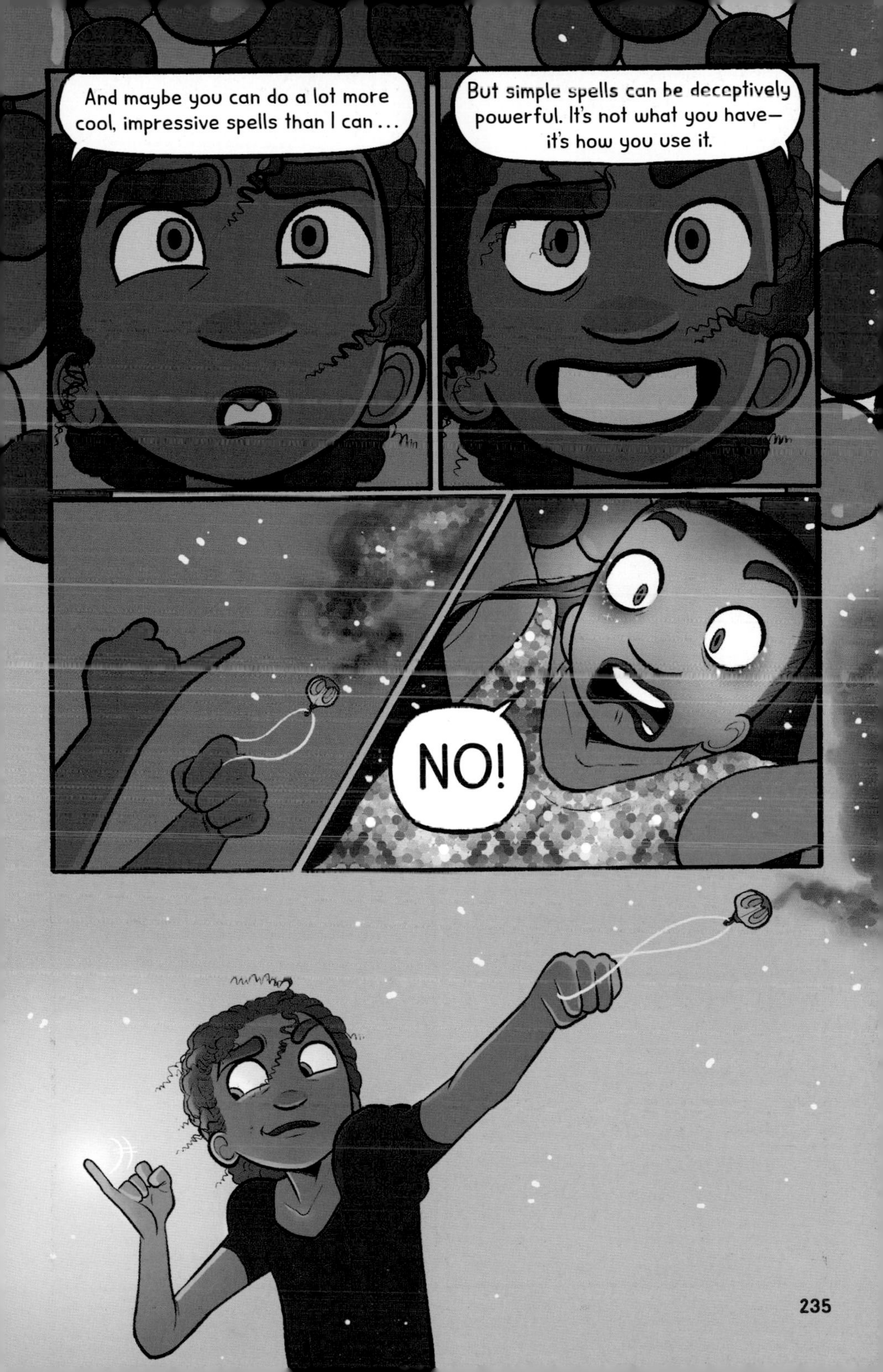
And maybe you can do a lot more cool, impressive spells than I can . . .
But simple spells can be deceptively powerful. It's not what you have—it's how you use it.
NO!

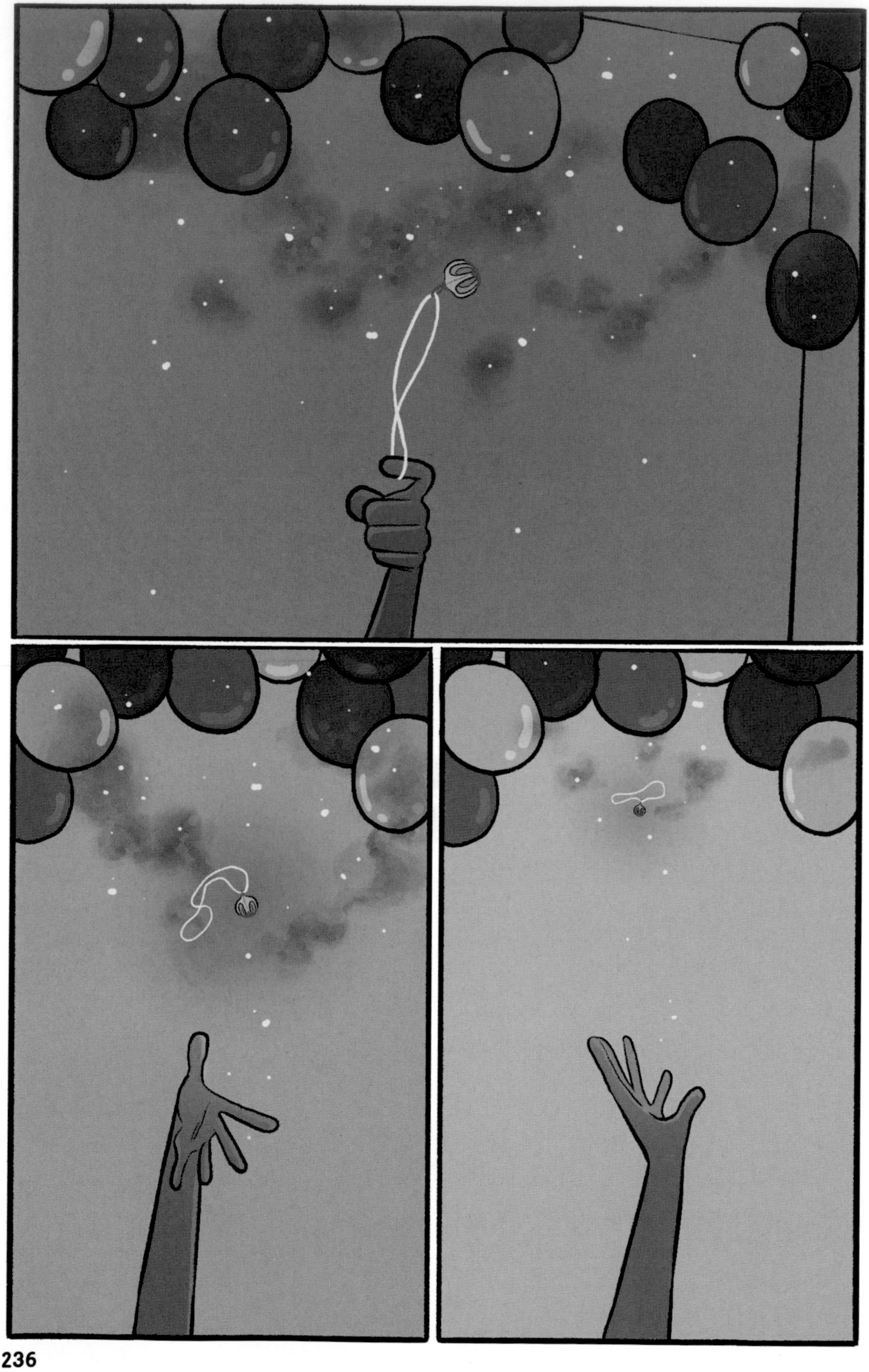

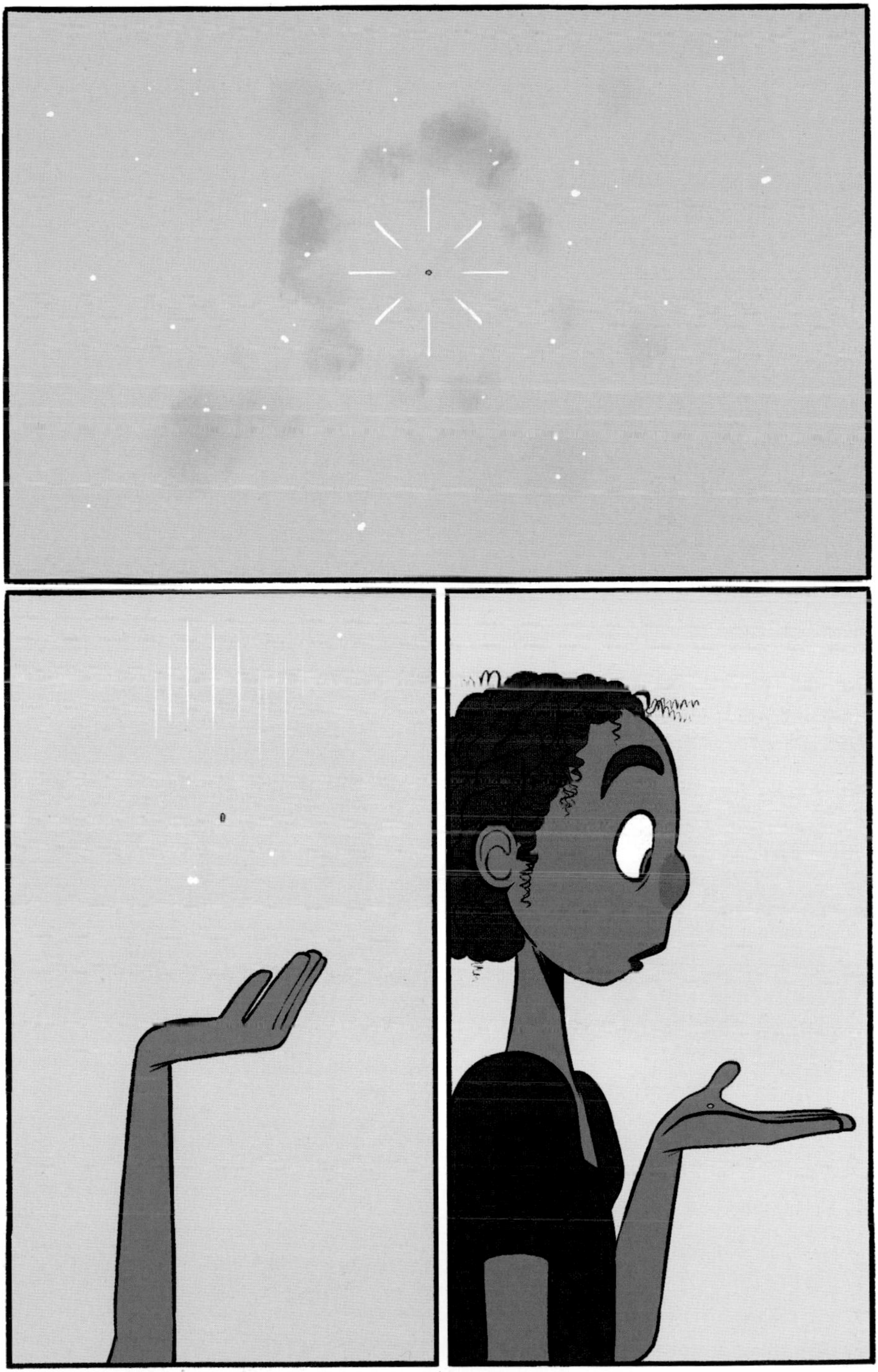

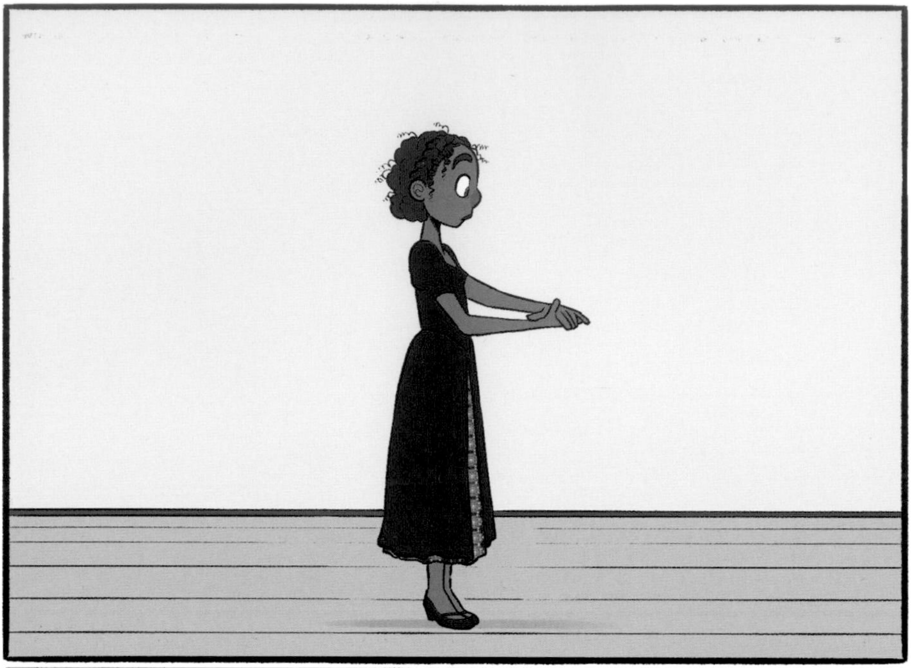

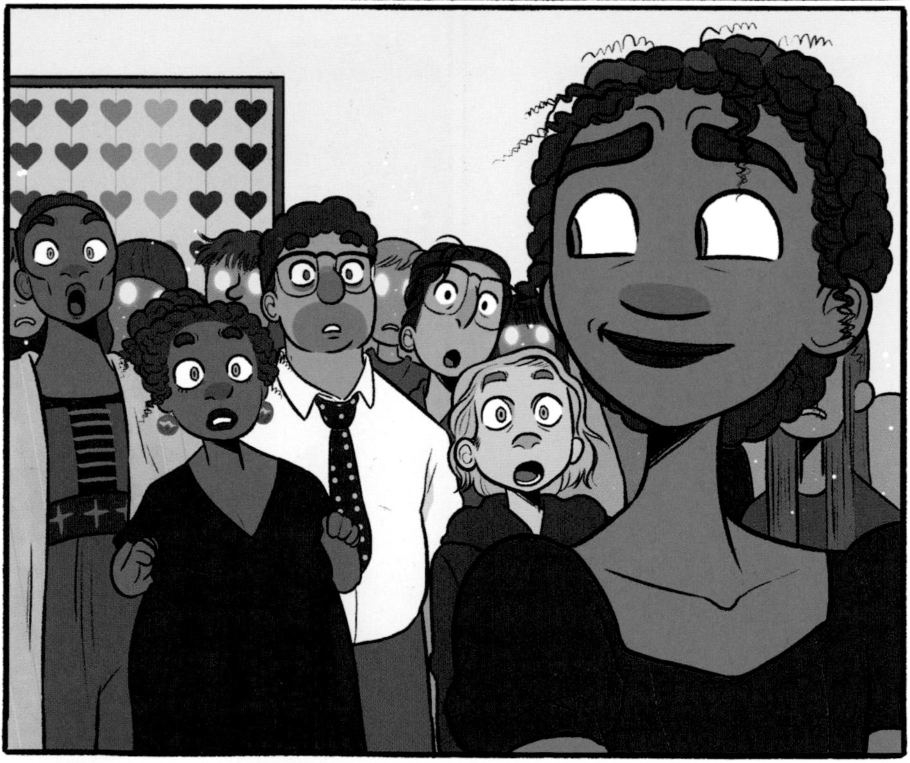

CHAPTER 13
Okay Is Magic

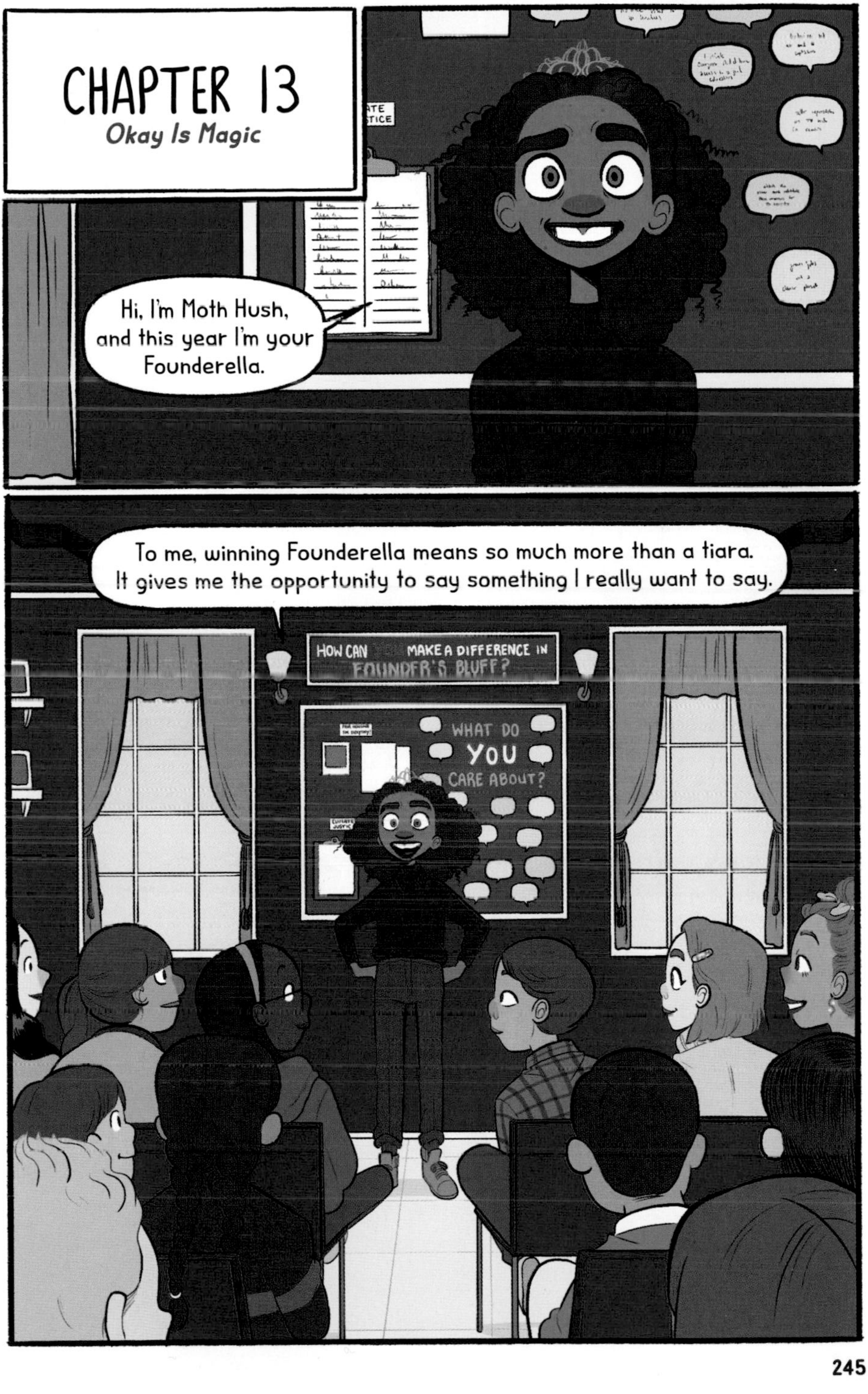
Hi, I'm Moth Hush, and this year I'm your Founderella.
To me, winning Founderella means so much more than a tiara. It gives me the opportunity to say something I really want to say.
WHAT DO YOU CARE ABOUT?

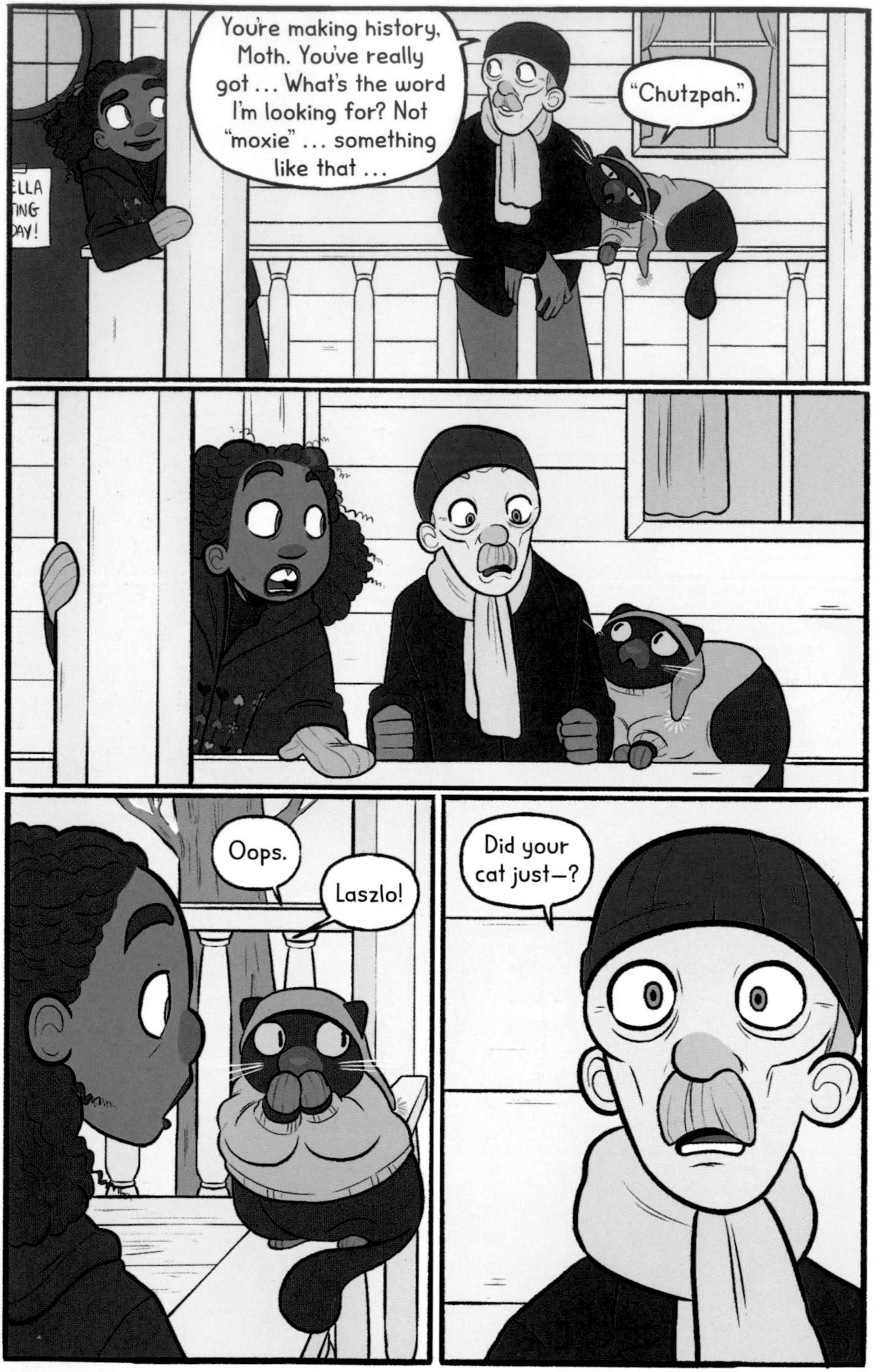
You're making history, Moth. You've really got . . . What's the word I'm looking for? Not "moxie" . . . something like that . . .
"Chutzpah."
Oops.
Laszlo!
Did your cat just—?

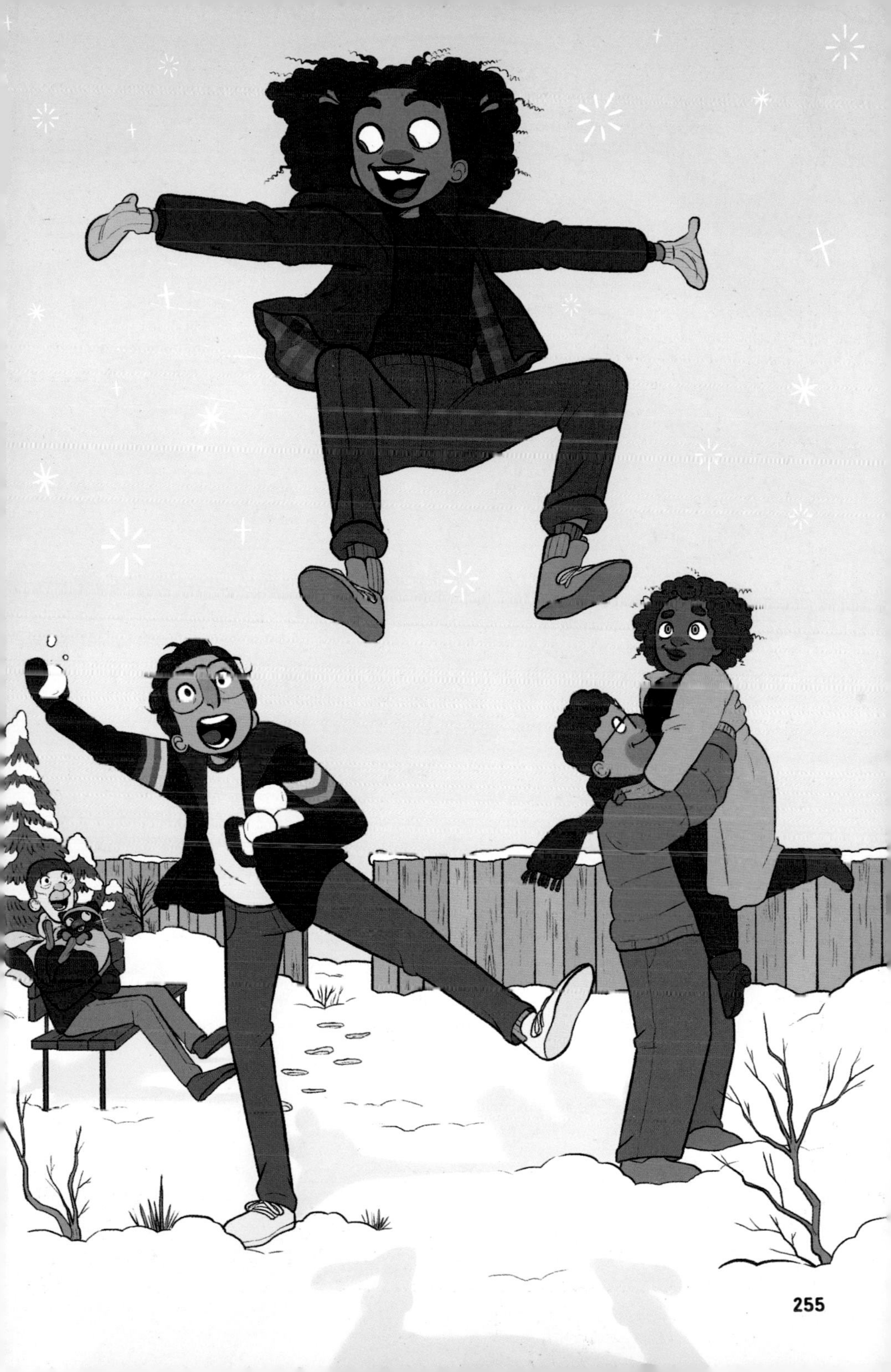

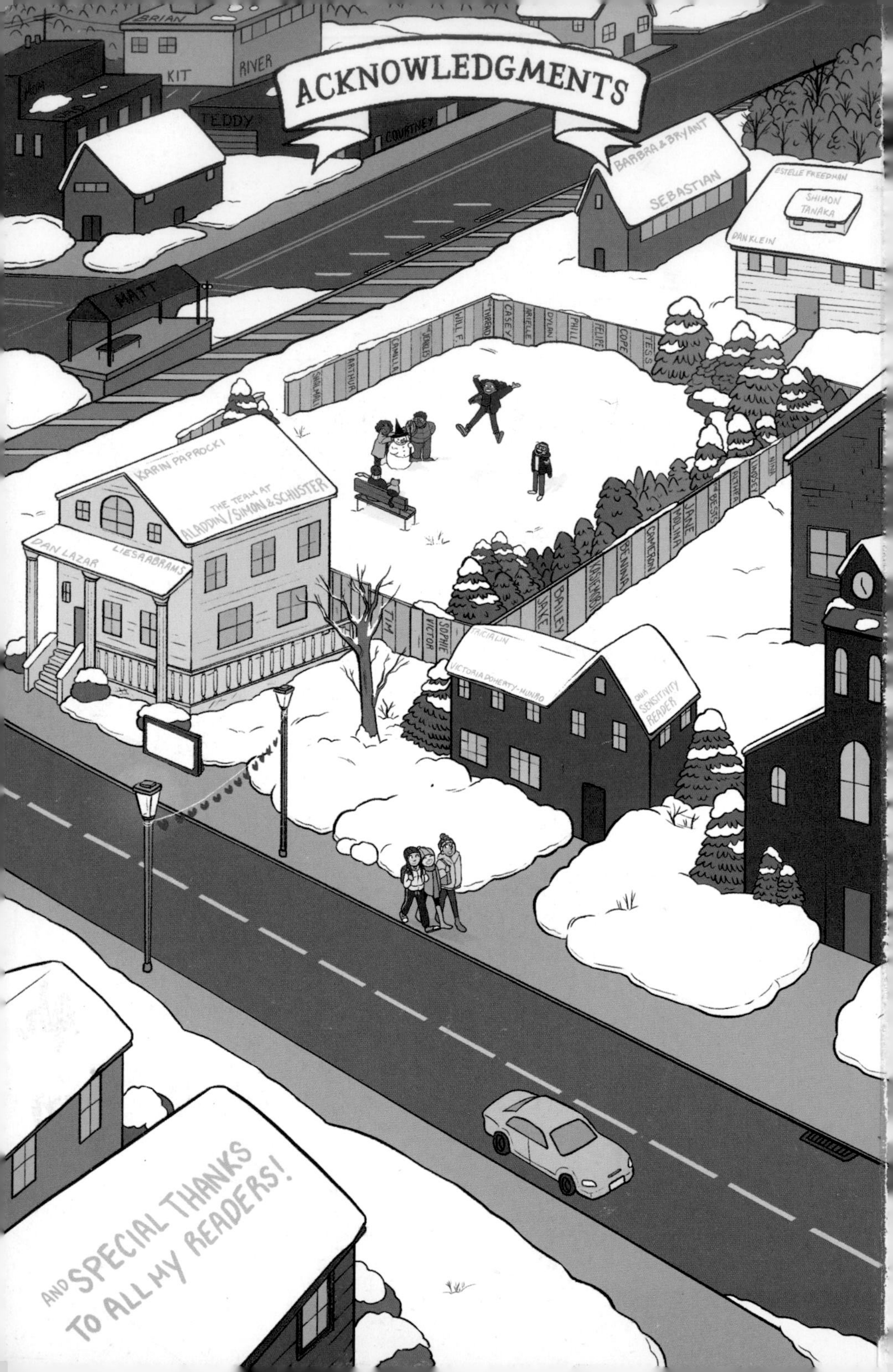

ACKNOWLEDGMENTS
BRIAN
KIT
RIVER
TEDDY
COURTNEY
MATT
BARBRA & BRYANT
SEBASTIAN
ESTELLE FREEDMAN
SHIMON TANAKA
DAN KLEIN
SHALMALI
ARTHUR
CAMILLA
WILL F.
CASEY
ARIELLE
DYLAN
PHILL
FELIPE
COPE
TESS
NINA
LINDSEY
ALTHEA
JANE MOLINA
CAMERON
BENJAMIN
BAILEY
JAKE
SOPHIE
VICTOR
TIM
KARIN PAPROCKI
THE TEAM AT ALADDIN/SIMON & SCHUSTER
DAN LAZAR
LIESA ABRAMS
TRICIA LIN
VICTORIA DOHERTY-MUNRO
SENSITIVITY READER
AND SPECIAL THANKS TO ALL MY READERS!